A TIME FOR SILENCE

Bestselling novelist Philippa Carr, who is also bestselling novelists Jean Plaidy and Victoria Holt, describes her well-loved 'Daughters of England' series as follows:

'Philippa Carr comes between Jean Plaidy and Victoria Holt. Jean Plaidy is writing authentic history in the form of the novel; Victoria Holt writes mystery and suspense with a strong dash of romance; but Philippa Carr, while giving a truly historical background, does not allow the history to overwhelm the story. The main concern of these books is what is happening to the people and to bring in the historical content only to show its effect on their lives.

'But the chief idea behind them all is to give the readers those unputdownable stories about characters whom they can love or hate (in other words, characters whom they can believe), and in which the historical content can be picked up as a bonus. They are first and foremost entertainment.'

PHILIPPA CARR

A Time for Silence

Fontana
An Imprint of HarperCollins*Publishers*

Fontana
An Imprint of HarperCollins*Publishers*
77–85 Fulham Palace Road,
Hammersmith, London W6 8JB

Published by Fontana 1992

1 3 5 7 9 10 8 6 4 2

First published in Great Britain by
HarperCollins*Publishers* 1991

The Author asserts the moral right to
be identified as the author of this work

ISBN 0 00 647102 1

Set in Times Roman

Printed in Great Britain by
HarperCollinsManufacturing Glasgow

CONTENTS

Prelude

I first met Carl Zimmerman in my father's house in Westminster when I was eleven years old. I remember the occasion well. We were, in common with the whole of London – or the entire country, for that matter – celebrating the new reign and the coronation of the King and Queen.

The old King had died. He had been a colourful character in his day, as Prince of Wales mostly. He had seemed to attract scandal which shocked the people – and the people love to be shocked. When he became King he appeared to be much more sober, but then, of course, he was much older.

I was born in the last year of the century – too young, as my mother had said, to remember the relief of Mafeking, though she had stood at the window of our London house with me in her arms looking down at the revelry in the streets below, and apparently I had appeared to be most amused.

The Prince of Wales had become Edward VII soon after that, on the death of his mother, the great Victoria, after which, I often heard, things were never the same again. Now Edward himself had passed on and we were welcoming his son George and George's Queen Mary to be our new sovereigns.

My father, Joel Greenham, was the Member of Parliament for Marchlands, a constituency close to Epping Forest which had been represented by a Greenham since the days of George II – as a Whig in those days, and a Liberal since the party changed its name.

I was accustomed to gatherings, for we entertained frequently, both at Westminster and Marchlands, where we had a delightful house which I loved. Here, in London, the parties

7

we gave were mostly political, and the guests were quite important well-known people whom I enjoyed meeting when I had the chance. It was different in the country where the guests would be neighbouring landowners and suchlike. They were more cosy.

My presence at the London parties was a secret one. I would be on the second floor, close to the banisters where I could get a good view and be able to draw back quickly if anyone should chance to look up. My parents knew I was there. They would sometimes look up and lift a hand surreptitiously to let me know they were aware of my presence. Robert Denver knew, too, but then he was like a member of the family.

There had always been close ties between us and the Denvers. My mother and Lady Denver had been brought up together in their early days; then Lady Denver, whom I called Aunt Belinda, had gone to Australia for some years and when she returned and married Sir Robert Denver, the relationship had been resumed. Aunt Belinda had two children. One was Robert, the other Annabelinda. Both were very important to me.

Robert was about five years older than I and one of the nicest people I had ever known. He was tall and lean; he had rather a disjointed look which was somehow endearing, as though, said his sister Annabelinda, he had been put together in a hurry and some parts had not fitted very well. He had a gentle nature and I had loved him from the first moment I knew him.

Annabelinda was two years older than I and not in the least like her brother; she was disturbing, unpredictable and immensely exciting.

'Annabelinda takes after her mother,' I had heard my own mother say on more than one occasion.

They had an estate in the country and when they came to London they stayed with us. Robert was going to take over the estate in time and he and his father were not such frequent visitors as Annabelinda and her mother. Those two much preferred London to the country.

On this occasion the whole family was with us. Sir Robert and Aunt Belinda and Robert were guests at the party. Annabelinda was with us on the stairs. She was a beauty already, with deep blue eyes, thick black hair and a beautifully smooth pale skin; she was full of vitality and outrageously adventurous. I could imagine that Aunt Belinda had been exactly like her in her youth and that she had plagued my mother as Annabelinda now plagued me.

'You must not let Annabelinda rule you,' said my mother. 'Make your own judgements. Don't let her lead you. She could be overpowering . . . just like her mother,' she added reminiscently.

I knew what she meant and determined to follow her advice.

On this occasion after Miss Grant, my governess, had sat with us while we drank our milk as we did every evening, Annabelinda had given vent to her annoyance.

'It's all very well for you, Lucinda,' she said. 'You are, after all, only eleven years old. I am thirteen and still treated like a child.'

'We can see them all arrive. That's fun, isn't it, Charles?' I said to my young brother.

'Oh yes,' he replied. 'And when they have all gone into the dining-room, we creep downstairs and wait in the cubbyhole till Robert brings us gorgeous things to eat.'

'Annabelinda knows all that,' I said. 'She's been with us at other times.'

'It's fun,' said Charles.

'Fun?' retorted Annabelinda. 'To be treated like a child . . . at my age!'

I studied her. She certainly did not look like a child.

'Annabelinda will develop early,' my mother had said.

It was true. She was already shapely. 'She's like her mother – born mature.' That was my mother again, who often expressed her deep knowledge of Aunt Belinda in a way which made it seem like a warning.

'*I* shall not come to look through the banisters at them,' went on Annabelinda. 'It is too childish for words.'

9

I shrugged my shoulders. I was looking forward to it. The guests would ascend the wide staircase from the hall to where my parents would be waiting to greet them under the big chandelier. The drawing-room and dining-room were on the first floor and there was a space at the top of the stairs where they talked together before they drifted into the other rooms. It was at this stage where we watched them through the banisters.

Then when they were in the dining-room, we would creep down and go into that small room which was reached by ascending a few steps of a back staircase which led to the upper rooms. There we waited. The room contained several cupboards in which all sorts of things were stored. There was a table and some chairs in it and it was around this that we would settle happily, eating whatever Robert brought us. He would creep in with a tray on which would be trifle, ice-cream or some such delicacy. He would sit with us in this room – which we called the cubbyhole – while we ate. It was the best part of the evening, and I think Robert enjoyed it, too.

When Miss Grant left us, we went to our point of vantage at the banisters and Annabelinda was with us. She did not explain her change of mind. She just squatted beside us and made critical comments on the appearances of the ladies while she gave most of her attention to the men.

When the guests had all gone into supper we prepared ourselves for the most exciting part of the evening. Silently we crept downstairs, sped under the chandelier, along to the end of the landing and up the four stairs to the cubbyhole.

Charles was finding it hard to suppress his giggles and almost immediately, just as I expected, Robert appeared with a tray on which were four glass dishes containing syllabub. He had guessed Annabelinda would be there.

She was a little ashamed, I believe, at being seen joining in with the young ones, but as her brother Robert had stooped from even greater heights – although he did not seem to be aware of this – she was to some extent reconciled.

We sat down at the table to enjoy the syllabub.

Charles said: 'I knew it would be syllabub. I heard Cook

say. She wasn't very pleased. Old-fangled stuff, she said it was.'

Everyone ignored him. Poor Charles! But when one is the youngest one gets used to being ignored, and Charles had a very cheerful disposition. He was content to attack the syllabub with relish.

'I brought you an extra large portion,' Robert told him. 'I thought you might need it.'

'Thanks,' replied Charles, and showed his appreciation with a beaming smile.

'What are they talking about down there?' asked Annabelinda.

'Politics mainly,' said Robert.

'Not still going on about that old election, are they?' I asked.

'Well, it's the House of Lords, really. That seems to be the main cause of the trouble.'

'They oppose everything the Government want to do,' I said. 'There is nothing new about that.'

'Perhaps the new King will do something about it,' suggested Annabelinda.

'Monarchs are constitutional now,' I reminded her, 'and the House of Lords is not so important as the Commons – though the laws have to be passed by them as well. My father says Mr Asquith should create more peers so that he has the balance in his favour.'

Annabelinda yawned, and I went on: 'It was wonderful of you, Robert, to bring this to us.'

'You know I always do at these affairs.'

'I know . . . and I like it.'

He gave me his special smile. 'The fact is,' he said, 'I like being here . . . rather than at the party, actually.'

'I should have liked a little more,' confessed Charles.

'What? After that big helping, you greedy creature,' I said.

'Have mine,' volunteered Robert, and Charles accepted with an, 'If you're sure you don't want it. It's a shame to waste it.'

11

It was at that moment that I thought I heard footsteps outside the door.

I paused and listened.

'What is it?' asked Robert.

'Someone's on the stairs. I heard that board creak. It always does . . . just outside the cubbyhole.'

I went to the door and opened it.

A young man was standing there. He looked startled when he saw me. I noticed his very fair hair and light blue eyes . . . as for a few seconds we stared at each other. He was in evening dress, so I knew he was one of the guests.

'Have you lost your way?' I asked.

'Yes . . . yes . . . I have lost my way.' He spoke with the faintest foreign accent.

The others had come to the door of the cubbyhole. He looked at us all in dismay.

'Oh,' he said, 'I am very sorry. I do not know how I got here. I am careless. I spill food on my coat. I think I must clean it off before it is seen. I find my way to the . . . little place . . . and I sponge it off. I come out . . . and I do not know where I am. I am lost.'

'You were trying to find your way to the dining-room. This house is full of odd nooks and crannies, but it is so conveniently near the Houses of Parliament. I can see where you went wrong. But you are almost back on the right floor now. I'll show you.'

'You are very kind.'

Annabelinda was studying him intently. 'Come and sit down for a moment,' she said. 'You haven't been in this house before, have you?'

'No. It is my first visit. I arrived in England only two weeks ago.'

'Where do you come from?' asked Annabelinda.

'From Switzerland.'

'How exciting . . . all those mountains and lakes.'

He smiled at her, looking less nervous now.

'What's your name?' I asked.

12

'Carl Zimmerman.'

'I'm Annabelinda Denver,' said Annabelinda. 'And this is my brother Robert. These two belong to the house. Lucinda and Charles Greenham.'

'Now,' he said, with a smile, 'we all know each other.'

'We weren't invited to the party. They think we're all too young . . . except Robert, of course. He brought up the syllabub for us.'

The young man's smile broadened.

'I understand. And I am happy to have met you.'

'Are you an important diplomat?' asked Annabelinda.

'Not an important one. This is my first assignment.'

'And you got lost on the stairs!' said Annabelinda with a little shriek.

'Anyone can get lost,' I said.

'I do it all the time,' added Robert.

'Are you staying in London for long?' asked Annabelinda.

He lifted his shoulders. 'I am not sure.'

'You must be quite important to have been invited here,' went on Annabelinda.

He shrugged his shoulders again. 'I am with my colleague. It is because of him.'

'Will they be missing you?' I asked.

'Oh, they'll be coming out of the dining-room now,' said Robert. 'Look, we'd better go. Come with me. I'll escort you back.'

'Thank you. You are very good.'

Annabelinda was not pleased. She scowled at her brother, but the young man had risen and was following Robert to the door.

'Thanks for the syllabub,' I said, and Robert smiled at me.

'And I thank you,' said the young man. 'I thank you all.'

Then he and Robert went back to the guests.

'Just as it was getting interesting!' grumbled Annabelinda. 'Really, Rob is a bit of a spoilsport.'

'He was right,' I defended him. 'They might have been

missed and it could have been awkward for him . . . as he must be new to all this.'

'I wanted him to stay. It was fun. Oh well . . . that's it. I'm going to my room.'

She went off and Charles and I retired to ours. We did not want to wait for the departure of the guests.

'The syllabub was good,' was Charles's final comment. 'I didn't mind its being old-fangled stuff.'

I think I, too, shared Annabelinda's feelings of vague disappointment.

It was not until next morning that I heard the news. Millie Jennings, one of the maids, told me when she brought in my hot water.

'Oh, such a to-do, Miss Lucinda. The police was here last night. Just midnight, it was. It wasn't till after all the guests were gone that Madam discovered.'

'What are you talking about, Millie?' I asked.

'The burglary, Miss, that's what. It was when Madam went up to her bedroom. She found one of the drawers open – her jewellery had been tampered with. They got the police, late as it was. You didn't hear them, then? Sleep like a log, you do, Miss.'

'Burglars! Last night! Then it must have been while the party was going on.'

'That's what they reckon. Some of Madam's emeralds have been taken, so it seems. Just fancy . . . us knowing nothing about it when all that was going on.'

I decided to get up and find out for myself what had happened, so I washed and dressed as quickly as I could and went down to find my mother. She was in the dining-room drinking a cup of coffee.

'Mama, what happened?' I asked.

She lifted her eyebrows. 'There appears to have been a burglary last night.'

'So Millie was saying. She said they took your emeralds.'

14

'Some of my jewellery is missing.'

'And it was while the party was going on!'

'It was a good time to do it, I suppose.'

'Millie said the police were here.'

'Yes, they came last night. They'll be here again this morning.'

'How could it have happened?'

'Apparently someone must have got in from the back of the house. The window of our bedroom was open so they could have come in that way. I think they may have been disturbed because there was so much they might have taken. They had been in your father's study, too.'

'Did they take anything from there?'

'Well, no. There is nothing of value there . . . except that paper knife with the sapphires set in the handle. They couldn't have noticed that. It seems they must have been disturbed before they really got started, and thought they'd better get out. You didn't hear anything, I suppose? What did you do after you'd finished the syllabub Robert brought you? I saw him sneaking out of the dining-room with the tray.'

'We just ate it. Oh yes, and there was someone on the stairs outside the cubbyhole.'

'What?'

'He had spilt something on his jacket and went off to clean it. Then he got lost when he was looking for the dining-room. Robert took him back there.'

'Oh, I see. Who was it?'

'Someone called Carl Zimmerman.'

'I remember. He came along with someone from one of the Embassies. A rather shy young man. Well, he would be new to all this.'

'Yes. He gave that impression.'

'I meant, did you hear anything suspicious? No noise or anything from above?'

'No. After that I went to bed and I don't remember any more until Millie came in.'

'I suppose we ought to be glad that it is no worse. I don't

15

like to think of people prowling about the house . . . especially when we're all in it. It gives one rather a creepy feeling.'

I agreed that it did.

The police came along that morning. Annabelinda, Charles and I watched them from an upper window. Annabelinda hoped they would question her. She began to wonder whether she had heard something after I had left her on the previous night. It was not that she would deliberately tell an untruth. She just liked excitement, and it was essential to her that she should be at the centre of it.

She was very disappointed when the police left without seeing her.

It was two days later. The Denvers were about to leave. I was sorry. I liked to feel that Robert was at hand. He was so kind and always wanted to be on good terms with everybody, whoever they were. I had mixed feelings about Annabelinda, as I knew my mother did about Aunt Belinda. We were attracted by them; we liked them, and yet in a way we were suspicious of them. Whenever I heard they were coming to visit us I would grow excited, and when they arrived faintly irritated. It was due to Annabelinda's somewhat patronizing manner, the admiration she demanded, the desire always to have attention focused on her and to jostle out of the way those who might attempt to rival her.

My mother knew exactly how I felt, because it had happened to her with Belinda. Yet when they went there would be a feeling of anticlimax; one would feel a mild depression; life was less interesting and one would find oneself hankering for their return.

It was almost as though Annabelinda was a part of me – not a part I greatly liked, but one which I found it difficult to do without.

We had just finished breakfast. Sir Robert was saying what a pleasant visit it had been and we must all come to Hampshire and stay with them. My father replied that things were happening in the House and he would be tied there for a while. Then he would have to do a spell at Marchlands. Constituencies could not be neglected.

'It is easier for you to come to London,' said my mother.

'Much easier,' said Aunt Belinda. 'Don't worry, Lucie dear. You will soon have to put up with us again. I know Annabelinda feels the same as I do, don't you, dear?'

'I love it here in London,' said Annabelinda fervently.

'Well then, we shall see you soon,' replied my mother.

At that moment Mrs Cherry, the housekeeper, came into the room in a most unceremonious manner, which was strange for her. She looked agitated. She was holding something in her hand.

'Oh, sir . . . madam . . . it's Jane. She just found these.'

We had all risen, for what Mrs Cherry was holding in her hand was my mother's emerald bracelet and ring, those which we thought had been stolen while the party was in progress.

'Mrs Cherry!' cried my mother. 'Where on earth . . . ?'

My father had gone to the housekeeper and taken the jewellery from her. 'Where were they found, Mrs Cherry?' he asked.

'In the bedroom, sir . . . caught in the valance round the bed.'

My mother stammered: 'It's . . . not possible. They were always kept in the case.'

'Jane found them, did she?' said my father.

'Yes, sir. I'll bring her along.'

We were all astounded. There was no doubt that these were the missing emeralds. How had they come to be caught in the valance round the bed?

My mother kept insisting that she had not worn the emeralds for a week and when she had she was sure she had put them back in their case. How could this possibly have happened?

The fact remained that the missing emeralds were recovered and the police had to be told.

The general feeling was that there had been no burglary and the emeralds could not have been put in their case; instead they had somehow been caught up in the bed valance; someone must have forgotten to close the window and when my parents had returned and seen it open they had assumed we had had a burglary.

There was an apology to the police for the trouble caused, a substantial contribution to police charities, and the case was closed.

It was for this reason that I remember so vividly my first meeting with Carl Zimmerman.

La Pinière

I often thought how lucky I was to have been born into a well-knit family. There had been a wonderful sense of security in those early days to know that besides my parents there were others such as Aunt Rebecca and her family in Cornwall where I went now and then for holidays. Then there were the Cartwrights – Rebecca's husband's people down there. They always made much of me.

Aunt Rebecca was my mother's half-sister and they were devoted to each other; then there was Uncle Gerald, my father's brother. He was a colonel in the Guards and was married to Aunt Hester, a very energetic lady who was immersed in Army life and her two sons, my cousins, George and Harold.

Apart from the family, there were the Denvers and through them Jean Pascal Bourdon – that fascinating and somewhat enigmatic character about whom, for me, there was an almost satanic aura. He was Aunt Belinda's father.

Closest to me was my mother, although my father came very near. I admired him deeply. He was a highly respected Member of Parliament. He was always busy, if not in London at the House of Commons, in the country at Marchlands, where he was 'nursing' the constituency. When the House was sitting late, my mother used to wait up for him with a little cold supper, so that they could talk together about the day's proceedings. She had done that for her own father who had also been in Parliament. In fact, that was how she had come to know the Greenhams and had married one of them, for the two families had been friends in her childhood. I had heard it

19

said that she had adopted the habit from Mrs Disraeli, who used to do it for the great Benjamin.

My father was very highly respected; his words were often quoted in the newspapers when he made a speech either in the House or at some meeting; yet although his party had been in power since 1905, he had never attained Cabinet status. And he never sought it.

In spite of the fact that he was a normal loving father and completely approachable, there was some mystery about him. For instance, there were occasions when he went away and we were never sure where he was going and when he was coming back. Whether my mother knew, I could never be sure. If she did, she would never tell.

'Oh, he's going on Government business,' she would say, but I, who knew her well, could detect a certain anxiety at such times, and she was always relieved when he returned.

I suppose it was because of this that I felt there was a little part of my father which I did not know, and this made him seem apart from me, as my mother never was. He was a good man and I loved him dearly but this mystery, vague and intangible, was always there.

I once told my mother that I was glad to be called Lucinda, because she was Lucie and that made us seem like a part of each other. She was touched and told me that she had always wanted a daughter, and the day I was born was the happiest in her life. And how different her life had been from mine. Not for her, in those early days, had there been the security of loving parents and a big family about her.

'Your Aunt Rebecca was like a mother to me,' she had told me. 'I often wonder what would have happened to me if it had not been for Rebecca.' In those early days she had not known who her father was and it was much later when she discovered that he was the well-known politician Benedict Lansdon and that she was Rebecca's half-sister.

Then, having learned of their relationship, she and Benedict Lansdon became very important to each other. She talked of him now and then; she would glow with pride and then be overcome by sadness, for one day, when he was about to step into his carriage which was to take him to the House of Commons, he was shot and killed by an Irish terrorist. She had been with him when it had happened.

I tried to imagine what it must have been like to see one's father killed, to see the life of a loved one snapped off suddenly. I believe she had never really recovered from it. And it was the beginning of troubles so bizarre through which she had to pass before she found happiness with my father.

She had been married before but she never talked of that, and I knew I must not ask. In fact, it was only rarely that she could bring herself to mention those days.

She did say once: 'Sometimes it is almost worthwhile going through great tribulation because when it is over you learn to appreciate what true happiness is, and you cherish it as perhaps people cannot who have never known the reverse.'

I was so happy that she had married my father and all that was behind her.

I said to her: 'You have us now . . . my father . . . Charles and me.'

'I thank God for you all,' she said. 'And, Lucinda, I want you to be happy. I hope you will have children of your own one day and then you will know the joy they can bring.'

Perhaps closer to us than our own blood relations were the Denvers. Aunt Belinda and her daughter would arrive at any time, but sometimes their visit was preceded by a short note announcing their imminent arrival. I had heard Mrs Cherry say that they treated the house like a hotel and she wondered Madam allowed it, she did really.

I stayed in Hampshire now and then. They had a wonderful manor house and Sir Robert owned a large estate which he, with Robert's help, took great pride in managing.

I always enjoyed my stays on the Caddington estate. I thought Caddington Manor was very exciting. It was considerably older than Marchlands and had been in existence since the Wars of the Roses. There had been a Denver there from the beginning. He did very well on the accession of Henry VII and had continued to prosper under the Tudors. Throughout the conflict the family had been staunchly Lancastrian and all over the manor were carvings of the Red Rose on walls, fireplaces and staircases. I learned quite a lot about the Wars of the Roses after even my first visit to Caddington Manor.

The picture gallery was a source of great interest to me. Annabelinda shrugged me aside when I wanted to ask about the people portrayed there.

'They're all dead,' she said. 'I wish we could live in London. My father would never agree. That's one thing he is firm about.'

'Well, you and your mother don't let that stop your coming,' I said.

That made Annabelinda laugh. She had a mild toleration for her father and I think Aunt Belinda felt the same. He was the provider, the kindly, tolerant figure in the background whom they did not allow to interfere with their pleasures.

Robert was a little like his father, but none of them was more interested in the past than I was, and I shared this with Robert.

One of the most exciting aspects arising from our intimacy was Annabelinda's fascinating French grandfather, Jean Pascal Bourdon.

He was quite different from anyone I had, as yet, known.

He was the brother of Aunt Celeste who had a house near us in London and we visited each other frequently. She was an unassuming woman who had married Benedict Lansdon after the death of my grandmother, and she had been his wife at the time of the murder. It was rather complicated – as I suppose such families are – but Celeste's brother had been the father of Aunt Belinda. It had all been rather shocking, for Aunt Belinda's mother had been a seamstress at the Bourdons' house and the birth had been kept secret for years. It must have been exciting for Aunt Belinda when this was discovered. Knowing Annabelinda well, and her being so much like her mother, I felt I knew a good deal about Aunt Belinda. She must have been delighted to learn that she was the daughter of this most fascinating man.

Jean Pascal Bourdon was rich, sophisticated and totally different from anyone else we knew. He had taken an interest in Aunt Belinda when he had discovered she was his daughter, and it was at his *château*, near Bordeaux, that she had met Sir Robert Denver.

Jean Pascal's interest was passed on to his granddaughter, and needless to say, Annabelinda was very impressed by him. She would spend a month or so with him, usually at the time of the wine harvest, and lately I had gone with her.

My mother did not greatly like my going. Nor did my Aunt Rebecca. But Annabelinda wanted me to go and Aunt Belinda said: 'Why on earth shouldn't she go? You can't keep the child tied to your apron strings forever, Lucie. It's time she saw something of the world. Bring her out of herself. She hasn't got Annabelinda's verve as it is.'

And in due course I went and became fascinated by the *château*, the mysterious grounds which surrounded it, the vineyards, the country and chiefly Monsieur Jean Pascal Bourdon himself.

Some two years before my tenth birthday, he had married a lady of mature years to match his own; she was of high rank in the French aristocracy – not that that meant a great deal nowadays – but at least it was a reminder of pre-revolutionary glory. And the fact that he was married made my mother and Aunt Rebecca a little reconciled to my visits to France. The Princesse would make sure that the household was conducted with appropriate propriety; and after that, as a matter of course, I went with Annabelinda.

I looked forward to the visits. I loved to roam the grounds and sit by the lake watching the swans. My mother had told me of the black swan who had lived on that lake when she was young, and how it had terrorized everyone who approached close to the water. They had called him Diable, and his mate, who was as docile as he was fierce, had been named Ange.

I loved that story, for the swan had attempted to attack my mother and she had been saved by Jean Pascal.

I was always made welcome at the *château*. Jean Pascal

used to talk to us as though we were grown up. Annabelinda loved that. He and the Princesse were the only people of whom she stood in awe.

One day when we had been sitting by the lake, Jean Pascal had come along; he sat beside me and talked. He told me how much he admired my mother. She had come to stay at the *château* with Aunt Belinda.

'It was her only visit,' he said. 'She was always a little suspicious of me. Quite wrongly, of course. I was devoted to her. I was so delighted that she married your father. He was just the man for her. That first marriage . . .' He shook his head.

I said: 'She never talks about it.'

'No. It's best forgotten. That's always a good idea. When something becomes unpleasant that is the time to forget it. That's what we should all do.'

'It's not always easy to forget.'

'It takes practice,' he admitted.

'Have you practised it throughout your life?'

'So much that I have become an adept at the art, little Lucinda. That is why you see me so content with life.'

He made me laugh, as he always did. He gave the impression that he was rather wicked and that, because of this, he understood other people's foibles and did not judge them as harshly as some people might.

'Beware the saint,' he said once. 'Beware the man – or woman – who flaunts his – or her – high standards. He – or she – often does not live up to them and will be very hard on others who fall short. Live your life as test you can, and by that I mean enjoy it and leave other people to do the same.'

Then he told me of how he came out one morning to find poor old Diable on the lake with his head down in the water. It was most unusual. He did not realize at once what had happened. He shouted. He took a stick and stirred the water. The swan did not move. Poor Diable. He was dead. It was the end of his dominance. 'It was rather sad,' he added.

'And poor little Ange?'

'She missed the old tyrant. She sailed the lake alone for a while and in less than a year she was dead. Now you see we have these white swans. Are they not beautiful, and peaceful too? Now you do not have to take a stick as you approach the lake in readiness for a surprise attack. But something has gone. Strange, is it not? How we grow to love the villains of this world! Unfair, it is true. But vice can sometimes be more attractive than virtue.'

'Can bad things be really more attractive than good ones?' I asked.

'Alas, the perversity of the world!' he sighed.

He was always interesting to listen to and I fancied he liked to talk to me. In fact, I was sure of this when Annabelinda showed signs of jealousy.

I should have been disappointed if I did not pay my yearly visit to the *château*.

Aunt Belinda came there sometimes. I could see that she amused her father. The Princesse found her agreeable, too. There was a great deal of entertaining since Jean Pascal's marriage and people with high-sounding titles were often present.

Annabelinda said: 'They are waiting for another revolution. This time in their favour so that they can all come back to past glory.'

I agreed with Annabelinda that one of the events of the year to look forward to most was our visit to France.

When we were at the *château* we were expected to speak French. It was supposed to be good for us. Jean Pascal laughed at our accents.

'You should be able to speak as fluently in French as I do in English,' he said. 'It is considered to be essential for the education of all but peasants and the English.'

It was in the year 1912, when I was thirteen years old, that the question of education arose.

Aunt Belinda had prevailed on Sir Robert to agree with her that Annabelinda should go to a school in Belgium. The school she had chosen belonged to a Frenchwoman, a friend of Jean

Pascal, an aristocrat naturally. From this school a girl would emerge speaking perfect French, fully equipped to converse with the highest in the land, perhaps not academically brilliant but blessed with all the social graces.

Annabelinda was enthusiastic, but there was one thing she needed to make the project wholly acceptable to her. I was faintly surprised to learn that it was my presence. Perhaps I should not have been. Annabelinda had always needed an audience and for so many years I had been the perfect one. Nothing would satisfy her but that I should go to Belgium with her.

My mother was against the idea at first.

'All that way!' she said. 'And for so long!'

'It's no farther than Scotland,' cried Aunt Belinda.

'We are not talking of going to Scotland.'

'You should think of your child. Children must always come first,' she added hypocritically, which exasperated my mother, because there had never been anyone who came first with Belinda. She herself had always occupied that place.

Aunt Celeste gave her opinion. 'I know Lucinda would get a first-class education,' she said. 'My brother assures me of this. The school has a high reputation. Girls of good family from all over Europe go there.'

'There are good schools in England,' said my mother.

My father thought it was not a bad idea for a girl to have a year or so in a foreign school. There was nothing like it for perfecting the language. 'They are teaching German, too. She would get the right accent and that makes all the difference.'

I myself was intrigued by the idea. I thought of the superiority which Annabelinda would display when she came home. I wanted to go, for I knew I had to go away to school sooner or later. I was getting beyond governesses. I knew as much as they did and was almost equipped to be a governess myself. Every day my desire to go with Annabelinda grew stronger. My mother knew this and was undecided.

Aunt Celeste, who said little and understood a good deal, realized that at the back of my mother's mind was the thought that I should be close to Jean Pascal, whom she did not trust.

'The Princesse has a high opinion of the school,' she told my mother. 'She will keep an eye on the girls. I know Madame Rochère. She is a very capable lady. Mind you, the school is not very near the *château*, but the Princesse has a house not very far from it and she and Jean Pascal stay there only very occasionally. The house is not in Belgium but close to the border in Valenciennes. Madame Rochère is a very responsible person – a little strict perhaps, but discipline is good. I am sure Annabelinda will benefit from it . . . and Lucinda too. They should go together, Lucie. It will be so much better for them if they have each other.'

At last my mother succumbed and this was largely due to my enthusiasm.

I wanted to go. It would be exciting, different from everything I had done before. Besides, Annabelinda would be with me.

So . . . it was to be. Annabelinda and I had an exciting month making our preparations, and on the third of September of that year 1912 we left England in the company of Aunt Celeste.

I had said a fond farewell to my parents who came to Dover with Aunt Belinda to see us depart with Aunt Celeste on the Channel ferry. We were to go to the Princesse's house in Valenciennes, where we would stay for the night before leaving for the school the next day. The Princesse would be waiting to greet us there. From there the distance to the school was not great, for it was situated some miles west of the city of Mons.

My mother was slightly less disturbed because of Aunt Celeste's presence and the fact that Jean Pascal was staying in the Médoc because his presence would be needed at the imminent wine harvest.

Aunt Celeste had assured my mother and Aunt Belinda that the Princesse would be most assiduous in her care of us. The school allowed pupils the occasional weekend if there was some relative or friend nearby to whom they could go, and the Princesse would be there if we needed her. Moreover, Celeste herself could go over frequently. I heard my mother say that she had rarely seen Celeste so contented as she was now she was taking part in the care of Annabelinda and me.

'It is a pity she did not have children,' she added. 'It would have made all the difference to her life.'

Well, we were now bringing her a little interest, and the truth was that although I hated leaving my parents, I could not help being excited at the prospect before me; and the fact that that excitement was mixed with apprehension did not spoil it in the least. I could see that Annabelinda felt much the same as I did.

After the night in Valenciennes we took the train across the border into Belgium. The Princesse accompanied us. It was not a very long journey to the town of Mons, and soon we were in the carriage driving the few miles from the station to the school.

We drew up before a large grey stone gatehouse. Beyond it I could see nothing but pine trees. There was a grey stone wall which seemed to extend for miles and on this was a large board painted white with black letters on it.

La Pinière.
Pension de Jeunes Demoiselles.

'The Pine Grove,' said Annabelinda. 'Doesn't it sound exciting?'

A man came out of the gatehouse and looked searchingly at us all.

'Mademoiselle Denver and Mademoiselle Greenham are the new pupils,' said Aunt Celeste.

The man pursed his lips and waved for us to continue.

'He did not look very pleased to see us,' I said.

'It's just his way,' replied Aunt Celeste.

We were driving down a wide path on either side of which pines grew thickly. Their redolent odour was strong in the air.

28

We had driven for half a mile or so before the school came into sight.

I caught my breath in wonder. I had not imagined anything like this. It was large and imposing, set back from well-kept lawns, on one of which a fountain played. It had clearly stood there for centuries – at least five, I guessed. I heard later that it had been built in the mid-fifteenth century and had been the property of the Rochère family for the past three hundred years, and that thirty years ago, when she must have been an enterprising twenty years of age, Madame Rochère realized that if she wished to keep the *château* she must find an income somehow. The school had seemed a good idea, and so it proved to be.

I had learned a little about architecture because of our house at Marchlands which was quite old, and the Denvers' place had always interested me. Robert had found a number of books in the library there which he had unearthed for me because he knew of my interest.

So now I recognized the conventionally Gothic style and later I delighted in the finials moulded in the granite and such details.

'It's ancient!' I cried. 'It's wonderful!'

The others were too concerned at our arrival to listen to me. We alighted and mounted the six stone steps to a door.

There was a huge knocker on the iron-studded door, held in place by the head of a fierce-looking warrior.

Aunt Celeste knocked and after a pause a shutter was drawn back.

'It is Madame Lansdon with the girls,' said Aunt Celeste.

The door was slowly opened. A man stood there. He surveyed us and nodded, gabbled something which I could not understand, and stood aside for us to enter. When we were inside, Celeste spoke to him; he nodded and disappeared.

It was then that I had my first encounter with Madame Rochère. She had come to meet us personally. I had a notion later that this was due to the presence of the Princesse, whom she greeted with respectful formality; and after a gracious acknowledgment of Celeste, who, as the sister of Jean Pascal, was worthy of some consideration also, she turned to us.

'And these are to be my girls,' she said.

'That is so,' answered Celeste.

Madame Rochère was silent for a few seconds, nodding her head as she assessed us. I was aware of Annabelinda's attempt to look nonchalant, but even she could not quite manage this in the presence of Madame Rochère.

She turned to Celeste and the Princesse.

'Madame la Princesse, Madame Lansdon, you will take a little wine to refresh you after your journey while the girls shall go straight to their dormitory and settle in?'

The Princesse bowed her head graciously and Aunt Celeste said it sounded an excellent idea.

Madame Rochère lifted a hand and, as though by magic, a woman appeared on the stairs.

'Ah, Mademoiselle Artois.' Madame Rochère turned to the Princesse and Celeste. 'Mademoiselle Artois is my house-mistress. She will take the girls. They may settle into their quarters and later be brought down to say goodbye to you before you leave. If that is what you wish, of course . . .'

'That would be very acceptable,' said Celeste.

Mademoiselle Artois was a woman in her mid-forties, I imagined. She might have seemed very severe, but after our meeting with Madame Rochère, she appeared to be comparatively mild.

She spoke to us in English, for which we were thankful, but although she had a fair command of the language, her accent and intonation now and then left us grappling for understanding.

She led us past the grey stone walls of the hall, which were hung with axes and murderous-looking weapons, to the wide staircase. We followed her up to the first floor and came to a long gallery in which I should have liked to pause to study the tapestry, which looked very ancient, and the portraits which lined the walls.

There were more stairs and more rooms to be passed through, for the dormitories were at the very top.

Mademoiselle Artois said to Annabelinda: 'You should have a room of your own because you are fifteen years of age. Most girls have their own room when they are fifteen.' She turned to me. 'You have thirteen years only. You will therefore share with three others . . . all of your age.'

I was rather glad. There was an eerieness about the place and I felt I should be more comfortable in the company of others.

We were in a corridor with a row of doors. As we passed, I saw one half open and I fancied there was someone behind trying to peep out – one of the pupils, I thought, anxious to take a look at the newcomers.

Mademoiselle Artois looked at Annabelinda. 'I know that you are fourteen, but unfortunately, there is not a room vacant until the end of term, so you must share. Yours will be a room for two. It may well be that the girl with whom you will share is there now waiting to greet you.'

We went past more doors and paused before one. Mademoiselle opened it and as she did so a girl who had been sitting on the bed rose. She was plumpish with long dark hair which was tied back with a red ribbon. I noticed her sparkling dark eyes.

'Ah, Lucia,' said Mademoiselle Artois. 'This is Annabelinda Denver, who will share with you until the end of term, or till another single room is available.' She turned back to Annabelinda. 'This is Lucia Durotti. Lucia is Italian. You will help each other with your languages.'

Lucia and Annabelinda surveyed each other with interest.

'You must tell Annabelinda which wardrobe is yours . . . and explain to her what she will want to know,' said Mademoiselle Artois. 'She will want to wash, I am sure, and unpack. Show her, Lucia.'

'Yes, mademoiselle,' said Lucia, turning to Annabelinda with a smile.

'And now it is your turn,' said Mademoiselle Artois to me, and we moved into the corridor.

She paused before another door and opened it.

A girl was in the room.

'You are here, Caroline,' said Mademoiselle Artois. 'Good. This is Lucinda Greenham, who will be in your dormitory. You will show her where things are and help her when need be.' She turned to me. 'There will be four of you in this room: Caroline Egerton, yourself, Yvonne Castelle, who is French, and Helga Spiegel, who is Austrian. We like to mix our nationalities, you see. It is helpful for languages. We cannot always do this, because there are more French and English girls than any others. But it is Madame Rochère's wish that we mix you as much as possible.'

'I understand, Mademoiselle Artois,' I said.

'Caroline is here to meet you because she is English and that will make it easier for you at first. I shall leave you now. Caroline will show you your wardrobe and before your family leave you may come down to say goodbye to them. I shall send someone to bring you down –' she looked at the watch pinned on her blouse – 'in, say . . . fifteen minutes. That should be about right.'

When she left us, Caroline Egerton and I stood surveying each other for a few minutes. She was brown-eyed, brown-haired and pleasantly smiling, so I felt it would not be difficult to be friends with her. Then she showed me where to put my clothes and helped me to unpack. She asked me where I came from and what my father did and why had I come with another girl? I answered all these questions and asked a few of my own. She told me that it was 'all right' at the school. She had been here two years. The older girls were given a fair amount of freedom and there was a great deal of attention given to the social side.

'Very French,' she said. 'Very formal. Madame Rochère is an old tyrant. Arty's all right. A bit soft, but not bad, because you could get away with things.'

I asked about Yvonne Castelle and Helga Spiegel.

'Oh, they're all right. We have some fun . . . talking after lights out and that sort of thing. Sometimes girls come in from

32

other rooms. That's forbidden. There would be trouble if we were caught.'

'Have you ever been?'

'Once. The fuss! We were kept in from recreation for a week . . . and had to write masses of lines. But it was worth it.'

'What do you do when the girls come in?'

'Talk.'

'What about?'

'School matters,' said Caroline mysteriously.

I was beginning to get intrigued and by the time I was taken down to say goodbye to Aunt Celeste and the Princesse, I felt I knew Caroline very well.

When I made the acquaintance of Yvonne Castelle and Helga Spiegel I discovered that Yvonne had been at the school for a year, Helga a little longer. They were all eager to instruct me into procedure and Caroline, who had a streak of motherliness in her nature, and having been instructed by Mademoiselle Artois to 'keep an eye on the newcomer', watched over me with assiduous care, which in those early days was comforting. Within a week I felt I had been there for much longer, and because I shared a dormitory with these three girls, they became my special friends.

Caroline was a sort of leader. She enjoyed her superiority and I noticed extended her motherliness to the others as well as myself, while Helga was very eager to do well at her studies because her parents had struggled hard to send her to such a school. She was more serious than the rest of us. Yvonne was the sophisticated one. She knew about Life, she told us.

I did fairly well at lessons and was assessed as adequate for my age, and I fitted comfortably into the group.

I did not see very much of Annabelinda. At school she was known as Anna B. Grace Hebburn, who was the daughter of a duke, and therefore was valued by Madame Rochère as 'good for the school', was a sort of head girl, having reached the dizzy pinnacle of seventeen years. Grace had decided – as she said somewhat inelegantly – that 'Annabelinda' was 'too much of a mouthful' and in future Annabelinda should be known as Anna B.

Grace's rival in Madame Rochère's esteem was Marie de Langeais, who was reputed to have come from the royal family of France. Marie was a rather languid girl of certain good looks who did little to feed the rivalry and Madame Rochère must have decided that an existing dukedom was worth more to the school than a connection with a monarchy now defunct for so many years. So Grace reigned supreme and her order that Anna B should be used in future was respected.

At La Pinière there was great emphasis on the social graces. The object was to mould us into young ladies who would be acceptable in the highest echelons of society rather than into scholars. Consequently great store was set on the dancing lessons, piano lessons and what was called 'Conversazione'.

This took place in the great hall, the walls of which were hung with faded tapestry and portraits. Here we would sit under the searching eyes of Madame Rochère herself, who would suddenly address one of us and expect us to carry on a lively and witty conversation which was usually about what is known as current events.

Each day we had a talk on what was happening in the world. This was delivered by a Monsieur Bourreau, who also gave piano lessons. Madame Rochère said the object was to turn us into young ladies who could be conversant on all matters of interest, and that included world affairs.

Anna B, as she was known now on Grace Hebburn's orders, was enjoying school. Her great crony was her room mate, Lucia Durotti. They were constantly whispering together. Anna B loved dancing and was commended for it. Occasionally our paths met, but she was two years older than I and at school age is often an insurmountable barrier.

I was informed by Caroline that there was going to be a feast in the dormitory. 'We have some biscuits and a tin of condensed milk – quite a big one. We also have a tin-opener and a spoon. I brought them with me from home. I was waiting until everyone settled in before we had the feast. It's my party, so I shall say who is to come. Everyone can bring a guest, so there'll be eight of us.'

I was excited and immediately asked Anna B. She received the invitation with some hauteur and could not immediately decide whether it was beneath her dignity to accept. When I confided to Helga that she thought she was too old to come, Helga said she was not sure whom she could ask so why shouldn't it be Lucia Durotti? Then there would be another old one and it wouldn't be so bad for Anna B.

When these invitations were offered the two girls accepted with alacrity.

Yvonne asked Thérèse de la Montaine, whose home was not far away from the school and who knew about the Rochère family and the old house before it had become a *pension* for *demoiselles*.

'It can be fun listening to her,' said Yvonne.

Caroline's guest was Marie Christine du Bray, who was very sad at this time. It was only six months since both her parents had been killed in a railway accident. Marie Christine had been with them at the time and had escaped. She had been ill and was not yet fully recovered. Her family had thought it would be best for her to be at school surrounded by people of her own age. Caroline had taken it upon herself to keep an eye on her.

We were all very excited about the feast. Secrecy was the order of the day.

'We do not want gatecrashers,' said Caroline. 'There would be noise and the possibility of exposure. And you know what that means. Detention! Lines! Weeping and wailing and gnashing of teeth. "Sometimes I despair of you girls."' Caroline was a good mimic and could give a fair imitation of Mademoiselle Artois.

Of course, the fact that what we were about to do was forbidden provided most of the excitement. There was nothing so very delectable about a biscuit and a few teaspoonsful of a rather sickly condensed milk taken from a communal spoon. The great point of the enterprise was the aura attached to midnight feasts . . . and forbidden fruit.

The time came. Eight of us were in our dormitory seated on two beds, four on one, four on another, facing each other.

The tin of milk was opened with some difficulty and there were squeals of excitement when some of it was spilled on the bedclothes, followed by frantic efforts to wipe it clean. The biscuits were handed round and consumed.

'Be careful of the crumbs,' warned Caroline. 'Arty has the eyes of a hawk.'

The conversation was carried on half in English and half in French, often embracing the two, which made it easy to speak, such as, 'Parlez doucement. Est-ce que vous want old Arty to hear?' There was a great deal of laughter, the more hilarious because it had to be suppressed; and there was no doubt that we were all enjoying ourselves immensely.

Then Yvonne remembered the reason why Thérèse de la Montaine had been asked, and she was eager for her guest to shine in the company; and when the conversation flagged and the giggles were less spontaneous, she said: 'Tell us about Madame Rochère and this house.'

'It's a very old house,' put in Caroline. 'There must be some stories about it. There are always stories about old houses. Does it have a ghost?'

'There is one ghost I know of,' said Thérèse. 'It's a lady who walks at night.'

We all looked round the room expectantly.

'Not here,' said Thérèse, 'though I reckon quite a lot of the old ancestors are cross about the house being changed. Ghosts don't like it when rooms are changed. Well, it would disturb them, wouldn't it?'

'Fancy having your haunting place changed!' said Helga.

'And a lot of girls put in it,' said Yvonne.

'Having midnight feasts in it,' said Anna B.

'I wonder they don't all come out and haunt *us*,' said Lucia.

'It's not our fault,' pointed out Caroline. 'We didn't make

the change. We're what you might call victims of circumstance. I think it is Madame Rochère who should look out.'

'She'd frighten any ghost away,' declared Lucia.

'How long is it since Madame Rochère made the change?' Yvonne prompted her guest.

'I think it was about thirty years ago. Old houses take a lot of money to keep up. The Rochères lost a lot of their property in the Revolution . . . and then they came to this one . . . just over the border. They lived here as they had in their French *château* . . . and then of course Madame Rochère couldn't afford to keep it up any longer. She'd married Monsieur Rochère, but hers was a great French family, too, and this house was very important to her. Monsieur Rochère died quite young and as she couldn't keep up the house she decided to turn it into a school.'

'We all know that,' said Anna B. 'What about the ghost?'

'Oh, that was long before . . . about two hundred years.'

'Time doesn't count with ghosts,' said Anna B. 'They can go on haunting for hundreds of years.'

'This was a lady . . .'

'It's always ladies,' retorted Anna B. 'They are better haunters than men.'

'It's because more awful things happen to them,' said Caroline. 'They have a reason to come back . . . for retribution.'

'Well, what about this ghost?' asked Yvonne.

'Well,' said Thérèse, 'it's a lady. She was young and beautiful.'

'They always are,' said Anna B.

'Do you want to hear about this ghost or not?' asked Lucia.

'Get on and tell us,' retorted Anna B.

'Well, she was young and beautiful. She had married the heir of La Pinière and then her husband caught a pox and his life was in danger.'

'You get spots all over,' said Lucia. 'And you are marked for life.'

'That's right,' went on Thérèse. 'She should have left him alone. It was very infectious. Everyone warned her, but she would nurse him herself. She would not let anyone else do it. She was with him night and day and she did it all herself. They said she was risking her life, for people died of it, you know.'

'We did know,' said Anna B. 'What happened to her? She died, I expect.'

'Not then. Her husband was cured. It was all due to her nursing. He was better and there were no marks on him at all. All the spots had gone and left no scars. He was more handsome than ever. But no sooner was he on the way to recovery than she found she was suffering from the pox which she had caught.'

'From him!' said Lucia.

'Of course from him,' said Anna B. 'Who else?'

'Get on with the story,' cried Yvonne.

'Well, her beauty had gone. She was covered in spots.'

'And he nursed her back to health,' cut in Lucia.

'He certainly did not. She got better but her face was all pitted. She wore a veil over it, and he . . . well, he didn't love her any more because she had lost her beauty . . . in caring for him.'

'What a sad tale,' said Helga.

'There's more to come. He neglected her. He had a . . . mistress.'

There was a long sigh from everyone present. The girls were all sitting up. The story had taken on a new dimension with the introduction of the mistress.

'You see, she had lost her looks in nursing him, and then he did this to her. And what did she do?'

'Killed the mistress . . . or him?' suggested Anna B.

'No, she did not. She went to the top of the tower and jumped right down and . . . killed herself.'

There was a shocked silence.

'And,' went on Thérèse, 'she now walks. She is the ghost. She can't rest. Every now and then she walks through the hall right up the spiral staircase . . . you know, the one that leads to the tower. You can hear her footsteps on the stone, they say.'

'I've never heard them,' said Helga.

'You have to be sensitive to hear them,' Thérèse told her.

'I'm sensitive,' said Caroline.

'So am I,' we all cried.

'Well, perhaps you'll hear them one day.'

'Has anyone seen her?'

'One of the girls said she did. She had long flowing hair and there was a veil over her face.'

'I'd like to see her,' said Anna B.

'Perhaps you will,' replied Yvonne.

'What do you say to a ghost?' asked Lucia.

'You don't say anything, of course,' retorted Thérèse. 'You're too frightened.'

'Perhaps one of us will see her,' I said.

'Who knows?' replied Thérèse.

After that we talked of ghosts. No one had seen any, but we had of course heard a great deal about them.

The clock in the tower struck two before the guests departed and after having made sure that there were no crumbs to attract Mademoiselle Artois's attention, we all went to bed.

After that night there was a good deal of talk about ghosts in general and particularly about that of the lady who had been disfigured by smallpox and had thrown herself from the top of the tower. An account of the midnight feast and the revelations of Thérèse were whispered from dormitory to dormitory.

We four used to talk about it continuously, after lights out. Anna B was quite interested too. She said it showed how you had to be on your guard with men and it was a lesson: if they caught smallpox, never nurse them.

Some girls said they had heard footsteps in the night . . . steps walking across the hall and out to the tower.

I saw a little more of Anna B after that night; the feast had brought us together more and those who could provide such an entertainment were not to be despised, even if they were only thirteen years old.

If I met her she would pause and talk and I was able to ask

how she was getting on. She said she quite liked it. She loved the dancing and she got on very well with Lucia. She did not ask how I was getting on. But that was typical of her.

One day I had a great surprise.

It was about half past four. We had finished lessons for the day and this was our rest period, when we could go to our dormitories to read or chat together.

I thought I would take a little walk in the gardens which were very beautiful. This we were allowed to do, providing we did not go beyond the grounds.

As I was coming out of the house, I caught sight of Anna B. She was hurrying towards the shrubbery and I went after her.

She was some way ahead and, fearing that when she entered the shrubbery I should lose sight of her, I called her name.

She looked round. 'Oh, it's you,' she said, and went on walking. I ran up to her.

'Where are you going?' I asked.

'Oh . . . nowhere.'

'Really, Anna B. One really doesn't go nowhere.'

'Just for a walk, that's all.'

And then I saw him. I could not believe it at first. It was so unexpected. For there, in the shrubbery, was Carl Zimmerman. My mind went back to the last time I had seen him standing uncertainly outside the cubbyhole and then again inside it talking to us until Robert took him to the dining-room.

He stared from me to Anna B.

'Why . . .' he began.

'You were at our home . . . do you remember?' I said.

He nodded.

'It is so strange to see you here . . . at our school.'

Anna B looked a little exasperated. She said: 'I knew Carl was here. I saw him the other day and he explained to me.'

'Explained . . . ?'

I could not stop myself from looking at him. He was very different from the previous occasion when he had been immaculately dressed for the evening. He was now wearing a loose

40

jacket which had smudges of earth on it; and so did his trousers; moreover, he was carrying a rake.

'Carl works here . . . in the gardens,' said Anna B.

He smiled at me. 'Yes,' he said. 'That is so.'

'He doesn't want anyone to know . . . exactly,' went on Anna B.

'What do you mean?'

Carl said: 'It is a . . . er . . . joke. A gamble . . . a bet I entered into. Ah, I mean a wager, I think. A friend of mine, he say I would not do manual labour for three months. He meant to take a job.'

'What about the embassy? Don't you belong to an embassy?'

'Yes . . . yes. This is something I must do because I say I can. I say I will do it for two months. My friend say, "You will not remain so long." I say I will, so I do.'

'A wager,' I said. 'I have heard of people doing things like that.'

'Yes . . . that is what it is. I will win . . . I have made up my mind.'

'Does Madame Rochère know that you are here on a . . . wager?'

'Oh no, no, no. She would send me off. She thinks I am a bona fide gardener's boy.'

'It's a bit of a joke,' said Anna B. 'And I think you are very brave to do it, Carl.'

'Oh, but it does not require bravery . . . just work.' He looked ruefully at his hands. 'It is work to which I am not accustomed.'

'You are doing very well,' said Anna B. 'I am sure they are very pleased with you. How marvellous it will be when you have won your wager! You will be rightly proud of yourself. How much is it, Carl?'

'Twenty thousand francs.'

Anna B pursed her lips and looked impressed.

'Oh, but it is not the money,' he said.

'The honour of Switzerland, eh?' said Anna B jocularly.

41

'Something like that.'

'Do you live here?' I asked.

He waved his hand. 'Over there. There are some little cottages . . . more like huts, really. But I manage . . . for my wager. The gardeners all live there together . . . with others employed here. It is adequate.'

'I see.'

'Well . . . I should not be speaking to young ladies from the school, of course.'

'We can't be seen here among all these trees,' said Anna B. 'At least, I hope not.'

We walked through the shrubbery and Carl pointed out his living quarters in the distance.

'There you see my dwelling,' he said. 'And now I take my leave.'

With that he bowed and left us.

Anna B looked a little cross and I gathered it was with me. I was about to mention this when she said: 'I wouldn't say anything about meeting Carl if I were you.'

'Why not?'

'Well, it's a bit secret, isn't it? I don't know what old Rochèrc's reaction would be – the old snob. She wouldn't want people coming to work here to settle wagers, would she? She would expect a properly trained gardener.'

'Well, he is only here for a little while.'

'She does not know that. So don't say anything, will you?'

'You didn't say you'd seen him.'

'It was only the other day I did. Then we came upon him accidentally . . . like that.'

'I suppose we might never have seen him if you hadn't come across him by chance.'

'No, we wouldn't.'

'Do you think he was a bit put out because we have discovered him?'

'Perhaps. He wouldn't want it generally known about the wager, would he?'

'He told you.'

'Well, I wouldn't mention it to Caroline or any of them. It would be all over the school if you did.'

'I won't.'

'What are you supposed to be doing now?'

'Just taking a little walk before I go back. It's Conversazione at six. I don't know what we are going to talk about.'

'Let's wait and see, eh?'

She walked with me a little and after that we went in.

It was a few days after my encounter with Carl and I had ceased to marvel at the coincidence of his choosing our school in which to work out his wager.

I said to Anna B: 'He seems to be one of those people who turn up in odd places.'

She smiled to herself.

'Well,' I went on, 'he was there at our house . . . outside the cubbyhole . . . and then to find him here. It's odd.'

'He's a diplomatic, of course.'

'He gets long holidays at that, I suppose. How strange for a diplomatic suddenly to become a gardener!'

'He explained. I reckon he has an exciting time.'

She was smiling. She looked different and had done for some little time. I thought it was because she was enjoying school. She and Lucia were always whispering together; there was a touch of superiority about them both as though they knew something which the rest of us didn't.

That night, when I had been fast asleep, I was abruptly awakened by someone calling. 'Lucinda . . . Lucinda!' It was insistent, dragging me out of a pleasant dream.

Caroline was standing by my bed. She was wearing her dressing-gown.

'Wake up,' she said. 'I can hear something. Listen.'

I sat up in bed, trying to shake off my drowsiness.

'What . . . ?' I mumbled.

'Footsteps,' whispered Caroline. 'I heard them go along the corridor and down to the hall.'

43

'The ghost!' I cried.

'Get up. I'm going to look. Come with me.'

'It's late . . .'

'Listen.'

I did and then I heard it, too. It was definitely the sound of footsteps and they were going down the staircase in the direction of the hall. I felt my heart begin to beat faster. Now I was as curious as Caroline.

Yvonne was awakened. 'What's wrong?' she asked.

'It's the ghost. We've both heard it.'

'Where?'

Caroline jerked her head towards the door. 'In the corridor and now on the stairs. Listen!'

We stood very still.

Helga was now awake. We explained quickly.

'We're going to look,' said Caroline.

Helga hastily got out of bed and put on her dressing-gown while Caroline quietly opened the door, and we went out into the corridor.

We descended the staircase and were in the hall. We gasped, for ahead of us, standing by one of the windows, was . . . the ghost.

It was the slim figure of a young woman, her hair loose about her shoulders; she had her back to us so we could not see whether she wore a veil over her scarred face, but in those first moments we were sure she did.

And then it dawned on us that she was not wearing the robes of an earlier century, but she was in a dressing-gown very like those we were wearing. As we stood there the figure turned and, instead of the pock-marked beauty, we saw that our ghost was Marie Christine du Bray.

'Marie Christine!' whispered Caroline.

She laid a hand on my arm and, as she did so, Marie Christine walked slowly towards us, her hands slightly outstretched, as though she were feeling her way. She gave no sign that she saw us.

Caroline whispered: 'She's walking in her sleep.'

'What do we do?' asked Yvonne.

'Go and get Mademoiselle Artois,' said Caroline.

'What?' cried Helga.

'Hush. We mustn't wake her. We don't know what to do. We ought to get her back to bed.'

Caroline herself took on the task and hurried upstairs to the room where Mademoiselle Artois slept. It was at the end of the dormitory where she had two rooms, her bedroom and study.

Marie Christine by this time had walked down to the end of the gallery and sat in an armchair. Caroline had told us to stay quietly and watch her, in case she went somewhere else.

It was not long before Mademoiselle appeared, looking unlike her daytime self, with two rather thin plaits hanging down her back, and a look of consternation on her face.

By this time several other girls had arrived on the scene, Anna B with Lucia among them.

Mademoiselle Artois immediately took charge.

'You girls go back at once to your dormitories. Marie Christine has walked in her sleep. Be very quiet. She must not be disturbed.'

The first shock of seeing Mademoiselle in *déshabille* had passed and the sound of her authoritative voice was as effective by night as it was by day. She went to Marie Christine and took her arm gently. 'It's all right,' she said soothingly. 'We shall go to your room. You will be comfortable there.'

Marie Christine stood up and allowed herself to be led. The girls silently watched as Marie Christine was taken up the stairs. Mademoiselle was too taken up with Marie Christine to have noticed that we were still there.

We all started to whisper.

'I thought it was the ghost.'

'So did I.'

'Marie Christine looked very strange.'

'So did Mademoiselle.'

Giggles followed.

'Do you think Marie Christine was looking for the ghost?'

'All that talk about it may have preyed on her mind.'

Mademoiselle appeared suddenly.

'Why are you not in your beds? Go to them at once. All is well. Marie Christine has merely been walking in her sleep. It is not unusual for people to do this. Now, back to bed, all of you.'

The next day everyone was talking about last night's adventure. In the morning Dr Crozier was called in to see Marie Christine. We were told that she was resting for the day.

At Conversazione when we were all assembled, Madame Rochère herself addressed us.

'You girls will be aware that there was a little disturbance in the night. I want to talk to you all very seriously. Marie Christine has suffered a great shock recently, and it has naturally unsettled her. Dr Crozier has seen her. There is nothing wrong, I am happy to say, except that she is a little disturbed, as we all should be in her position. This has made her uneasy at night when she should be resting, and it has resulted in this sleepwalking. She may not do it again, but if she did and you girls heard her, I want you to do nothing. Do not speak to her or disturb her in any way. Dr Crozier informs me that it is best to leave her. She will go back to her bed when she is ready and be unaware of what has happened. I am assured that this is the best way to deal with the matter. She is resting now and will do so during the day. I want no more gathering together and talking, whispering, disturbing everyone, as there was last night.

'Be very gentle with Marie Christine in your contacts with her. Remember that she has suffered a great ordeal from which she is recovering. And remember this: I want no more walking about in the night. Mademoiselle Artois will deal with everything. That is all.'

Madame Rochère had spoken in French and her speech was immediately repeated in English, Italian and German –

to make sure that everyone understood perfectly what was expected of them.

This impressed upon us that the matter was very serious, although there was nothing unusual about sleepwalking. Lots of people did it. If it had been the ghost, that would have been far more exciting. As it was, what most people remembered about that night were Mademoiselle Artois's plaits.

The nights were getting darker. We were approaching Christmas and there was a great deal of excitement because most of the girls were going home for the holiday. Aunt Celeste wrote that she would come to the school and take Anna B and me to the Princesse's house, where we would spend a night before making the journey home. The girls talked continuously of the arrangements which were being made.

It was November as yet – dark days, just the time for ghosts. Mists in the air, shadows in the rooms, to remind people of them.

Marie Christine seemed better. We would see her laughing now and then; she was going to her aunt for Christmas and she had several jolly cousins.

Then rumours about the ghost were started.

One of the senior girls declared she had actually seen it; and it was not Marie Christine sleepwalking. She had heard footsteps in the corridor and had opened her door and looked out. She thought that she ought to report it to Mademoiselle Artois if it were Marie Christine sleepwalking, but as it was not, she did no such thing. What she had seen was a figure, a girl, her hair hanging loosely about her shoulders and over her face was a veil. She had seen it distinctly. There was a full moon and it shone right through the window. There was no mistake. She had seen the veiled woman.

Everyone was talking about it. Janet Carew, the girl who had seen the ghost, was seventeen and therefore her word should be respected. She had been at the school for three years and was known to be an unperturbable type, not given to flights of fancy. Instead, she was predictable – in other words, in the opinion of the girls, rather dull. Yet she insisted that she had seen the ghost.

'What did it do?' she was asked.

'It just . . . walked.'

'Where did it go?'

'Into one of the dormitories.'

'Which one?'

'I couldn't see. I think it possibly disappeared into the wall.'

After that, other people said they saw it. There was an uneasiness throughout the school. We were all watchful, anxious not to be alone in any of the big rooms after dark.

There was one night when I could not sleep. It was surprising because we had all had rather an exhausting day. There had been a long ramble in the afternoon. Miss Carruthers, who taught English and physical training, had said the winter would soon be upon us and we must make the most of the fine days, the 'season of mists and mellow fruitfulness' she said. She was always happy to bring literature and physical exercise together. 'A healthy mind and a healthy body' was one of her favourite maxims.

So we had sprinted through fields and thickets almost to the edge of the town of Mons, which we saw in the distance. It was invigorating but we were all a little weary at Conversazione, and as soon as we were in bed most of us were fast asleep.

I had dozed and awoke. The others were all asleep. I could see them clearly because the moon shining through the window was so bright.

I lay there for some time but sleep seemed elusive, and suddenly I thought I heard a sound below.

I got out of bed and went to the window. The dormitories looked out from the back of the house on to the kitchen garden and the orchard. I started with amazement. There was someone down there. I saw her clearly, speeding across from the orchard to the back door.

It was Anna B. I would know her anywhere. Her black hair

was loose and she was coming purposefully towards the house. I stood watching her . . . fascinated. She came to the side of the house, opened a window and climbed in.

Where had she been? What had she been doing? It was strange but, in spite of her somewhat superior attitude towards me, I always felt a need to look after her. I had a feeling that she might get into serious trouble.

I turned to look at my room mates. They were all fast asleep.

Anna B would have to come up to her dormitory. I would surprise her. I would tell her what a dangerous thing she was doing. It could result in her expulsion.

I crept out of the room, shutting the door quietly behind me. I went swiftly along the corridor and waited in the shadows.

She came. She did not look like the girl who had recently climbed through the window. She was wearing a veil over her face.

The ghost, of course!

She came silently up the stairs. I saw her clearly in the light from the window. She would never have deceived me into thinking she was the ghost. I would have known her anywhere.

She opened the door of her dormitory. I followed her in. Lucia lifted herself from her bed and said: 'You're late.'

Then both she and Anna B were staring at me.

'What are you doing?' demanded Anna B.

'Where have you been?' I countered.

She just continued to stare at me, puzzled and furious.

'You should be more careful,' I said. 'I heard you below. I looked out and saw you come in through the window. I waited for you.'

'You . . . you spy!'

'Be quiet!' said Lucia. 'Do you want to wake the school?'

'You'll be in trouble, young Lucinda,' said Anna B. 'Walking about the dormitories at night.'

'Not as much as you will be, going out and climbing through a window.'

'Listen to me,' said Lucia. 'Go back to your dorm. Talk in the morning.'

I could see that was good sense.

I nodded. 'All right. I'll see you in the morning.'

Anna B sat on her bed glowering at me. She was still holding the veil in her hand. Lucia had begun to giggle.

I crept back to my room. The three girls were still fast asleep and unaware that I had been away.

I got into bed and lay there shivering. What could she have been doing? And this was not the first time. I guessed Anna B was the 'ghost' whom Janet Carew had seen.

But where did she go? One thing was certain: Lucia was in the secret.

I had to wait until the following afternoon before I could encounter Anna B, for we attended different classes and our paths did not often cross.

When I did, she said: 'Come into the garden.'

I followed her there.

'What do you mean by spying on me?' she demanded in a bellicose manner. She was clearly on the defensive and distinctly rattled.

'I was not spying!' I retorted. 'I heard you and I looked out as anyone would. It could have been someone else who saw you . . . Mademoiselle Artois for instance.'

'That old fool!'

'She's not an old fool. She's probably a good deal wiser than you are. Tell me, where did you go? Why did you go? It's not the first time, is it?'

'Who are you – the Grand Inquisitor?'

'No. Just someone to whom you owe an explanation.'

'I owe you nothing.'

'I could go along and tell Mademoiselle Artois what I saw last night . . . creeping into the house . . . pretending to be a ghost. So you are the ghost Janet Carew saw!'

She began to laugh. 'So you are a sneak as well as a spy! It was a jolly good idea. It scared them. I got the idea when Marie Christine went walking. I thought if they heard me, they'd think she was sleepwalking again and wouldn't bother. I thought the veil would be a good idea if anyone should see. They wouldn't recognize me under it.'

'I recognized you.'

'Oh well, you're my dear old friend Lucinda, aren't you?'

'Annabelinda,' I said, reverting to her proper name. 'What were you doing?'

'That's better,' she said. 'I hate "Anna B". Never call me that again once we are away from here.'

'You're changing the subject. What were you doing?'

'I felt like a walk.'

'Where to?'

'Just round the grounds. Perhaps I liked playing the ghost.'

'It was very dangerous. Do you want to be expelled?'

'I wouldn't be.'

'I guess you would.'

'Of course not. Grandpère Bourdon is a great friend of Madame Rochère. They would work something out. He would plead for me.'

'You were taking a risk.'

'Haven't you yet learned that I like taking risks?'

'Tell me what all this is about. I don't believe you did all that just because you felt like a midnight stroll in the grounds.'

'You're getting too clever, little Lucinda.'

'Which means you are not going to tell me. But Lucia knows.'

'Lucia's a good sort.'

'She's another such as you are.'

'Well, that may be so.'

'Where did you go, Annabelinda?'

'I'll tell you when you're eighteen.'

'Don't be absurd!'

'You'll understand then. And perhaps you will have done the same thing yourself.'

51

Her eyes were dancing. I felt it was so mysterious, but I knew she was not going to tell me.

She said: 'I'm going in now. Mustn't be late for Conversazione, must we? So let's be good little girls. Come on.'

Later, when I saw her giggling with Lucia, as though they shared secrets, I felt bitterly hurt.

The Indiscretion

Christmas was now almost upon us. Bustle and preparations permeated the house.

A party of us went into Mons, in the company of Miss Carruthers and Mademoiselle du Pont who taught French, to buy presents for friends at home.

It was only a short train journey and Miss Carruthers was very eager that we should see some of what she called 'the points of interest' before we spent our time in the frivolous pleasure of gift-selecting.

She lectured us as we chuffed along.

'Now, girls, you must know that Mons is situated between the Trouille and Haine rivers at the junction of two canals. One of these was built by Napoleon. It was at one time a Roman camp and it is the capital of the province of Hainault.'

None of us was paying full attention to this; we were all consulting our present lists. Anna B was looking a little preoccupied. She was sitting with Lucia and now and then talking to her, but I thought she was somewhat bored with the whole proceedings.

Arriving in the town, we had to do a little sight-seeing. Miss Carruthers insisted on it and we were all afraid that we would have too little time for shopping. We went to see the Church of St Waufru and the belfry famous for its forty-seven-bell carillon.

'And, girls,' added Miss Carruthers, 'the Battle of Malplaquet was fought and won by our own great Duke of Marlborough not far from here.'

At last we were allowed our freedom and I have to admit

that the large store to which we were taken was of greater interest to me than the exploits of the great Duke and when, at length, we were allowed our freedom, I bought some sugar almonds in a beautiful blue and silver box for my mother, a model of the church for my father and a penknife for Charles.

When we went back I sat with Annabelinda. I asked what she had bought.

'Nothing,' she replied briefly.

'You look bored,' I said.

'Who wouldn't be?'

'I wasn't.'

'Oh, you'd like anything.'

She was genuinely disgruntled and when I asked if she were annoyed about something she snapped at me: 'Of course not. Why should I be? But old Carruthers did go on about that church and the bells.'

In due course we left for home.

Aunt Celeste came for us and we spent a night at Valenciennes. Neither the Princesse nor Jean Pascal was there, and soon we were on our way home.

My parents were at Dover to meet us. We kept hugging each other and they wanted to hear all about school. Annabelinda was staying the night with us, and Aunt Belinda was coming to London on the following day.

It was a wonderful homecoming. I told them all about school life and described Madame Rochère and the only slightly less formidable Mademoiselle Artois, Miss Carruthers, the whole lot. They wanted to hear about the midnight feasts and Marie Christine's sleepwalking.

I was on the point of mentioning the ghost, but I held back. Somehow I felt that Annabelinda, in her present mood, would want that.

'It is quite clear to me,' said my mother, 'that you enjoy that school.'

I assured her I did, although I wished it were not so far away. The Princesse had been wonderful, I went on, and her title did much to enhance our prestige with Madame Rochère.

'What of Jean Pascal Bourdon?' she said. 'I have not heard you mention him.'

'We haven't seen him.'

'He is busy at Château Bourdon, I suppose. The wine and all that.'

'Yes, and Aunt Celeste just took us to their house at Valenciennes, didn't she, Anna B? That's what the girls call her at school. They say Annabelinda is too long.'

'I don't like it,' said Annabelinda. 'I forbid you to call me by anything but my proper name.'

When we were alone, my mother said: 'What's wrong with Annabelinda? She doesn't seem so enamoured of the school as you are.'

'Oh, she likes it. She would have liked to stay on and not come home for the holidays, I believe.'

'Oh dear, we must try to make her change her mind.'

There was so much to do during those holidays, so many things to talk about, that I forgot Annabelinda.

The Denvers spent Christmas week with us and after that I went down to Cornwall to be with Aunt Rebecca. That was always enjoyable and Aunt Rebecca was as eager to hear about the school as my mother had been.

We came back to London and preparations for the return to school began in earnest. A few days before we were due to leave, Annabelinda and her mother came to London.

Annabelinda looked no better than she had when the holiday began. She did not seem to want to talk to me, but the night before we left, I was feeling so anxious about her that I went along to her room, determined to talk.

I knocked and without waiting for an answer went in.

She was in bed but not asleep.

'Oh, it's you,' she said ungraciously.

'Annabelinda,' I said. 'I'm worried about you. Are you ill or something? Why don't you tell me? There might be something I could do.'

'You can't do anything,' she replied. 'I shall never see him again.'

'Who?'

'Carl.'

'Carl . . . you mean the gardener?'

'He wasn't really a gardener. That was only a bet. He just left without saying. I didn't know he was going. He didn't tell me.'

'Was there any reason why he should tell you?'

'Every reason,' she said. 'We were friends.'

'Friends,' I repeated. 'You only saw him in the gardens – apart from that night in this house.'

'That's nothing to do with it,' she retorted. 'We were friends, special friends. You know what I mean . . . well, lovers.'

'Lovers!' I gasped.

'Don't keep repeating what I say. You don't understand anything.'

'I would if you told me.'

'Well, Carl and I were special friends. It was great fun. I used to see him often. Sometimes in the days and . . .'

Memories of her creeping into the house, coming up the stairs, playing the ghost, came to me. 'And at night,' I added.

She smiled and looked a little like her old self at the recollection.

'It was great fun. Lucia knew. She was a real sport. Well, she'd had adventures herself. She helped me a lot. She used to put a bundle in my bed so that it looked as though I were there, asleep . . . just in case old Arty came in.'

'Is this why you are so upset? He was your friend and he didn't even tell you that he was going?'

She nodded, miserable again.

'He couldn't have been much of a friend.'

'It must have been a sudden call from somewhere.'

'He could have left a message.'

'Well, not easily. He wasn't supposed to have anything to do with the girls.'

I felt shocked and bewildered. All I could say was: 'Well, fancy . . . you and Carl.'

'He is very handsome.'

'I suppose so.'

'And rather unusual. I mean, doing all that for a bet.'

'There is certainly something unusual about him. Perhaps he'll appear again somewhere.'

'That will be too late. Oh, we did have some fun together. He was ever so interested in the school. He used to ask me a lot of questions about it. He made me draw a plan of it. One night I let him in.'

'Let him in!'

She nodded. 'We climbed through the window.'

'As I saw *you* do.'

'Yes. It was easy. I just unbolted it and left it unbolted so that I could get back. I had an arrangement with Lucia that if I did not get back by two in the morning she would come down and make sure someone hadn't bolted the window. Lucia was a great help.'

'And you brought him into the school!'

'Only once. There was something he wanted to see about the building. It was so exciting . . . creeping round in the dark . . . with a torch, of course.'

'You might have been caught!'

'Disaster!' she said, raising her eyes to the ceiling.

'You would have been expelled.'

'I don't think so. Grandpère Bourdon would have stopped that. Madame Rochère is very fond of him. I think he must have been her lover years ago when she was young and beautiful. I believe my grandfather has been the lover of half the women in France. He wouldn't let me be expelled.'

'You are very daring . . . and now you are wretched because of this Carl.'

She was silent.

'Well,' I said. 'I'm glad I know. You are just a deserted maiden, pining for her lover.'

'Don't tell anyone. I don't know why I've told you.'

'Because, in spite of everything, we are still friends.'

'I suppose so . . .'

'I was getting quite worried about you. You'll get over this. There will be others.'

She smiled at me faintly.

'Thanks for coming, Lucinda.'

She was more gracious than she had been for a long time.

'I'm glad I did,' I answered. 'Good night.'

The next day we made the journey back to school. My parents came with us as far as Dover, as they had before, Aunt Belinda with them. Then they went back to London and we spent the night with Aunt Celeste at Valenciennes. Jean Pascal Bourdon and the Princesse were still at the Château Bourdon in the Médoc.

Soon we were settling in for the term. I was glad to find that I had the same dormitory companions and we all greeted each other joyously. Lucia had left and Annabelinda had a room to herself.

I thought: She will like that. But I was sure she would miss Lucia.

It must have been about a week after we were back when Annabelinda fainted during the English class. I was not there, of course, but I heard about it immediately.

She was taken to her room and the doctor was sent for.

I was worried about her. I knew she was not herself. I was beginning to think that it must be more than the melancholy over a lost lover.

The doctor was closeted with Madame Rochère for some time after he had seen Annabelinda. I went along to her room, but was stopped by Mademoiselle Artois as I was about to enter it.

'Where are you going, Lucinda?' she asked.

'To see Annabelinda. I have heard that the doctor has been to see her.'

'Annabelinda is not to be disturbed.'

'I shan't disturb her. She is really like my sister. We have been together a great deal . . . always.'

58

'That may be, but Annabelinda is not to be disturbed. Now, go to your class.' She looked at her watch. 'Or you will be late,' she added.

I could not concentrate on anything. She was ill. I wanted to be with her. However much we sparred, she was like a part of me. Like my parents . . . Aunt Celeste . . . I could not bear to be shut out.

For two days she remained in her room and I was not allowed to visit her. I began to think she was suffering from some infectious disease.

Then Jean Pascal Bourdon arrived at the school with the Princesse. He was taken straight to Madame Rochère and stayed with her for a long time.

During the day I was sent for by Madame Rochère.

'The Princesse and Monsieur Bourdon are here,' she told me – as if I did not know. 'They would like to speak to you. They are waiting for you in my sitting-room. You may go along to them now.'

I wondered what this could mean, and I hurried along.

The Princesse kissed me on both cheeks. Jean Pascal was standing a few paces behind her; then he came forward and, taking both my hands in his, kissed me as the Princesse had and smiled at me tenderly.

'My dear Lucinda,' he said. 'I can see that you are anxious about Annabelinda. The poor child is quite ill. We are going to take her back with us to Bourdon. We shall look after her there and we hope that, in a few months, she will be her old self.'

'Months!' I said.

'Oh yes, my dear,' put in the Princesse. 'It will be several months.'

Jean Pascal went on: 'I am telling her parents that she will need special care, which naturally she cannot get at school. After all, it is a school, not a hospital. I am asking my daughter and her husband to come over to Bourdon where we shall be. So they will soon be here, I hope. You will miss Annabelinda, I know. But you have settled in now, have you not?'

I murmured that I had. I felt bewildered. I could not believe that Annabelinda was so ill that she had to leave school for several months.

He was watching me covertly. He said suddenly: 'Has Annabelinda talked to you?'

'Well . . . she did a little.'

'About . . . how she was feeling?'

'Oh er . . . yes. We did talk in London before we left. She was upset about . . . er . . .'

'About . . . er . . . ?'

'About a friend of hers.'

'She told you that, did she?'

'Yes.'

'This friend of hers?'

'He came here as a gardener.'

'I see,' said Jean Pascal abruptly. 'Well, she is ill, you know, and she will need some time to recover.'

'Is she coming back to school?'

'I dare say she will when she is well. I wouldn't say anything about this gardener, if I were you.'

'Oh, I wouldn't. I thought Annabelinda didn't want me to.'

'I am sure she wouldn't. She just spoke to him in the gardens, of course.'

'Oh,' I began, and stopped abruptly. Jean Pascal gave me an intent look; then he was smiling.

'I hope you will come to the *château* sometimes,' he said. 'Perhaps before you go home for the summer holiday. That's a good time of year . . . when the grapes are nearly ripe, you know.'

'Thank you,' I said.

'We are leaving today and taking Annabelinda with us. I hope you won't be lonely without her.'

'I have Caroline, Helga and Yvonne and others.'

'I am sure you have lots of friends.'

'Annabelinda is not going to . . .' They both looked at me in horror as I stammered: 'Not going . . . to die?'

Jean Pascal laughed. '*Mon Dieu, non, non, non,*' he cried.

'She will be all right. She just needs quiet and rest and attention which she can get at Bourdon. When you see her in the summer it will be the old Annabelinda whom you knew.'

'I have been worried.'

'Of course you have, dear child. But there is no need. We're going to nurse her to health. You will be amazed when you see her. In the meantime you must work hard and please Madame Rochère, who gives you quite a good report, I might tell you. And . . . just don't talk too much about Annabelinda. She doesn't like being ill. Nobody does, and when she comes back she won't want people to think of her as an invalid.'

'I understand.'

'I knew you would. Bless you, my dear. I am so looking forward to seeing you in the summer.'

'I too, my dear,' said the Princesse.

That afternoon they left, taking Annabelinda with them.

I missed her very much. I would always feel an emptiness when she was out of my life. I missed the skirmishes, her scorn, her contempt, for I knew that beneath it all there was a certain affection.

I wondered how she was progressing and I was delighted when I received a letter from her.

Dear Lucinda [she wrote],

How are you getting on at school without me? My mother came to Bourdon. They have all decided that I must stay here for a while. They say the climate is so much better for me than it is at home. I shall be all right in time, they tell me. Grandpère has a lot of influence here and knows all the people who can be of use. He suggests you come here before you go home in the summer. He's confident that I shall be completely recovered by then. But I may need a little rest, so I'm to stay on here until I'm ready to go back home.

I wish you were here. I will look forward to your coming when school finishes at the end of July for the long summer

61

break. Don't say you must hurry home to see your parents and that brother of yours. You must come and be with me first.

Annabelinda.

She sounded more like herself. I wrote and told her that I would stay for two weeks at the Château Bourdon before going home, if that were agreeable. That was long enough, I stressed, for I was longing to see my parents after the long term away.

School went on as usual. There was a midnight feast. Caroline had brought a cake with icing on the top when she came back from the Christmas holidays and this was a great treat. But nothing seemed quite the same without Annabelinda.

'What's wrong with her?' asked Caroline.

'Some awful illness which takes months to cure.'

'Consumption, I suppose,' said Caroline wisely.

'I don't think so.'

'People do go into declines.'

'She hasn't looked well for some time. So perhaps it is that.'

'They usually go to Switzerland for a cure,' said Helga. 'It's the mountain air or something.'

Switzerland? I thought. Carl Zimmerman came from there.

I was thinking more and more of Carl Zimmerman. The illness had started after he had left. It was pining for him which had brought it on.

I started to wonder about him. I would walk about the grounds remembering our encounter with him. I went to look at the cottages, one of which had been occupied by him.

There seemed to be someone in one of them. I studied it. It was clearly inhabited. I strolled round and then went back to the house.

And the next afternoon I found myself wandering that way again.

I walked round to the back of the cottages. They had gardens there and in one of them was a woman hanging out washing.

She called good-afternoon to me and added: 'You're from

the school. I've seen you round here before.'

'Yes,' I said, and added: 'I suppose you work for the school?'

'Not me. My husband does. He works in the gardens. There's plenty of work there.'

'I suppose so.'

She came towards me. She had a pleasant happy face. I noticed that she was going to have a baby . . . and quite soon. She leaned her arms on the wall and surveyed me.

'Have you been long at the school?' she asked.

'I came last September.'

'Where do you come from? England, I guess.'

'How did you know?'

'Well, you pick them out. It is the way you speak French, perhaps.'

'Is it as bad as that?'

'Never mind,' she said. 'And it is not bad at all. I know what you are saying.'

'Oh, good. Did you know Carl who worked here for a time?'

'Oh yes. Not much of a gardener, my Jacques said. I knew him. Didn't stay long.'

'Why did he go away so soon?'

'I don't think he ever meant to stay. One of those here-today-and-gone-tomorrow types.'

'Well, I'd better get back.'

'Goodbye,' she said cheerfully.

A week or so later I saw her again. She looked a little larger.

'Hello. You again,' she said. 'You seem to like this place.'

'I like to get out at this time of the day, and it is pleasant in the gardens.'

'Spring really is here.'

'Yes. It's lovely.'

'It's time for my rest. I have to rest now, you know.'

I knew what she meant. 'You're very pleased about it, aren't you? I mean . . . the baby.'

'So you've noticed.' She laughed loudly, indicating this was a joke, as her condition was so obvious.

'Well . . . er . . . I did.'

'A young girl like you!'

'I'm not really so young.'

'No. Of course you're not. Young people know about such things nowadays. You've guessed right. I am pleased. We always wanted a child, Jacques and me. Thought we were never going to have one and then the good God saw fit to grant our wish.'

'It must be wonderful for you.'

She nodded, blissfully serene.

I went away thinking about her.

One day when Miss Carruthers took us on a tour of Mons we had a chance to visit the shops again and I bought a baby's jacket which I proposed to take to the woman. I had discovered her name. It was Marguerite Plantain. Jacques Plantain had been employed on the school estate for many years and his father and grandfather had worked for the Rochères before there had been a school.

Marguerite was delighted with the jacket. She told me how she enjoyed our little chats over the wall. I was invited into the cottage on that occasion. It was very small, with two rooms upstairs, two downstairs and a wash-house at the back.

She took great pleasure in showing me the things she had prepared for the baby. I was very interested and told her that I hoped it would arrive before I left for the summer holidays.

'School closes at the very end of July,' she said. 'Leastways it always has. Well, the baby should be here a week or so before that.'

'I shall want to know whether it's a girl or boy. I'd like a little girl.'

'*You* would!' She laughed at me. 'Well, it is for the good God to decide that. Jacques wants a boy but I reckon he'll be mightily pleased with whatever is sent us. All I want is to hold this little one in my arms.'

Spring was passing. Summer had come. Only one more month before school finished. I was enjoying school more than ever. Caroline and I had become firm friends and I was quite fond of the other two.

Country walks, paper chases, plenty of fresh air. That was the best medicine, said Miss Carruthers. There were complaints from Mademoiselle Artois because we left the dormitory untidy. Dancing lessons, piano lessons . . . through the long warm days. But I was always missing Annabelinda and waiting eagerly for some news of her.

She did write now and then. She was getting better. She thought she would soon be really well by the time I joined her. It was very hot in Bourdon and they were all complaining about the effect the weather was having on the grapes.

'I look forward to seeing you, Lucinda,' she said, 'and hearing about all that's been going on in that old school.'

And I was certainly looking forward to seeing her.

In the middle of July Marguerite gave birth to a stillborn son. I felt very unhappy because I could not bear to think of her suffering. I had known how desperately she had wanted that child and now, poor Marguerite, all her plans and hopes had been in vain.

The blinds were drawn at the cottage. I could not bring myself to call. I feared she would remember our conversation about the baby and that would make her more unhappy.

I did not go near the cottage for two weeks, but I continued to think about her and then one day, when I did walk that way, I went to the back of the cottage and looked over the wall. In the garden, in a perambulator, lay a baby.

I could not contain my curiosity. The next day I went there again. The perambulator and the baby were in the garden. I went round to the front of the cottage and knocked on the door.

Marguerite opened it and looked at me. I felt the tears in my eyes. She saw them and turned her head away for a second or two.

Then she said: 'My dear, it was good of you to come.'

'I didn't like to before . . . but I thought of you.'

She laid a hand on my arm. 'Come inside,' she said.

I did so. 'I was so very sorry . . .' I began.

'It was a bitter blow. I just wanted to die. All our hopes . . . all our plans . . . and then to end like that. Sit down. I am glad you came. I'll not forget. The little coat you bought . . . it will be used.'

'It seems so cruel.'

She nodded. 'I was wicked. I cursed the good God. Jacques did, too. We were beside ourselves with grief. It was our dream, you see . . . both of us. We waited so long, and then . . . it ended like that. It was more than we could endure. And I cursed the good God. I said how could He do this? What have we done to deserve it? But God is good. He had His reasons. And now He has given me this little one to care for. It is one of His miracles. It eases the pain and I love him already. It is not like my own . . . but they say it will come to be like that. And it seems so . . . a little more every day.'

'So you have a baby after all?'

'Yes. He is mine now. Mine forever. He needs me and I need him. Poor mite. He has no mother, no one to care for him. So I am going to give him that loving care I would have given my own.'

'Tell me about it.'

'It was Madame Rochère. She heard of this little one. She said, how would it be if I took him in place of the one I had lost? I didn't say yes then. I didn't feel there was anything that could replace my own. Then she said this little one needed me . . . and although I might not realize it, I needed him. It wasn't the money, of course.'

'The money?'

'Oh yes. He's being paid for. He's got no mother but there are relations who will pay to have him cared for. Jacques and I, we shall be richer than we ever dreamed. But it is not the money . . .'

'I am sure it isn't.'

'We talked it over. I said, that baby will be ours forever. I

66

don't want anyone to come and take him away. If he's mine, he's to be mine for always. And they said that was how they wanted it to be. There's money put away for him. Every year it will be sent. He's not to want for anything. And, my dear, I love him already.'

'It's a wonderful story, Madame Plantain. It's like a miracle. You lost your own baby and if you hadn't this little baby wouldn't have had you to look after him.'

'Oh, they'd have found someone to do that. Those sort of people have money and can arrange things. But with me it's not the money. It's the baby. He's a little dear. I reckon he knows me already.'

'May I see him?'

'Of course you can. I'll fetch him in. He's only a little thing as yet. Might be a week or so older than mine . . . no more.'

'When did he come?'

'A few weeks back. Madame Rochère arranged it. I think it must have been someone from the lawyers who brought him. There was a paper. We had to put our mark on it . . . both Jacques and me. And it's all signed and sealed. I said, there's only one thing I want to know. The baby is mine for ever . . . just as though I'd given life to him. And they said that was in the paper. But you must see him. Just a moment. I'll fetch him.'

She brought him in. He was a very young baby with fine fair hair. His eyes were closed for he was sleeping so I could not see what colour they were, but I guessed they were blue. He seemed to be a healthy child.

'What's his name?' I asked.

'Edouard. That was given him. And of course he'll take our name. I would not have it otherwise.'

'So he will be yours, Madame Plantain, yours entirely.'

'That's so. And I'll never forget what he is doing for us. The first thing Jacques looks for when he comes in is this little fellow.'

She sat rocking the baby who continued to sleep.

I said: 'I think it is wonderful that it has ended like this.'

67

'It was like a miracle from heaven,' she said. 'And I shall always believe it was such.'

It was on the first day of August when the term finished. The Princesse came to the school. She was going to take me straight to the *château*.

Madame Rochère treated her with the respect due to her rank and they spent a little time together.

As we left I was reminded of my arrival in the previous September, and I thought what a lot had happened in one short year.

The Princesse was as affable and gracious as ever and we had a pleasant journey down to Bordeaux. At the station the Bourdon carriage was waiting to collect us and we made the journey comfortably to the *château*.

I was very much looking forward to seeing Annabelinda. The Princesse had told me that she had made a good recovery and was almost her old self.

'We make her rest a little each day, because it was a long and trying illness. However, we feel that we have pulled her through most satisfactorily.'

Annabelinda was waiting to greet us with Jean Pascal beside her. She looked well and even blooming.

'It's lovely to see you, Lucinda,' she cried. She hugged me warmly and I felt very emotional.

'Annabelinda, it's wonderful to see you again.'

'It was an awful time.'

Jean Pascal had taken my hands and was kissing them.

'Welcome, dear child. How happy we all are that you are here. And how do you think Annabelinda is looking, eh?'

'She looks better than she ever did.'

He laughed. 'That's what I tell her. You see, my dear, you and I think alike.'

'And she really is completely recovered?'

'Yes . . . yes. There is no doubt of that. We are going to take care of her and make sure there is not a relapse.'

We went into the *château*, which always overawed me. My mother said she had felt the same about it when she was there. The past seemed to encroach on the present and one thought of all the people who had lived there through the ages and had perhaps left something of themselves behind.

We dined in the intimate dining-room and Jean Pascal and the Princesse did seem genuinely happy to have me there; as for Annabelinda, she made me feel very welcome.

'I only hope your parents are not angry with us for keeping you away from them,' said Jean Pascal.

'They will spare us a little time, I am sure,' said the Princesse.

'If Annabelinda can come back with me, they will be very pleased,' I said.

'I think it is certain that she will be well enough to do that,' answered Jean Pascal.

The conversation continued in such a manner but I felt there was a certain strain and that Jean Pascal was aware of it.

I was glad when we retired to our rooms, and I could not resist going along to Annabelinda's.

She was in bed but not asleep.

She smiled at me. 'I guessed you'd come along,' she said.

'Well, it's so long since we've had a real talk.'

'Tell me about school. How were they when I left so suddenly? Was there a lot of talk?'

'They could talk of nothing else. They gave you all manner of diseases . . . from scarlet fever to beri-beri.'

She smiled. 'It was all rather grim, wasn't it?'

'It's all over now. You're as well as ever. Tell me about it. What was really wrong?'

'Grandpère says I am not to talk about it. He says it will be better for me not to. I've got to put it all behind me. It could spoil my chances.'

'Spoil your chances . . . chances of what?'

'Making the right sort of marriage. They are thinking about marriage for me. After all, I am getting old.'

'Sixteen?'

'Another year.'

'How would it spoil your chances?'

'Oh, nothing. Forget it.'

But I refused to. 'How?' I persisted.

'Well, with the grand sort of family that Grandpère wants for me, they think all the time of children, carrying on the family name and all that. They want their heirs to be strong. They would be wary of a wife who had . . . had what I've had.'

'What did you have? It's all been rather mysterious. Was it consumption? If so, why not say so?'

'Grandpère says we should forget it and never mention it.'

'I see. You mean people think that once you've had that, you might pass it on to your children.'

'Yes. That's the idea. So not a word.'

'And they cured you here!'

'Well, not here. I had to go away. I haven't been at the *château* all the time.'

'I gathered that.'

'I told you it was all rather secret. Grandpère's idea. He arranged it all.'

'I remember I did get a letter from you with the postmark Bergerac.'

'Bergerac! I never want to go there again.'

'Isn't it somewhere near here?'

'Well, some miles. I must have posted the letter when we were passing through.'

'Passing through . . . to where?'

'Oh, I don't remember. I was rather ill at the time.'

'Why don't you want to see Bergerac again?'

'Well, I want to forget that time . . . and your mentioning the place reminded me. All those places round about do. I had this terrible thing, you see.'

'It *was* consumption, wasn't it?'

She nodded . . . and then shook her head. 'I don't want to say . . . exactly . . . but . . . promise you won't tell anyone I told you.'

'I promise. Was it Switzerland? That's where people go. Up in the mountains.'

She nodded again.

'And they cured you?' I said.

'Completely. All I have to do in the future is . . . be careful. Grandpère says this is a warning. Once you've had this sort of thing, people are suspicious.'

'They think it can be passed on.'

'Grandpère thinks it could spoil my chances for the sort of marriage he wants for me.'

'What was it like in the sanatorium?'

'Oh, they were very strict. You had to do what you were told.'

'It sounds like La Pinière.'

She laughed. 'But it's all over and I want to forget it ever happened. I'm well now. I am going to be all right. I'm looking forward to going to London.'

'I expect your family will want you to be in the country with them.'

'Oh, Mama will want to be in London, I expect. As for my father and dear brother Robert, they've got their beloved estate to think about. They won't worry about me.'

'I missed you, Annabelinda.'

'Don't you think I missed you?'

'It must have been awful, so far away from everyone. I suppose your grandfather and the Princesse visited you during the time you were there?'

'Of course. They were marvellous to me. But I don't want to talk about it. Please, Lucinda.'

'All right. Not another word.'

'And don't forget. Don't tell anyone about Switzerland. I shouldn't have mentioned it to you, but you wormed it out of me.'

'I'll be silent.'

'Good old Lucinda.'

*

71

A week passed. We rode a good deal, usually in the company of Jean Pascal. Visitors came to the *château* and there were one or two dinner-parties.

I was longing to go home but I found a great pleasure in walking in the grounds of the *château*. I liked to be alone there. I used to sit by the lake, watching the swans and the little brown duck who came waddling by. I would take a few crumbs for him and was amused by the way he would come to the edge of the lake and wait patiently for the offering.

Sometimes as I sat there I would think how strange life was and would imagine my mother as a young girl, not much older than I was now, sitting on this very seat. There had been a black swan then. She often talked of it and how it defended its territory with venom.

How peaceful it was now, with the beautiful docile swans in place of the black one. And yet there were undercurrents . . . mysterious, seeming not quite what they were represented to be.

One early afternoon when I had been sitting by the lake and was returning to the *château*, I met the postman in the grounds. He was coming to the house with some mail.

He called a greeting. He knew who I was, for I had collected the mail from him before.

'Ah,' he said, 'once more, Mademoiselle, you have saved my legs. I am running a little late. Would you take this one for Monsieur Bourdon?'

I said I would and took the letter. It was a foolscap envelope with the name written on it in bold black capitals.

The postman thanked me and went on his way.

I thought Jean Pascal might be in his study, so I took the letter up there. I knocked on the door. There was no answer, so I opened the door and went in. The window was open and as I entered a gust of wind picked up the papers which were lying on the desk and scattered them over the floor.

I shut the door, hurried in, put the letter I had brought on the desk and stooped to pick up the papers.

As I did so, a phrase on one of them caught my eye. It was 'Jacques and Marguerite Plantain – 10,000 francs'.

I stared at it. There was some writing in French which I could not entirely understand, and the address on the letter was that of solicitors in Bordeaux.

Understanding flashed into my mind. It was as though pieces of a puzzle had suddenly and miraculously fitted themselves together and presented me with a picture.

'Interesting?' said a voice behind me.

Jean Pascal had come into the room.

I felt myself blushing hotly as he took the paper from my hand.

Then he said in a cool voice which struck terror into me: 'What are you doing with my papers, Lucinda?'

I heard myself stammering: 'I . . . er . . . I . . . brought a letter. The postman gave it to me because I was in the grounds. I did knock. There was no answer, so I opened the door. The window was open, you see, and the draught . . . the papers fell on the floor. I was picking them up.'

'Of course.'

He picked up the rest of the papers and put them on the desk. He smiled at me. 'It was very helpful of you, Lucinda. And how good of you to bring my mail.'

I escaped and went out of the *château*, letting the air cool my burning cheeks.

'Ten thousand francs to Jacques and Marguerite Plantain.' It was clear. It was for taking the baby. Why should Jean Pascal want them to take a baby?

I should have seen it before. Carl and Annabelinda had met . . . secretly. They had been lovers. The result of love-making was babies. And Carl had left her to face the consequences. No wonder she had changed. How could I not have guessed? She had fainted in class. Madame Rochère had sent for the doctor and immediately afterwards Jean Pascal came. In his suave, sophisticated manner, he had known exactly how to deal with such a situation.

She had not been to Switzerland. She had been to Bergerac which the map showed me was near enough for convenience and far enough for anonymity. Annabelinda would agree with

73

everything her grandfather suggested. She would realize the wisdom of his instructions about the need for secrecy.

She had had a baby and it was the one in the Plantains' cottage. And because Marguerite had lost her baby, she was eager to have another. Moreover, she had been paid handsomely to look after him and would be paid regularly throughout his life. The child would ease her pain over her own loss and give her and her husband security throughout their lives. Annabelinda's misfortune was the Plantains' blessing.

Now I knew, I could think only of the baby who would have that love and care from Marguerite which his mother could not give him.

I felt overburdened by this dark secret. I almost wished I had not discovered it. I myself had a secret now. I must never let anyone know that I was aware of what had happened.

As I sat looking at the swans I heard the sound of footsteps, and my heart started to pound in terror, for Jean Pascal was coming towards me.

He sat down beside me.

'I am glad I found you,' he said. 'I think you and I have something to say to each other.'

'I assure you I only went into your study to take the letter. The papers had blown to the floor and naturally I thought I should pick them up.'

'But naturally. And what you saw on one, you found of great interest?'

'But I . . .'

'Please, Lucinda, let there be no subterfuge between us. Let me say at once that I believe what you tell me. But something did attract your attention . . . well, it astonished you. It was on the paper you read.'

I was silent.

'Lucinda, my dear, you must be frank with me, as I shall be with you. What was on that paper?'

I took a deep breath. I did not know how to begin.

'It . . . it was the name of two people who live on the school estate, was it?' he urged.

74

'Yes,' I answered.

'You know these people?'

'Yes. At least, I know Madame Plantain. I talked to her when I walked past the cottage in the grounds. We talked at first. I knew she was going to have a baby.'

'Yes?'

'I knew the baby died and she adopted another.'

'You are a clever girl, Lucinda. You say to yourself: Why should Jean Pascal Bourdon pay her money . . . as I have seen he has done by that paper.'

'Well . . .'

'Oh, come, we have finished with innuendoes. If we are to understand this little matter we must be frank. You thought how strange it was that the grandfather of Annabelinda should be paying money to these people. You think: Annabelinda has been away for some months. She suffered from a mysterious illness, and then there is a baby. Well, I am sure the situation has become clear to clever little Lucinda, who, let us admit, was somewhat puzzled about the mysterious happenings before. And when she saw that paper with the names of people she knew, she began to understand. Is that so?'

'I began to think . . . yes.'

'Of course.' He slipped an arm through mine and pressed it against him.

'Lucinda,' he went on, 'you and I are good friends, are we not? I have always had a softness in my heart for you. You are the daughter of my dear Lucie, whom I always adored. You have been the companion of my granddaughter. I regard you as my own family.'

'It is kind of you, and I am sorry I took the letter up to your study. I should have left it in the hall.'

'Well, no. Perhaps it is as well. Now we shall have this matter cleared up. You will share our secret, and I know I can trust you not to reveal it. You are fond of Annabelinda. She has committed an indiscretion. It is not the first time it has happened in my family . . . your family . . . anybody's family. It is nature's way. Deplorable. But it can be set right . . . and forgotten. It is always wise in life to forget that which is unpleasant. Remorse is very good for us, but it should be indulged with caution and taken in small doses, and never enough to impair the zest for living. Do you agree?'

'I expect you are right.'

'But of course I am right. You suspect much. Suspicion is an ugly thing. Quite often it distorts the truth and makes it uglier than it is. You have guessed what Annabelinda's illness was all about, that it was discovered by the doctor whom Madame Rochère called in, and you can imagine that good lady's consternation when she learned what had befallen one of her pupils. But she is a wise woman. Annabelinda is my granddaughter, so she sent for me. She knew she could rely on me in this little contretemps.'

I nodded. It was all I had imagined in that flash of understanding which came to me when I read the paper.

'Annabelinda had dallied with one of the gardeners,' he went on. 'Madame Rochère was extremely shocked that it should be a gardener, but I pointed out to her that the outcome could have been the same whatever the rank of the man in the case, and we must suppress our outrage with sound common sense. The first thing was to get Annabelinda out of school. We could not have let her stay much longer. There would be gossip. We could not let it be known throughout the neighbourhood that my granddaughter had committed such an indiscretion. So she went away to a clinic where she would be taken care of.'

'In Bergerac,' I said.

For a moment he was astonished, then he said: 'I see you are fully conversant with all this. How did you know?'

'It slipped out in conversation with Annabelinda that she had been there.'

'She should be more careful. It is a most reliable place. I know the lady who owns it. She will be the soul of discretion. So there went Annabelinda, and later of course there arose the problem of finding a home for the child.'

'It worked out very conveniently for you,' I said. 'Of one

thing I am sure. Madame Plantain will make a very good mother.'

'Madame Rochère assured me of that. You do not think I would put my great-grandchild with someone who would not be good to him?'

'And you were ready to put him out to be cared for?'

'I detect a note of criticism. Dear Lucinda, could I have him here? Adopt a child, at my age? Only for one reason. I have to think of Annabelinda. What would her future be if this were known? She would be classed as a fallen woman before she had a chance to stand up and show what she has to offer. She would never have married into appropriate circles.'

'She might have found someone to love her and she could have her baby with her.'

He leaned towards me and kissed my hair lightly.

'Dear Lucinda, you see the world through the eyes of innocence. Charming, very charming. But life is not like that. I want what is best for Annabelinda. She is a very beautiful and attractive girl. I should hate to see her chances ruined at the start.'

'What of the child?' I asked.

'He will have the best of homes. You yourself have said so. But I confess I am a little uneasy that he should be so near the school.'

'You think Annabelinda will recognize her son?'

'All babies look alike. They change as they grow up, but in the first weeks they are different. They come into the world like wizened old men and in a few weeks they are plump and beautiful. But you see how careful we must be. You see how the odd coincidence can leap up to confound you. Your acquaintance with this good woman, your seeing that paper. Who would have thought that would have happened? And yet it is all so simple, so natural. Mind you, I did wonder at the wisdom of placing the child so near to the school. But Madame Rochère gave the woman such a good character, and she, of course, had no notion of where the child came from.'

I said: 'You have gone to a great deal of trouble to do this for Annabelinda.'

'For her and the honour of the family,' he said. 'That means a great deal to people such as I am. Perhaps we are too proud, a little arrogant. *Mon Dieu*, we should have learned our lessons, should we not, all those years ago? But does one ever learn lessons? A little perhaps . . . but rarely entirely. Well, now you know what happened, and I am placing my trust in you. The incident must be forgotten. I shall make sure that the child is well cared for . . . educated when the time comes. There is no need to fear for his future. And what I ask of you, dear Lucinda, is never to divulge to any person what you have learned. I have a high respect for your integrity, I know I can rely on you. Annabelinda is wayward . . . a little irresponsible. It is part of her charm. Do not let her know that you are aware of what happened. Help her to keep up the myth. And please, I beg of you, do not tell her that the child who is being brought up by the Plantains is hers. I can rely on you, can I not, Lucinda?'

'I shall tell no one,' I said.

He put his hand over mine and pressed it.

'I place my trust in you,' he said.

Then we sat silent for a few moments watching the white swans gliding gracefully on the lake.

After the summer holidays, in September we returned to La Pinière. It was a year since I had first seen it and I felt that I had grown a long way from the naïve girl I had been then. I had learned much and although the dramatic events had not happened to me, I had been close enough to them to be deeply affected.

I thought of Jean Pascal Bourdon as some powerful god who arranged people's lives – cynically, yet benignly . . . amorally in a way. And yet what would Annabelinda have done without him?

I thought often of the child in the care of Marguerite

Plantain. He would never know his mother and what trouble had been caused by his coming into the world. He would be well cared for, educated when the time came. Cheques would arrive regularly for the Plantains and they would have no idea from whom they came. By one powerful stroke, Jean Pascal had changed their lives even more than Annabelinda's, because I was sure that, in time, Annabelinda would convince herself that this episode in her life had never happened, while the Plantains would have Edouard, the constant reminder.

Caroline said I had changed since the holidays.

'You look so serious. Do you know, sometimes when I speak to you, you don't answer. Was it such a wonderful holiday?'

'Wonderful,' I told her.

Annabelinda was received at school with a sort of awe. They were all convinced that she had been, as one of them remarked, 'snatched from the jaws of death'. And any to whom that had happened must be of very special interest.

Annabelinda exploited the situation, as I would have expected. She was quite a figure at school now. She had her own room, and although Madame Rochère was a little cool towards her – and, I believe, watchful – Annabelinda shrugged that aside. She was enjoying school. 'The wages of sin,' I told myself, feeling it was the sort of comment Jean Pascal might have made.

Oddly, Annabelinda seemed to have forgotten the episode more easily than I. But I supposed she wanted to, and Annabelinda always did what she wanted. *I* could not forget, and there was the baby to remind me.

I became fascinated by the child, and could not resist taking walks past the cottage. Whereas before I had been fond of the company of my fellow pupils, I now wanted to escape from them and make my way to the cottage . . . alone. On warm days the perambulator would almost always be in the Plantain garden.

Marguerite was recovering from her tragedy, and I think this was largely due to little Edouard. She doted on the child.

79

She told me: 'Jacques is beginning to love him. It was hard for him at first. It was his own he wanted. But Edouard has such winning ways. Just look at the little angel.'

Sometimes I would hold Edouard on my lap. I would look for a likeness to his parents. There was none. He was just like any other baby.

Sometimes I would go into the Plantain garden and sit by him. I would watch him and think of Annabelinda and Carl together . . . clandestinely meeting in that cottage of his which would be rather like the Plantains' . . . creeping out of school at night. How daring she was! This would be the first of many adventures in her life, I imagined. This was just a beginning. And what a beginning . . . bringing another life into the world. I suppose she had not given this possibility a thought when she was with Carl. And Carl himself? The man of mystery. He would not even know he had a son. Would he care? What sort of man was he? I had only seen him twice. Yet he was the father of this child. He was the reason why all this had happened, the reason why Jean Pascal Bourdon had had to be called in to come with his cynical knowledge of the world and its foibles, to manipulate everyone so that this child's birth would not spoil Annabelinda's prospects of making a brilliant marriage.

It was no wonder that I felt older, a little blasé. I had been shown such a new light on worldly affairs. I had grown only one year in time but many in experience.

School life continued as usual. I was in a higher class and even more time was given to social pursuits. There were more dancing lessons, more piano lessons, singing lessons, and deportment.

I was realizing that fourteen was quite a mature age – a time when I would have to think of the future.

Annabelinda, with her sixteen years and aura of mystery, was far above me. We did not see a great deal of each other during school hours, and when I had a little time to myself I liked to wander off to the Plantain cottage.

Annabelinda was unaware of the cottage; she certainly

knew nothing of the baby who lay in his perambulator in the garden on warm days. I thought it all very strange and mysterious, but it did give a certain flavour to life.

Christmas came. Aunt Celeste collected us as usual and we stayed a night in Valenciennes and then went home. Everything was according to plan and in due course we were back again for the January term, and would not go home until the summer, for the journey was too long to be undertaken at mid-term, so we went down to spend the brief holiday at Château Bourdon.

'It won't be long,' my mother wrote, 'until you are coming home again. How time flies!'

I knew that she was not very happy about my going to France, although Aunt Celeste assured her that the education I was getting was excellent and the fact that I should have several languages when it was completed was a real asset.

My mother agreed with this, but said she wished it were nearer.

At mid-term, when we went to the *château*, Annabelinda was her merry self. I marvelled that she could be so. Did she never wonder what had happened to her child? It occurred to me that, in his infinite wisdom, Jean Pascal might have told her that her baby had died at his birth. In any case, I could not ask her.

At the *château* we rode a great deal; we inspected the vineyards; we dined with distinguished guests whom Jean Pascal and the Princesse gathered about them; and I often sat by the lake and thought of all that had happened over the last year.

Jean Pascal did not mention it. This was part of his policy. One forgot unpleasant things and in time it seemed as though they had never happened.

I was glad to get back to school.

During Conversazione a frequent topic was the Balkan war.

As well-educated young ladies, we were expected to be able to discuss world affairs, especially those which were happening fairly close to us. This was the reason for so much emphasis being laid on the Conversazione.

Most of us found the subject of the Balkans exceptionally boring and there had been rejoicing when the wretched war was over. Their affairs had been the source of some discussion. I had learned that the war which had broken out during the previous year had been between the Balkan States, which had included Serbia, Bulgaria, Greece and Montenegro on one side, and the Ottoman Empire on the other.

In the May of last year the Balkan States had been victorious and a treaty was signed in London, the result of which was that the Ottoman Empire lost most of its territory in Europe.

'Thank goodness that's over,' Caroline said. 'Now we can forget the wretched lot of them.'

'My dear Caroline,' said Miss Carruthers. 'You are extremely thoughtless. These matters can be of the greatest importance to us. I know the Balkans seem remote to you, but we are part of Europe and anything that happens there could have its effect on us. Wars are good for no one and when one's neighbours indulge in them, events must be closely watched. One never knows when one's country may be brought in.'

However, it was pleasant to be able to forget the war and discuss the capital cities of Europe such as Paris, Brussels and Rome, all of which we read about and talked of with a certain amount of aplomb – the Bois de Boulogne, Les Invalides, the Colosseum of Rome, the art galleries of Florence – just as though we knew them well. This made us feel very sophisticated, knowledgeable and much-travelled – in our minds at least.

There were moans of dismay when war broke out again. Serbia, Greece and Roumania were quarrelling with Bulgaria over the division of the spoils gained from the last war. We were delighted when Bulgaria was quickly defeated and peace returned.

However, Madame Rochère seemed a little grave – and so did some of the other teachers, and the atmosphere became a little uneasy. All the same, it was a delightful summer; the weather was perfect and the days sped by. Soon the term would be at an end and we should be on our way home once more for the summer holidays. Aunt Celeste would come for us on the first day of August. School broke up on the last day of July.

We were coming towards the end of June. There was just over a month to go and Annabelinda and I were already making plans.

'This time next year, I shall be thinking of leaving,' she said. 'I shall have a Season. Do they have Seasons in France? I must ask Grandpère. Of course, they haven't got a King and Queen. It wouldn't be the same. I suppose my Season will be in London. I shall see the King and Queen. Queen Mary looks a little stern, doesn't she?'

I thought: How can she talk so lightly of such things? Does she ever give a thought to the baby?

Little Edouard was now nearly a year old. He was beginning to take notice. He could crawl and was learning to stand up. Sometimes he would take a few tottering steps. I would sit opposite Marguerite and he would stand there, his face alight with pleasure. It was a game to him, to totter from Marguerite's arms to mine without falling. She would hold back, ready to catch him should the need arise. Then he would take his faltering steps and fall into mine, which were waiting to receive him. We would clap, applauding his triumph, and he would put his hands together and do the same, beaming with pride in his achievement.

It was amazing what pleasure I found in that child. Perhaps it was because I knew he was Annabelinda's that he was so important to me. I felt that he belonged to our family. One day I should have to leave him. When my days at La Pinière were over, that would be the end. No. I should come back. I should pay a visit now and then . . . so that I could see how he was growing up. Marguerite would welcome me. She under stood my feelings for the child. She shared them.

Edouard had done so much for her. He had assuaged her grief. I sometimes believed she could not have loved her own child more than she loved Edouard.

I had returned from the cottage, and when I went up to the dormitory, Caroline was there with Helga.

'You're late,' said Caroline. 'Why do you always go off on your own?'

'Because I like it.'

'To get away from us. That's not very polite.'

'It's to get away from school. I like . . . to walk around.'

'You haven't got a secret lover, have you?'

I flushed a little, thinking of Annabelinda creeping out to meet Carl.

'You have! You have!' shrieked Caroline.

'Don't be silly! How could I?'

'There are ways. Some do.'

Again that feeling of unease. Did they guess about Annabelinda? Why should I feel guilty because of her?

'I'd better get ready,' I said. 'I'll be late for Conversazione.'

When we reached the hall Madame Rochère was already there. She looked as though she had an important announcement to make. She had. She stood up and waited until we were seated, then she began.

'Something has happened, girls,' she said. 'Yesterday in Sarajevo, which as you know is the capital of Bosnia in Yugoslavia, the heir apparent to the throne of Austria and Hungary, the Archduke Francis Ferdinand, with his wife, was assassinated by a Bosnian Serb called Gavrilo Princip.'

It was obvious that the girls were not greatly impressed by the news. Most of us were thinking: Oh dear, we thought we had finished with those tiresome people. Now it will all be brought up again, and there will be little talk of the new dances and fashions, and those great cities of the world, and all the delightful things one can do in them. Haven't we had enough of those people with their two wars? And now they go round killing people!

'This is grave news,' Madame Rochère was saying. 'It has happened far away, it is true, but it may have an effect on us. We must wait and see, and be prepared.'

*

July was with us. We were all preoccupied with plans for going home.

I said to Marguerite: 'I shall be away for about two months.'

'You will see a change in Edouard when you come back,' she commented.

Aunt Celeste wrote that she would be coming to Valenciennes as usual. She would arrive at the school on the first of August. I wondered if Jean Pascal and the Princesse would be at Valenciennes. We always spent a day at the house there before beginning our journey home.

We had no notion at that time that this was going to be any different from our usual homecoming.

Then on the twenty-eighth of July, Austria–Hungary declared war on Serbia. Relations between the two countries had been deteriorating since the murder of the Archduke Francis Ferdinand, and this was the result.

Madame Rochère was looking grave. It was clear that she thought this was happening at an unfortunate time. A month later and all the girls would have been at their respective homes and not her responsibility. The enormity of the situation was, at that time, of course, not apparent to us, but it was only a matter of days before this became clear.

I awoke on the morning of the first of August with mixed feelings. I longed to see my parents and my brother Charles; on the other hand I should miss Edouard. It was amazing how I had grown so fond of a baby who could do little more than smile blandly when I picked him up and made little cooing noises which Marguerite and I tried to interpret into words. Yet I did not want to leave the child. Yet there was so much to look forward to.

We were ready to leave, as were most of the girls. Some had gone on the previous day.

The morning seemed long. Celeste usually came early so that we could leave at once for Valenciennes. It seemed strange that she had not appeared.

The strange thing was that all the English girls who had been expecting to leave that day were in the same position as ourselves. Helga had gone with the German contingent some days earlier; and most of the French girls were able to leave.

It was disconcerting and we knew something was very wrong.

There was tension throughout the school. Everyone was whispering, conjuring up what had happened. Then we heard that Germany was involved by declaring war against Russia.

Another day passed and there was no news of Celeste.

We had no notion of what was going on and why Celeste had not come for us. It was consoling that we were not the only ones whose arrangements had undergone this mysterious change.

A few more girls left, but there was still no sign of Celeste.

On the third of August Germany declared war on France and then we understood that something very grave was happening.

That was a nightmare day. The gardens looked so peaceful; everything was quiet; there was a dramatic quality in the air. The flowers, the insects, the birds . . . they all seemed to be waiting . . . just as we were. We knew the calm could not go on.

On the afternoon of that day a man came riding into the grounds on a motorcycle.

Caroline came bursting into the dormitory. I had just come back from visiting Edouard. Marguerite had told me that she and Jacques were very uneasy. She had a fear of the Germans.

'We are too near them,' she kept saying. 'Too close . . . Too close.'

Even Edouard seemed to sense the tension and was a little fretful.

I was filled with misgivings. I had expected to be home by now. It was all so unusual.

Caroline was saying: 'There's a man with Madame Rochère. He is asking for you and Anna B. He's brought letters or something. I distinctly heard him mention your name.'

'Where is he?'

'With Madame Rochère.'

At that moment Mademoiselle Artois appeared at the door.

'Lucinda, you are to go to Madame Rochère's study at once.'

I hurried off.

Madame Rochère was seated at her desk. A man in the uniform of a British soldier sat opposite her.

He rose as I entered and said: 'Good afternoon, Miss.'

'This,' said Madame Rochère, 'is Sergeant Clark. He has brought a letter from your parents. I also have heard from them.'

Sergeant Clark produced the letter.

'You should read it now,' said Madame Rochère. 'Sit down and do so.'

I obeyed with alacrity.

My dearest Lucinda [I read],

You will be aware that there is trouble in Europe and it has been impossible for Aunt Celeste to meet you as usual. Travel at the ports is disrupted. We are all very anxious that you should come home as soon as possible.

Your Uncle Gerald is having this letter brought to you. He is sending out someone to bring you and Annabelinda back to England. It might be difficult getting across France and finding the necessary transport. A Major Merrivale will be coming to the school to bring you both home. You must stay there until he arrives, which will be as soon as it can be arranged. Your Uncle Gerald thinks this is the best way of getting you back safely in these unfortunate circumstances.

Your father and I are very worried about you, but we are sure Uncle Gerald will see that you are brought safely back.

All our love, darling,

Mama.

There was a note from my father, telling me to take great care and follow Major Merrivale's instructions, then we should all soon be together.

Enclosed was a note from Charles. 'Lucky you. Having all the fun. Charles.'

I lifted my eyes to Madame Rochère who was watching me closely.

'Your parents are very wise,' she said. 'I know your uncle is Colonel Greenham and he will be able to arrange for the safe conduct of both you and Annabelinda. Now we must await the arrival of Major Merrivale, and you must be ready to leave as soon as he comes.'

'Yes, Madame Rochère.'

I said goodbye to the soldier and thanked him. Then I sped away to the dormitories to find Annabelinda and tell her what had happened.

That evening we heard the startling news. Germany had invaded Belgium, and on the following day, the fourth of August, Great Britain declared war on Germany.

Two days passed. Most of the girls had left by now. Miss Carruthers stayed on. She said she could not leave until all the English girls had gone. The trains were running intermittently.

Had we not been told to wait for Major Merrivale, we should have gone to Valenciennes; but that might have been unwise, as the French were now at war.

The most immediate danger was the invasion of Belgium, and each hour we lived in trepidation of what might happen to us. We knew that Belgium was defenceless against the might of Germany's army; and we did not have to be told that each day they were penetrating further and coming nearer and nearer.

We did not stray far from the school in case Major Merrivale arrived. I thought of the anxiety my parents would be suffering. It would be even greater than ours, for they were completely in the dark.

Then came a day of terror. We had heard rumours that the Germans were advancing rapidly. We were not quite sure how far we could trust that rumour, but I could not help wondering whether they would reach us before Major Merrivale came.

I was in the gardens close to the school with Annabelinda, when disaster struck from the sky. I had never seen a Zeppelin before and was unsure what it was up there among the clouds. I was soon to discover.

As the light caught this large, rather cumbersome cylindrical airship, it looked as though it were made of silver.

It was almost overhead. I stood still, watching, and saw something fall. There was a loud explosion which nearly knocked me down; then I saw the smoke and flames.

To my horror I realized that the bomb had fallen near the cottages.

My throat was dry. I shouted: 'They've struck the cottages. There are people there. The Plantains . . . the baby!'

I started to run towards them. Annabelinda tried to restrain me.

'Keep away,' she cried. 'You'll get hurt.'

I pushed aside her restraining hand. I heard myself crying out: 'There's the baby.'

And I ran. I forgot Annabelinda. I could only think of the Plantains and Edouard. I could see the cottage. Smoke was in my eyes; the acrid smell filled my nostrils. I saw the airship floating further away. It was going now that it had deposited its lethal cargo.

Where the cottage had been was a pile of rubble. A fire was burning. I found my way to the wall round the garden. The perambulator was still there. And . . . Edouard was in it.

I dashed to it and looked at him. He smiled at me when he saw me and gurgled something.

I took him out of the pram and hugged him.

'Oh, thank God . . . thank God,' I cried.

I did not realize that I was weeping. I just stood there, holding him. He tried to wriggle free. I was hugging him too tightly for his comfort.

With a calmness which astonished me, for my mind was in a turmoil, I put him back into his perambulator and strapped him in. Then I walked with him to the spot where the cottage had been. Marguerite must be there somewhere. She would never have gone out and left the baby.

'Marguerite,' I called. 'Where are you?'

There was silence.

I moved towards that mass of broken walls and rubble which had been his home. I could see the fire smouldering there and a terrible fear seized me. I dreaded what I might find.

I should call for help, perhaps. It would be dangerous to walk about here. I must rouse people. I must get help. But I had to assure myself that Marguerite was there.

I found her. Jacques was beside her, and I could see that he was dead. There was blood and froth about his mouth; his coat was stained with blood and there was something unnatural about the way he lay. Marguerite was lying under a beam which pinned her to the ground.

I cried: 'Marguerite!'

She opened her eyes.

I said: 'Oh, thank God. Marguerite, I must get help. They'll come and get you out of here.'

'Edouard . . .' she whispered.

I said: 'He is safe. Unharmed. I have him. He is in his pram.'

She smiled and closed her eyes.

'Marguerite,' I said. 'I am going back to the school . . . taking Edouard. I'll get help. They'll come and look after you.'

'Jacques . . .' she said. Her eyes turned. She saw him lying there and I guessed she knew that he was dead. I saw the stricken look in her eyes.

'Oh, Jacques,' she murmured. 'Oh, Jacques . . .'

I did not know how to comfort her, but I must get help. They must remove that plank across her body. They must get her to a hospital or somewhere safe. But there was no safety. What had happened here could happen again at any moment . . . to any of us. This was war.

I stood up and she opened her eyes. 'Don't go,' she said.

'I am going to get help, Marguerite.'

She shook her head. 'Stay here . . . Edouard.'

'Edouard is safe,' I said.

'Who . . . who will care for him?'

'I'm going to get help.'

'No . . . no . . . I am finished. I know it. I feel it. Edouard . . .'

'He is safe,' I repeated.

'Who will care for him?' she asked again.

'You will. You are going to get well.'

I saw a look of impatience cross her face.

'You,' she said. 'You will care for him. You love him, too.'

I did not know what she meant at first, but all her thoughts were for Edouard. I knew how she had planned for his future, because she had told me of it. The cheques which came regularly would buy him such things as he needed, things which had never come the way of Jacques and Marguerite. She had planned for Edouard. He had saved her from her abject misery; he had replaced her lost child; he had given her something to live for. Her life was to have been dedicated to him . . . and now she was being taken from him.

All her concern was for him. She believed she was dying. Jacques was dead. He had been talking to her one minute and the next he was lying dead beside her. And all because of this stupid war. How could those men in the airships do such a thing? Did they stop to think what misery they were causing to people whom they had never known?

I started to rise. I said: 'I must get help. I'm wasting time. They'll come, and you'll be all right. They'll look after you.'

'No, no. I shall never be all right. Do not go . . . not yet. Edouard, what will become of him? They sent him away. They paid money . . . but money's not love. Poor child. Poor little baby. Who will love him? Who will care for him? Not those who sent him away . . . farmed him out.'

'He made you happy, Marguerite,' I said.

'Oh yes . . . happy. My little baby. But what will become of him? There is only one I wish him to be with.'

I could only say: 'All will be well. They will come soon. I must bring them here.'

91

She shook her head. 'You, Lucinda. You love him and he loves you. He knows so little of the world. He knows you are safe . . . you, me and Jacques. Only one of us will do. He would be frightened without any of us. He is so little. It must be you.'

I thought her mind was wandering; then I realized how earnest she was. She clutched my hand. I looked into her eyes. They were imploring . . . begging.

'Miss Lucinda, you must do this. It is my dying wish. Promise me that I may die happy.'

'Marguerite . . .'

'Take him with you. Take him away. You will go home to England. You will be safe there. Take my baby with you. Please, please take him. You must. What will become of him if you do not?'

'We must find those who brought him to you.'

'I do not know them.'

'There is the solicitor, you said.'

'I have never seen him. The money comes. I have no address. I do not know where it comes from. They do not care for him. They do not love him. They gave him away. They pay to keep him out of the way. To them he is nothing . . . something to be forgotten. How could they ever love him? Lucinda, it is my dying wish. Promise me. I trust you. You have a good mother and a good father. You have spoken of them and I hear the love in your voice when you do so. They are good people. Tell them how a dying woman begged of you. Your mother will understand. But take my baby. You take him. Take little Edouard . . . please. Let me die happy.'

Her breath was coming in gasps. What was I doing here? Why was I not running for help? I was here because I was aware that there was no help for her. She was dying. She knew it and I knew it, and her only desire now was to extract a promise from me before it was too late.

'Lucinda . . . Lucinda . . .' Her voice was a whisper now.

I bent over her. I said: 'Don't worry. I will take Edouard with me when I go to England. I know that when my mother hears what has happened, she will want to care for him.'

I saw the smile which spread across her face. It was one of peace.

'But, Marguerite,' I went on, 'you are going to get well. They will come and take you to a hospital.'

She smiled. She was still holding my hand in hers.

'I will go now,' I said. 'I will take Edouard with me. A soldier is coming to take us across France to England. I promise Edouard shall go with us. Trust me, Marguerite.'

She opened her eyes and looked straight into mine. 'I trust you,' she said. 'You will keep your word and I will die content.'

Her grip on my hand slackened. She was finding it more and more difficult to breathe. Then . . . I knew that she was dead.

I rose. I took the perambulator and went across the gardens to the house.

As I came into the hall I saw Madame Rochère with Mademoiselle Artois, Miss Carruthers and some of the servants. There was a shocked silence as I wheeled in the perambulator.

I looked straight at Madame Rochère and said: 'The Plantains' cottage is destroyed. Monsieur and Madame Plantain have both been killed. The baby was in his perambulator in the garden. He is unharmed. So I brought him here. I shall look after him.'

It was the first time I had spoken to Madame Rochère with authority. I was determined. I had made a solemn promise to a dead woman, and I intended to keep it.

Madame Rochère looked shocked – as indeed they all did – and I was amazed that she showed no surprise at my announcement, nor at the sight of the baby.

She said: 'Help is coming. Those poor people. So soon . . . We will arrange something for the child.'

'I am looking after him,' I said. 'He knows me. He will miss Madame Plantain. He must be with me.'

She took no notice and walked past me, so I lifted Edouard up and took him to my dormitory.

I was glad I had it to myself. The others had gone, Caroline with them. She had taken the train to the French border on the previous day with the other English girls.

Miss Carruthers came in.

'Do you know how to care for a child?' she asked. 'I think it would be best to hand him over to Madame Printemps. She will know what to do.'

Madame Printemps worked in the kitchens, a plump, middle-aged woman who had had eight children.

I said: 'He knows me. He will be frightened by strangers. I have promised to look after him.'

I realized that taking that solemn oath had had an effect on me. I spoke with a resolution that made some impression on those who heard it. Previously I should have been told not to be foolish, and to hand over the baby to Madame Printemps without delay.

But perhaps they were all suffering from the shock of the bombardment by air. Perhaps they were thinking: It was the Plantains today, who will it be tomorrow?

However, no attempt was made to take Edouard from me. I put him to bed and lay down beside him.

'Edouard,' I said, 'you are going to be my baby from now on. There is nothing to fear. My mother will help me look after you. She knows a great deal about babies. She will understand when I tell her I have made a solemn promise to Madame Plantain so that she could die happy.'

Then I lay very still, weeping for Marguerite Plantain who had cared so much for this child. Edouard stared at me solemnly and put out a finger to touch a tear. I took his hand and kissed it, and I said: 'Edouard, we shall be together. You will be safe with me.'

While I lay there Annabelinda came in. She stared at us.

'I heard,' she said. 'I think you must be mad.'

'What do you mean?'

'Bringing in a baby like that.'

I said: 'He had no one to look after him. The Plantains are both dead . . . killed by that cruel bomb. I have promised Madame Plantain to take him to England.'

'Take him to England! It won't be allowed.'

'It will be.'

'What about Madame Rochère? Do you think she will let you do such a thing?'

'She will have to, because I have made up my mind. It's not for her to say.'

'What about this Major Merrivale?'

'If he takes me, he will take the baby.'

'I can't understand you, Lucinda. You seem to have lost your senses. Do you realize what an awkward position we are in?'

'I do indeed,' I heard myself say. 'Perhaps I understand a lot more than you realize.'

'What do you mean?'

I said: 'I am taking the baby with me. I am going to look after him. Someone has to. His parents didn't want to bother with him.'

She said: 'I know it's sad. But he's Belgian. Someone here can look after him. He belongs here. We have enough to do. We've got to get home before it gets worse.'

'He does not belong here,' I said slowly and deliberately, and I was amazed at the strength of my anger towards her, sitting there, smug, caring only for herself. I could not stop myself. I forgot my promise to Jean Pascal. I forgot everything but my concern for the child and my anger against Annabelinda. 'He does belong here, with us,' I went on. 'With us . . . with *you*. You want him left behind because to you he is an encumbrance . . . just as he was when he was born. Edouard is your son, Annabelinda, the child who was put out with the Plantains to get rid of him, so that you might not have an impediment in your life.'

She had turned pale, and then the colour rushed into her face. 'What . . . what are you saying?' she whispered.

I could not understand myself. I was overwrought. I had

95

been more deeply shocked by my experience than I realized. I could not control myself. It was too late to try to now, and I was not sure in that moment that I wanted to.

I went on: 'I have grown fond of Edouard. I used to go to the cottage to see him. He knows me. I found out about . . . everything . . . by chance. I know that you were not ill and that you had to go away because you were going to have a child . . . Carl's child. Your grandfather and the Princesse arranged it. They paid the Plantains to take Edouard, so that no one would know of your . . . indiscretion, and you could make some grand marriage when the time came and live happily ever after, just as though Edouard did not exist. But he does exist. You can't move people around just because they may be a nuisance to you. Edouard is your son. He will be alone in the world. I dare say your grandfather would find someone else to take him in and would pay them well for doing so. Oh yes, he would do all that. But Edouard is a person now. He has lost the one he loved . . . who was a mother to him. He only has me now and I am going to look after him.'

She was staring at me incredulously. 'You . . . you can't rush into this . . .' she stammered. 'People can't just pick up children.'

'I can and I'm going to. He is going to England with me.'

'And what . . . when we get there?'

I felt a twinge of pity for her. She was frightened, and I had rarely seen Annabelinda in that state. I relented a little. I had broken a promise and I was ashamed of myself in a way, and yet, I asked myself, why should I be silent now? Why should she not know who Edouard was? Why should she not shoulder her responsibilities? This helpless child, lying on the bed, looking from one to the other of us, was hers.

Yet I felt he was mine. She would never give him the love and care he needed.

Then I relented. She was having that effect on me which she always had. She was wayward Annabelinda and whatever she did could not alter my affection for her.

I was calmer now. The storm was passing. I must try to do

all I could to mend the damage I had done by breaking my promise.

I said: 'Listen, Annabelinda. I know what happened because I found out. I know your grandfather and the Princesse took you away. You went to a clinic in Bergerac; the child was born there. Madame Rochère was in the secret. She wanted no scandals at the school, and she was a strong ally of your grandfather. She knew that Madame Plantain had just lost a child, and it seemed an opportunity too good to miss. There must have been some misgiving about putting Edouard so near the school. However, it all seemed remote enough, and you would be there only for another year. It appeared to be a satisfactory solution. I suppose it would have been. I discovered so much because I had been visiting the Plantains. Anyway, I was in the secret. That wouldn't have mattered. I would have said nothing. Then the war came and changed everything. So I have planned what I shall do. I shall take Edouard home with me. My mother will help me.'

'You will tell her . . .'

'I shall just say that his foster-parents were killed. I had visited them and was fond of him and could not leave him behind. I know it will be all right. He will be like a brother to me and to Charles. I know I can rely on my parents.'

'Don't tell them, Lucinda. Promise you won't tell.'

'I won't promise. But I will only tell them if it is necessary to do so.'

'But . . . no one must know. It would be awful!'

'I shall tell no one. I know I burst out with it . . . but that was to you.'

'I didn't know he was my baby.'

'I was aware of that. The arrangement with the Plantains was between them and your grandfather's solicitors.'

'Oh, Lucinda, it's terrible! And I thought it was all over. What terrible bad luck.'

I could not help smiling at her. Her secret was disclosed because there was a war. I thought of Jacques Plantain lying dead in the remains of his home, and Madame Plantain's last thoughts for the welfare of the child she loved. And this, to Annabelinda, was her bad luck.

Well, she was Annabelinda. She would see every event as it affected her. Perhaps we all did. Perhaps I should not think too badly of Annabelinda.

I said to her: 'What is done is done. We just have to go on from here. Edouard will have a good home with my parents. You know my mother. She will welcome him. I will make her understand that I had to bring him.'

'And so no one need know,' said Annabelinda. 'He will be just a child who lost his parents in an air raid in Belgium. And you brought him home with you because you could not leave a child.'

'It's the truth, isn't it?'

She nodded. 'Lucinda, if it ever came out . . .'

'It need not,' I assured her.

'You have always been my best friend. We are fond of each other, in spite of . . .'

'Yes, Annabelinda, that's true. I want to help you. You behaved very foolishly over that young man.'

'I know.'

'But it is over now. We have to forget. We shall take the baby home with us. I am sure everything will go smoothly. My parents will raise no objections. I only have to let them see how important Edouard is to me. It will all seem quite plausible because it is wartime. It is going to be all right, Annabelinda.'

She threw herself into my arms and hugged me. The baby crowed with pleasure, as though he found the scene very amusing.

I went to him and picked him up. I said: 'Look, Annabelinda. Isn't he a little darling?'

They regarded each other speculatively.

'Sit down,' I said. She did and I put him on her lap. He studied her with curiosity. Then he began to whimper suddenly; he turned away from her and held out his arms to me.

Exodus

It was mid-morning of the next day when Major Merrivale arrived at La Pinière.

From the moment I saw him my spirits rose; and that was the effect he had on everyone. There was about him a certain quality – a rare one – of changing the atmosphere merely by his coming. He had an air of extreme confidence; his manner implied that all was well with his world and he was going to make it so for others. In the first place he was tall – a little over six feet; he had brown eyes which sparkled with merriment; his features were not set in a classical mould but they were well formed; he had a kindly expression: but it was that conviction that all was well with him, and would be with all those around him, which was just what we needed at that time.

Madame Rochère was clearly extremely relieved, for she had become very worried about our continued stay at La Pinière, as she did not know from one hour to the next how close the Germans were to the school, and that our rescuer should be a man of overwhelming charm who inspired such confidence was a blessing indeed.

He drove up in an army car – a large vehicle – and came striding into the hall.

'I'm Merrivale,' he announced. 'I believe you are expecting me.'

We were all very quickly in the hall, for we had been on the alert for his arrival for some time.

Madame Rochère said: 'Yes, yes, we have been waiting for you. The girls are ready to leave whenever you wish. I expect you would like a little refreshment before you leave. It shall be prepared at once. I will have the girls brought here.'

There was no need. Having heard the arrival, we were already there.

I said: 'I'm Lucinda Greenham and this is Annabelinda Denver.'

He took my hand and smiled at me. I felt a deep pleasure. There was something so completely confident about him that one felt there was now nothing to fear. We should soon be home.

'I'm sorry for the delay,' he said. 'There was congestion all along the route. People are realizing that the enemy is on the way.'

Annabelinda was smiling at him and he took her hand as he had mine.

'I'm glad I'm here at last. We'll have you out of this place very soon. When can you leave?'

'Madame Printemps will serve a light luncheon,' said Madame Rochère. 'Then you can get away. Most of the servants have gone. They are afraid the Germans will come here. They are trying to get over the border.'

He nodded. 'That's the general idea,' he said.

Miss Carruthers came into the hall.

I said: 'Oh, Miss Carruthers, this is Major Merrivale.'

'Ah yes,' she replied. 'How do you do? You have come to take the girls home. I wondered if . . .' she began, and hesitated. 'Well, I have to get home, too. I didn't feel I could leave while these two were here . . . and, of course, I wasn't sure how to get to the coast myself.'

'You mean you want to come along with us,' said the Major with a smile. 'But of course. There's plenty of room.'

Miss Carruthers's face expressed her joy and relief. I could see that he had the same effect on her as he had on the rest of us.

'Now,' put in Madame Rochère. 'You girls have everything ready. *Déjeuner* will be served now . . . and then you can leave. Come along into the dining-room and we can start.'

We followed her there. I walked beside the Major and said: 'I must tell you, there is a baby.'

He turned and looked at me. He had a way of raising his eyebrows which was very attractive and somehow made one feel that it would be easy to make him understand.

'A baby?' he said.

'The cottages near the school were destroyed by a Zeppelin. The people there, a husband and wife, were killed. They left a baby. I knew them. I used to visit them. I brought the baby here.'

'And you want to take the child along with you?'

'I must. I made a solemn promise. It was when she was dying . . .'

'I see. And you promised the mother to take care of the child. Do you know how to look after it?'

'Oh yes. You don't mind . . . ?'

He laughed. 'I don't think I should be very good at looking after it. But you ladies will see to that, I am sure.'

I laughed with him. I thought he was wonderful. I turned away to hide my emotion and he took my arm and pressed it.

Not only was he capable and light-hearted, he had understood at once.

After the meal, which made me think of the Feast of the Passover, our pieces of baggage were put in the army vehicle and in a short time we were driving to the border.

We were very soon in heavy traffic. It seemed as though the entire population of Belgium was eager to get out of the country. It was a pathetic sight to see that lost, bewildered look on the faces of so many. There were vehicles of all sorts, people on bicycles, some with wheelbarrows, some on foot – all with one purpose: to get away before the invading army caught up with them.

Major Merrivale was in complete command. He sat at the driver's wheel and Annabelinda had contrived it so that she was in the front beside him. Miss Carruthers and I, with Edouard, sat at the back.

The Major kept up a conversation most of the time. He told us that the British Army was already coming into France.

'It won't be long before we are driving the Germans back,' he said. 'In the meantime, we have to prepare. We were all caught a little on the hop, as the saying goes, while the Germans had been planning this for years. The Kaiser was determined on it. He has been trying to get at us for years . . . ever since he sent that telegram of congratulations to Kruger at the time of the South African war – and that's going back a bit. We shall have to teach him a lesson. Are you comfortable at the back?'

'Oh yes, thanks,' we both said.

'And Monsieur Edouard?'

'He's happy. He's finding it all very amusing.'

'Wise child. That's the right attitude.'

'It can't be very amusing for these people who are leaving their homes,' I said.

'It will only be temporarily,' he replied. 'Soon they will all be going back.'

'When do you think the Germans will reach Mons, Major?' asked Miss Carruthers.

'That's hard to say, but if they keep up their present speed, I'd say a week or so.'

'Is it as bad as that?'

'Oh, it was a foul thing to do – to plunge into a country which has nothing whatever to do with this just because it is easy to get to the enemy that way. Poor little Belgium . . . completely without the means to resist. Never mind, we'll soon make those Germans wish they hadn't started this.'

'You are very confident,' I said.

'I've always been like this. Often I'm wrong, but at least I've had the pleasure of believing everything will come right . . . even if it does go the other way. So you see, it's not such a foolish attitude to take.'

'I think it is the right attitude,' said Annabelinda, smiling at him.

He returned the smile. I thought: He is finding her attractive . . . and for the simple reason that she is.

'It is a matter of opinion,' put in Miss Carruthers. 'It's like everything in life. There is a good side and a bad side. But the Major is right when he says it is good to be optimistic, as long as one is prepared to face the truth when one is proved to be wrong.'

'Ah,' said the Major, 'we have a philosopher here. A Sibyl.'

'Actually,' said Miss Carruthers, 'my name is Sybil, though it is spelt differently.'

The Major gave his infectious laugh and we all joined in, Miss Carruthers as heartily as any.

I thought then: Here we are, in this hazardous situation, in circumstances which are tragic to so many, and yet there are times when we can laugh and, yes, really be happy.

And we were on our way. I had Edouard with me and there had been no opposition to his coming. Miss Carruthers was different from what she had ever been before. Annabelinda had put that upsetting scene between us right out of her mind.

And this was all due to Major Merrivale.

It was evening before we crossed the frontier.

Major Merrivale had told us that his name was Marcus and, as he did not see any reason why we should stand on ceremony, he suggested we should drop the 'Major' and address him by his christian name.

'This,' he said, 'is a very special occasion, is it not? We are going to remember this for a long time. Don't you agree?'

We all did wholeheartedly.

'Now I think that young man at the back will be wondering why he is kept from his slumbers.'

'Actually,' I replied, 'he is deep in them now, so I am sure he is wondering no such thing.'

'All the same, he ought to be made comfortable for the

night. I think we all deserve that and, now that the desire for speed is not so intense, I am going to find an inn where we can stay the night.'

'That would be wonderful,' said Annabelinda.

We all agreed that it would be.

'There's a little place near St Armand. We might make for that,' he said.

'You seem to know the country well,' said Annabelinda.

'I studied the map and I discussed it with a brother officer who did know something. There is an inn called Le Cerf. The Stag. Sounds homely, doesn't it? The sort of place you'd find in the New Forest, say. So we'll look for that. There will probably be a board outside depicting the creature. If we can't find that we'll soon find something else.'

There was not so much traffic on the roads now, and I was glad. It was so depressing to see those poor people driven from their homes. I hoped they were all safely over the border by now . . . and that they would soon be on the way back to their homes.

We found Le Cerf. It was a fair-sized inn with tables in the gardens surrounding it. There was a somewhat loquacious host who greeted us effusively, largely, I think, because of Marcus Merrivale's presence. He was a member of the British Army and therefore an ally.

There were three rooms available; one was allotted to the Major, one to Miss Carruthers: and Annabelinda and I shared the third with Edouard. We went to them to wash and all agreed to meet in the lounge when we were ready.

There were two beds in our room, and first I looked after Edouard. Some soup and a creamy pudding were sent up to him. I fed him, prepared him for bed and soon he was fast asleep.

Annabelinda in the meantime was washing. She sat before the mirror studying her face while I went on dealing with Edouard.

She said contentedly: 'This is quite an adventure.'

'We can certainly call it that.'

'We shall soon be home now. I wonder if we shall see Major Merrivale after he has taken us there.'

'Perhaps he will call. He will know my Uncle Gerald well, I expect.'

'Of course. It was your Uncle Gerald who gave him the task of bringing us back. It's rather romantic, isn't it?' She laughed.

'Not too loudly, please, Annabelinda. Edouard's just going off to sleep.'

'Perhaps I should go down. You could come when you are ready.'

'All right. I may be some little time. I want to make sure he's fast asleep. I wouldn't want him waking up in a strange place and finding himself alone.'

She went with alacrity.

She was clearly enjoying the adventure, largely because of Major Merrivale's presence. And I shared her euphoria. We should soon be home. I longed to see my parents. My mother would know exactly what was best for Edouard and she would understand my feelings about him immediately. How lucky I was in my parents!

Then I began to wonder if Major Merrivale would call on us. I felt sure he would.

I was elated on that night. I kept telling myself that it was because we were on our way home and, in Major Merrivale's care, must soon be there.

There was a gentle tap on the door. I called 'Come in' and Miss Carruthers entered. It was strange to think of her as Sybil.

'I thought I'd come along and see how you were managing with the baby.'

I pointed to Edouard. 'He has just had some soup and pudding and he's asleep now. I think he is reasonably pleased with life.'

Miss Carruthers went over to look at him. 'Poor little mite,' she said.

'I intend that he shall be a lucky and happy little mite.'

'You're a good girl, Lucinda,' she said. I was surprised. I had not expected such a compliment from her. But everything was different today. It was something to do with Major Merrivale. He was having an effect on us all.

'What a charming man the Major is,' she went on. 'He makes no trouble of anything. He just inspires one with confidence.'

I agreed and, as we went along to the lounge, I said: 'I shall come up again soon just to make sure Edouard is all right. I don't know how this has affected him. I'm glad he isn't any older. Then I feel he would have been most upset.'

'Oh, he is too young to know what is happening. I think he is very fond of you and while you are around he will feel safe.'

'He will surely miss Madame Plantain.'

'Yes. He'll miss his mother. My dear Lucinda, you have taken on a great deal, you know.'

'My mother will help me. She is wonderful and she will know exactly what to do.'

'I hope I shall meet her.'

'But of course you must. Have you far to go to your home?'

She was silent for a few moments. 'Well,' she said at length, 'I stay with my cousin during holidays. I was going there for two months when school broke up. We don't know what will be happening now, do we?'

'Do you think we shall all be going back next term?'

She looked sombre and shook her head emphatically. 'I have a feeling that it is not going to be over as quickly as that. And what damage the Germans will do as they pass through the country one can never know. They have already killed the Plantains and destroyed their home. That sort of thing is happening all over Belgium. I'm afraid, Lucinda, that everything is rather uncertain. Come . . . they will be waiting for us.'

In the lounge Annabelinda was talking animatedly to Major Merrivale, and they were both laughing.

'You've been ages,' said Annabelinda. 'We're starving.'

'Lucinda has to care for the baby,' retorted Miss Carruthers rather reprovingly.

'Dear Lucinda! She's so efficient, Marcus.'

'I'm sure she is.'

The host came and said that dinner was about to be served, and we went into the dining-room. Two people were already sitting there. They were both young . . . not much more than twenty, I imagined.

The young man looked up as we entered and said: 'Good evening.' The girl said nothing.

Then the host's wife came in with hot soup, which was followed by cold beef with baked potatoes in their jackets.

Marcus Merrivale kept up a steady stream of conversation in which we all joined, and just as we were finishing the beef, the girl stood up abruptly and hurried from the room. The young man went out after her.

'What was all that about?' said Annabelinda. 'That girl seemed upset.'

'I think a great number of people are upset tonight,' I remarked.

After a short while the young man returned to the dining-room. He seemed upset and he looked across to our table almost apologetically.

'Can we do anything to help?' asked the Major.

There was a brief silence while apple tart was brought.

'Would you like to join us?' went on Marcus 'You look rather lonely sitting there.'

'Thank you,' replied the young man. He seemed grateful. We made a place for him at our table and he brought his plate over and sat down.

There was something disarming about him. He looked so young and he was clearly worried. As he seated himself at the table, I noticed there was something unusual about one of his hands. He had lost half his little finger.

I was ashamed when he caught me looking at it.

He said: 'It was my own fault. I was playing with fireworks.'

'How terrible!'

'Yes, one careless moment and one has a reminder for the rest of one's life.'

'It is not very noticeable.'

He smiled at me ruefully. 'One is conscious of it.'

'You shouldn't be.'

'I suppose one is really more conscious of one's disabilities than other people are.' He smiled and went on: 'We have had a terrible shock, my sister and I. We have lost our home and our parents. I can't believe it now. One day we were all there together, just as we had always been, and then suddenly – our home is gone, our parents killed. I can't believe it even now.'

'It's happening all over Belgium, I'm afraid,' said Marcus.

'I know. But because others are suffering in the same way, that does not make it any easier.'

'Where are you going now?' asked Marcus.

'I am going to join the French Army, but I am worried about Andrée. You see, there isn't anyone now . . .'

'Where do you come from?' asked Marcus.

'Just outside Charleroi. We have lived there all our lives, and now . . . Well, I had thought about joining the army some little time ago, and now, of course, it seems the only thing. But there is Andrée.'

'Where were you going?'

'I wanted Andrée to go to England. We've got an aunt there. Andrée visited her only last year. She lives in a place called Somerset. Our aunt married an Englishman. But . . . er . . . Andrée does not want to go there. She wants to stay with me. But if I am going into the army . . . Poor Andrée, she can't grasp what has happened to us. The sound of the guns was terrible. They were only a few miles away. Everyone was getting out. My parents didn't want to leave the farm. They'd been there all their married life. How can you get up and leave everything you've ever known? And then it was too late. It all went up in a sort of cloud . . . the fields . . . the house itself. And my parents were in the house. Andrée and I were in the fields some way off. That is why we are here now.'

'It is a sad story,' said Miss Carruthers. 'It wouldn't have seemed possible a few weeks ago, and now it is happening all round us.'

'It is a difficult decision to make,' went on the young man. 'I don't want to leave Andrée, but I'll feel happier if she is in England. I feel I must get into the army somehow. I have always wanted to, and now I feel I have to fight this vicious enemy.'

'Your great anxiety is for your sister,' said Marcus.

The young man nodded. He had not touched his apple tart.

'I should try to eat, if I were you,' said Marcus gently. But the young man shook his head and pushed the plate away.

As soon as the meal was over, I went up to see Edouard. He was sleeping peacefully. I felt depressed by the conversation with the young man, who was just another of those who were enduring terrible suffering at this time.

When I rejoined the party, he was still there. He obviously found comfort in the society of sympathetic listeners.

He was still talking about his sister Andrée and stressing how relieved he would be if she were safe in England.

At length Marcus reminded us that we had to make an early start in the morning and what we needed was a good night's sleep, so we said goodbye to the young man, whom we had by this time discovered was Georges Latour, wished him the best of luck and went to our rooms.

I was pleased to see that Edouard was still sleeping peacefully. I slept in the bed with him and Annabelinda took the other; and in spite of the excitement of the day, I was soon fast asleep.

When I awoke and looked round the room, I wondered where I was until I saw Edouard beside me and Annabelinda asleep in the other bed.

I yawned, got up, wondering what this day would bring.

In the dining-room there was coffee and crusty bread, hot from the oven. Georges Latour was at the table.

He said: 'Andrée is not up yet.'

'Is she feeling better?' I asked.

'A little, I think. Things never seem quite so bad in the morning, do they?'

'I suppose not.'

I fed Edouard, who regarded Georges Latour solemnly. He said: 'Whose is the baby?'

I told him about the Zeppelin raid and the deaths of Jacques and Marguerite Plantain, and how I had found Edouard in his perambulator in the garden.

'I knew him, you see. I used to visit them. It wasn't as though he were a stranger to me. I could not leave him.'

'What a tragedy this war is for so many!' said Georges.

And I was sorry to have reminded him of his own tragedy. We sat in gloomy silence for a few minutes, and then Marcus came. The atmosphere changed. Even Georges Latour seemed to brighten a little.

'Ah, up in good time, I see,' said Marcus. 'And young Edouard? How is he finding life this morning?'

'Much as usual. He seems to be rather indifferent to his surroundings.'

'As long as he has someone to see to his comforts, what does he care where he is?' said Marcus. 'You really are very good at looking after him.'

'It's easy, and he is a good child.'

Marcus said to Georges: 'And you – you'll be leaving soon, I suppose?'

'As soon as my sister is ready.'

'How is she this morning?'

'More or less the same.'

'I hope it all works out.'

Marcus drank some coffee and ate some of the bread. Miss Carruthers joined us. She said: 'It will be wonderful if we can get across the Channel tonight.'

'We'll try,' said Marcus. 'There'll be troopships coming over so there may be a little delay. But we'll make it, never fear. If not tonight, tomorrow.'

'It will be wonderful to be home,' I said.

Then Annabelinda came in.

'Oh, am I late?' she asked.

'Not really,' Marcus assured her. 'Just let us say the others were early.'

'How kind you are! I do like people who make excuses for me! Oh, what delicious-looking bread! And coffee, too!'

We chatted for a while and Marcus said could we all be ready to leave in fifteen minutes? Then we would set off. We all declared we could be and he went out to get the car.

But we did not leave in fifteen minutes.

We were assembled in the lounge. Andrée had come down, ready for departure. She smiled at us wanly. We did not like to ask how she was in case she thought the enquiry referred to her abrupt departure from the dining-room on the previous night.

We were sitting there rather uneasily when Marcus came in.

'There's a hitch,' he said. 'Something wrong with the vehicle.'

We all looked dismayed, and he smiled his bright smile.

'It can't be much. I'm sure we'll get it fixed in no time.'

Georges Latour, who was also preparing to leave, said he would go to a garage and get someone to call.

'That will delay your start,' said Marcus.

'That's nothing. It won't take long in the car. I'll bring someone back. Talk to Andrée while I'm gone.'

'A little delay won't hurt,' said Marcus. 'We may get to the coast in time to board a ferry. If not, there's tomorrow.'

We sat waiting.

Miss Carruthers said to Andrée: 'I am afraid this is delaying you, too.'

She shrugged her shoulders. 'It is of no importance,' she said.

'I wonder what is happening at La Pinière,' I said. 'Poor Madame Rochère. Whatever is she feeling now?'

'She should have left,' remarked Annabelinda.

'She could not bear to leave her home. She spent all her

married life there, and then she had the school all those years. It must be terrible for her. But if the Germans come . . .'

'She will know how to deal with them,' said Annabelinda. 'They'll be terrified of her . . . as we all were.'

'What nonsense! We were schoolgirls. She will be confronted by a conquering army.'

'Oh, she'll be all right.'

We waited for about an hour before Georges came back. He looked helpless.

'Sorry,' he said. 'I couldn't get anyone. You've no idea of the confusion everywhere. They are working on a lot of vehicles they are going to need at any moment. No one has anyone to send.'

'I'll see if I can discover what is wrong,' said Marcus.

'Do you know much about motors?' asked Georges.

'Not my line, really. There is usually a mechanic around.'

'I have a little knowledge,' said Georges. 'I might be able to see what's wrong. I'll have a try.'

They went out.

Edouard had awakened and was taking stock of us all. I took him on to my lap and he gripped my coat and kept hold of it as though to ensure that I did not leave him. Apart from that, he seemed quite undisturbed.

Andrée was talking a little now. She said that she must not stand in Georges's way. He had always been keen to join the army. She thought they would be eager to take him now. They would want as many men as they could get.

'I shall have to go to my aunt in England,' she said. 'I suppose I ought to be glad I've somewhere to go to. I don't want Georges to worry about me and he is very worried, but I don't want to live with my aunt.' She lifted her shoulders. 'I do not know how long it will be. This war could go on and on, but I must not be a burden to Georges. Young men do not want their sisters clinging to them. I should like to do some work in England. Do you think that is a possibility? I wouldn't mind going if I could do something. Georges will be in the army and that will help him, but myself . . .'

'I dare say there will be all sorts of work for people to do,' said Miss Carruthers. 'Wars make work.'

'It is good to be able to talk,' said Andrée. 'I feel you understand.'

'What sort of work would you want to do?' I asked.

'Anything. I wouldn't mind working in a house at first.'

'Do you mean as a servant?'

'I wouldn't mind. I'd rather do that than go to Aunt Berthe. In any case, I should be doing dusting and cooking with her. Why not do it somewhere else?'

'Then you'll easily find something,' said Annabelinda.

Andrée had brightened considerably. She looked almost animated.

'Do you . . . er . . . know anybody?' she asked.

'We know a lot of people, don't we, Annabelinda?'

'Oh yes. Our families do.'

'I'm quite good at looking after babies,' said Andrée. 'I've always loved them.'

'Oh, then it shouldn't be difficult . . . in London or in the country.'

'If you would help me . . .'

'But of course we will, if we can,' said Annabelinda.

'That would be wonderful. I was just thinking . . .'

We waited for her to go on, but she said: 'Oh no, it would be asking too much.'

'What were you going to say?' asked Miss Carruthers.

'Well . . . Oh no, I can't. You'd think me . . . oh no.'

'Please say it,' I said.

'Well . . . if I could travel with you . . . Georges need not come as far as the coast. He could go straight to Paris and find out about joining the army. I need not go to Aunt Berthe. If I could come with you . . . if you would help me.'

Annabelinda and I exchanged glances. We should arrive home with a baby, a schoolmistress and a girl who had been a stranger to us on the previous night. It would be a surprise – I might say a shock – for my parents. But these were unusual times and when tragedies overtook people, one must do all one

113

could to help them. I was sure my parents would understand that.

Annabelinda said: 'We could, couldn't we, Lucinda?'

'Yes, I should think so,' I replied. 'Yes, you must travel with us. I'll take you to my home. We don't know what is happening there. My mother will surely know someone who needs a maid . . . that's if you don't mind what you do.'

'Do you really mean that?'

'Of course.'

Miss Carruthers said: 'I hope there won't be any difficulty in getting you into England. I don't know what the regulations are. Wartime, you know, and all that.'

Andrée looked alarmed. Then she said: 'I have my papers. I was in England only last year, visiting my aunt. It was all right then.'

'The Major will be able to make it right, I'm sure,' said Annabelinda.

Andrée was talking excitedly. 'Oh . . . how can I thank you? I feel so much better. I really couldn't face Aunt Berthe, and there's poor Georges. If I could come with you, he could go straight to Paris. It would be such a help to us. I just have a feeling that this is going to work out well for us. We both of us want a complete change. We want to get away from all that . . .'

Her voice broke, and we all murmured our understanding and sympathy.

While we were talking, Marcus and Georges came in. They were beaming with pleasure.

'It's done,' cried Marcus. 'It's all right, thanks to Monsieur Latour.'

'I just found the trouble,' said Georges modestly. 'I've always enjoyed tinkering with cars.'

'So it is all right for us to leave?' asked Miss Carruthers.

'Absolutely,' replied Marcus. 'But look at the time! It's almost noon. I suggest that we all have a meal here at the inn. We should have to stop for food otherwise on our way. I'll tell the landlord.'

Andrée Latour said to her brother: 'Georges, I have some wonderful news.'

'Why? What's happened?'

'These kind people are going to allow me to travel with them. And, Georges, I am not going to Tante Berthe. Please don't try to persuade me to. I have made up my mind. They are going to help me find something I could do . . .'

'Andrée, you must go to Tante Berthe. You have to. It's the only thing to do.'

'No, no. Listen. Mademoiselle Greenham and Mademoiselle Denver, they will take me to their home. They will find a place for me. I can work where I want to. I will try anything – anything – rather than go to Tante Berthe. So you see, Georges, you need not come with me to England. You can go straight to Paris. I couldn't bear to go to Tante Berthe. Georges . . . say you are pleased.'

Georges was looking bewildered. I could understand. He would be leaving his sister with strangers. In ordinary circumstances that would have been out of the question, but these were no ordinary circumstances.

'But . . I . . . I'm sure . . .' he began.

'It's all so simple,' I put in. 'I'll take her to my home with us. My mother will be very helpful. She always is. My father is a Member of Parliament and there are always people around. They are certain to know someone who wants help in the house.'

But Georges was still looking uneasy and quite bemused.

We ate a good luncheon and talked a great deal.

I fed Edouard and afterwards Andrée took him on to her lap, and to my surprise he did not protest.

'What a good little boy he is!' she commented and kissed the top of his head. Edouard grunted in a manner intended to express approval.

The thought occurred to me that Andrée might help with him. We should have to have a nursery for him and we should need someone there.

I felt as though I were living in a dream. Every little detail

115

seemed of the utmost importance. If the car had not broken down, we should have set out early this morning as we had planned; we should have said goodbye to Georges and Andrée and almost certainly would never have seen them again.

How strange life was! One could never be certain what would happen next – particularly in a situation like this.

There was barely room for Andrée in the car, but we managed. Georges followed us along the road in his own car. We should be together until he branched off for Paris. Andrée took Edouard from me and sang a little song to him:

> *'Il pleut, il pleut, bergère,*
> *Presse tes blancs moutons.*
> *Allons à la chaumière,*
> *Bergère, vite, allons . . .'*

Edouard, who was beginning to be fretful, watched her mouth closely as she sang, and a beautiful smile spread over his face.

There was no doubt that he liked Andrée.

There was a tearful scene when we parted from Georges. That dreamlike quality had returned. Everything that was happening seemed so extraordinary. Andrée, a stranger this time yesterday, was now one of us.

What would happen next, I wondered?

And so we made our way towards the coast.

We reached Calais in the late afternoon, and soon learned that there was no hope of a sailing that night, so we put up at an inn close by the harbour. There was an uneasy atmosphere throughout the town. People looked dismayed and bewildered. We were in a country which had recently been plunged into war. The enemy were making rapid progress through Belgium and were almost at the frontier – a feat they had achieved in a matter of days.

What next? was the question on everyone's lips.

116

All through the night I could hear the rhythm of the waves as they rose and fell. Tomorrow, I kept saying to myself, I shall be home.

Marcus was in his usual high spirits. The following morning he went off to assess the situation and to make arrangements to get us out of France as quickly as possible.

He was gone some time and, when he returned, found us all eagerly awaiting him in the parlour. He told us there were difficulties, but he hoped to sort them out before long. The fact was we could not leave immediately.

All through that day we waited, and by nightfall we were still at the inn.

Marcus had gone off in the early morning. He said he might be some time, but he was sure we should be able to sail the next day.

I was surprised to discover that people can get to know each other more thoroughly in such circumstances than in months of conventional living.

I was drawn towards Andrée, largely because she had taken to Edouard, and he to her. She appeared to have a knowledge of the needs of babies. When he cried or had a bout of indigestion, she knew how to soothe him. She would rub his stomach, talking to him as she did so. The snatches of French songs which she sang to him always seemed to amuse him.

It was evening. Marcus was still out trying to arrange for us to get on a ferry. We had had dinner and had gone up to the bedroom I shared with Annabelinda and Edouard, who was fast asleep at this time. Annabelinda, Andrée and Miss Carruthers had joined us there.

It was an attic room with a ceiling which sloped almost to the floor on one side, and there was a small window which looked out on the harbour.

We were talking in a rather desultory manner when suddenly the atmosphere changed and it became a time of revelation. I do not know how these things happen. It might have been because we were all uneasy and that grey sea outside seemed like a mighty barrier between us and home, reminding

117

us of the difficulties, mocking us as it beat against the harbour walls, reminding us that we were far from home, that we might be caught up in this war and never cross that sea.

Perhaps I was too fanciful and the others were not thinking along similar lines, but the desire to get close to each other seemed to be with us all, to brush aside that façade we showed to the world and to reveal ourselves as we really were.

Andrée began it. She said: 'I feel something of a fraud. It is not the tragedy I have made you think it is for me to be here. I have dreamed and longed to start a new life. I have hoped and prayed that it would come about. Perhaps I prayed too fervently. Perhaps if you believe that something will come to you, if you pray for it night and day, it comes – not in the way you think, but in God's way . . . and you have to pay for it.'

She had our attention, even Annabelinda's whose concentration was apt to stray if the subject did not include her.

Andrée looked round the room at each of us in turn. She went on: 'Has it occurred to you that people are hardly ever what they seem? We all have our secrets hidden right away. If we brought them out . . . if we showed them . . . we should not be the people others believe us to be.'

Miss Carruthers said: 'I dare say you are right, but perhaps it is more comfortable to go on as we are. More pleasant, making life run more smoothly.'

'There are sometimes occasions when one wants to confess,' said Andrée. 'To examine oneself, perhaps. To find out all sorts of things one did not know about oneself.'

'Confession is good for the soul,' said Miss Carruthers. 'But perhaps it is better not to make a habit of it.'

'I was thinking of myself,' went on Andrée. 'You are all so sorry for me. I lost my home . . . my parents. "What a terrible thing," you say. "Poor girl! What a tragedy she has gone through." But I did not love my home. For a long time I have wanted to get away from it . . . and my parents. I knew I would never be happy until I did. My father was a farmer, a deeply religious man. There was little laughter in our house. Laughter was a sin. I yearned to get away. I went to my aunt in England.

118

She had married an Englishman. I was to help her when her husband died. It was as bad as being at home. I vowed I would never go back to her. Then you found me upset at Le Cerf. It was going back to her that I was so miserable about, not the death of my parents and the loss of the home I wanted to leave. I never loved my parents. We had no tenderness from them. I was beginning to think I should never get away unless I ran away. I often contemplated it. And then suddenly . . . that explosion . . . the farm destroyed . . . it was gone . . . they were gone. And I am free.'

'Well,' said Annabelinda. 'We shan't be sorry for you any more.'

'That is what I want. I feel free. I feel excited. A new life is opening for me.' She turned to me. 'I have you to thank. I can't tell you what your promise to help me means to me.'

'It is so little,' I said.

'I see that it means a great deal to Andrée,' put in Miss Carruthers. She turned to Andrée. 'Well, my dear, you have been frank with us and I admire you for it. You have made me consider my own case.'

It occurred to me then how much she had changed. She was still in a measure the old formidable Miss Carruthers, but a new woman had emerged, the woman who was showing herself to be as vulnerable as the rest of us, for she went on: 'One cannot go on teaching for ever. There comes a time when one has to stop, and then . . . what is to become of one? For me, there is my cousin Mary – one might say the counterpart of Andrée's Aunt Berthe. I was an only child. My father died when I was eight years old, my mother had died soon after my birth. Uncle Bertram, Mary's father, was in comfortable circumstances. He was my mother's brother. He helped a good deal. He took over my education, but he never let me forget it. He is dead now, but there is Cousin Mary to remind me of my debt. And you see, there is no one to whom I can go but Cousin Mary. Hers is the only home I have. Holidays, when I have to leave the school, are something I have always dreaded . . .'

I could not believe I was listening to Miss Carruthers, who had always been so unassailable.

'And now,' said Annabelinda, 'you are going to her . . . and there could be no school for you to return to.'

'That is how life goes,' said Miss Carruthers. 'We must needs accept what is meted out to us.'

I think she was already regretting her frankness. I felt a fondness for this new version of our severe mistress which would have been impossible at school.

I started to tell them about myself.

'I have had a very happy childhood,' I said. 'My father is a Member of Parliament. He is often away and then, of course, when we are in London, he is busy at the Houses of Parliament, and when we are in the country, there is constituency business. My mother and I have been very close to each other all my life. She is the most understanding person I know.'

'How lucky you are!' said Andrée.

'I have always known it. I think she is a particularly wonderful person, because she suffered a terrible tragedy when she was young. Her father, of whom she was very fond, was shot dead when she was with him. He was on his way to the Houses of Parliament, and she was saying goodbye to him as he got into his carriage. She saw the man who did it and it was her evidence which convicted him. He was an Irish terrorist, and it had something to do with Mr Gladstone's Home Rule Bill which my grandfather was opposing. It took her a long time to get over it; she married and that went wrong; but eventually she and my father were married.'

'And lived happily ever after,' added Annabelinda.

'Well, they did,' I said. 'They had always loved each other but all those terrible things happened, not only to my mother but to my father, too. He was missing at one time. They thought he was dead. That's quite a story.'

'Do tell us,' said Andrée.

'I don't really know what it was all about. They don't talk of it much. But it was when they thought he was dead that my mother married this other man. One day I think she will tell me more about it.'

'What an exciting time she must have had,' said Annabelinda.

'Excitement is not always a happy state, Annabelinda,' remarked Miss Carruthers. 'You learn as you go through life that there are events which are exciting to anticipate, amusing and entertaining to relate after they have happened, but extremely uncomfortable when they are in progress.'

'Now it's your turn,' said André to Annabelinda.

'Oh, my mother is a beauty. She's had an exciting life. She lived in Australia for a time. When she came back to England she married Sir Robert Denver. I've got a brother, too. He's Robert, after my father. He's nice but rather dull.'

'He's not dull,' I protested. 'He's just . . . good.'

'Oh well . . .'

'Why should good people be called dull?' I demanded hotly. 'I think they are a whole lot nicer than selfish people. *And* more interesting. Robert is one of the nicest people I know.'

'And she knows so many,' mocked Annabelinda.

'You ought to be proud of him,' I said.

Annabelinda grinned. 'Robert,' she said, 'is very fond of Lucinda. That's why she likes him so much.'

Before I could speak, André said: 'This is like a confessional. Why is it that we all have the urge to lay bare our souls tonight?'

'It's rather fun,' said Annabelinda. She caught my eye and grinned at me. She had told us nothing about herself. Her secrets were too dangerous to be divulged.

'I know what it is,' said Miss Carruthers. 'It is the uncertainty of our lives. We are waiting, listening to the waves. There is a wind blowing up. Shall we ever be able to get away? It is at such times that people feel the urge to reveal themselves, to show themselves to the world as they really are.'

I believed there was some truth in that, but Annabelinda would never reveal her weaknesses.

At that moment Edouard woke up and began to cry. Andrée immediately soothed him and Annabelinda said: 'Marcus will have arranged something. It won't be long now before we are home.'

We spent another night in that inn and in the early morning of the following day we boarded a Channel ferry. At last we were on the way home. Marcus had made it possible.

I sat on deck in the semi-darkness, holding Edouard on my lap. Andrée was beside me.

'I don't know what we should have done without you,' I said to her. 'I know so little about the needs of children.'

'You learn quickly,' she said. 'It comes naturally to some of us. I don't know what *I* could have done without *you*. When I think of how you have helped me . . .'

'We must all help each other at times like this.'

Annabelinda was close by with Marcus Merrivale and Miss Carruthers. I felt very comforted to watch them.

How silent it was! There was a coolish breeze sweeping over the sea. We were all tired but too emotionally disturbed to think of sleep.

When I shut my eyes I could see the remains of the cottage. I could see Marguerite's appealing eyes. And I knew that was something I should never forget.

I looked across at Marcus Merrivale. His task was nearly over. He would deposit us at my parents' house and then report to Uncle Gerald. 'Mission accomplished!'

I smiled. What a fine man he was! What a hero! Not once had I seen him in the least perturbed. He had accepted everything with something like jaunty nonchalance and a certain belief that he would be able to overcome all difficulties. And he had.

We shall see him again, I assured myself. My parents would want to thank him and he was, after all, a friend of Uncle Gerald.

That thought gave me a certain warm comfort.

And then in the dawn light, I saw the outline of the white cliffs.

We had come safely home.

Milton Priory

They were there to greet us when we arrived – my parents, Charles, Aunt Belinda and Uncle Robert – all, except Robert. My mother seized me and hugged me again and again. She seemed as though she must keep reassuring herself that I was really there.

Miss Carruthers stood a little apart with Andrée, who was holding the baby. My mother had given them a quick glance but she was too intent on me to take in immediately the fact that we had brought strangers with us.

My father stood by, awaiting his turn to embrace me. He was almost as emotional as my mother. Charles was dancing around. 'Did you see any soldiers?' he asked.

It was a wonderful homecoming.

Marcus stood by, watching and smiling.

'How can we thank you enough?' my father was saying to him. 'How grateful we are to my brother for arranging for you to bring them home . . . and especially to you.'

Aunt Belinda was talking excitedly and kissed Annabelinda and then me. Uncle Robert stood by, smiling benignly on us all. Dear Uncle Robert. He reminded me so much of his son, my own dear Robert.

'Where is Robert?' I asked.

'Robert joined the Army immediately war was declared,' my mother told me.

'He's in training now,' added Aunt Belinda. 'Somewhere on Salisbury Plain, I think.'

'I'm going to join when I'm old enough,' said Charles. Nobody took any notice of him.

My mother seemed suddenly aware that there were strangers present. Her eyes lingered on Andrée and the baby.

'I'll tell you everything later,' I said to her. 'This is Miss Carruthers, who has travelled with us from the school. She really doesn't want to go down to the country just yet. If she could stay . . .'

'But of course you must stay, Miss Carruthers,' said my mother. 'Lucinda has mentioned you in her letters. You must be exhausted after all this. I'll have a room made ready.'

'And this is Mademoiselle Andrée Latour. We met while we were getting across France.'

'Welcome to England,' said my mother.

'She must stay here too, Mama,' I said.

'Of course. Look, here are some of the servants. They have all been so anxious about you. Mrs Cherry . . . isn't this wonderful?'

'It is indeed, M'am,' replied Mrs Cherry. 'We are so glad you've come back safe and sound, Miss Lucinda.'

'We want two rooms made ready. Three, perhaps. Major Merrivale . . . ?'

'Thank you,' he said. 'But I shall be reporting to Colonel Greenham to let him know that all has gone according to plan.'

'But you'll stay for a meal?'

'That would be delightful.'

My mother, in her usual way, was getting the practical details sorted out. I was longing to be alone with her. I could see she had the same thought in mind.

Aunt Belinda and Uncle Robert went off with Annabelinda and I went to my room. I had not been there long when my mother arrived.

As soon as she entered the room, she took me into her arms.

'We have been so worried,' she said. 'I have scarcely slept since war was declared. And you out there, in Belgium of all places, with the Germans sweeping across the country. Oh yes, we were sick with worry, your father and I . . . although he didn't show it as much as I did. We can't be grateful enough to your Uncle Gerald who said he would get you out the best way. I wanted to come out, but he said that was ridiculous and impossible. So he sent that charming Major. What a pleasant man!'

'Yes,' I said. 'Everyone liked him. He was so imperturbable.'

'God bless him.'

'I must explain to you about these people with us. Do you mind their coming here?'

She looked at me in astonishment. 'My darling, I'd welcome anyone who came with you. It's all I care about, to have you back. But who are they? I know Miss Carruthers, of course. I mean the girl with the baby.'

'First the baby. I've got to keep him. I promised his mother. You see, she was dying . . .'

I told her how I had visited Edouard, how Marguerite had lost her own child and become foster-mother to Edouard. She listened intently as I described the scene with Marguerite when she was dying.

'I've got to look after him, Mama. I could never be happy if I didn't,' I finished.

She understood perfectly. She said: 'It's a big undertaking. Poor little mite . . . without a mother.'

'She loved him so much. He took the place of her own child.'

'Yes, I see.'

'But he will stay here, won't he? He must not become one of those babies for whom a home has to be found.'

'He has already been that once, poor lamb.'

'I don't want it to happen again.'

'Don't worry about the child. It will be impossible for you to adopt him at your age. But we'll see to him. Poor little refugee. I wish these people who make wars would pause a while first to think of the misery they are causing.'

'The only thing they think about is power and they don't care who suffers if they can get that. But Edouard will be all right here.'

126

'Edouard? That's his name, is it? We'll call him Edward. That will go down better here.'

I hugged her. She had reacted to the baby just as I had known she would.

'I thought,' she said, 'that his mother was that Andrée.'

'Oh no. We found her in an inn just over the border between Belgium and France. Her home was blown up, her parents killed, and she was on her way to an aunt whom she loathes. She wants to get work here. I thought we could help her. She's very good with babies.'

'You have brought home some problems with you, my darling. And you not yet out of the schoolroom! You're something of a manipulator . . . but I love you for it, and I'm deliriously happy because I've got you back.'

'And then there is Miss Carruthers. She is quite different from what I thought her. At school she was indomitable . . . really formidable, and now I realize that she is just a little frightened about the future.'

'I've known governesses like that. They wonder what will happen to them when they can no longer teach.'

'It seems there's a cousin who lets her know she's living on her bounty. It must be horrible. I know she would love to stay here for a few days.'

'I can see no reason why she shouldn't. She came with you all the way and that makes her a rather special person to me.'

'How lucky I am to have you and Papa instead of a horrible old cousin and an aunt like Andrée's. Tell me about Robert.'

'He's been very worried about you. We'll have to let him know at once that you are safely home. He joined up right at the start, and of course he couldn't get away. On the first opportunity he'll be here, you see.'

'Robert a soldier . . . how strange that seems!'

'I think we are going to find lots of strange things happening in the next months. But at the moment all I care about is that you are home.'

At that moment the door opened and my father came in.

127

He did not speak but put his arms round me and held me tightly. He stroked my hair. 'We are so pleased that you have come back to us,' was all he said.

It was a wonderful homecoming.

The next day was given over to frenetic planning. My mother threw herself into this with an almost maniacal energy. She kept telling me how thankful she was that I was home and of the terrible anxiety they had suffered, of her wild imaginings as to what was happening. 'I never want to go through that again,' she said more than once.

'Our first concern,' she went on, 'must be the baby.' The nursery was to be opened up. The servants were delighted. They cooed over Edouard – Edward as he had now become – and he was clearly delighted with the attention.

'Poor little mite,' said Mrs Cherry. 'His home blown up by them Germans. I'd blow them up if I had my way. You'd think they'd have some pity for a helpless little baby. It's a good thing we're going to show them what's what.'

'We'll have to get a nanny,' said my mother. 'In the meantime, Andrée will stay and help. I must say Edward seems to have taken a fancy to her . . . almost as much as he has to you.'

'That will suit her beautifully. We've got to help her, Mama. She seems so happy now that she can stay here. She was very upset about going to that old aunt of hers.'

'Poor girl! What a lot she has gone through. Thank God, Edward is too young to know what happened to his home.'

So the problem of Edward and Andrée had settled itself. The next was Miss Carruthers. My father had taken quite a liking to her. He found her conversation stimulating. On the first evening, she impressed him with her knowledge of government and political matters.

During that first meal they had a discussion about the merits and drawbacks of a coalition government. Miss Carruthers offered the opinion that, though this could be a somewhat hazardous procedure in peacetime, it might be quite the reverse when we were at war.

'To have all parties working together with one aim – the successful conclusion of the war – would be preferable to having them carping for the sake of carping. To have them thinking of the good of the country rather than scoring political points, as is, alas, their usual practice, could not fail to be beneficial.'

My father agreed with her, and they chatted at ease and with obvious enjoyment.

A few days passed. My mother suggested that Miss Carruthers should stay a little longer, unless she was in a hurry to get to the country. Miss Carruthers accepted the invitation with obvious pleasure.

Annabelinda went back to Hampshire with her parents, declaring that she would be coming back to London soon.

My mother often came to my room immediately after we had retired. Just for a little bedtime chat, she used to say.

During one of these, she said: 'I think it is unlikely that you will be going back to La Pinière. It's no use our deceiving ourselves that all this is going to be over in a week or two. The Germans are flooding into Belgium. They'll be in France before long. I've been talking this over with your father. You are only fifteen years old and your education is not finished.'

'It's holiday time now.'

'I know, but that will soon be over. We have to think ahead. Your father and I could not bear to let you go away to school again, even in England. What you went through . . .'

'Oh, it wasn't so bad for us. We got away in time, thanks to Major Merrivale. It would have been difficult without him.'

'Oh yes, indeed. We're going to ask him to dinner – perhaps on the twenty-third, if he can manage it – and your Uncle Gerald with him. But then he may not be able to spare the time. But what I was going to say was that you have to continue your education, war or no war, and your father thought it might be a good idea to ask Miss Carruthers if she would stay and act as governess.'

I looked at my mother and laughed.

'What's the matter?' she asked. 'Have I said something funny?'

'No . . . no. Not at all. It is just that you are like some sort of magician. You're making it all work out. Andrée, Edward . . . and now Miss Carruthers.'

'You like her, don't you? Your father thinks she is a very intelligent woman.'

'Yes, I do like her. I like her quite a lot now I've got to know her. She's different away from school. There she was so stern. When we were coming across France, she seemed to become human.'

'I think she is a nice woman and she would be a very good governess.'

'Have you mentioned it to her?'

'Not yet. Your father and I decided we would see how you felt about it first.'

'I think it's a wonderful idea. She was so hating the thought of going back to that cousin. I can't help laughing. It's so wonderful now we are home. We talked one night in the inn at Calais, with the waves dashing against the harbour walls . . . we talked about ourselves and our fears of what would happen if we ever got away and came home. We talked of our problems and I could see that Miss Carruthers was just a little frightened about the future. So was Andrée. Now it's solved. It's like a fairy-tale ending.'

She was silent for a while and then she said: 'We've got to keep it so, Lucinda. Will you talk to Miss Carruthers? But perhaps I should.'

'Yes,' I said. 'You ask her. Tell her how grateful you will be if she stays.'

'I will do that.'

I looked round my room and said: 'It is wonderful to be home.'

The days passed quickly. Miss Carruthers was clearly delighted at the prospect of her new post. She discussed what she called

130

our curriculum with me. She would concentrate rather specially on literature, she thought; through this I should get a good grounding in the classics and would be able to show erudition when conversing with my father's guests. I agreed. I would have agreed to anything because I was so happy to see her pleasure. It was the same with Andrée. They were two contented people.

I wrote to Annabelinda. I had to tell her that Miss Carruthers was going to be my governess. I was sure that would amuse her. She, at the mature age of seventeen, would doubtless persuade her mother that no further education was necessary.

Nothing much has changed here [I wrote]. Of course, everyone talks of the war and little else. Most people seem to think it will be over by Christmas. Perhaps it will, once our forces get over there.

We haven't seen Uncle Gerald yet. Aunt Hester says he is very busy. I am sure it won't be long before he is overseas. He is involved now at the War Office. He is coming to dinner on the twenty-third. And guess what? Major Merrivale is coming too. Mama thought it would be best to invite him when Uncle Gerald comes. It will be fun to see him again.

Andrée is very happy. I can't help thinking how strange it was, meeting them at Le Cerf. Don't you agree? One chance meeting and people's lives are changed.

Edward is very happy here. He is no longer Edouard. My mother thought it best to anglicize him, as he'll be brought up here. She has been wonderful about everything. But then I knew she would be.

Have you heard any news of Robert?

Give my love to your parents, and of course I send the same to you.

Lucinda.

I did not hear from Annabelinda. She rarely answered letters unless there was something she particularly wanted to say.

Aunt Hester came over to see us from Camberley where she and Uncle Gerald had lived for most of their married life. She was in London to do some shopping, she said, and had taken the opportunity to call.

'It saves writing,' she said. 'It's about this dinner. Gerald can't possibly come on the twenty-third. Things are moving fast over there. The Germans are approaching Mons and the situation is getting more and more alarming.'

Mons! I thought of Madame Rochère, and wondered what she was doing. I had a feeling she would never leave La Pinière.

'I understand, of course,' said my mother. 'But what a pity! I did want to let Major Merrivale know how grateful we are to him. I suppose he will be involved with Gerald?'

'Oh yes. They'll leave at the same time, I expect. They do work closely together.'

'It was wonderful of him to arrange to get the girls home.'

'Gerald would do a lot for the family. But what I was going to say was, could we have this dinner-party earlier? I think – but I can't be absolutely certain – that Gerald will be leaving on the twenty-second. The nineteenth would be just about the latest he could come.'

'Well, we'll make it the nineteenth. Why not? That will suit us just as well.'

'I feel sure that will be all right,' said Aunt Hester. 'But you'll understand if we have to cancel. These times are so uncertain.'

'But of course,' said my mother.

My mother decided that it should be a very small party. 'Really a family affair. I dare say both Uncle Gerald and Major Merrivale have had enough of functions in their positions. I shall ask Miss Carruthers and Andrée to join us. After all, they were members of the party and I am sure Major Merrivale would like to know that they are safely settled.'

I was looking forward to it with pleasure and, I have to admit, with a certain amount of excitement. Marcus Merrivale had been in my thoughts a great deal. He was the kind of man who left a deep impression.

I was afraid that the party might be cancelled. My mother said we must be prepared for that. Wars made everything uncertain.

However, the nineteenth arrived and there was Marcus Merrivale with Uncle Gerald and Aunt Hester. Marcus looked just as he had during the journey across France.

He took both my hands. 'Miss Lucinda! What a pleasure to see you! And Miss Carruthers and Mademoiselle Latour. Well, this is a gathering of the clan, is it not?'

My father said: 'I don't know how we are ever going to thank you, Major. What you did . . .'

'It was nothing . . . but pleasure all the way, I do assure you.'

'I knew Marcus would pull it off,' said Uncle Gerald. 'He was just the man for the job.'

'Well, come along in,' said my mother. 'I only hope you are not going to be called away. One never knows at times like this with you military people. Anything can happen from hour to hour.'

My mother had arranged that the Major should sit on her right hand and I was next to him. Uncle Gerald was between Miss Carruthers and Andrée.

My parents asked the Major a lot of questions about the journey, most of which I had already answered; and again my mother thanked him for what he had done. He replied again that it had been a pleasure.

'A change from my usual duties,' he added. 'And you know how we all love a change. By the way,' he added, 'how is Master Edouard faring? Has he deigned to accept his new home?'

'With supreme indifference,' replied my mother. 'Lucinda will tell you all about him. He is her favourite topic. By the way, we call him Edward now. We thought it best to anglicize him.'

'What an excellent idea!' He turned to me. 'I am so glad

Mademoiselle is with you. She is so happy.' He smiled across at her.

'Oh, I am,' Andrée said fervently.

My father was talking to Aunt Hester about her sons, Harold and George. George had been going into the Army in any case, but Harold had immediately joined up. 'Of course, he is rather young,' said Aunt Hester.

'We're going to need all the men we can get,' said Marcus, and then the talk turned to the war.

After dinner, when we had all retired to the drawing-room, Marcus was beside me once more.

He asked about Annabelinda. I told him she was in Hampshire with her family and, as her brother had joined the Army, I had therefore not seen him since my return to England.

'He's training on Salisbury Plain,' I added.

'It must be the Royal Field Artillery.'

'Yes, it is. I expect he'll come and see us as soon as he can.'

'He's a favourite of yours, is he?'

'Oh yes. He's one of the nicest people I know.'

He nodded. 'I did not expect to see Miss Carruthers here tonight.'

'She is going to teach me. My parents think I need a governess for a while.'

'Yes, of course. You are very young.' He grinned at me. 'Don't be downcast on that account. It is something which will quickly be rectified, you know.'

'I suppose you will be going away soon?'

'At any moment . . . by the look of things.'

'I heard the Germans were close to Mons. How close, do you know?'

'Only that it is too close.'

'It's hateful. I can't stop thinking of Madame Rochère. What will she do? She will be so haughty and unrelenting.'

'I dare say she will have to submit to the conquerors. She would have been wise to get away.'

'I can't believe she will ever leave La Pinière of her own

free will. Just imagine how it must be for her! Losing her home.'

'Still, better than losing one's life.'

I was sombre and he put a hand over mine. 'Don't be sad, Miss Lucinda. I hate to see you sad.'

'It's a sad time for so many.'

'Nothing is entirely bad, you know. There is always some little bit of good lurking among the troubles. Just think! But for all this, we should never have met.'

I smiled at him and he went on: 'I hope you will think of this meeting as one of the good things in all this.'

'My mother has told you many times how grateful we all are to you, so I won't repeat it. But I mean it just the same.'

'You overrate what I did. Never mind. I like it. I shall take the first opportunity of coming to see you again.'

'Oh . . . shall you?'

'It is what I shall look forward to most.'

'What of your family?'

'Ask me what you want to know.'

'Where do they live? Have you a big family? Have you a wife?'

'Sussex. Parents, brother and sister. Not yet.'

I laughed. 'You're very laconic.'

'You asked for answers and you got them.'

'Why did you say "not yet" about being married? It sounds as though you might soon.'

'I shall have to wait until I find the perfect woman . . . and then would she have me?'

'I feel sure she would.'

'Nothing is sure in this life, but it is nice of you to say so. I fear the perfect woman would look for a perfect man.'

'When people are in love, the ones they love seem perfect in their eyes.'

'How comforting. But the imperfections come to light later. Perhaps after all perfection is a sort of compromise.'

'Are you a little cynical?'

135

'Me? Never for a moment. I am a romantic. An optimist. Probably a very unwise man.'

'Well, I hope you find the perfect woman.'

'I shall. Even if I have to wait until she grows up a little.'

He was looking at me, smiling, lifting his eyebrow a little in a quizzical way. I was disconcerted but happy.

Andrée was coming towards us.

'Major Merrivale,' she said. 'I have heard the Germans are advancing across Belgium and that they are almost at the borders of France. Is it true?'

'It is not wise to listen to rumours, Mademoiselle Latour. But I fear the advance is rapid.'

'Shall you be going overseas again soon?'

'In a few days, I expect.'

'How I wish it were all over!'

'You can be sure we are all with you in that.'

Miss Carruthers joined us.

'It has been such a pleasure to see you, Major Merrivale,' she said. 'I shall never forget how you looked after us.'

'Like the good shepherd,' added Andrée.

'Don't say that,' I protested with a laugh. 'It makes us all sound like sheep. I always thinks that "shepherd" in that respect is not a very good analogy. After all, the shepherd looks after the sheep to prepare them for the slaughter-house.'

'Some die of old age,' said Miss Carruthers.

'But even they are kept just for their wool.'

'What about the Pied Piper?' suggested Miss Carruthers, with a rare look of roguishness.

'Well, he led the children into the mountainside, didn't he?' I said.

'Ladies,' said Marcus. 'I am no shepherd and no piper . . . just an ordinary fellow who was overjoyed to be of service to you. What I did was something anyone could have done.'

'Well, I think you were very resourceful in a difficult situation,' declared Miss Carruthers. 'It was an experience I shall never forget and will always be grateful for.'

My mother joined us with Aunt Hester and the conversation became general.

I was sure that everyone thought it was a successful evening, and after it was over Marcus Merrivale remained in my thoughts. I was discovering that I liked him very much. I noticed that even the servants were impressed by the charm he extended to them. He had stepped into our lives as a hero. He was the kind of man who seemed to care about other people's feelings and he had a smiling consideration for everyone; and I was beginning to think that there was something special in his attitude to me.

The next day Uncle Gerald called to say goodbye.

The news was bad. The Germans were on the outskirts of Mons and a great battle was in progress.

'We've got to hold them,' said Uncle Gerald. 'We're stepping up the movements of men and ammunition. The regiment's leaving tomorrow at dawn.'

'Major Merrivale will be with you, I suppose,' said my mother.

'Oh yes. Nice fellow, isn't he?'

'Most attractive and, of course, we are especially grateful to him. And to you, naturally.'

'You've made that plain. I knew he could be trusted to do the job. Rather dashing, don't you think? Popular with the ladies.'

'That does not surprise me,' replied my mother.

'Good family, too. Branch of the Luckleys. The Duke would be a second cousin, I believe. Army tradition in the family. Marcus will go far. He's got the flair and the background.'

'He seemed to get on well with Lucinda,' said my mother. 'I suppose, when something like this happens, it brings people close together. I hope we shall see more of him.'

'He'll have his hands full while this goes on. And so will most of us.'

'It's got to be over some time.'

'The sooner the better. But I think it may be later than

sooner. There's a lot of determination on both sides. I have a notion it might be rather a long struggle.'

'People seem to think it will be over by Christmas.'

'That's what the press tell them, and they repeat it like parrots. Well, I suppose it is a good thing to look on the bright side.'

'Bring that nice Major to see us when you can,' said my mother.

'You can trust me to do just that,' replied Uncle Gerald.

Annabelinda arrived in London with her mother.

'We have some shopping to do,' said Aunt Belinda. 'I said to Robert, we can't allow this dreadful war to stop everything. We've got to get on with our lives, haven't we?'

'So you have left Robert behind?'

'There's so much to do, he said. What with young Robert in the Army and some of the people on the estate joining up . . .'

'I suppose it makes things difficult. However, *you* are here.'

'How's that nice Major? Robert knows the family.'

'Gerald said he was connected with the Luckleys.'

'I'm impressed,' said Aunt Belinda. 'Annabelinda told me what a charmer he is. I hear he is coming to dinner. I'm looking forward to seeing him again.'

'I'm afraid not. He has been to dinner. We had to put it forward because he and Gerald were going overseas earlier than they thought.'

Annabelinda's face darkened. 'Oh,' she murmured. 'But Lucinda told me there was to be a dinner-party. I've got a special dress.'

'I'm sorry,' said my mother. 'But never mind. It couldn't be helped. They had to leave earlier than they thought at first. Things are rather bad over there.'

I could see how bitterly disappointed Annabelinda was. The thought crossed my mind that she had persuaded her

138

mother to come because of this dinner-party. I was certain of this that evening.

She burst into my bedroom, her face distorted with anger.

'You sly, deceitful creature,' she said. 'You did it on purpose. I understand why.'

'What are you talking about?' I asked.

'You . . . and Marcus. You knew he wasn't coming on the twenty-third but earlier, and you didn't let me know.'

'Why should I?'

'Because I should have been there.'

'You weren't invited.'

'Of course I wasn't. You saw to that.'

'I didn't think about it. If you had been here, of course you would have been. But you weren't. We don't invite you every time we have a dinner-party. You're too far away anyway.'

'Why didn't you tell me about the change of dates?'

'It didn't occur to me that I should.'

'You didn't want me there, did you?'

'You would have been there if you had been in London.'

'You told me that the party was to be on the twenty-third when you knew it was the nineteenth.'

'When I mentioned in my letter that the party was going to be on the twenty-third I thought it was.'

'And when the date was changed you deliberately held that back.'

'I did not hold it back deliberately. The date was changed after I had written to you and I did not think it necessary to tell you of the alteration.'

'You were afraid I would come up. You didn't want me to. You were afraid that if I were there he wouldn't take any notice of you.'

'I thought no such thing.'

'Oh yes you did. You were jealous. It's always the same. You were trying to make him notice you and you were angry because he showed clearly that he liked me better. You like him, don't you? You try to attract him. Well, let me tell you, he is more interested in me than in you . . . and that's why you didn't want me here.'

'You're talking the most arrant nonsense. I thought nothing of the sort. You think everybody is in love with you. Just because . . .'

'Because what?'

'Because of Carl Zimmerman.'

Her face darkened. I thought she was going to hit me.

'Don't you ever mention him again!'

'Well, please don't talk nonsense to me.'

She looked stricken suddenly. I had hated her a few minutes before. Now I felt that old affection stealing over me.

She said quietly: 'That was mean of you, Lucinda.'

'I didn't think to remind you of the dinner,' I said. 'And it never occurred to me to attract his attention. If you had been here you would have come to the party. It wasn't very grand.'

'You're so *young*,' she said. 'And it really seemed as though you were trying to keep me out. He's a man of experience. He wouldn't be interested in a schoolgirl. I'd hate to see you make a fool of yourself, Lucinda.'

'*I* was not the one to make a fool of *myself*. I'm not likely to over a man.'

'You throw yourself at him. You must let him do the chasing. The fact is, he is quite interested in *me*. I know it. One does know these things. I know how you feel about him. He really is rather fascinating, but you know absolutely nothing. He thinks of you as a child. He told me so. You mustn't start thinking . . .'

'Thinking what?'

'That he likes you particularly. You'll only get hurt.'

'As you did?' I could not help retorting. 'Are *you* the one to give advice, Annabelinda?'

'Yes. If one is experienced, one is.'

'You are certainly experienced.'

'You should have let me know he was coming. However, it's done and he is now over there . . . fighting, I suppose. I

140

dare say he was terribly disappointed not to see me. Did he ask after me?'

'You were mentioned.'

'What did he say?'

'He just asked how you were.'

She nodded slowly. She said: 'All I want to do is look after you, to stop you getting hurt.'

'I don't need looking after and, remember, you were the one who got hurt.'

'You do need looking after. Don't get romantic thoughts about Marcus Merrivale. I know he is charming to everybody, but he is a man of the world. He's got a reputation with women. Don't go imagining him as the romantic lover, because you simply don't know anything about such things.'

She left me soon after that and I lay thinking about what she had said.

The weeks passed slowly. We settled down to a routine. My father was often away on what my mother called 'House business', by which she meant the House of Commons. One did not ask questions about such business.

With her usual efficiency, Miss Carruthers had begun her duties and we had lessons every day. Andrée had taken charge of Edward and, for the moment, my mother said that would suffice and we need not think about a nanny for a while. Andrée was very capable and too many changes would not be good for the child.

My mother herself was very busy with all sorts of charities to aid what was called the war effort – mainly the Red Cross, in which she took a special interest. We were all called in to help from time to time.

It was one dark November day when Mrs Cherry came to my room to tell me a gentleman had called to see me. He was waiting in the drawing-room. I immediately thought of Marcus Merrivale. I glanced at myself in the mirror. My cheeks were pink, my eyes shining. I was excited.

141

I hurried down to the drawing-room in a mood of pleasurable anticipation. I opened the door and there was Robert.

Delight swept over me. I had forgotten I was expecting Marcus.

'Robert!' I cried.

He was grinning at me rather sheepishly. He looked different in khaki. It was not really becoming. It would be later when he gained his commission and a smart uniform with it – but he was not yet in that position. He looked very fit and well. His skin was slightly tanned and he had lost just a little of that gangling look which had been so essentially Robert.

I rushed to him and we hugged each other.

'It is wonderful to see you,' I cried. 'I have been wondering when I should.'

'I feel the same,' he replied. 'It seems ages. I've heard all about your journey home. That must have been quite an adventure.'

'Oh, it was.'

'It was lucky that your uncle was able to arrange to have you brought out.'

'Otherwise we should have had to go with the refugees.'

'It was a Major Merrivale, I heard, who brought you home.'

'Yes. He was so good.'

'He would be. And his position helped, of course. I was dreadfully worried when I thought of you in that school. Belgium, of all places!'

'I often wonder what is happening there now. Madame Rochère, who owned the school, is a very aristocratic, haughty lady. I try to think of what might be happening to her.'

'It's very unpleasant to be in an occupied country – something I hope we shall never have to face.'

'Of course we shall not have to! That would be quite unthinkable. There is always the Channel. It won't be the same for the French.'

'That's so. I often think about my grandfather. So does my mother. We don't hear what's happening in Bordeaux.'

142

'I think that Monsieur Bourdon will know how to look after himself.'

'So do I, but we should like to hear.'

'Robert, tell me about yourself.'

'Well, it's a hard life at first, but I'm getting used to it. We do a lot of riding which I enjoy, as you can guess, and one gets used to the long day and the shouting and the orders which have to be obeyed instantly. One doesn't dislike it. There's some wonderful comradeship, and it's a good feeling when you drop into bed absolutely worn out, to sleep and sleep until reveillé.'

'Are you longing to be home, Robert?'

'For a lot of reasons, yes. But we've got to fight this war and win it. If we all stayed at home, we'd never do that.'

'How long leave have you got?'

'Three days more. I've had two at home and the rest I'm spending in London.'

'Oh, good.'

'My sister and mother came up with me. They're here now. My father had to stay behind. There's so much work to do.'

'Does he mind your coming here?'

'You know what he is. He always sees the point and wants to do what the family want. And of course, my mother and Annabelinda said we should spend the time in London to see you and your family.'

'I'm so glad you're here.'

'It's so long since I've seen you. It was last Christmas. Just think of that. We've never been away from each other so long before.'

'I don't believe we have. How are you going to spend your leave now you're here?'

'With you . . . and . . .'

'With Annabelinda, your mother and the rest of us.'

'I dare say they'll want to be off into the town.'

'What a lovely prospect!'

He caught my hand and looked into my face. 'Do you really mean that, Lucinda?'

'Of course I do.'

'You've changed a little.'

'In what way?'

'Grown up.'

'We're doing that all the time.'

'By more than a year, I mean. I suppose it's the war and all you must have seen on that awful journey. I heard about the baby.'

'Oh yes. You must see Edward.'

'It must have been a terrible experience, seeing that woman dying . . . and it was wonderful of you to care about the baby.'

'I knew you'd understand.'

'There was nothing else you could have done. I hear he's a fine little fellow.'

'And did you hear about Andrée Latour?'

'Yes, Annabelinda told me. She said Major Merrivale was wonderful.'

'Yes, he was.'

'I wish I'd been the one, Lucinda.'

'Well, you were in training, weren't you, and I suppose Uncle Gerald thought he would do it very well. Which he did.'

'It must have been extraordinary . . . the whole thing . . . and you just out of school.'

'I'm home now and things seem more or less normal. Miss Carruthers, one of the mistresses from the school, came with us. She's acting as governess to me now.'

'Well, you're only fifteen, of course.'

He sighed, and I said: 'You seem to find that regrettable.'

'Well,' he admitted, 'I wish you were a little older. Seventeen, say.'

'Seventeen? Is that such a ripe old age?'

'It's an age when you can start thinking about the future.'

'I suppose one can start thinking about the future at any time.'

'I mean making plans . . . reasonable plans.'

I looked puzzled and he went on: 'Never mind. We'll talk about all that later. What would you like to do? Go to a theatre? A pity we can't go riding. We wouldn't want to go in the Row. I'd like to gallop over fields.'

'We could do a little walking in the Park. Just as we used to.'

'That would be fun. Could we get away from everyone?'

'Is that what you want?'

'Yes,' he said.

'I think that as this is your leave, you should make the choice.'

Annabelinda had come into the room. She kissed me fondly.

'I thought I'd let my big brother give you a surprise before letting you know we were here. What do you think of him?'

'I think he looks very well, and it is wonderful to see him.'

'I knew you'd think that. Lucinda's a great admirer of yours, Robert.'

'The admiration is mutual.'

Annabelinda laughed. She was in good spirits.

Her mother came in. She looked very elegant; she was remarkably like her daughter. She swept me into her embrace.

'Dear Lucinda! How wonderful to see you!' My mother was with her.

'Isn't it a lovely surprise to see Robert?' she said.

I agreed that it was.

'I'm so glad you came here,' she added to Robert.

'Oh, I wanted to see you all.'

'And particularly his dear Lucinda,' added Annabelinda.

'Robert was just saying what he would like to do,' I said. 'I told him he must make the decisions as it is his leave.'

'And only three days of it,' added my mother.

'Never mind,' said Robert. 'I'll make the most of it.'

We went in to luncheon.

Annabelinda asked after Miss Carruthers and Andrée Latour.

'Miss Carruthers is a stickler for convention,' explained my mother. 'She dines with us on certain occasions, but I fancy she does so with a certain reluctance. She is very much aware of her place – and I really think prefers to eat alone. As for

Andrée, she is in the nursery with Edward during the day, but very often dines with us.'

'And is it all working out well with this baby?' asked Aunt Belinda.

'Wonderfully. We wouldn't be without him.'

'How cosy!' said Aunt Belinda. 'But then you were always a cosy person, Lucie.'

'I'm not sure whether that is a compliment or not,' laughed my mother.

'Oh, it's a compliment, Lucie dear. By the way, did you see any more of that nice Major Merrivale?'

Annabelinda was alert . . . watching me.

'No,' replied my mother. 'Soldiers are kept very busy at a time like this.'

'What a pity. We missed him that time he came to dinner. I thought he was such a charming man.'

'Very charming,' said my mother.

'And of such a good family. This dreadful war . . . it just spoils everything.'

'It goes on and on,' said my mother. 'And now we've declared war on Turkey. So . . . more trouble in that quarter, and wasn't the sinking of the *Good Hope* and the *Monmouth* terrible?'

'I refuse to talk of these horrible things,' said Aunt Belinda. 'I have had enough of it and so must you, Lucie. I expect Joel brings home all the horrible news, doesn't he?'

'We don't have to wait for that,' retorted my mother. 'It's in the papers.'

'My Robert is concerned about the land. We should all be producing more and more crops. But as I said, enough! Are the shops still exciting? I don't think we should neglect ourselves just because there is a war on.'

My mother laughed at her, just as she must have laughed all through the years – and as I did with Annabelinda.

Then Robert told us some amusing stories about life on Salisbury Plain.

'You learn how to be spartan and stoical,' he said. He

imitated the sergeant-major and told us some of the sarcastic remarks made about the pampered lives of some of the recruits before they had fallen into his hands. 'You're in the Army now,' and 'Mummy's not there to kiss her little darling and tuck him in at night.' Apparently there was one who took a sadistic delight in harassing any who showed signs of weakness.

He told us how one night they had all been celebrating in the local inn, and the sadistic riding instructor became so intoxicated that he did not know what was happening to him. Some of the recruits took him out on to the Plain, stripped him of his clothes and, folding them up and putting them beside him, left him.

'I have to report,' said Robert, 'that next morning he was at the stables, none the worse for his adventure, and he behaved as though nothing had happened, making no reference to the incident.'

'He deserved it,' said Aunt Belinda.

'Still, it showed he had some good in him, to accept the revenge of those he had humiliated,' said my mother.

'Trust Lucie to see good in everything!' retorted Aunt Belinda.

'Well, there *is* usually something good in everyone,' I said.

'I see you are bringing up your daughter to be like you, Lucie,' said Aunt Belinda.

'Which seems to me a very good idea,' added Robert. He went on: 'At least the fellow was a good sport. We respected him more after that. He was ready to take what he gave. I suppose he looked upon it as rough justice.'

'Well, Annabelinda and I are not as nice as you and your daughter, Lucie,' said Aunt Belinda. 'We would have gloated, wouldn't we, darling? We would have left him without his clothes, too. Then you'd see whether he was back on duty, nobly ignoring the wrong done to him.'

'We don't hate him all that much,' explained Robert. 'He is a bit of a brute, but it couldn't have been all that easy training a lot of raw recruits.'

'We must go to the theatre while we are in town,' said Aunt Belinda, changing the subject.

Robert and I were together a good deal during those three days. We enjoying walking about London. We were in complete harmony, liked the same things and were almost aware of what the other was thinking.

When we walked over Westminster Bridge, we would pause and look round us and think of earlier days. We remembered that I had left my gloves on a seat in Green Park and we had gone back to look for them. He could recall, as I did, that immense joy and excitement when we found them on the seat, just where I had left them. We were both overawed as we passed the magnificent Houses of Parliament, with the river running past and those great gothic-like towers looking as though they had been there for centuries, though they were not yet a hundred years old. They represented something precious to us – home, our country, and we had always been proud and grateful to be part of it. Now that feeling was intensified. We were fighting to save ourselves from foreign domination; we were fighting so that little countries like Belgium should not be violently invaded without warning. And Robert was going into battle. I was both apprehensive for and proud of him.

All this we felt as we walked together. We often made our way to Green Park and looked at the ducks. We found the seat on which I had left my gloves. That made us laugh, and we began recalling more incidents from the past.

'It seems, Lucinda,' said Robert, 'that our lives have always been entwined.'

'It is because of the friendship between our mothers.'

'You and Annabelinda are like sisters.'

'Yes. It has always been like that. Although I have not seen much of her this visit.'

'I think they have conspired to leave us together.'

'Do you?'

'Oh, obviously. I'm not complaining.'

'Nor I. I think they have been busy shopping. They are always like that when they come to London.'

'They would like to have a place up here, but while your parents give us shelter, I suppose they think it is not essential. And my father is against it.'

'But I suppose he would give way.'

'I suppose so. This has been a wonderful leave.'

'I hope you are not going to mind going back to that awful riding instructor too much.'

'What I am going to mind is leaving you.'

'Oh Robert, I do hate your going.'

He took my hand and pressed it. 'Write to me, Lucinda.'

'Of course.'

'And tell me everything that's happening.'

'I will . . . and you, too.'

'I expect our letters will be censored.'

'I don't want to hear war news. I want to hear *your* news.'

He laughed. 'There'll be another leave and then I should get my commission.'

'And that could mean going right away.'

'I suppose so.'

'Perhaps it will be over by then.'

'Who knows? Lucinda, you seem quite a bit older these days. I mean more than your years.'

'Do I? I think it must be because of what happened. That sort of thing jerks you out of your childhood.'

'Fifteen. You'll soon be sixteen. Sixteen would be quite mature.'

'You make me feel like some old crone.'

'Oh no. I just wish you were a little nearer to my age, that's all.'

'If I had been, you might not have been the nice big brother to me whom you have been all my life.'

'That's just it.'

'What?'

'Grow up quickly, Lucinda, there's a good girl.'

'I promise to do all I can about the matter.'

He turned to me and kissed my cheek. 'It is lovely to be with you,' he said. 'We understand each other.'

'Yes. I think we do. I shall be very sad when you go back tomorrow, Robert.'

'Let's plan for my next leave, then.'

'What a good idea! And in the meantime I'll see what I can do to speed up the growing process.'

'Just do that,' he said.

And after that we walked back to the house. We were both a little quieter than usual.

We all went to the station to see Robert off. Aunt Belinda and Annabelinda were staying a few more days.

I was surprised and more than a little shocked that Annabelinda showed no interest whatsoever in Edward; and if he were referred to a mask would come over her face and she would affect indifference. I was sure she could not feel this but she gave the impression that she was annoyed with me for bringing him to England. She would have preferred that he had remained in Belgium, conveniently out of the way.

I suppose her point was logical enough. That was an episode in her life that she wanted to forget, and my action had brought the result of it right out into the open to remind her whenever she visited us.

But it seemed to me inhuman that a woman should have no interest in, no curiosity about, her own son.

She was full of high spirits and seemed to have forgiven me for not telling her that the dinner for Marcus Merrivale had had to be changed to a different date.

She came to my room to have a little chat now and then, away from everyone. We talked about school and what might be happening to Madame Rochère.

'I am sure she will be directing the army of occupation,' said Annabelinda.

'Poor Madame Rochère, I hardly think it will be like that.'

'You can't imagine Rochy knuckling under to anyone, can you?'

'In the circumstances, yes.'

'I can't help thinking how neatly it all worked out. That was due to the incomparable Major. You haven't heard anything of him, have you?'

'No.'

'Are you sure?'

'Of course.'

'You were a bit secretive about him once. I just wondered.'

'I'm not secretive at all. I did not know when I wrote to you. I suppose he is now somewhere in France . . . or Belgium.'

'I thought perhaps that, as he is in the same regiment as your uncle, you might know.'

'I don't know where Uncle Gerald is. This is war. There are lots of things which have to be kept secret.'

'I know that. We're not allowed to forget it, are we? I expect he is having a jolly time.'

'I should imagine it is not so very jolly out there.'

'He would always have a good time. He was such fun to be with. You and Robert get on very well, don't you?'

'Yes. You know we always did.'

'He's a good sort, Robert. You and he are just right for each other.'

'What do you mean?'

She laughed scornfully. 'You know what I mean. I think the families have always had it in mind. It's what they want.'

'You mean . . . ?'

'Of course, you idiot. Wedding bells and all that. If you were a year or two older, he would have asked you by now. I should have thought that was obvious.'

'It wasn't obvious at all. I've always liked Robert. We've always been good friends.'

'The best basis for marriage, they say. You like him, don't you? Wouldn't it be fun to be sisters-in-law? It's what they all want, you know.'

'I don't believe my parents give a thought to all that. As for you, Annabelinda, I think you should concern yourself with your affairs and leave mine to me.'

'Oh!' she said mockingly. 'Dear Lucinda, Robert adores you and you adore him. You're the perfect match. You're so alike. When you marry him, you'll go down to the country, have ten children and be the perfect married couple who'll live happily ever after.'

'Annabelinda, will you stop arranging my life?'

'I'm not arranging it. I'm just saying what it will be – and it will be the best thing for you.'

'Are you adding clairvoyance to your many accomplishments?'

'I am just being logical and seeing what is right under my eyes. You look really cross. Do you want me to go?'

'Yes . . . if you are going to foretell the future. Why don't you look to your own?'

'I do, Lucinda. I do all the time.'

I looked at her steadily. I could see how her mind worked. She had taken a great fancy to Marcus Merrivale. His family were rich and socially desirable, while he himself was so attractive – a perfect combination. She was hoping to see him again, to enchant him – something which she felt herself capable of doing, and she was just a little fearful that, simply because of the advantage I had of being the niece of his superior officer, I might have opportunities which were denied to her.

I laughed at her, but after she had gone I began to think of the implication of what she had said.

Was it true my family were eager for me to marry Robert? I knew they would welcome it, because they were fond of him. And Robert? He had been very tender and a little cryptic . . . if one could imagine his ever being so. He had intimated that if I were older he might propose marriage to me.

The thought gave me a pleasurable, comfortable feeling.

Perhaps I was flattered. I liked Robert very much. On the other hand, images of Marcus Merrivale kept intruding. I remembered him on the road through to the border between

France and Belgium . . . travelling to Calais . . . and later in our own drawing-room.

I was rather excited because Annabelinda clearly saw me as a rival.

Christmas had come – a Christmas of curtailed activities. There was a war on and people remembered that earlier it had been said that it would be over by Christmas; and here was Christmas and the war was still with us.

The easy victory was not to be. Some of the wounded were being brought back across the Channel, and still it went on.

From the first, my mother had been deeply involved in charities. Now she saw an opportunity to do more.

It was in April of the following year that she had the idea of turning Marchlands into a hospital for wounded soldiers.

Marchlands was convenient. It was not too far from the coast or from London. It was in a good situation, surrounded by forest, and the pure air would make it ideal for convalescence. The house was large and suited to the project.

There was a great deal of excitement. My mother was completely absorbed; my father, of course, would have to stay in London for the week, but he could come down for weekends. The household would be moved down there. Two doctors would be employed with several nurses. Miss Carruthers and I could be of use. We were not trained, of course, but there were lots of jobs to be done in a hospital which did not demand that skill. We were all caught up in it. There were journeys to and from Marchlands. Everything seemed to have been overshadowed by the plan – even the war.

It was in May when Marcus came again. He was with Uncle Gerald and they were both preparing to leave for Gallipoli in a few days' time, although the week before they had just come back from France.

It was a lively meal we had, with Uncle Gerald and Marcus talking most of the time about military matters. Uncle Gerald had always been like that, my mother had told me once. He loved fighting battles on the tablecloth with the pepperpot representing some fortress and the salt for the guns. He would pick up some dish to stand for the opposing forces.

My father listened intently. He was very occupied these days. There was anxiety in high places. The war was not proving as easy to win as some had calculated.

'The whole operation is to relieve the Russians,' Uncle Gerald was saying. 'That's why we are coming to grips with the Turks on the Dardanelles.'

'Fisher doesn't approve,' said my father. 'And you know he is in charge.'

'That's bad,' said Uncle Gerald. 'The First Sea Lord creating the wrong impression.'

'Churchill's opinion is that a combined military and naval operation could knock Turkey out of the war.'

'That's what we're aiming to do.'

'This will be a little different from France,' said Marcus. 'We're getting tired of trench warfare.'

'An awful way to go to war,' agreed Uncle Gerald. 'Living like troglodytes, almost. Dodging the enemy instead of going out to fight him.'

Afterwards I had a few words with Marcus in the drawing-room.

'When are you leaving?' I asked.

'Any moment. When the call comes. One is never absolutely sure.'

'How uncertain everything is in wartime!'

'I believe, dear Lucinda, that it can even be so in peacetime.'

'Do you think it will soon be over?'

'One becomes a little wary of prophecy. Only one thing is certain. We are all growing older every day.'

'You speak as though that is something to be pleased about. Lots of people hate getting old.'

'That depends where you stand in life. Perverse, is it not? Some would do anything to hold back the years; others would like to advance them.'

'Into which category do you fall?'

'I should like you to rush on a few years while I stayed where I am.'

It was the second time the question of my youth had arisen – first with Robert, now with Marcus. It must be significant.

I could not resist saying: 'Whatever for?'

'Because there are things I should like to say to you and I cannot say them now.'

'I might like to hear them.'

'Don't tempt me, dear little Lucinda. Just grow up, please. You are sixteen years old, or you will be this year.'

'Not until September.'

'I shall remember that. This time next year you will be all but seventeen and, being a very clever young lady, I am sure you will have the wisdom of a seventeen-year-old before you reach that age.'

'You seem to think seventeen is a significant age.'

'Oh yes, it is. It is when the maiden is on the brink of womanhood.'

'It sounds very poetic.'

'You bring out the poet in me. In fact, such is your influence that you bring out the good in me. So we must see each other as often as possible, so that good may prevail.'

'How? When you will be away?'

'We will think about each other every day. And at the first opportunity I will come to see whether you have kept your promise to grow up quickly.'

'Did I make such a promise? And in any case I cannot do so if you persist in treating me like a child.'

He looked at me intently and said: 'Forgive me. If we were anywhere else but in your parents' drawing-room, I should be tempted to forget your age.'

There was no mistaking his meaning. I thought of Anna-belinda. This was what she feared. The thought excited me.

Two days later he left for Gallipoli.

I thought about him a great deal. Was he really telling me he cared for me? Or was that light-hearted caressing manner the one he bestowed on all females? I was a little bemused, but I had to confess that I was attracted by him. Annabelinda had shown a certain perception. I wondered what she would say if she had heard our conversation.

I followed the campaign in Gallipoli. It seemed very far away and particularly dangerous. If only it could all be over!

What would happen then?

We should soon be leaving for Marchlands. The hospital was almost ready. Miss Carruthers was very enthusiastic about it. There would be no curtailment of lessons, she said, but it would be illuminating for us to learn something of the procedure in hospitals and at the same time gratifying to contribute to the war effort. Andrée agreed with her and hoped that Edward would spare her for the occasional hour.

I was thinking a great deal about Marcus, wondering when I should see him again and whether he would continue in the same strain of flirtatious innuendo. I had to admit I found it all exciting. He was a most attractive man – in fact, the most attractive I had ever met – and that was not just in my eyes. Most people would agree with me; and the fact that he had noticed me was very gratifying.

I tried to get all the information I could about the campaign in the Dardanelles, and I was very anxious when I heard that all was not going well.

But what did go well in this war? There was bad news from across the Channel. It seemed as though the end was by no means in sight.

I tried to catch some of my mother's enthusiasm for the hospital project and to stop my thoughts continually straying to Marcus.

One night, when there was a full moon, I suddenly awoke. It may have been the brightness of that moon shining on me which aroused me. Something had, and I was not sure whether I had been dreaming.

Everything seemed so still outside. Ever since the first

Zeppelin had been sighted crossing the coast in early December of the previous year, people had looked up anxiously at the full moon. What was so delightful in peacetime could be a hazard in war. When the enemy came in their airships they would choose a moonlit night. They would attempt to devastate our houses as they had that of Jacques and Marguerite.

I was wide awake suddenly. Yes, something had awakened me. I listened. A light footfall; the creak of a floorboard. Someone was walking about the house.

I glanced at the clock by my bed. It was nearly two o'clock. I got out of bed, felt for my slippers, caught up my dressing-gown and opened the door.

I looked out. There was no one in the corridor. Then I heard it again. Someone was on the stairs.

I hurried to the landing and, as I looked down, I saw a figure descending cautiously.

To my amazement it was Andrée.

'Andrée,' I whispered. 'Andrée, what's wrong?'

She turned and for a second I saw a look of fear on her face. Then she said: 'Oh . . . it's you. For a moment I thought . . . I've awakened you. I'm so sorry, Lucinda.'

'Is something wrong?'

'No. I don't think so. You know how anxious I get about Edward.'

'What's wrong with him?'

'Nothing much.' She had come up the stairs and stood beside me.

'What were you doing?' I asked.

'I was just doing down to the kitchen to get some honey.'

'Honey! At this time of night? It's nearly two.'

'Well, he has a little cough, you see. It kept him awake for a bit. He's sleeping now, so I thought I'd slip down and get the honey which does soothe him. Don't worry. It's just a slight chill. He's been a little poorly the last day, I thought. And the cough was threatening to keep him awake.'

'I'll get the doctor in the morning.'

'That may not be necessary. It's just that this cough kept

157

him awake for a while, and then when he did doze off . . . I slipped down to get the honey.'

'It's a good idea. I'll come with you.'

'Do you know where they keep the honey?'

'No, but we'll find it. They must have some. It would be with the preserves . . . jams and things. You really don't think it's anything serious, do you?'

'*Mon Dieu*, no. I just fuss over him, I'm afraid. But you understand that. You are as bad as I am. I do know that children get these little ailments and are over them in no time. He'll probably be all right in the morning.'

We reached the kitchen and, after a little exploring, found the honey.

'It's wonderful the way you look after him,' I said.

'He's such a darling.'

'I think so too. But you are so good with him.'

'What I have done suits me, so please, you mustn't make a heroine of me. I enjoy looking after Edward. I wanted somewhere to come. You and your family have done everything for me. If I could repay you even a little, I should be overjoyed. But what I do is nothing, nothing compared with what you have done for me. To be here, to have escaped . . .'

I put my hand over hers and pressed it.

'It's odd how something good comes out of so much that is evil,' I said.

'And evil out of good, perhaps.'

'Oh?'

'Oh, nothing. I suppose I must hurry back. His lordship may wake up. He'd be put out if there was no one there to look after him.'

'I do hope the cough is not going to develop. We'll have to watch it, Andrée.'

'Trust me to do that.'

We went up the stairs together.

'I'll come right up,' I said.

'Perhaps it's better not,' she said. 'If he woke up he'd wonder what was happening, then he'd never get to sleep. I'm hoping he is still asleep. If so, all is well. I'll have the honey if he needs it. If anything was really wrong, I'd come to you right away.'

'Perhaps you're right,' I said.

At the door of my room we paused.

'I'm so sorry I disturbed you,' she said. 'I tried hard not to make a noise.'

'You looked quite scared when you saw me. I'm afraid I frightened you.'

She laughed. 'I must have thought you were a ghost. Are you a light sleeper? I tried so hard not to make a noise.'

'Not more than normally, I suppose. I just happened to wake up then. I think it was the moon. It shines right into my room. Oh, how I wish this wretched war was over! I think it puts our nerves on edge.'

'We won't have much time to think of anything other than the hospital when we get to Marchlands.'

'Perhaps that will be good for us.'

'We will make it so,' said Andrée. 'Good night, Lucinda. And once more, I'm sorry.'

I went back to bed. I thought of Andrée's anxiety about Edward and hoped he was all right. What an excellent nurse she had turned out to be. I fell to thinking of the meeting in the inn. Then I went through that journey across France. Pictures flashed in and out of my mind. I kept seeing the bewildered faces of the refugees – an old woman pushing a bassinet containing all the possessions she had been able to bring with her; an old car loaded with people and goods; little children clinging to their mother's skirts – all suddenly rooted up from their homes.

Such sights stamped themselves on the memory and would remain there for ever.

Thus I fell asleep.

Edward was quite well in the morning and a week or so later the hospital was ready. My mother was completely delighted and indeed it was a great achievement. Several bedrooms had been turned into wards. There was an operating theatre, many storerooms, a dispensary; in fact, all that a hospital should have.

We had two doctors: Dr Egerton, who was about forty, and Dr May who was more mature; we had a staff of nurses – most of them young and fresh from training, and at the head of them an experienced dragon – Sister Gamage – who struck terror not only into her nurses but into all of us. Then there was the staff of servants who had been at Marchlands as long as I could remember. They were all dedicated to making a success of the hospital and delighted to be able to do something for the country.

As I guessed she would be, Miss Carruthers was a great asset. That authoritative air of hers was very useful and she and Sister Gamage took a great liking to each other at once. My mother said she was a wonderful help.

During the weeks that followed, we were all very busy settling into the hospital. My mother was realizing what a tremendous undertaking she had embarked on; but she was very appreciative of all those who helped. We were all immersed in the exercise, which was a good thing because it kept our minds off the progress of the war.

Disaster followed disaster. The *Lusitania*, on its way from New York to Liverpool, had been sunk in May by a German submarine with the loss of almost twelve hundred people. This shocked the nation, and there was speculation as to whether this would bring the United States of America into the war.

The coalition government which Mr Asquith had formed, bringing in Conservative leaders like Bonar Law and Austen Chamberlain, was not proving to be entirely successful. The fact that the Dardanelles venture was threatening to be disastrous could not be hidden. Winston Churchill was being criticized because of his wholehearted support for it. The Prime Minister was being called inept and not the man needed to lead the country to victory.

We were all adjusting ourselves to the new way of life. Miss

160

Carruthers and I were at our desks in the morning. In the afternoon we had two hours during which we often rode out. Miss Carruthers had ridden in her youth but had not been on a horse for some years, but she quickly remembered her old training, and she was a tolerably good horsewoman. Andrée took lessons and occasionally the three of us rode out together.

Andrée, I discovered, had a great capacity for enjoyment, and it was gratifying that she was so grateful to us for taking her away from a life which would have been distasteful to her. Miss Carruthers felt something similar, but not to the same extent; and in any case she did not show her feelings as readily as Andrée did.

'I love old houses,' Andrée said one day, 'particularly those with a history.' She wanted to know all about Marchlands and would study the portraits of past Greenhams and ask questions about them. I knew very little of them.

'You will have to ask my father,' I said.

'He would be too busy just now, with all that is going on, to bother with my curiosity,' replied Andrée. 'By the way, what of that house . . . is it Milton Priory? I heard some of the servants talking about it. I'd love to have a look at it.'

'It's about two miles from here,' I said. 'We could go and take a look at it. It has stood empty for some years. It's one of those places that get a reputation for being haunted.'

'So some of the servants were saying.'

'Strange noises?' I said. 'Weeping and wailing and lights appearing in the windows. That's the usual thing.'

'Something like that.'

'It's quite derelict really. I don't know who owns it. There's nothing much to see.'

'Still, I'd like to look at it some time.'

'Tomorrow, then. Let's ride there. I don't suppose Miss Carruthers will mind.'

The next day, when we went to the stables, Andrée reminded me of my promise to go to Milton Priory.

'All right,' I said. 'But prepare for a disappointment.'

'Is that the old place surrounded by shrubs?' asked Miss Carruthers.

'That sounds like an apt description,' I replied.

I had not seen the place for about two years. I noticed at once that it had changed. The shrubs were as unkempt as ever, but it had lost that unlived-in look. Was it because the windows had been cleaned?

'Fascinating,' said Andrée. 'Yes, it does look haunted. Do you know its history?'

'No, nothing at all,' I replied. 'Except that it has been empty for a long time and nobody seems to want to buy it. I don't know whether it's up for sale or not. I've not heard of its being so.'

'Could we go a little nearer?' asked Andrée.

'I can't imagine anyone would mind if we did,' I said.

We urged our horses towards the shrubs and, as we did so, a large Alsatian dog came bounding towards us. He looked fierce and forbidding.

'Angus,' said a voice. 'What is it, boyo?'

A man was coming towards us. His shabby tweeds and unkempt appearance fitted the house. He was middle-aged, with a tawny beard and he carried a gun.

'Sit, Angus,' he said.

Angus sat but continued to regard us in a glowering and threatening manner.

'What are you doing here?' asked the man. 'Do you know you are trespassing?'

I said: 'I'm sorry. We didn't think we were. The house is empty, isn't it? We were just looking.'

'You don't come any farther until I know your business.'

I was amazed. I said: 'I'm from Marchlands.'

'Oh, aye,' he replied.

'We just thought we would look round. We have done before. Please tell us who you are.'

'I'm the caretaker,' he said.

'Caretaker at Milton Priory!'

'From now on.'

162

'Is it up for sale?' I asked.

'Reckon.'

'I hadn't heard.'

He shrugged his shoulders.

'Someone must have bought it,' I said.

'Could be so.'

'I see. I'm sorry. It has been empty so long and no one ever minded before. We just thought we'd explore a little.'

'Well, I wouldn't try exploring round here any more, if I were you. Angus wouldn't like it and Angus can be a pretty fierce customer, I can tell you.'

'Well, now we know,' I said. 'I'm sorry, Andrée. That's all you are going to see of Milton Priory.'

'It's disappointing,' she said. 'I should have loved to know the history of the place. I wonder who will come here?'

'No doubt we shall know in good time. They will be my father's constituents, so he will soon be after their votes.'

Miss Carruthers said it was an interesting place. A little too early for William and Mary, she mused. There was a touch of the Stuart . . . early Stuart. 'It will need a good deal of restoration, I imagine. How long did you say it had been empty, Lucinda?'

'I'm not sure. But a long time.'

We rode back to Marchlands and then we went to the hospital to see if our services were wanted.

At the weekend my father came down, as he often did. My mother was eager to tell him how everything was progressing.

I remember, at dinner that night, he told us how unpopular the Prime Minister was becoming.

'The war is still going on, so they look round for a scapegoat. Poor Asquith! He fits the case very well. Especially with Lloyd George waiting to spring into his shoes. Margot Asquith is furious. If anyone can keep the old man going, it will be his formidable wife.'

Dr Egerton was dining with us that night. He was seated next to Miss Carruthers.

'Lloyd George is a very able man, I believe,' said the doctor.

'Perhaps that fiery Welshman will have all the energy which Asquith lacks,' suggested Miss Carruthers.

'Oh, I'm not sure of that,' replied the doctor, and he and Miss Carruthers went into a discussion about the merits of Lloyd George and Asquith.

My father said: 'I'm sorry for the old man, but people are beginning to wonder whether it wouldn't be better if he resigned in favour of L.G.'

'What of Churchill?' asked my mother.

'Oh, he's in disgrace over the Dardanelles. He was so sure it was the right course to take. I suppose he is not all that certain now.'

'Are things very bad?' I asked.

'Never so bad as the press makes out. It's the bad news they find sensational. And if there is someone they can possibly blame, they will. People are always more interested in the bad than the good. Let us say that things could be better.'

My mother said: 'We were talking about Milton Priory the other day. Lucinda was saying that they have a caretaker there with a fierce dog.'

I fancied my father looked alert. 'Milton Priory?' he said. 'What's this about it?'

'It seems someone's making it ready to sell. Lucinda went there to have a look at the house . . . to show Andrée, in fact.'

'I was with them,' said Miss Carruthers. 'The caretaker was rather officious and told us to keep away in no uncertain terms.'

I explained to my father exactly what had happened. 'The dog was very fierce. He looked as though all he needed was his master's command to tear us all apart.'

'I expect the man knew how to handle him. Did you get the idea that they were preparing the house for sale?'

'That seemed most likely.'

'We shall know in good time,' said my mother. 'I wonder who the new owners will be?'

'I hope they will be good Liberals,' I said. 'Otherwise we shall have to convert them.'

My father smiled at me. 'How was the place different?' he asked.

'I think the windows had been cleaned . . . and then, of course, there was the caretaker. I suppose they will have to smarten it up if they hope to sell at a reasonable price.'

'We'll watch and await developments,' put in my mother.

'I should keep away from it, if I were you,' said my father. 'I don't like the sound of that dog.'

'We're certain to hear when it's sold,' added my mother. 'You can't keep things like that secret here.'

Then the talk switched back to the coalition and the possibility of Mr Asquith's handing over the premiership to Mr Lloyd George.

Very soon after that Robert Denver came to see us. He looked really handsome in his uniform. He was still too thin and looked taller than ever, but less 'disjointed', as Annabelinda had once described her brother's physique.

I was delighted to see him. I studied him with awe.

'Oh, Robert,' I cried. 'You're through. You've got your commission!'

'I'm pleased,' he admitted. 'I feel like a man again.'

'Free of those bullying sergeant-majors. Poor Robert. I could imagine how you felt about it.'

'Necessary, I suppose. But hard to take at times.'

'So it is goodbye, Salisbury Plain.' My face fell. 'And . . . now . . . the battlefield.'

'The battlefield is to be postponed, probably for a month or more. What do you think? I'm going on a course.'

'A course? I thought you'd just come through your training.'

'So I have. But this is different. Do you know, Lucinda, I was by no means a model soldier. It's a bit of luck that I got my commission. But I discovered a method of memorizing the Morse Code. The others couldn't understand how I did it. To tell the truth, I couldn't myself. Well, as I could work the thing more quickly than the others, I was selected to go on this course.'

'That means you'll be sending messages . . . on the battle-field.'

'Something like that, I imagine. I'll have my mechanic with me. He'll fix the 'phones . . . that sort of thing would be beyond me. I'll take the messages and send others. Something like that, I suppose.'

'Oh Robert, I'm proud of you.'

'I've done nothing to be proud of.'

'You have and you will do more.'

'Oh, I'm not made in the heroic mould. That's for people like Major Merrivale. By the way, have you seen him lately?'

'No. He's in Gallipoli.'

Robert looked grim.

'So is Uncle Gerald,' I went on. 'We're quite anxious.'

Robert nodded in understanding.

My mother greeted him warmly. So did Aunt Celeste, who was often at Marchlands and enjoyed helping in the hospital.

There was a good deal of talk. Miss Carruthers and Andrée joined us, and my mother and I, with Andrée, took Robert along to see Edward.

'He's growing fast,' commented Robert.

Andrée looked at Edward with pride. 'He's going to be a big boy, aren't you, Edward?'

Edward muttered something and smiled benignly.

We had lunch and afterwards my mother said: 'Why don't you and Robert go for a little ride, Lucinda? You used to love to ride round these lanes.'

Robert said: 'I like the idea. Don't you, Lucinda?'

'I do,' I said.

Soon we were out, riding through the familiar countryside, as we used to before I went away to school and there was a war.

We kept recalling incidents from the past.

'Do you remember when we found the baby blackbird lying in the road?'

'Oh yes. He'd fallen out of the nest. And you climbed a tree because we guessed the nest would be up there . . . and we put him back. And the next day we came to see if he was all right.'

'Do you remember when your horse tripped over a log in the forest and you landed in a heap of leaves?'

We laughed at the memory. There was so much to remember.

'It seems so long ago,' I said, 'because everything has changed.'

'It will come back to normal.'

'Do you think so?'

'I do. I shall be back with the estate and in time it will seem as though this never happened.'

'I think that when this sort of thing comes it changes people and they can never be the same again.'

'You're not changing, are you, Lucinda?'

'I feel different. I notice it . . . riding with you like this, and talking about what happened in the old days. Little things like the baby bird and the tumble in the forest. It takes me back and for a moment I am as I was then . . . and then I can see that there is a lot of difference between that person and what I am today.'

'I suppose we are all touched by experience, but what I mean is, are you the same Lucinda, my special friend?'

'I hope I shall always be that, Robert.'

'You must always be, no matter what happens.'

'It's a comfort to hear that. I've always been able to rely on you.'

'The old predictable, as my sister calls me.'

'She says it's why I'm so dull. She always knows what I am going to do.'

'Well, Annabelinda always believes she is right. *She*'s predictable enough in that. It's true that I am predictable in most things, and I suppose that can be called unexciting.'

'Well, I was excited when I saw you this morning in officer's uniform.'

'You were the first one I wanted to show it off to.'

'Are you going to your parents?'

'Yes, this evening.'

'And shall I see you before you go on your course?'

'I plan to stay at home for two days. Then have one more day at Marchlands, if that is agreeable to you?'

'I suppose you have to go home?'

'I must. My father will have so much to tell me about the estate.'

'You love the land, don't you, Robert?'

'I've been brought up to know that it will be mine one day . . . in the far distant future, I hope. I feel the same about it as my father does. As you know, he and I have always been the best of friends.'

'My mother often says you are just like him.'

'That's the general opinion. My mother and sister are quite different.'

'It's odd to have such contrasts in one family. People say I am like my mother, but my mother says I have a lot of my father in me. I don't know who Charles takes after. I reckon he'll go into politics. At the moment he is the only person I know who is praying for the war to go on until he is old enough to join the Army.'

'A good patriotic spirit!'

'I think he is more concerned with the glory of Charles Greenham! He sees himself dashing into battle and winning the war in a week.'

'He'll grow up.'

'I'm glad you are going on this course, Robert . . . because it will delay your going . . . out there.'

'I'll be all right, Lucinda. The old predictable. You'll see me just obeying orders from my superior commanders. I'm the sort who muddles through.'

'Don't change, will you?'

'I couldn't if I tried. May I make the same request of you?'

'Oh, look!' I said. 'There's the old priory.'

'What a difference! What have they done to it?'

'There are new people there.'

'Have they bought it?'

'I think they must have. The old owners were so careless about it. Now there is a caretaker with a fierce dog to keep people out. Mind you, people did wander in and out. There were some broken windows and people used to get into the house. I suppose there's a good reason for a caretaker.'

'They've cleaned it up, haven't they?'

'Yes. I expect the new people will be moving in soon.'

'Let's hope they'll be agreeable and add something to the social life of Marchlands.'

'My parents are hoping they are good Liberals.'

'Well, the Liberals haven't got the monopoly now, have they? With this coalition a Conservative has as good a chance of getting into the Cabinet.'

'When my father comes home we hear something of what is going on. They are still harrying poor old Asquith.'

'He won't last much longer.'

'Is that a good thing?'

'The only good thing would be to finish off this war and get back to peace.'

That evening Robert left us to join his family.

'I shall see you in two days' time,' he said. 'Make sure that you keep the days free.'

'I might even get Miss Carruthers to let me off lessons.'

'I always forget you are a schoolgirl, Lucinda. But it is not for much longer, is it?'

When he had gone I fell to thinking of Marcus Merrivale. He, with Robert, was looking forward to the time when I grew up.

I felt honoured, and at the same time uneasy. When I was with Robert I knew exactly that it was where I wanted to be; but then, the exhilarating company of Marcus Merrivale was quite intoxicating.

It was Christmas again and then the New Year, 1916. Nothing was going well. It was acknowledged that the plan to capture the Dardanelles had been a failure.

There were some who agreed with Churchill that it was a brilliant idea but that it had been badly carried out.

The Secretary of State for War, Lord Kitchener, had gone out to the Dardanelles to advise withdrawal. There was no hope of victory there and it was a waste of men and ammunition to carry on. And now, in January of that year, the troops from Gallipoli began to arrive back in England.

It was at the end of that month when Uncle Gerald came to see us. He looked older than he had when he left. He told us that the campaign should never have been undertaken.

He played it out at lunch at the table.

'Doomed to fail from the start,' he said. 'A lack of surprise, for one thing. They sent us part-time soldiers. We lacked experienced men and, believe me, that's what was needed for an enterprise like this. There weren't enough supplies. There was an acute shortage of shells. Asquith must go!'

'Churchill has already gone,' my father reminded him.

'Churchill's idea was all right. That could have worked. It was the way it was tackled which destroyed us. You see, here we are –' My mother looked apprehensively at his wine glass. 'And here –' he swung the cruet into line – 'the Turk.'

For a moment we watched him moving plates and dishes round the table. It did not look in the least like a battlefield to me and I was longing to ask for news of Marcus Merrivale.

'It hasn't done much for our prestige. This is the beginning of the end for Asquith. Consider our losses, Joel . . . nearly a quarter of a million men, some from the Empire. It's a disaster, Joel. A disaster. I dare say you've been hearing about it all in the House.'

'They've talked of little else since Kitchener's verdict.'

'Heads will fall, Joel. Heads will fall.'

'I dare say you are glad to be back, Gerald,' said my mother. 'What about Major Merrivale? Is he back with you?'

'They are all coming back. Merrivale was wounded.'

'Wounded!' said my mother. 'Badly?'

'Hm. He went straight to the hospital.'

'He could have come here,' said my mother.

'My dear Lucie, I think he was really rather badly hurt.'

My mother bristled and Uncle Gerald relented a little.

'In cases like this,' he said, 'they're taken off to one of the London hospitals.'

'How badly hurt is he?' I asked.

'Oh, he'll come through. Trust Merrivale for that. But it was a bit more than a sniper's bullet.'

'Which hospital is he in?' asked my mother.

'I'm not sure.'

'What happened to him?'

'I don't know the details . . . just that he was a stretcher case.'

I felt sick. I could imagine . . . a stretcher case. How was he? I wanted to see him.

My mother said: 'We have a special interest in him, you know, Gerald, after he brought Lucinda, Edward and the others out of Belgium.'

'Oh, I know. A great fellow. He's not at death's door. Just needs a bit of patching up.'

'You must find out more details and let us know. I think that if he is in a London hospital, the least Lucinda and I can do is visit him, Joel, and I don't forget what he did for Lucinda. Heaven knows what might have happened if he hadn't looked after her, and we shall always be grateful to you, Gerald, for sending him to do so.'

'Seemed the best thing to do. He's a very resourceful fellow. Well, you'd expect that. There's only one Merrivale.'

'Well, do let us know, Gerald. We'd love to go and see him, wouldn't we, Lucinda?'

'Yes,' I answered. 'We would.'

In his precise way, Uncle Gerald sent the information to us in a few days.

My mother said it was not easy to leave the hospital but in the circumstances she thought it necessary.

Andrée said she would like to come with us. Not that she would accompany us to the hospital, for she was sure three people would be too many, but she wanted to go to London to get some things for Edward.

'Do you remember that musical box he had? It played the Brahms Cradle Song when it opened. I know he misses it. He was opening a box yesterday and clearly listening. He looked so disappointed because there was no tune.'

'Fancy his remembering all that time,' said my mother. 'But it's a haunting melody and I suppose even a child would be aware of that.'

'It is that and a few other things I should like to get,' said Andrée.

'It seems a good idea,' replied my mother.

So we went.

Marcus was in a ward with several other officers. He was lying on his back and not quite his usual exuberant self; but he grinned at us.

'This is wonderful,' he said. 'How good of you to come and see this poor old crock.'

'I don't think the term applies,' said my mother. 'Gerald told us you were improving every day.'

'My progress will leap forward after this visit. Do sit down.'

'Please don't move,' said my mother.

'It would be impossible, I fear. They've got me strapped up a bit.'

'How do you feel?'

'Wonderful . . . because you and Lucinda have come to see me.'

My mother laughed. 'I'm serious, Major Merrivale.'

'So am I. And please don't call me Major.'

'Marcus,' said my mother. 'We are so glad that you are home.'

'Does that go for Miss Lucinda also?'

'Of course it does,' I said. 'We were worried about you when we heard things were not going well.'

He grimaced. 'Something of a shambles, eh? However, it's brought me home.'

172

'Where you will be staying for some time,' added my mother.

'That seems very likely.'

'We were disappointed that you did not come to our hospital,' I told him.

'What a pleasure that would have been . . . worth getting hit for.'

'Oh, don't say that!' said my mother. 'Marchlands is an excellent place for convalescence. The forest, you know. Perhaps later on . . .'

'You mean I might come to Marchlands? Nothing could help me more to make a speedy recovery.'

'Then we shall do what we can to arrange it. I dare say Gerald could do something. He can fix most things.'

'From henceforth I shall make myself a nuisance here, so that they will be only too glad to get rid of me.'

I did not think that would be the case. It was clear that that inimitable charm worked here as everywhere else and the nurses enjoyed looking after him.

The matron came in while we were there – a stern-faced, middle-aged woman who looked as though she would be capable of keeping a regiment in order; and even she softened and chided him gently because he was getting too excited.

Our visit was not a long one, but it was the maximum time allowed.

I felt a little uneasy as we left the ward, for I was sure Marcus was putting on a show of being in a much better condition than he actually was.

My mother was able to have a word with the doctor before we left. Marchlands was now known in the medical world as one of those country houses given over to the wounded since the beginning of the war, and therefore a certain respect was accorded her.

We were taken into a small room and seated at a desk was Dr Glenning.

He told us to be seated and my mother then said: 'Major

Merrivale is a very special friend. How badly has he been wounded?'

'Well, there are worse cases.'

'And better,' added my mother.

The doctor nodded. 'Some internal injuries. A bullet . . . most fortunately . . . just missed his lungs. However, that has been extracted, but as you know, it is a vital area and we have to be watchful. There is some damage to the right leg. But that is minor compared with the internal trouble.'

'I see. He is not in danger?'

The doctor shook his head. 'Oh, he's got a good chance of recovery. He's very strong . . . in excellent condition. I'd say his chances of getting back to normal are good, but it is going to take time.'

'My daughter and I were thinking that Marchlands would be a good place for him to come for convalescence. We were wondering if the Major could come to us.'

'I could not allow him to be moved just now, and this is going to be a long job. Later, if he continues to improve, I don't see why not. He's going to need convalescence and to be among friends would be good for him. Yes, I think in due course, Mrs Greenham, he might well go to Marchlands.'

I put in: 'And he really is not in danger?'

'No more than most. We're never quite sure how these things are going to turn out. You probably know, Mrs Greenham . . . but I would say he has a fair chance of recovery.'

'That's good news,' said my mother. 'Have you any idea about when . . . ?'

The doctor pursed his lips and looked thoughtful.

'Well, I should think at least a couple of months.'

'As long as that!'

'Rather a grave injury, Mrs Greenham.'

'Well, we shall look forward to receiving him at Marchlands. Will you let us know when it will be safe for him to come?'

'Indeed I will do that.'

'In the meanwhile we shall be visiting him. We came up especially today.'

'Marchlands keeps you busy, I've heard.'

'Very busy all the time.'

'We've had a rush of casualties after the Dardanelles débâcle. Not that there are not a large number coming from France all the time.'

'Let's hope it will soon be over.'

'I'd second that, Mrs Greenham.'

He shook hands and repeated his promise that he would let us know when Marcus was well enough to travel, and we left the hospital in a happier mood than that in which we had arrived.

We had seen him. He was ill, but not so ill that he would not recover – and in time he would come to Marchlands.

Returning to Marchlands, I felt a sense of elation. I realized I was happier than I had been since the ill-fated Dardanelles venture had begun. I had been thinking about Marcus a great deal and every time the campaign had been mentioned, I had been conscious of a cold fear. Now it was over. He was wounded, yes; but he was still alive, and with his irrepressible spirits he would recover.

And in time we should have him under our care in Marchlands.

My mother sensed my mood and shared it.

'He is such a charming man,' she said. 'I could not bear to think of anything happening to change him. He'll recover quicker than most. Since the hospital started, I've noticed that optimism is one of the best cures to help a patient along the road to recovery.'

Andrée was eager to hear the news of Marcus, but I could see she wanted to get back to Marchlands and Edward. She hated leaving him even for a day.

It was about a week after our visit to London when I was awakened in the night by the sound of an explosion. My thoughts immediately went to the Zeppelin I had seen when the cottage near La Pinière had been attacked. We had to expect air raids. The Zeppelins were cumbersome objects and a good target for a firing squad, but they did present a great danger.

I leaped out of bed, put on my dressing-gown and slippers and went out of my room.

Immediately I heard my mother's voice. 'Lucinda, are you all right? Charles . . . ?'

Charles was already in the corridor. Some of the servants were there and I saw Miss Carruthers.

'That was a bomb, I am sure,' she said. 'It must have been rather close.'

Mrs Grey, the cook, had appeared.

'What was it, do you think, Mrs Grey?' asked my mother.

'Sounded just like one of them bombs, Mrs Greenham.'

'I'm afraid so. I wonder . . .'

We all gathered in the hall where some of the nurses joined us.

'What time is it?' asked my mother.

'Just after midnight,' someone replied.

'Do you think it's an air raid?'

'Most likely.'

'I can't hear anything more. Do you think they'll come back?'

'Perhaps.'

Mrs Grey said she thought everyone could do with a cup of tea, and if we would like to go to the drawing-room, she'd have it sent there. The others could have theirs in the kitchen.

My mother thought that was a good idea. Everything seemed quiet now and we should hear all about it in the morning.

Miss Carruthers said: 'We must be prepared for any emergency. One only hopes they will not drop anything on the hospital.'

'They would drop anything anywhere,' said my mother. 'Charles, come away from that window. You never know . . .'

Reluctantly, Charles moved away.

'I'd like to fly,' he said. 'Fancy being up there in the sky!'

'Not dropping bombs on people, I hope,' I said.

'Oh, I wouldn't do that.'

'Very noble of you,' I retorted.

'I'm going to join the Royal Flying Corps.'

Nobody expressed surprise. Charles was going to take up some adventurous profession every few weeks.

Nothing much happened that night, but we were astonished next morning to learn that it was not a Zeppelin which had dropped the bomb. What we had heard was an explosion which had taken place at Milton Priory.

We learned it from the postman. Jenner, the butler, had seen him when he came with the post and thought what the man had to tell was so interesting that he brought him into the dining-room where we were having breakfast.

'I thought you would like to hear what the postman has to say, Mrs Greenham,' he said. 'It's about that explosion in the night.'

'Yes, M'am,' said the postman. 'It's up at the old Priory . . . that place where things have been going on lately. They won't be putting that up for sale now. Looks as if they's destroyed the place . . . completely.'

'How could it have happened?' asked my mother.

'Well, there's a mystery for you. Something was wrong. Gas, perhaps. You know what that can do. Whatever it might be, that's the end of Milton Priory.'

'How very strange!' said Miss Carruthers. 'I wonder what the explanation is?'

'No doubt we shall find out in time,' said my mother.

When I saw Andrée, she said: 'I heard the explosion in the night.'

'You should have joined us in the drawing-room,' I told her. 'We did not get to bed until about an hour later. We just sat there talking and speculating as to what might have happened. We all thought then that it was a bomb dropped by a Zeppelin.'

'Was it?'

'No. Apparently not. It was caused by something in the house . . . gas, they say.'

'How dreadful! I didn't come down because it had awakened Edward. He was a bit fretful. I couldn't leave him.'

'Yes. I guessed that. Was he frightened?'

'Just a bit. I soothed him and finally he got to sleep.'

'I expect we shall hear more about this explosion.'

'I'd like to take a look at it.'

'Perhaps when Edward is having his nap, we could ride over.'

We did. The police were at the scene. We rode as close as we could. It was a sight to shock – twisted girders, collapsed walls, piles of bricks, where once that rather lovely old house had stood.

'There's little left of it,' said Andrée with a shiver.

'They'll never sell it now.'

'It's a complete ruin,' went on Andrée. 'Have they any idea yet how it happened?'

'I expect they will soon find out. I wonder who the owners are?'

'Didn't someone buy it recently?'

'I'm not sure whether it was sold or being prepared for a sale.'

'Well, whatever it was, that's the end of it.'

We rode back no wiser.

Later we heard that the explosion was due to a leakage of gas.

My father arrived later that afternoon.

He went over to look at the Priory. He met some official there and, as a Member of Parliament, I suppose, was allowed to go over the remains of the house. It occurred to me that the man might be from one of the ministries and my father, because the Priory was situated in his constituency, had come down to investigate the mystery.

I thought he looked distinctly worried.

Two of the men with whom he had been at the Priory came to dine with us. And at the dinner table it became clear that my father and his guests did not want to talk about the explosion.

However, the rest of us, my mother, Miss Carruthers, Dr Egerton and myself could not easily dismiss a matter which was uppermost in our thoughts.

'Lucinda was very curious about the Priory when she saw how changed it was,' my mother was saying. 'That was some time ago. We had all made up our minds that it must have been one of those horrible Zeppelins.'

'We can't be sure that it was not,' said my father.

'Oh no, Joel,' protested my mother. 'Those things are so huge. They just seem to hang in the sky. Someone would have seen it.'

'It is just possible that it quickly dropped the bomb and got away.'

'But the explosion was so loud,' I said. 'People nearby would go out to look. It couldn't have got away so quickly without being seen.'

'Well then, perhaps it was not a Zeppelin.'

'I've just thought of something,' I said. 'There's no gas at Milton Priory. How could there be? Nobody ever put it in.'

'They must have been putting it in now,' replied my father.

'If they were, surely we should have known? No, it wasn't gas. It wasn't dropped from the air. So what was it? What a mystery! No doubt we shall find out sooner or later. How I should love to know! It's really very intriguing. I shan't rest until I find out.'

'Well,' said my father, 'in the words of our Prime Minister, we must "wait and see".'

It was the following day. I had just finished my session with Miss Carruthers and as I came out of the schoolroom I saw my mother on the stairs.

She said: 'Lucinda, I wanted to talk to you.'

'Yes?'

'Come into my sitting-room. I don't want anyone to hear.'

I was eager to learn what she had to say, and when we reached her room she shut the door and, looking at me anxiously, said: 'Sit down.'

I did so, very puzzled.

'Lucinda,' she began, 'this is very important. It is also secret. But your father and I know you will be discreet, and, after all, you are no longer a child.'

I waited apprehensively as she paused, for she was staring ahead, frowning.

'I know you have been aware of the fact for a long time that your father is . . . well, something more than an ordinary Member of Parliament.'

'Yes . . . vaguely. He does go off sometimes, and I know you are a little anxious when he does, and there is, of course, the implication that no questions should be asked.'

'I wish he were not engaged in all this secrecy. I'm always afraid he will come to some harm. It could have ruined our lives in the beginning, when he was engaged on secret work and I thought he was dead. I married . . .' She shook her head. 'If he had been here, it would have been so different.'

'I do know something about that.'

I guessed this preamble was because she was trying to make up her mind to tell me what all this was about.

'Your father is doing a wonderful job for the country,' she went on. 'He has never taken Cabinet rank because of this work. It would not be possible for a minister to do what he is doing. So he just sits in Parliament. Well, that is a Greenham tradition, and he had to follow it. But it's all part of the same thing. It's working for the country.'

'Yes, I know.'

'There is a matter which has come up. He is going to tell you about it himself. He was reluctant to, but we both thought it best. He asked me to . . . well, prepare you, as it were. I think he wants to be sure that it will be all right to take you into this secret. In fact, he thinks it might be necessary to.'

'What is this secret?'

'He is going to tell you. We were discussing it last night and

180

we came to the conclusion that it is the best way. Your father thought at first that you were too young but, well, everything that has been happening lately has jerked you out of your childhood. You'll understand and do all you can to help, I know. I've convinced him of this. He's in the study now. Let's go to him.'

My father was waiting for us.

'Here she is,' said my mother. 'We can rely on Lucinda. She understands.'

'Sit down, my dear,' said my father. 'This must sound very mysterious to you.'

'It does,' I answered.

'Your mother has told you that I am involved in certain matters.'

'Yes, she has.'

'It's about Milton Priory.'

I was taken aback. 'Milton Priory!' I said.

'Yes, Milton Priory,' he repeated. 'You know, don't you, that you must not give an indication to anyone at any time of this?'

'I understand that.'

'I don't want people talking about it . . . as you were inclined to do. I want it believed that the explosion was caused by a Zeppelin or a gas leak, something that could happen in any place at any time. I know you were especially interested in the place, but you must stop speculating about it. Keeping the mystery alive arouses people's curiosity, so you must stop talking of it and if the subject is raised in your presence, do everything you can to divert the conversation away from it. I don't want people prying . . . investigating . . .'

'Why not?'

'Listen, Lucinda. The Priory was being used by the Government as a research centre. Important experiments were being carried out there. A secret place was needed for these experiments. We are surrounded by spies, as countries are in war. We cannot trust anyone. It was very important for the location of this research to be kept secret. It was on my recommendation that the Priory was chosen. There it was, an almost derelict house, empty for some years. A great amount of work was needed to make it habitable as a residence. It would be acceptable in the neighbourhood that people should be there. And there was a show of restoring the place while the essential work was being carried out. That was what was happening at the Priory.'

My father paused and looked at me.

I said: 'And you think that spies discovered this and blew it up?'

He nodded. 'That is exactly what I think. But who? I feel very deeply involved as it was my suggestion that the work should take place there. I had secret documents in London giving important details of the place and the work which was being done.'

'What work was it?'

'Too complicated to explain. Experiments with a new armoured vehicle which would be valuable on the battlefield. It was being perfected. And now much of the work has been destroyed.'

'Completely?' I asked.

'Oh no. But it will set us back months. The worrying fact is that certain documents in my possession must have been seen by someone who has made use of them – with this result. In the first place, the nature of the work has been revealed to the enemy; in the second place, they have learned where it was being carried out; and in the third place, they have found a means of blowing up the house.'

'I remember the caretaker and the dog. He was guarding the place, of course.'

'Now, Lucinda, one of the most alarming aspects of the whole matter is that someone must have got into the London house – someone who had seen secret papers which were kept there for safety. Who could it be? There was no break-in. At least, if there was, I knew nothing about it.'

'You mean, it could be someone in the house?'

'Well, not necessarily living there. It could be someone who has access. Perhaps a workman coming to do some job. Your mother and I have talked this over. You were so interested in the Priory. I have explained why I want you to stop talking about it. But there is something more. I want you to be watchful, Lucinda. If you see anything . . . anyone acting suspiciously . . . let me or your mother know at once, whoever it is. We cannot eliminate anyone from this. You can see what danger there is. I want to know who saw those secret papers in my room, who made it possible for the Priory to be destroyed.'

'Yes,' I said. 'I want to know, too.'

My mother took my hand. 'I'm glad you know about this, Lucinda,' she said.

'The idea of someone's coming into the house, going through my papers, is intolerable,' said my father. 'It makes one realize how dangerous the times are. So, Lucinda, keep quiet about the Priory. Avoid bringing up the matter . . . and keep your eyes open.'

'I will,' I said. 'Oh, I will.'

The Hero

The spring had come and little seemed to have changed. It would be two years in August since the war had started, and those who had prophesied that it would not last six months were silent. Even the most optimistic no longer believed that the end was in sight.

I had had two letters from Robert, heavily censored, and I had no idea where he was except that it was 'somewhere in France'. He was often in my thoughts, and so was Marcus. I think I was more anxious about Robert, who was out there in acute danger. Marcus at least was safe in a hospital bed, although he must have been badly wounded to have been there so long.

I had seen Annabelinda at infrequent intervals. She and her mother came to London and stayed at our house, even though we were at Marchlands.

It was May – a beautiful month, I had always thought – on the brink of summer, the days not yet too hot, and the hedges white with wild parsley and stitchwort. I took long walks in the forest. It was quiet, just as it had been when William the Conqueror and Henry VIII had hunted there.

Then I thought of that terrible battlefield where Robert would be. I dreamed about him in the trenches. I could see him with that rather deprecating grin, and I knew I could not bear it if he did not come back. What I wanted to hear more than anything was that he was coming home on one of the troopships – perhaps slightly wounded, enough to keep him with us, as Marcus was.

We saw little of Uncle Gerald. He was in France now.

People were looking grim. There was no longer any excitement about the war – except for people like Charles, whose idea of it were far from reality.

Annabelinda came to Marchlands with her mother.

Aunt Belinda was very effusive. She was involved in all sorts of charities but, knowing Aunt Belinda, I guessed that her main task would be delegation. She would arrange for others to do the work and take credit for it when it was done.

Perhaps I was unfair in my judgement and exaggerated a little, but when I saw how my mother worked, I did feel a little impatient with the Aunt Belindas and Annabelindas of this world.

'Dear Lucie,' gushed Aunt Belinda. 'So busy with all this wonderful work. You'll be decorated before the war's over, I'm sure. And you deserve it, dear.'

My mother replied: 'I am rewarded without that. It is a joy when you see these men getting better. And we are lucky to have the forest so close.'

Annabelinda and I rode through the trees. She was rather disgruntled.

'I've had enough of this wretched war,' she said.

'Do you think you are the only one?'

'Certainly I don't. That's why someone should put a stop to it. Do you realize I am nearly nineteen years old?'

'Well, I suppose you must be. I shall be seventeen in September.'

'We're getting old. If this miserable war goes on for another two years, just think! What about us?'

I laughed at her.

'What's amusing?' she demanded.

'I was just thinking about all those men who are out there fighting. Your own brother, for instance. And you ask, what about us!'

'Oh, Robert will be all right. He always has been.'

'This is war!'

'Don't I know it! I should have had a Season by now.'

'That really is world-shattering.'

'Don't try to be a cynic. You're not clever enough for it. It's so boring in the country. You must find it so, too. What do you do all day? Old Carruthers must be a bit of a hard task mistress.'

'We get on well. I enjoy our lessons.'

'You would. You were always a bit of a swot.'

'*You* were never interested in anything but yourself. Edward is a lot of fun. You might have shared in that.'

She flushed. 'You are a beast, Lucinda.'

'You're so unnatural.'

'It isn't what I want to be, but what can I do?'

'Being you, only what you do, I suppose. I'm not complaining. He's a darling. Andrée and I spend a good deal of time with him, so you see, we are not bored. Then I do a little in the hospital.'

'What sort of thing?'

'I go round and talk to some of them . . . those who are well enough to talk. Actually, we don't have a lot of bad cases here. I think they consider we are more of a convalescent home.'

'That sounds interesting. As a matter of fact, it's what I wanted to talk to you about. I thought I might come and help a bit.'

'I can't quite see you . . .'

'I'm bright and amusing. I could help with the patients and do anything else that had to be done. One wants to do one's share. My mother was saying I ought to do something. I help her a lot with her charities and things. I'm quite good at it. But I should like to do more. My mother is talking to yours about my coming here for a while to help.'

'You could train as a nurse.'

She looked at me in horror. 'That would take ages.'

'There are places you can go to for a period.'

'Oh no,' she said. 'The war would be over before I could be of any use. I want just to come and help. And what about you? You're not a trained nurse.'

'No, but then this is my home and I can be called on at any time.'

'Well, it's my home in a way. We're like a family. Your mother and my mother . . . their upbringing and all that. They were in the same nursery together.'

'I know. You'd find the country boring.'

'You're trying to put me off. Don't think I don't know why.'

'What do you mean?'

'You were always jealous of me . . . and Marcus.'

'Jealous of you? Why?'

'Because he was more attracted to me than to you. I know you thought he liked you at one time. He's like that with every girl. It's just his way. It doesn't mean a thing.'

'What's that got to do with your coming here?'

She smiled slyly. 'He'll be ever so pleased when he finds I'm here,' she said.

I still said nothing.

'I've been to see him in that hospital,' she went on. 'My mother and I went. It was so interesting. Poor Marcus! He really did get it, didn't he? That ghastly place. Gallipoli. And it was all a mistake. They should never have gone there. Well, he's home now. They wouldn't let him out of the hospital. And they won't for another month, he reckons. He says he's looking forward to his convalescence . . . here.'

'I now see the reason for your sudden desire to serve your country, which really means serving your own ends.'

'Don't be so pompous! Of course, Marcus is an added attraction, but I have been thinking for a long time that I should like to come here. I shall be very good at helping to enliven the days of those poor soldiers. They've had such a miserable time in the trenches and everywhere. So I shall be coming to help in the good work. I shall go back to London to do some shopping and get myself ready. Then I shall descend on you.'

I was silent. I could imagine her with those men who were getting better and were ready to indulge in a little recreation

187

which, with Annabelinda, would mean flirtation.

There was no doubt that they would enjoy her company.

It was two weeks before she arrived. I have to admit that she was an immediate success with the men – less so with the staff.

My mother talked about her to me when we were alone.

'She reminds me so much of her mother. At times I imagine I am eighteen again and she is Belinda. They are so animated . . . vital . . . both of them. That is their great attraction, though they both have a rather unusual kind of beauty. I think it is the French in them. I can see a good deal of Jean Pascal Bourdon there. I wonder how he is getting on? I suppose he could have got away, but he is the typical French aristocrat: he would not desert his country. And I should imagine he will be wily enough to get by. About Annabelinda: I think, on the whole, she's an asset. I saw her wheeling out Captain Gregory. He is so depressed about his disability. I don't think he will ever be any better. She was doing her usual line of innocent flirtation and for the first time I saw him actually smile.'

'She's certainly good in that respect,' I said.

'One can't help liking her. It was the same with her mother. They are both so naïvely selfish.'

There was still no news of Marcus. He must have been four months in that hospital.

We had had some startling news. On June 5th, Lord Kitchener was on his way to a meeting with the Russians, when the *Hampshire*, the ship in which he was sailing, was struck by a German mine, and he was drowned.

England was plunged in mourning. And still the war went on.

To cheer us came news of Marcus's imminent arrival. He was brought in in an army vehicle and was able to walk with a stick, though with some difficulty.

We were all waiting to greet him.

He looked a little thin, slightly paler, but he was as full of life as ever.

He took my hand and gazed at me with such delight that I felt my spirits rising.

Then he saw Annabelinda. 'And Miss Annabelinda too!' he exclaimed. 'A double blessing! How fortunate! Mrs Greenham . . . and Miss Carruthers! And the capable Mademoiselle Latour. And where is Master Edward?'

'He's sleeping at the moment,' said Andrée.

'Our band of adventurers! Mrs Greenham, I cannot thank you enough for allowing me to come.'

'We have all been very impatient for your arrival and quite put out because it took so long,' said my mother.

So there he was, installed at Marchlands. Immediately the place seemed different – and I was not the only one who felt this.

He was put into a small ward with three other officers. One of the assets of Marchlands was that we had several of these small wards. It meant that, instead of the long rooms with rows of beds, such as are found in most hospitals, we had these cosy apartments which before had been large airy bedrooms.

The three men with Marcus were a middle-aged major, a captain of about thirty and a young lieutenant. My mother had said they would be the sort who would get on well together.

It soon became clear that Marcus was a welcome newcomer. We often heard laughter coming from the ward, and the nurses vied with each other for the pleasure of looking after that particular quartet.

Annabelinda took charge of them. She referred to theirs as her ward, and she was constantly in and out. Of course, she was a favourite with the men.

I could not help but be a little put out. For so long I had looked forward to Marcus's arrival, and now it was like an anticlimax.

Marcus could walk out into the gardens and he used to like to sit there under the sycamore trees on the lawn. I was very rarely there with him alone. If I did manage it, in a few minutes Annabelinda would be there.

I was not sure whether he resented this as I did. He gave no sign of doing so – but then he would not.

Annabelinda would chatter away, asking questions about the fighting in Gallipoli, and not listening to the answers. She said how wonderful it was to feel one was doing something towards the progress of victory, and how much she admired the brave men who were fighting for the cause. Then we would talk about that journey we had all made together; we would remember little incidents which had seemed far from funny at the time and now seemed quite hilarious.

Marcus frequently told us how delighted he was to be at Marchlands.

'I used to lie in my narrow hospital bed and wonder if I was ever going to get here,' he said. 'The weeks went on and on and they would not let me go.'

'You have been very ill, Marcus,' I said.

'Oh, not really. It was just that stubborn doctor. The more eager I was to go, the more determined he seemed to be to keep me.'

'You are so brave,' said Annabelinda. 'You make light of your wounds. And if you are glad to be here, we are twice as glad to have you in our clutches.'

'This is where I would rather be than anywhere else.'

'I am so pleased,' said Annabelinda, looking at him earnestly, 'that they can't take you away from us . . . not yet anyway. We shall insist on keeping you until this silly old war is over.'

'You are too good to me,' he told her.

'You will see how good I can be,' she said, her eyes full of promise.

Then one day I found him alone under the sycamore tree.

'This is wonderful,' he exclaimed. 'I hardly ever see you alone.'

'You always seem quite happy.'

'I'm happier at this moment.'

'You always say the things people want to hear. Do you really mean them?'

He put his hand over mine. 'Not always, but at this moment, yes.'

I laughed. 'Flattery comes as easily to you as breathing.'

'Well, it pleases people . . . and what's wrong with that?'

'But if you don't mean it . . .'

'It serves a purpose. As I said, it pleases people. You would not want me to go around displeasing them, would you?'

'That's very laudable, but in time, of course, people will realize you don't mean what you say.'

'Only the wise ones . . . like you. Most lap it up. It's what they want to hear, so why not give it to them? But I assure you, I will be absolutely truthful with you. You are so astute that it would be pointless to be otherwise. At this moment, I am happy to see you and to have you to myself, and to see that you are growing up into a very attractive young lady. You were so young when we first met.'

'I'm nearly two years older now.'

'About to reach the magic age. But don't grow up too soon, will you?'

'I thought you were urging me to.'

'I want you to keep that bloom of innocence. Sweet sixteen, they say, don't they? How right they are! Don't learn about the wicked ways of the world too soon, will you?'

'I think I have learned quite a lot about them in the last two years.'

'But it hasn't spoilt you. You still have that adorable innocence. You will soon be seventeen. When is your birthday?'

'In September. The first.'

'Almost three months away.'

'I wonder if you will still be here?'

'I am going to be. If necessary I shall malinger. I shall pull the wool over Dr Egerton's eyes and make him insist on my remaining here.'

'But surely you will have recovered by then?'

He shrugged his shoulders and touched his chest. 'That bullet did something. The old leg might get back to something like normal. I believe they are not much concerned about that. I don't think it would qualify me to be here. But I have to take care of this other thing.'

'I am glad in a way that you won't be able to go to the front.'

'You would mind very much if I did?'

'Of course. I thought a great deal about you when you were in Gallipoli.'

'I wish I'd known.'

'But you must have guessed. We were all thinking of you . . . you and Uncle Gerald.'

'It's your thinking of me that interests me.'

We were silent for a few moments, then I said: 'You know a great deal about me and my family. I know little about you and yours.'

'There is not a great deal to know. I have been in the Army from the time I was eighteen. Destined for it, you know. It's all tradition in my family.'

'Uncle Gerald did say something about your coming from an ancient family.'

'We all come from ancient families. Heaven knows how far our ancestors go back . . . to the days when they were all living in trees or caves, perhaps.'

'The difference is that you know what your family were and what they were doing hundreds of years ago. You're from one of those families who –'

'Came over with the Conqueror? That's what you mean, is it? Oh, I dare say. There was always a lot of pride in the family . . . all that sort of thing.'

'Tradition,' I supplied.

'That's it. The family has been doing certain things for centuries. We have to remember that and go on doing them. The second son always goes into the Army. The first, of course, runs the estate. The third goes into politics and if there is a fourth, the poor devil is destined for the Church. The idea in the past was to have the family represented in all the influential fields. Thus we played our part in governing the country.

What was done in the sixteenth century must be done in the twentieth.'

'And do you all meekly obey?'

'There have been rebels. Last century one went into business. Unheard of! He made a fortune, bolstered up the crumbling ancestral home and set the family on its feet. But that did not stop them thinking there was something shameful about his life.'

'Well, at least you have done your duty and haven't become a black sheep.'

'But not an entirely white one either.'

'I should have thought they would have been proud of you.'

'No. I should have become a field marshal, or at least a colonel by now. I haven't a hope. Wars are the time for promotion. But I'm knocked out of it, as it were.'

'Won't the family recognize that?'

'Oh yes, but it doesn't really count. I should at least have got a medal, preferably the Victoria Cross.'

'Poor Marcus! Perhaps it would have been better to have been born into an ordinary family like mine.'

'Yours is far from ordinary. Consider your mother. Turning her home into a hospital!'

'Do you feel restricted, having to conform to such high standards?' I asked.

'No. Because I don't always. One gets accustomed to compromise. That is our secret motto. As long as it all looks well, that's all that matters.'

'But you went into the Army.'

'It suited me in a way. I was too feckless at eighteen to have any ambitions of my own.'

'And now?'

'Oh, I shall be a good Merrivale to the end of my days. I shall stay in the Army until I retire, then possibly settle on the estate. There's a fine old house, not quite so imposing as the ancestral home, but it has been used by one of the younger sons through the ages. My uncle, who lived there, died recently and his son is living there now. I believe he has plans to move to one of the family's smaller estates up north some time. Then that house could be mine . . . when I retire from the Army. I could settle down there and give my brother a hand with the estate. That life would suit me.'

'So you will do your duty to the family.'

'I shall marry and settle. I must marry before I am thirty.'

'Is that a family law?'

'It's expected of us. Sons should have settled by the time they are thirty and begin to replenish the earth . . . or shall we say, the family. Time is running out for me. Do you know I am twenty-eight?'

'Is that really so?'

'Quite old, compared with you.'

'You will never be old.'

'Ah. Who is flattering now?'

'If it is the truth, it is not flattering, is it?'

'But you were saying this to please me.'

'I was merely saying what I think.'

'Oh, hello . . . there you are.' Annabelinda was coming towards us.

'Marcus,' she went on, 'how long have you been sitting there? I'm not sure that you should. There's quite a chill in the air.'

'Ah,' said Marcus. 'The fair Annabelinda! Have you come to join us?'

'I have brought your jacket.' She put it round his shoulders. 'I saw you from one of the windows and I thought you needed it.'

'How I love to be pampered!'

'I was looking for Lucinda actually,' said Annabelinda. 'Your mother was asking for you a little while ago. I thought you might be somewhere in the gardens.'

'I'll go and see what she wants,' I said. Marcus raised his eyebrows into an expression of resignation.

'Goodbye for now,' I added.

When I reached the house, I looked back. Annabelinda was sitting close to him on the seat and they were laughing together.

I found my mother.

'Did you want me?' I asked.

'Well, not especially, but now you're here, you might take these towels along to Sister Burroughs.'

A few days later, after we had closed our books for the morning, Miss Carruthers said: 'Lucinda, I have something to tell you. You will be the first to know.'

I waited expectantly.

'You are aware that your seventeenth birthday is coming up soon.'

'The first of September.'

'Exactly. You will then not really be in need of a governess.'

'Has my mother said anything about that?'

'No. But it is the case, is it not?'

'I suppose so. But I hope . . . well, my mother always said how useful you are in the hospital. She says she does not know what she would do without all her helpers.'

'The fact is I am going to be married.'

'Miss Carruthers!'

She glanced down, smiling. It was hard to imagine Miss Carruthers coy, but that was how she seemed at that moment.

'Dr Egerton has asked me to marry him.'

'Congratulations! I am so pleased. He is such a nice man.'

'I think so,' said Miss Carruthers. 'We got on well from the first and now . . . he has asked me.'

I thought of what I had heard of Dr Egerton. His wife had died six years before. He must be about forty. He had a son and daughter, both married and not living at home. I thought it sounded ideal. My first thought was: Now she will never have to go to that cousin. How wonderful for her!

She clearly thought so, too.

'I have told David – Dr Egerton – that I shall not leave my post until you are seventeen.'

'Oh, you must not think of me. I am as near seventeen as is necessary, and in any case, it will soon be the school holidays.'

'Dr Egerton understands. We are going to make the

195

announcement on your seventeenth birthday. We shall be married in October. If your mother will allow me to stay here until then.'

'But of course! I'm so surprised. I think it is wonderful. I am so pleased about it.'

I threw my arms round her and hugged her.

'Oh, Lucinda.' She laughed indulgently. 'You are so exuberant. We have been through a great deal together, and I wanted you to be the first one to know. Now I shall tell your mother.'

'She will be so happy for you. And you can continue to help in the hospital. Won't that be marvellous! Mrs Egerton!' I added slowly, savouring it.

'You are quite ridiculous,' said Miss Carruthers happily. 'But it does seem to have worked out very well.'

She looked different. There was a radiance about her. Was it due to the fact that she was in love, or was it the happiness which came from the knowledge that her future was secure? A governess's life was so precarious.

I sat with her for a while and we talked about how she and Dr Egerton had become good friends right from the beginning.

'Of course, we met now and then in the hospital,' she said. 'And often we would walk in the gardens. It grew from that.'

'I think it is wonderful,' I told her.

'And when you realize that if this terrible war had not come upon us . . . if we had not had to leave the school in such a hurry . . . if I had left with some of the other teachers . . .'

'But you did not. I remember you said you would not leave until all the English girls had got away.'

'And your mother was so good. It was a chain of events with chance playing a big part.'

'Doesn't it show that things are not all bad? Something good can come out of the worst. Perhaps we should always remember that.'

'I think it is something I shall remember all my life,' said Miss Carruthers.

*

My mother was delighted to hear the news.

'I have thought a lot about Miss Carruthers,' she said. 'I knew she would be wondering how much longer you would need her. I was going to ask her to stay on and help in the hospital. I suppose she will do that now, Dr Egerton being so closely involved. This is the best thing that could have happened for them both. I've always thought Dr Egerton is one of those men who needed a wife. He has been a little lost since Mary went. So I am very pleased about this, and Miss Carruthers is like a different person. She always had that concern about the future. So many governesses do. And we don't have to worry about you, now that you are just on seventeen. And Charles is all right going to the rectory for lessons every day. Of course, we shall have to think about his going away to school one day, but we can shelve that for a while. I don't want him to go away while we're at war. I want you all at hand. I don't like it when your father is in London, but at least he is here most weekends.'

About this time there was a subtle change in Marcus's attitude towards me. At first I thought I had imagined it, but later it seemed more marked.

Annabelinda was constantly in his company, and I hardly ever saw him alone. I could not blame her for this entirely, although she contributed to it considerably.

If he went to sit on the seat under the sycamore tree, Annabelinda was always with him. At first I used to join them until I had a distinct feeling that I was in the way. I must say that feeling was engendered by Annabelinda, never by him. He was as gracious and courtly as ever, except that I sensed a certain superficiality in his manner.

During that August, my mother said: 'It will be your birthday soon. I can't believe it is seventeen years since you came into the world. What a wonderful day that was! I am determined to do something to celebrate. We'll have a party. It will cheer everyone up. We need cheering up in these gloomy days. The news doesn't get any better, does it?'

She was right. Everyone was excited by the prospect of a party.

At first we thought that if it were a fine day we would have it on the lawn. We would have a buffet for all those who were mobile, but we must not forget those who were not.

This idea was abandoned, for so many would be too ill to be moved and we did not want to accentuate their disability by having two parties. We could have them brought down to the main hall and there we would have a concert. We could use the dais at one end for a stage. It would be all local talent. Anyone of the staff and patients who were well enough should perform.

'You are going to a good deal of trouble,' I told my mother.

'My dear Lucinda, it is your birthday, and seventeen is like a milestone. It should be celebrated in style. Your father will have to be here for it. Everyone must know what a special occasion it is.'

They were all talking about the birthday, the highlight of which was the concert. There were serious discussions about what the performers would do.

'Anyone would think this was Drury Lane,' said Mrs Grey, who, I was sure, had no idea what it was like at Drury Lane. But we all understood what she meant.

The day arrived. There were well-wishers with gifts and everyone behaved as though I had done something very clever in having lived for seventeen years.

The concert was to start at two-thirty that afternoon.

In the morning I escaped to the garden. I kept thinking of my conversation with Marcus and how he had continually referred to my seventeenth birthday. The fact was that I had begun to believe he was in love with me and that thought had excited me tremendously. I had hardly admitted it to myself, but I had the idea firmly fixed in my mind that my seventeenth birthday would be some landmark in our relationship – which after all was what he had implied.

Lately I had begun to doubt this, but the thought would not go away.

I blamed Annabelinda. She was so determined to be with him and exclude me. I told myself he did not wish it, but was too polite to tell her to go away. I clung to this belief and tried to stifle my doubts.

I saw him in the gardens then and I was happy because I had the impression that he was looking for me.

He was walking more easily now. In fact, my mother had said only yesterday that Dr Egerton had told her Marcus might well be released from the hospital in a week or so.

He used a stick but moved with apparent ease.

I called: 'Hello, Marcus.'

He stopped. 'Lucinda! The birthday lady. Congratulations! So, at last you have made it.'

'It was rather inevitable.'

'And there are such celebrations! You must be very proud.'

'Oh, that is all due to my mother. She is determined that all shall be aware of my great age.'

'And rightly so.'

'My mother was saying that you might be discharged from the hospital soon.'

'I cannot malinger much longer.'

'You know very well you have not been malingering.'

'Well, perhaps not. But I am a bit of an old crock, you know.'

'They won't send you . . . ?'

'To the front line? Not for some time. Actually, I am going to the War Office for a while. It will be something for me to do.'

'That will be interesting.'

He grimaced. We passed the seat and I said: 'Would you like to sit down?'

'Doctor's orders that I should exercise. Actually, I should be rehearsing.'

'Oh, are you performing this afternoon?'

'Yes, I've been roped in.'

'What are you doing?'

'"*The Road to Mandalay*."'

'Do you add a good voice to your many accomplishments?'

'I am not sure of the accomplishments. I think some would

question that I have any. The voice is, well . . . just a voice. It makes a noise. That's all.'

'How modest you are!'

'Not at all. I should never have allowed myself to be persuaded. You wait until you hear my performance. It's a very popular song, so perhaps I'll get by.'

I guessed it would not be long before Annabelinda discovered that we were together – and I was right.

She came hurrying out.

'Oh, there you are, Marcus. Dr Egerton told you not to tire yourself.'

'On the contrary, he told me to take exercise.'

'He meant in moderation.'

'I have been very moderate.'

'Isn't it exciting about the concert? I am longing to hear "*Mandalay*".'

'I think I shall plead stage fright.'

'Nobody would believe you,' I said. 'I am sure it will be a great success. They are not expecting Caruso.'

'I imagine,' added Annabelinda, 'that the rest of them will be very amateurish. You will be the star turn, Marcus.'

'My stage fright increases with every moment. You must not have too high an opinion of me, my dear Annabelinda.'

'I shall form my own opinions, Marcus.'

'You are a strong-minded young lady, I know. But please do not expect too much. I can make myself heard, and that is about all.'

'I am longing to hear you,' said Annabelinda.

'I think I shall go in,' I told them. 'There is a good deal to do.'

'We will see you later,' said Annabelinda blithely.

So I left them and went in, feeling deflated. He was not going to say anything special to me. He had talked so earnestly about my birthday, indicating that he was waiting for it, and then all he talked about was '*The Road to Mandalay*'.

The concert was a success, though more remarkable for the paucity of the performances than the discovery of talent. But it was greatly enjoyed and the more mishaps there were the more appreciative the merriment.

Marcus's '*Mandalay*' was a great success. He performed with aplomb rather than genius, but he had an agreeable voice which was strong enough to be heard all over the hall. It was his impersonation of a temperamental opera star which amused the audience and was without doubt the success of the show.

There were songs from others, several from the beginning of the century. '*Soldiers of the Queen*' was very well received, though not applicable to the times; then there was '*Goodbye, Dolly Gray*', another favourite. And someone recited 'Gunga Din'. All were vociferously applauded and everyone agreed it had been a memorable day.

I would always remember it, too, and when I did I would think of Marcus, making light conversation in the gardens, declining my unspoken invitation to talk. I could not help feeling a certain humiliation.

I had been foolish in imagining what was not there.

Three weeks later Marcus left. My father was with us on his last weekend and Marcus dined with us.

He said how much he had enjoyed his stay with us and that my mother deserved a medal for all she had done.

It was all very merry. Annabelinda looked especially attractive. She sat next to Marcus and I felt there was a certain understanding between them.

How could I have been so vain as to think he was in love with me? He was a man of the world and I had temporarily amused him because I was young and innocent. Had he not stressed my innocence? He had wanted me to retain it when I grew up. Why should he? What could it matter to him? It was just idle talk and I had been naïve enough to take it seriously.

He talked to my father at dinner, explaining that he would be at the War Office.

'You will have to be in London,' said my father. 'Where will you stay?'

'I'll see if I can get a small place . . . a pied-à-terre. I shall

201

go down to the family at weekends. If invited, I might come to Marchlands to see how you are all getting on without me.'

'You will be welcome at any time,' my mother told him. 'But I must warn you: guests often get pressed into service.'

'That would be interesting. But I must warn *you*. I should be an awful dud.'

'We'd teach you,' replied my mother.

'Then that's a promise.'

'It's wonderful to see you recovered.'

'Well, yes . . . but not fit enough to go out there again.'

'I can't say that greatly grieves me.'

'The War Office will be interesting,' said my father.

'All the red tape and that.'

'But quite an experience.'

'How are things getting on in the House?'

'Something has to happen. We've got to win this war soon. It's been going on too long.'

'You mean Asquith will go.'

'Lloyd George is waiting in the wings. There'll be a change soon. I'd say before Christmas. L.G. will be going to the Palace to kiss hands.'

'As soon as that! Poor old Asquith!'

'Another Christmas,' said my mother, 'and we are still at war.'

'It has got to end soon,' said my father. 'If the Americans come in, I'd say the end was in sight.'

'And will they?'

'It seems possible.'

'I just long for it to be over,' said my mother.

'It will be . . . in time.'

A week after Marcus left, Annabelinda announced that her mother needed her at home and she thought she ought to go to her.

'You'll manage very well without me,' she said.

I could not resist saying: 'As you devoted yourself almost

entirely to Major Merrivale and he is no longer with us, I dare say we *shall* manage very well.'

She smirked. 'Poor Lucinda,' she said.

I was glad to see her go. She reminded me too bitterly of my humiliation over Marcus.

At the end of October, Miss Carruthers was married to Dr Egerton. It was a simple ceremony and there was a small reception at Marchlands afterwards.

I was very pleased to see Miss Carruthers so happy. The cousin came for the ceremony, and I could see immediately why Miss Carruthers had not been eager to share her home. She was a formidable lady, but at this time quite affable and clearly not displeased by the marriage. So all was extremely satisfactory in that respect.

The new Mrs Egerton made herself useful in the hospital every afternoon, just as she had when teaching me.

'It is very comforting that all has turned out so well,' said my mother. 'I wonder what will happen to Andrée.'

'We wouldn't want her to leave us,' I replied. 'She is so good with Edward. Were you thinking of a husband for her?'

'I do often think of people who are working as she does and Miss Carruthers did. Think of the care Andrée gives to Edward . . . as most nannies do give to the children they look after, and in time they have to face the fact that those children do not belong to them. I wonder what she will want to do when the war is over? Perhaps go back to Belgium.'

'She was very anxious to get away,' I said.

'There is that brother of hers. I suppose she doesn't hear anything of him. It must be very sad for her.'

'She is sure he is with the French Army.'

'Anything might have happened to him. She's a strange girl.'

'Do you think so?'

'She seems so . . . contented.'

'Does that make her strange? She was glad to get away; she did not want to go to her aunt; and she loved Edward dearly. He is such a darling. I can see why she feels contented.'

'But she must worry about her brother.'

'I believe she was not very close to any of her family.'

'I wonder what will happen to her?'

'Who knows what will happen to anyone?'

My mother looked at me sharply. I think she had an inkling of my feelings for Marcus. I was beginning to realize I was rather naïve. I had probably betrayed them.

The days passed – one very like another. I spent more time in the hospital now as I had greater leisure without Miss Carruthers's lessons. I walked a good deal in the forest and I felt very melancholy during those days.

It was December. As my father had prophesied, Lloyd George had taken over the Government. Marcus had not come to Marchlands, in spite of his promise to do so.

I told myself I should have known by now that he did not mean half what he said. Had he not admitted that to me on one occasion? He said he did because it was what people wanted to hear.

We celebrated Christmas at the hospital, and then it was New Year. 1917 – and the war still with us and showing no more sign of ending than it had two years ago.

The days passed slowly. How I missed Marcus! I think many people did. He had added a gaiety to the place. He was right, of course. He said the things people wanted to hear and made them laugh and be happy – as long as they remembered he did not really mean them. He joked about most things and that made life pleasant.

I thought of him continually during those long and dreary winter days.

News filtered through – mostly gloomy and bringing little hope of a speedy victory. There was a gleam of hope with the coming of April when America declared war on Germany. Soon they would be coming to stand beside us.

Everyone was saying: This must be the beginning of the end.

It was the end of April when news came to cheer me. My mother came to me in great excitement.

'What do you think? I've heard from Gerald. Robert's coming here.'

My first thought was: He's been wounded.

'Is he badly hurt?' I asked.

'It's his leg. He's been in hospital in London for about two weeks, Gerald said. He's well enough to come here to convalesce. Gerald said it will do him good to have a spell with us.'

'Oh . . . that's wonderful!'

My mother smiled. 'Yes, it will be. You'll enjoy his being here. You two were always special friends, weren't you? Gerald said Robert can't wait to get here. He'll be coming tomorrow.'

My mother was looking at me with that expression of apprehension which I had known over the years. She had understood my feelings for Marcus, for I had been simple enough to betray them. So she was delighted that my good friend Robert would be here to cheer me up.

I rose early next morning. We had discussed where we would put him. 'In one of the four-bed wards,' said my mother. 'Dear Robert! We must do the best possible for him.'

'As if we don't for everyone!'

'Oh, but there is something special about Robert.'

He arrived in the early afternoon. When I saw him standing there with his crutches, I felt overcome with emotion. He had the same grin, but was thinner, which accentuated what Annabelinda had called his 'disjointed look'. He was paler and somehow he looked vulnerable.

I ran to him and threw my arms round him.

'It's so good to see you, Robert,' I said.

'And for me to see you.'

'We're so glad you have come.'

'Your uncle said you would be.'

'And he was right.'

My mother came out and kissed him.

'We were so delighted when we heard the news,' she said.

'You can imagine how I felt. You both look wonderfully well.'

'It's the thought of having you at our mercy. We are going to give you the special treatment, aren't we, Lucinda?'

'We are,' I replied.

I felt I had been lifted out of my melancholy.

The great matter for rejoicing was that he was not badly wounded. He could go out into the gardens and did not have to rely completely on the nurses. We found that patients who could help themselves recovered more quickly than the others.

He knew Marchlands well, of course, and it was for him, he said, like coming home.

I was happier now. Robert's presence had made a great difference. I no longer brooded on my folly. It was wonderful to be with someone as uncomplicated as him – someone I could understand and be sure that he meant what he said.

I could see that my mother was delighted. She could not conceal her feelings from me, any more than I could mine from her. So Robert's coming had made a difference to us both.

In the afternoons he would sit in the gardens. The spring days were delightful – long and warm, with just a slight nip in the air to remind us that summer was not yet with us.

We used to sit together, but not under the sycamore tree. I did not want to be there with Robert because I still remembered too much of my conversations with Marcus. I said I preferred the seat under the oak on the other side of the lawn and that was enough for Robert. He always made his way to the seat under the oak.

We talked. We spoke of the old days, recalling incidents which I thought I had forgotten. We laughed a good deal – laughter which meant a happy contentment, because Robert was safely home for a while and we could be together as we had been in the old days.

I looked forward to every day now. I found I was not thinking of Marcus all the time. It was only occasionally that some memory would come back to me with its little pangs of disappointment . . . of humiliation and longing.

I was anxious because when Robert fully recovered it was very likely that he would have to go to war again. But I learned to live for each day as it came along, which was not easy but which I knew was wise. To think of the future when we could not know what would happen, could result in fearful apprehension. In wartime there was a feeling of fatality. I guessed, from Robert's attitude, that he had acquired the skill of living in the present, and talking to him of the life out there on the battlefields of France and Belgium, I caught it from him.

So . . . I was happy during those days with Robert.

· He had changed a little. Such experiences as he had had must change anyone. He was more serious than he had been; there was a certain recklessness – an odd term to apply to Robert. What I mean is that I sensed a determination to savour the pleasures of the moment.

He used to tell me about his experiences so vividly that, as he talked, I could almost hear the gunfire, see the shells exploding round him; I could feel the claustrophobic atmosphere of trench warfare . . . the horror of going 'over the top' . . . of eating the ever-present tinned food.

'I was lucky in a way,' he said. 'A lot of my work was done in the field. It was this Morse thing. I didn't really understand it but by some fluke I could receive and transmit at a greater speed than most. It was just a knack . . . some odd way of my own of connecting the dots and dashes with certain landmarks. I won't attempt to explain, because it is quite crazy. But they thought I was this Morse genius. So my job was to go out with the mechanic who would fix up the telephones. Then I would spy out the land with my binoculars, discover where the enemy was massing . . . or where they had set up their guns . . . and send the message back to our lines. It was quite easy, quite simple. Jim, my mechanic, did all the hard work.'

'You always denigrate yourself, Robert. You are not a bit like most people.'

'Really, it was nothing, Lucinda. Quite easy. I was the lucky one . . . just because by chance I had this formula.'

'It was very clever of you to work it out.'

'I didn't work it out. It just came. However, that was what I was doing when I was hit.'

'You might have been left out there.'

'Oh, it wasn't all that bad. I was able to wait for the advance, and then I was taken back to base. After that, home. Your Uncle Gerald came to see me in the hospital. He said: "I don't see why you shouldn't go to Marchlands." I can tell you, Lucinda, it was like saying I was going to Heaven.'

'Oh . . . don't say that.'

'Heaven on Earth,' he corrected.

'Robert, how bad is your leg?'

'It's getting better. I don't suppose I shall ever walk as I did before, though.'

'Then . . . you couldn't go back.'

'Not at the moment certainly.'

'Not ever, Robert,' I said. 'I just could not bear it. You've told me so much about it. You've made me see it. I shall pray that your leg gets better . . . but slowly and that it is not really well until this wretched war is over.'

'Dear Lucinda,' he said. 'What a nice thing to say.'

There was great excitement in the hospital when the news came. Robert had won the Military Cross. Nobody was more astonished than Robert himself. He showed the letter to my mother who called me at once.

'Just listen to this,' she cried. 'Robert is a hero. He's got the Military Cross.'

'Really!'

'He was out in what they call No-Man's-Land, and sending messages back as to the enemy's whereabouts. He was wounded and could, for that reason, have returned to base, but he did not do so. He remained at his post and continued sending messages which were so vital that the guns which would otherwise have been destroyed by the enemy were saved. That's the gist of it. Robert is being decorated for his bravery.'

I embraced him, kissed him and wept over him.

'There wasn't anything else I could have done,' said Robert. 'I just went on . . . that was all.'

'Stop it, Robert,' I commanded. 'You were wonderful. You're a hero. You'll go to Buckingham Palace and have a medal pinned on you by the King.'

There were celebrations throughout the hospital.

Robert was embarrassed. 'Too much fuss,' he said. 'It might be a mistake. Really, I was just sending back those messages . . .'

'And saving the guns,' I cried. 'Shut up, Robert. You're a hero and we are going to see that everyone knows it.'

I think he was more pleased to see our delight than in his own success.

Aunt Belinda arrived at Marchlands with Annabelinda. They were both exuberant.

'Isn't it wonderful? Fancy, Robert . . .' cried Annabelinda.

Aunt Belinda said: 'We shall go to Buckingham Palace. The other Robert will come up for the occasion. We're so proud of him.'

'I'm glad to hear it,' I said.

'You look better, Lucinda,' said Annabelinda.

'Thank you.'

'I've got lots to tell you.'

'What have you been doing?'

'We're going to have a long talk . . . alone.'

Aunt Belinda was fussing round Robert. How was he, she wanted to know. She had been so pleased when she had heard he was going to Marchlands.

'I said to Robert: "Darling Lucie will look after him better than anyone. And Lucinda will be there. They were always such friends." It will be wonderful to go to the Palace.'

'Don't think it is going to be too grand,' said Robert. 'There'll be plenty of others there.'

'It's no use pretending it isn't wonderful, Robbie darling. I'm so proud of you. My little Robbie . . . a hero!'

'Oh, Mother, please . . .'

'He's just like his father,' said Aunt Belinda. 'They don't know how to get the best out of things. You're a hero, darling.

You saved those guns. Don't forget that and everyone is going to know it.'

Robert looked resigned and he and I exchanged smiles.

I should have liked to have been the one to go to the Palace with him, but of course too many could not go, and Uncle Robert, Aunt Belinda and Annabelinda were his immediate family.

I did have my chat with Annabelinda on the first day of their arrival. It was evening. Annabelinda had always liked bedtime chats.

She came to my room and sat on my bed.

'I have such news,' she said. 'It's not out yet, but it will be next week. You shall be the first to know.'

'What is it?'

'I'm going to be married. I am engaged . . . not officially yet. There has to be a proper announcement. His family, you see.'

'Engaged?' I said.

She lowered her eyes, as though she feared to look at me.

'To Marcus,' she said.

'Oh . . . congratulations.'

'Thank you. It's not supposed to be known yet, but I couldn't keep it from you. Besides, I wanted to tell you myself. His people . . . you've no idea. Their house is like a castle. That's the main house, where his parents live. When we're married, our house will be on the estate. It's quite grand . . . but you should see the ancestral home.'

'So you are very pleased.'

She grimaced. 'The family are a bit overpowering. I went up there with my parents. They've inspected me. It's like going back in time. All those old conventions. I can't imagine how I shall live up to them.'

'No,' I said. 'Nor can I.'

'Well, Marcus is marvellous. Right from the first, I knew.' She looked faintly defiant. 'So did he. And we'll have fun. I shall get him to buy a house in London. If he is going to stay at the War Office, he will have to. That wound makes him unfit for military service. It's going to be wonderful. It's only his old family that frightens me. Everything has to be just as it always has been . . . ceremonial. You've no idea. That's why Marcus is so different. You'd never guess, talking to him, that there had been all that discipline in his life.'

'When are you going to be married?'

'Well, first we have to announce the engagement. I've only just passed the first test. There will be more vetting, I imagine. They wanted to know all about my family. Marcus said that I'd charm his father and he'll know how to tackle his mother. I shall be all right. You know how respectable Daddy is. He's passed muster – socially and financially.'

'And your mother?'

'You know how charming she can be.'

'And you?'

She looked smug, and I said: 'Have you told Marcus?'

'Told him what?'

'About your past.'

'What do you mean?' she asked abruptly.

'Annabelinda, you know. I mean about Edward.'

She flushed scarlet. 'How can you be so unkind when I'm so happy?' she demanded.

'You haven't told him, then?'

'How could I?'

'Don't you think he ought to know?'

'It's all over. It was just a slip.'

'There is Edward.'

'He's just the little boy you brought from France. People do things like that in wartime. His parents were dead and you took him. Your people have adopted him because of your promise to his mother when she was dying. It's all . . . settled.'

'I thought perhaps you would feel that you must tell your future husband.'

'How could I? Lucinda, don't ever talk to me about it. It makes me so unhappy. You're jealous, I believe.'

'I am not. I should not like to have a secret like that on my conscience, and I could not be jealous of someone who had.

But it is not on your conscience, is it – for the simple reason that you haven't one.'

I was talking wildly. I was not sure whether I was angry with her because she was going to marry Marcus or because she talked of Edward as though he were not important.

She got up and went to the door.

'I shan't talk to you any more. I thought you would like to know. I thought you would be pleased that I had told you first.' She turned and faced me and went on appealingly: 'Lucinda, you wouldn't say a word . . . ?'

'Of course not. I haven't ever, have I? And I have known for a long time.'

'I think it would spoil everything.'

'I am sure Marcus would understand.'

'It's his family. I was surprised. I shouldn't have thought he would be afraid of anything. But he is in awe of his family. They've got to approve, Lucinda. I reckon he'd be cut off like that.' She snapped her fingers. 'Yes, he would, if he did something which was not in the family tradition.'

'Such as marrying a girl who had had an illegitimate child?'

'You're making it sound so awful.'

'It could have been for poor little Edward.'

'Well, it wasn't. And my grandfather Bourdon didn't think it was so strange. He said it happens here and there in families and the best thing is to get over it with as little fuss as possible. Lucinda, promise me, you'll never mention it again . . . to anyone.'

'I promise. I kept quiet before and perhaps it has turned out for the best. Edward is happy here. He has a good home and he'll be all right.'

'Then it is happily settled, isn't it? He's all right. That's all that matters.'

'Yes,' I said. 'I suppose so.'

She was looking happy again and I was sorry I had said what I had. That was how it was with Annabelinda. I might rail against her one moment, and the next I would be trying to placate her.

212

She came over and kissed me. 'I know I can always rely on you, Lucinda.'

'Well, I suppose you can.'

After she left, I could not stop myself thinking of Marcus. I was not really surprised that it had turned out in this way.

I did wonder whether at one time he had begun to care seriously for me. With Marcus one would never know. As for Annabelinda, she would go through life untroubled, I suspected. She would feel no guilt about her secret and her unacknowledged child simply because she had the gift of being able to shut out anything that was detrimental to herself. She was able to convince herself that it had never happened until someone – as I did – brought it up in such a way as to make it impossible to deny it had taken place.

Two weeks later there was an announcement in the papers of the engagement of Major Merrivale to Annabelinda Denver.

In due course Robert went to the Palace to receive his medal, Aunt Belinda, Uncle Robert and Annabelinda with him.

And afterwards he returned to Marchlands. Someone from the press came down; there was a piece in the paper about his gallantry and pictures were taken.

I thought Robert looked very fine in his uniform with the silver and mauve ribbon attached to his coat. There was no doubt that his family were very proud of him. There were tears in Uncle Robert's eyes and Aunt Belinda positively beamed.

She was very contented with life. Her son decorated for bravery, and her daughter – without a Season which would not have been possible during the war – was engaged to a very eligible young man.

The war was not so bad for Aunt Belinda and her family after all.

A Revelation

I was staying for a few days in London, as I did now and then. As I was spending more time in the hospital after Miss Carruthers's marriage, on this occasion I had come to town to make some arrangements about patients who would shortly be sent to Marchlands from one of the big hospitals. I also had some purchases to make.

It was pleasant to be with my father who would return with me to Marchlands at the weekend. He was very preoccupied at this time. I knew that he had a great deal on his mind, and I think he enjoyed dining quietly with me alone. In some respects he was more hopeful about the war. He told me that the first contingent of Americans was expected in June.

'This will have a demoralizing effect on the enemy,' he said. 'And we can do with their help, of course.'

'Do you think the end is in sight?'

'Well, perhaps not exactly in sight. Round the corner maybe. There's one thing that makes me uneasy.'

He sat biting his lips while I waited for him to go on.

Then he looked at me steadily and said: 'There's something wrong somewhere. Secrets – top secrets – are being betrayed.'

'How?'

He shrugged his shoulders. 'There are bound to be spies around. Even in peacetime they are here, and in wartime, although it is more difficult for them to operate, their efforts are intensified. But lately . . . You remember the affair at Milton Priory?'

'You never found out how that came about?'

He shook his head. 'Unfortunately, I was deeply involved

in that. I felt responsible. I am sure someone had been at my papers. It's unsettling. Well, we can only be watchful. But some of these people are devilishly clever.'

'Perhaps it will all be over soon. Won't that be wonderful?'

He agreed that it would.

It was the next day when Tom Green, one of the men from the stables at Marchlands, arrived at the house.

I was astonished to see him, and thought for the moment that something must be very wrong.

I must have betrayed my anxiety, for he said quickly: 'All's well at Marchlands, Miss Lucinda. It's just that a woman came. She seemed to be most upset, like . . . and wanted to give a letter to you, and, as I had to come up to London on an errand for Mrs Greenham to the hospital here, I thought I'd kill two birds with one stone, as the saying goes.'

'A woman?'

'Yes, Miss. Really upset she was . . . in quite a state. She asked for you. She didn't want to see anyone else. She was real distressed when I told her you were away.'

'Did she give her name?'

'No, Miss. All she said was she wanted to see Miss Lucinda Greenham, and when I said I wasn't sure when you'd be back, she said she would write a note to you. So I settled her down with pen and paper and she wrote and I gave her an envelope and she said to put this with a letter she'd brought and she said would I give it to you the moment you came back? I said I would. I was right down sorry for her. So I took the opportunity, like . . .'

'Give me the letters.'

He felt in his pocket and produced them. My name was written on one. It said: PRIVATE. URGENT.

I did not want to open it under the groom's curious eyes, so I said: 'Thanks. I'll see what this is all about.'

I went up to my room.

The other envelope was rather bulky and it was addressed to Major Merrivale.

I slit the envelope addressed to me. I took out the note. At the top of it was the address 23 Adelaide Villas, Maida Vale, London.

Dear Miss Greenham [I read],

I don't know whether I'm right in this, but it is something I must do.

Would you please give this letter to Major Merrivale? I don't know whether I should write to him in this way, but as he is in your hospital and he should know what's happening, I had to. I thought you looked like a kind young lady, and perhaps I could explain to you. But as you are away, I don't want to trust it with anyone else.

I saw your picture in the paper with the gentleman who won the medal and there was a bit about the hospital. I just thought you looked like the sort who would understand and help me.

Would you give this letter to Major Merrivale as soon as you can? I hope it won't be too late. It is very important to someone.

Yours truly,
Miss Emma Johns

I sat for a moment reading the letter and wondering what it could mean. Hadn't the stableman told her that Major Merrivale was no longer at the hospital? Of course not. She had not mentioned his name. She had just asked for me. It was clear that she did not want to tell anyone else to get a message to him. It must be something very important as she would only entrust it to me . . . because I had a kind face!

It was very mysterious.

Obviously I should get the letter to Major Merrivale without delay. But I did not know where he was. I had heard that he had a small pied-à-terre in London, but where, I did not know. Nor had I ever heard the address of his home in the country.

Annabelinda could help me. But would it be wise to give her the letter? I detected some urgent plea in the note addressed to me that I alone should deliver the envelope.

I was not sure what to do.

I read the note again. '23 Adelaide Villas, Maida Vale.' As I was in London, I could go there. I could explain to Miss Emma Johns that the Major was no longer at the hospital and that I did not know how to reach him, unless she would wish me to pass on the letter to his fiancée.

The more I thought of it, the more I liked the idea, for I must confess that I was very curious to know what this was all about.

So that very morning I took a cab to Maida Vale.

Adelaide Villas was a pleasant crescent of small houses, all alike and not without charm. I knocked at No. 23. The door was opened by a woman of about thirty and I guessed at once that she was Miss Emma Johns.

I said: 'Miss Emma Johns?'

She nodded, staring at me, and I saw recognition dawn in her eyes. The picture which had been taken of me with Robert when the local press had come down to write a little piece about his getting his decoration must have been a good likeness.

I went on: 'I'm Lucinda Greenham.'

'Oh . . . please come in.'

I stepped into a small hall. She opened a door and I was in what was obviously a sitting-room – neat, tidy and well cared for.

She told me to sit down and I said at once: 'I came because I was unsure what to do. The fact is, Major Merrivale is no longer at Marchlands Hospital.'

'Oh,' she said blankly.

'I thought the best thing to do was to come and see you, as I happened to be in London. I was not quite sure how to act. There seemed a certain amount of secrecy.'

She was clasping and unclasping her hands.

'It's an awkward situation,' she said at length. 'I wouldn't have dreamed of writing to the Major but for Janet being so ill. She's not got long, you see.'

'Janet?'

'She's my sister. I look after her and the children.'

217

'And . . . er . . . you wanted . . . ?'

She was silent again, frowning.

'You've been so good to come,' she went on. 'That was kind. I knew you'd be kind. And I thought if I could get to see you and talk to you, it would be all right. You could have given him the letter and no one else know . . . if you see what I mean.'

'Up to a point,' I replied. 'But I think if I knew what this was all about, I might be able to help more.'

'Well, you see, I have always been with them. Janet . . . she's my sister. She's a bit younger than me . . . eight years. She was always so pretty. I'd looked after her since our mother died. Soon after Janet was born, in fact. She's always been like my baby. I don't rightly know . . .'

'Is it something you'd rather not tell me?'

'I'm that uncertain. I really want her to see him before she goes.'

'Goes?'

'She hasn't got long to live. It's her chest. I knew it was coming. She's had this weakness for some years, and there are the little ones. Oh, I know they'll be all right. But it's just that she wants to see him before she goes, like.'

'I'll do what I can to help. I don't know where the Major is living, but I can find out. But as there was all this secrecy I wondered how to act and whether I ought to see you first.'

'I don't know. The young lady he is going to marry . . . You see, I don't know whether it would be right. I don't want to upset the Major. He's been so good. It would finish Janet off if she thought she'd made trouble for him. She loves him, you see. Otherwise it would never have been. And he's always been so good to us all.'

'I am just wondering how I can help. If you told me . . .'

She hesitated and then seemed to come to a decision.

'Well,' she said, 'there was never any deceiving or that sort of thing. Janet went as parlourmaid in some grand house in the country. He was a guest. He saw her and that was that. He made it quite clear in the beginning and Janet, who knew how these things worked out, understood right away. It was her decision, and she's never regretted it. He bought this place for her and when Martin came along, I moved in with her. It suited us all. And then there was Eva. It was a happy little family. We had some good times. And there was never any trouble about how we were to live. There was always the money coming, regular as clockwork. Oh, he was good to us. Special presents and all that sort of thing. Janet was a very happy woman. She'd always known there couldn't be a marriage and she got along very well without it.'

'I understand,' I said.

'The last thing Janet would want would be to make trouble for him when he's been so good to her. But you see, she hasn't got long and if he knew, he'd want to see her as much as she wants to see him. She knows the children will be all right . . . but she wants to make sure.'

'Yes, of course.'

'And if anyone got to know . . . if it came out, I mean . . . she'd never forgive me for bringing it out like this. There was that bit in the paper about him being engaged . . . so I thought . . . well, I had to do something.'

I said: 'An idea has just struck me. I don't know why I didn't think of it before. My uncle is in the same regiment. It is very likely that he would know the Major's address in London. He is in London just now . . . briefly . . . but I could get in touch with him. And if you would like me to deliver the letter to the Major, I would do so.'

'Oh yes . . . yes, I'd trust you.'

'Then that is what I will do.'

'Thank you. Poor Janet. She doesn't complain, but it is her dearest wish to see him. She just wants to thank him for all the happiness he has given her, and tell him she doesn't regret it. She wants to make sure for the children, too. I have an idea that, now he will soon be married, he doesn't regret anything from the past any more than she does . . .'

The door opened and a boy looked in. He must have been about eight or nine years old.

'It's all right, Martin,' said Miss Emma Johns. 'Where's Eva?'

A very pretty little girl put her head round the door.

'Well, both of you, run along. There's good children. I'll be with you soon.'

They both eyed me with a certain curiosity, as I did them. I fancied there was a look of Marcus about them.

The door shut on them and I rose to go.

I said: 'If I am successful in getting the address from my uncle, I will take the letter and let you know I have done so. I expect the Major will come to see you then.'

'It is a long time since we have seen him. Since the war started, he has been away fighting and then in the hospital. There was no holding up of the money. That's paid into a bank. There is some solicitor doing it. I've never seen any letters from them. It was all arranged like that. I didn't know which way to turn. You've been a great help, Miss Greenham.'

'Well, if I couldn't get in touch with my uncle, I could ask the . . . the fiancée. But perhaps you wouldn't want that?'

'Oh no, Miss Greenham. I wouldn't want it to get to her ears. You never know . . . you understand?'

I did understand perfectly. I said: 'Well, I will let you know what happens. And if I can get the address, I will deliver the letter personally into the hands of Major Merrivale.'

I left her then and made my way home.

I thought it was an ironical twist of fate that both the prospective bride and groom should have children whose identity must remain secret from the other.

I went immediately to Uncle Gerald's London house. As I had expected, he was not at home, but Aunt Hester was very helpful.

'Oh yes,' she said. 'I can give you Marcus's address. He won't be in the country just now. He'll be in London. He's taken a house temporarily but I believe he often goes to the country for weekends . . . when he can get away. Or he might be at the Denvers'. There is all this preparation for the wedding. I think they are all very pleased about it, and it will be good to see Annabelinda settled. Let me get the address for you.'

Aunt Hester was a very practical woman, without much imagination, and such people can be very useful at times. She did not ask any awkward questions as some might have done, and very soon I was on my way to Marcus's London address.

I could not hope that I should find him there and I did not, so I left a note asking him to get in touch with me immediately, telling me when I could see him, as I had something for him which I believed was urgent.

It was about five in the afternoon when he called at the house. My father was not at home, so I could see him without any questions being asked.

I received him in the drawing-room and I could not suppress a certain exhilaration as he came into the room. He looked even more handsome than I remembered, and his slight limp did not make him less attractive. He looked at me as though I were the one person in the world whom he most wanted to see.

'Lucinda!' he said. 'What a pleasure to see you! I can't tell you how delighted I was to receive your note.'

'I'm so glad you came. I've been rather anxious about this.'

He looked gravely concerned and I told him what had happened. I was amazed how calmly he received the information.

'And this is the letter I have for you.'

He took it, glanced at it and put it into his pocket.

'I believe it is very urgent,' I said. 'Miss Emma Johns was rather distressed.'

'I understand,' he said. 'I will deal with it at once.'

'Then I had better not keep you.'

He looked distressed and I reminded myself that he did not mean that he wanted to be with me so much. It was all playacting. I should never allow myself to be so deceived again.

'And how are *you*, Lucinda?' he said.

'Well, thank you, and I see you have recovered your health.'

221

'Yes, but they won't let me go out again. I'm stuck here in London.'

'There are many, I dare say, who are pleased about that.'

'Does that include you, Lucinda?'

'Naturally, one likes to think one's friends are in comparative safety.'

'And I hear you have Robert Denver with you.'

'Yes. He has a leg wound too.'

'Which you are hoping will keep him in comparative safety?'

'Of course.'

'He's a noble hero, isn't he?'

'He is very brave and I am glad that his bravery has been recognized.'

'It is always good when people get their deserts.' He grimaced slightly, and I could not help smiling.

I said: 'I think that letter needs your immediate attention.'

'Would you excuse me if I read it now?'

'I think you should do that.'

He sat down and slit the envelope. I watched him as he read.

His expression remained impassive. I did not know what he was feeling. He was a superb actor.

'If you feel you should leave . . .'

'How understanding you are! I think I must leave. It is disappointing that our meeting should be so brief.' He took my hands and looked searchingly into my face. 'But we shall meet again . . . often. It has been so long.'

'You are going to be busy,' I reminded him. 'Weddings need much preparation.'

'I often think of you, Lucinda.'

'Oh, do you? Well, I wish you happiness, and I hope everything goes as you wish.'

There was no mistaking his show of reluctance at leaving, and I wondered how much of it was genuine.

I was very disturbed. All that day I could not stop myself thinking of him and his affairs.

*

222

The next morning I called at the Maida Vale address. Miss Emma Johns opened the door and invited me in.

'It was so good of you,' she said. 'I knew that I could trust you to do all that should be done.'

'I am sure he will come,' I said.

'Oh, he came last night.'

'It must have been just after I gave him the letter. I discovered his address through my aunt, and I went at once to see him.'

'Thank you. Thank you. I can't tell you what happiness his visit brought to Janet. She'll die peacefully now. He saw the children too. He's always been good to them. He has assured her that everything will be all right. Their future is taken care of and there is nothing for us to worry about. He is such a good man . . . a dear man. I don't know how to thank you, Miss Greenham, I knew you'd help. I knew I shouldn't have to worry if I could see you and explain.'

'I am so pleased I was able to be of use.'

'Janet's sleeping peacefully now. She blessed him and said she hoped he'd be happy in his marriage. She said his bride was the luckiest woman in the world. Poor Janet, she did love him so much. He was wonderful with her. I heard her laughing. I know now she'll die happy. She knows he still cares for her and she always understood how it had to be. Thank you again, Miss Greenham, for all you have done.'

'It was really very little.'

'You'll never know how much.'

I came away from Maida Vale feeling I had learned another vital lesson about human nature.

I wondered what the general opinion would be about Marcus and his secret family hidden away in Maida Vale. But what happiness he had brought to that family. The unselfishness of genuine love was brought home to me. Janet Johns was prepared to remain the mistress in the background of his life; she was happy to accept what he could give her and be content. She must have loved him very much.

I learned something about him too. He was superficial, but

223

he certainly knew how to inspire devotion. It occurred to me that we were all complicated beings and that none of us should stand in judgement against any other.

A few days later I received a letter from Marcus.

My dear Lucinda.

How kind of you to act as go-between in this matter! You especially would understand. Thank you for all the trouble you took. Everyone concerned is most grateful. You have acted as I would expect you to . . . with the utmost kindness and tact.

I hope all goes well with you always. Annabelinda has told me how delighted you are to have her brother with you. She has explained to me what truly great friends you are.

I am hoping to see you soon.

Admiring you, as ever,

Marcus.

I thought how typical of him that letter was. He treated the matter of his secret family as though it were nothing unusual; and the fact that I shared in the secrecy did not perturb him in the least. Who but Marcus would have skimmed over the exposure of his liaison with such composure?

I still found myself thinking of him rather tenderly.

The Man in the Forest

In the July of 1917 Annabelinda and Marcus were married.

With my parents, Aunt Celeste and Robert, I went down to the Denver home for the occasion.

Aunt Belinda greeted us with suppressed excitement. There was no doubt of her satisfaction in the marriage.

'Marcus's parents will be arriving the day before the ceremony,' she told us. 'I think they will be leaving the day after.' She grimaced. 'They are very grand, of course, not like Marcus, who is the dearest man. I think he is a little in awe of them. Annabelinda says she feels very much as if she is on approval. However, they can't do much after the wedding, can they? I'm exaggerating, of course. I'm sure they'll be very nice guests. They'll adore Big Robert . . . and my young one too. Those two get on with most people. In any case, the Denver family goes back as far as theirs. It just happens they didn't manage to secure a dukedom on the way. All they got was a baronetcy.'

'I wouldn't worry about such a trivial matter, if I were you,' said my mother.

'Who's talking about being worried, Lucie? Certainly I'm not. Nothing can go wrong. Once this ring is on my daughter's finger and it is all signed and sealed, the matter is closed. And at least Marcus is a darling. We all adore him. They will be leaving almost immediately after the ceremony for the honeymoon. It's a pity they can't go somewhere romantic like Florence or Venice. But it will have to be Torquay . . . and then Marcus has to get back to work. Wars are such a bore. They spoil everything.'

'Yes,' said my mother. 'People's lives and even honey-moons.'

'Still the same old Lucie. But in spite of everything, this is fun. Wait till you see Annabelinda's wedding dress.'

'I am sure it's magnificent,' said my mother.

Marcus's parents arrived. His father was affable and obviously quite fascinated by Aunt Belinda, who had made a great effort to attract him. His mother was undoubtedly formidable. She was gracious rather than friendly; and I guessed at once that it was she who was so insistent in reminding them of their ancient lineage and *noblesse oblige*.

Fleetingly I wondered what she would have said if she had known of Annabelinda's lapse from virtue. I had a feeling that she would have done everything in her power to prevent the marriage – and that power would have been great.

I sat in church next to Robert. I watched Annabelinda come down the aisle on Sir Robert's arm. They looked very well together; he tall and very pleasant-looking, because of that expression of goodwill towards the world of which I had always been aware, chiefly because his son had inherited it. As for Annabelinda, she was startlingly beautiful in a dress of white satin and lace, and there was a wreath of orange blossom in her hair.

The marriage ceremony began and I saw Marcus put the ring on her finger. I listened to them taking their vows. And I could not stop myself imagining that I was there in her place. I had had my dreams and an occasion like this brought home to me how ridiculous I had been.

'It is experience,' my mother would have said. 'You learn something from it.'

What I had learned was that I must never deceive myself again.

The strains of the Wedding March flowed out and there they were – surely one of the most handsome couples who had ever been married in this church, coming down the aisle and looking wonderfully happy.

Then we went back to the Denver home for the reception.

Aunt Belinda was greeting everyone, saying what a beautiful service it had been, what a handsome bridegroom, what a beautiful bride. They were cutting the cake . . . Annabelinda wielding the knife and Marcus helping her, then drinking the champagne from the Denver cellars. Speeches followed.

Aunt Celeste was standing beside me.

'Aren't they charming?' she said. 'Just what a bride and groom should be. I wish my brother were here to see them.'

'I wonder what Monsieur Jean Pascal is doing now?'

She shook her head.

'You haven't heard anything?' I asked.

She shook her head again. 'It could not be easy to get news. I don't know where the enemy is in his area. One doesn't hear anything.'

'They wouldn't have gone to Valenciennes, I suppose. That would be very close to the fighting.'

'My brother himself was hardly ever there. The Princesse went now and then. I dare say they are at the *château*. I wish I could get some news.'

'It's nearly three years since all this started. I can't believe it.'

Aunt Celeste nodded. 'I am so relieved that you and Annabelinda were able to get home.'

'Yes, thanks to Marcus.'

'And how romantic this has turned out. It has made me think a lot about my brother. It would have been wonderful if he had been able to be here today.'

Robert came up.

'You look sad,' he said. 'Why is it that there is always an element of sadness about weddings?'

'They remind people of so much,' I said.

'Yes, I suppose so. Let me fill your glasses.'

He signed to the waiters while Aunt Celeste stared ahead, thinking of her brother who was somewhere in France.

The speeches were over, the bride and groom had left for Torquay. Robert said to me: 'It's hot in here. Too many people. Let's slip outside.'

I was glad to and we went into the gardens.

'It's beautiful out here,' I said.

'You like it, don't you?'

'I always have. I used to love coming here when I was little. You were always nice to me, Robert. Although I was quite a bit younger than you, you never reminded me of it, like Annabelinda, who did all the time.'

'Oh, no one takes any notice of Annabelinda.'

'I did. She's two years older than I and never let me forget it.'

'Well, you are old enough now not to be concerned about those two years.' He stood still, looking about him. 'There is something special about one's own home,' he said. 'Somehow it seems as though it is a part of you.'

'I know.'

'The paddock over there. I used to ride round and round on my pony, feeling very adventurous. I'll never forget the first day I was let off the leading rein. There's the old oak tree. I climbed that once. I'd done something I shouldn't have and I thought I'd hide myself so that they couldn't find me.'

'I can't think you ever did anything very bad.'

'Oh, please,' he said. 'You make me sound impossible. I was always in trouble with Nanny Aldridge, I can tell you.'

'Well, very minor peccadilloes, I am sure.'

'You're laughing at me.'

'Well, you are, and always have been, good. One could rely on you . . . unlike Annabelinda.'

'You mean dull.'

'Why do people think goodness is synonymous with dullness?'

'Because it is often a kind way of saying one is unimaginative.'

'And winning medals on the battlefield?'

'That was chance. A lot of people deserved them and didn't get noticed.'

'I won't listen to such talk. You were never dull and I always loved it when you arrived.'

'Lucinda, will you marry me?'

I was silent and he went on: 'It is what I have always wanted. I know that both our families will be delighted.'

I could still find nothing to say. I could not plead surprise, for there had always been this very special friendship between us, but on Annabelinda's wedding day, when I was admitting to myself that I had had very tender feelings towards her bridegroom, was not the time. My emotions were in too much of a turmoil.

I heard myself stammer: 'Robert . . . it's too soon. I hadn't thought . . .'

'I understand,' he said. 'You want to think about it. Marriage is a serious undertaking.'

Still I was silent. To marry Robert! Everything would be pleasant, comforting. I should live here in this beautiful place. My mother would be delighted. She loved Robert, as so many people did. Annabelinda would be my sister-in-law. It was strange that that should be one of the first thoughts that occurred to me.

Robert was saying: 'I know you like me, Lucinda. I mean *you* don't really find me dull.'

'Do get that foolish notion out of your head. You are not dull and I am very, very fond of you.'

'But . . .' he said sadly.

'It's just too soon.'

A smile crossed his face. 'I didn't lead up to it, did I? I just blundered in. Trust me.'

'No, Robert. It's not that at all. It is just that I don't feel ready.'

'Let's leave it. Forget I said anything. We'll talk about it some other time.'

'Yes, do let's. You know how happy I always am with you. I was so pleased when you came to Marchlands. But just now . . .'

'You don't have to explain. I am going to ask you again.'

I turned to him and put my arms round him and for a few seconds he held me against him.

'Yes, Robert,' I said. 'Just a little time, please.'

'That's fine. I'll ask you again. There's one thing I haven't told you.'

'What is that?'

'I have to go before a medical board in three weeks' time.'

'What does that mean?' I asked in alarm.

'They'll assess how fit I am.'

'They couldn't possibly send you out there again!'

'We'll have to see.'

Some of the guests were coming out into the garden and Aunt Celeste joined us.

I felt very unsettled and disturbed. I could not bear the thought of Robert's leaving England.

I was relieved when Robert's visit to the medical board had to be postponed. There was a slight complication with his leg. It needed more rest, Dr Egerton decided, and therefore the medical board would have to wait for a few weeks.

Edward was now four years old. I was not sure of the actual date of his birth, but my mother had suggested we make it the fourth of August. That was the date when Britain had declared war on Germany.

'Let us have something pleasant to remember it by, as well as all the horror,' said my mother.

Edward was now quite a person. He was very curious about everything, full of energy, quite fluent and very amusing. We all thought he was an exceptionally bright child, and it was a little more than prejudice, I do believe, that made us feel this.

He was interested in birthdays because they meant parties. He had been to one or two with other children in the neighbourhood and now it was his turn.

We invited about ten local children. There was a cake with four candles and Andrée and I, with help from my mother when she could spare the time, planned some games which would be suitable for the children.

Edward was devoted to Andrée, but I think he had a rather special feeling for me. I had always tried to be with him as much as possible. In spite of the fact that I myself had had an excellent nanny, my mother had always been closer to me than anyone else. I wanted Edward to feel the same about me. I wanted to make up for his mother's callous desertion and the loss of his loving foster-mother. I did not want him to be deprived of anything in life.

I used to read a story to him every night before he went to sleep, and I knew how much he looked forward to that.

Andrée used to say: 'He loves me as his nanny, but you as his mother.'

'Poor child,' I said. 'How sad it all was for him.'

'Don't expect me to feel pity for him!' she retorted. 'I think he is one of the luckiest of children. Here he is, with every luxury . . . surrounded by love. He's got your mother, you, me . . . and the servants all dote on him and would spoil him if I didn't look out.'

'It's because he is adorable.'

I could see she was thinking of her own childhood which had been so different. Poor Andrée! I was so glad that she seemed happier with us.

There were ten children in all at the party. But the nursery was a big room. It would be the schoolroom later, as it had been such a short time ago when I had studied with Miss Carruthers. Books were stacked in the cupboard; the big table with the ink-stains on it was covered by a white cloth on which stood jellies, tarts and scones, and in pride of place, the birthday cake.

There was great fun with Edward's trying to blow out the candles while the others crowded round and consumed with relish, and after the food was cleared away, we played games.

There was a good deal of laughing and shouting. 'Pass the parcel' was a great favourite, with everyone shrieking with delight when the music stopped and the one who was holding the parcel took off another wrapper, and more expressions of delight when the music started again and the parcel went on its way, to fall as a prize into the hands of the child who held it when the music finally stopped and a painting box was revealed.

They scrambled their way through musical chairs and statues. Andrée was a very good organizer and was able to control the children with the right amount of benevolent authority, which is essential on such occasions.

As it was a fine day, we went into the garden and there they could run about as much as they wished. When it was time for the guests to go, Edward, standing beside me, received their thanks with dignity. Andrée had gone up to the nursery and Edward and I were alone.

I smiled down at him. 'It was a good party, wasn't it?' I said.

'It was a good party.' He had a habit of repeating such statements as if he were in agreement with them.

'So now,' I went on, 'you are well and truly four years old.'

'Next time I'll be five.'

'Yes, five years old.'

'Then six, seven and eight.'

'You're making the years go too quickly.'

'When I'm ten, I'll go riding without James.'

'Yes, I dare say. Where do you like to ride best?'

'I like the forest best.'

'Do you ride there with Andrée?'

He nodded. 'James too. Sometimes just Andrée.'

'And you like that?'

He nodded again. 'I like the forest.'

'Why?'

'Trees,' he said. 'And people.'

'People?'

'The man.'

'What man?'

'Andrée's man.'

'Andrée meets a man, does she?'

He nodded.

'What? Every time?'

232

'A lot of times. They talk. They walk the horses. Andrée keeps looking at me. She says, "Stay there, Edward."'

'And do you stay there?'

He nodded.

'Do you know the man? Is he someone from the hospital?'

He shook his head vigorously.

'So, he's a stranger?'

'He's a stranger.' He mouthed the word and repeated it as he often did when he heard a word for the first time.

'The forest's nice,' he said. 'When I'm five I won't have a leading rein. I'll ride fast. I'll gallop . . .'

'I am sure you will.'

I was thinking about Andrée's meeting with a stranger. A man. Well, she was young; she was quite good-looking. It hadn't occurred to me before that she might have an admirer.

We were half way through September and Robert was still with us. Dr Egerton still was not entirely satisfied and thought that a little more rest was needed. He said he wanted to keep his eye on this patient for a little longer.

We were all relieved. Often I would feel Robert's eyes on me wistfully and I wanted then to do anything to comfort him, and I was fully aware of how miserable I should be if he went away, and what terrible anxiety I should suffer wondering what was happening to him. The third Battle of Ypres had begun and there was particularly bitter fighting at this time. The casualties were great. I used to shudder when bad cases were brought to us, and I always thought: That might have been Robert.

Sybil Egerton talked about him to me. We had grown accustomed to calling her Sybil now. Mrs Egerton was too formal and she was no longer Miss Carruthers. She was at the hospital every day, arriving with her husband and staying until early evening. She was very efficient, practical, a little brisk and quite unsentimental. This suited some of those who were severely wounded, for she made them feel that they were not so badly off as they had imagined, and that there were others far worse. She used to read to those whose eyesight was damaged, and it made my mother and me smile to see her in one of the little rooms with those who could get there, reading Dickens to them. It was like a small class and she was very much the schoolmistress, but it happened to be just the treatment they needed. Marrying the doctor had added to her stature.

She announced to me in her straightforward manner: 'Robert Denver is in love with you.'

I did not answer and she went on: 'He is a good man and you could not find anyone more suited to you.'

'I've known him all my life,' I said.

'So much the better. He is the antithesis of his sister.'

'I know.'

'I'm sure he would make you happy. Marriage is the ideal state . . . providing it is the right marriage.'

Having found satisfaction herself in this state, she felt herself qualified to help others to do likewise.

She was smiling wisely at me, indicating that if I needed any advice on the matter, I should come to her.

My mother also talked to me of Robert.

'It seems odd to want to hold back someone's recovery, but I do hope Robert stays with us a little longer. Surely this miserable war must come to an end soon. He does care for you, you know.'

'Sybil was talking about him.'

'Oh yes, she was telling me how pleased she would be to see you settled. I think you are very fond of Robert.'

'Yes, I am. He . . . he has asked me.'

'You haven't said no.'

'I am not sure . . .'

'I see. He's a good man, Lucinda. One of the best. He's like his father. Who but Sir Robert would have put up with Belinda all these years?'

'I can't be hurried into anything so serious.'

'You're not still thinking of . . . ?'

It was always thus between us. We knew each other's minds so well that we followed the working of them without having to put it into words.

'My dear Lucinda,' she said. 'It's all for the best that it ended like this. I don't think you would have been happy with him. He is very attractive, has all the social graces, but there is something superficial about him . . . something too worldly. You would have been disappointed. You're not like that at all. You're honest and sincere. He was brought up in a different atmosphere from the one you were. There would have been irritations in time.'

'Whereas I've known Robert all my life.'

'That's no drawback.'

'There are no surprises,' I said. 'It's all so predictable.'

'Marcus came to you in a dramatic way. It was all rather romantic . . . not so much while you were living it perhaps, but when you look back. That's what so often happens in life. The things we anticipate with such excitement and look back on and find so amusing are often quite uncomfortable while we are actually living them. As I say, he appeared on the scene; he took charge of everything; he took you out of danger. Of course he seems romantic. At one time I thought you and he . . . I tried to reconcile myself, but I didn't really like it because I felt it wouldn't work. He's charming, but he's suave. I know people like him. He goes out of his way to please, but somehow I don't think his feelings go deep . . . if you know what I mean. He seemed to be very interested in you . . . until Annabelinda appeared again. I know she made a dead set at him, but she couldn't have forced him to ask her to marry him, could she? He had to want to . . . and he asked her so soon. Sometimes, my dearest Lucinda, something happens in life which hurts, but when it's past you can look back on it and see that it is all for the best.'

I nodded and she came to me and kissed me.

'The war must soon be over,' she said. 'Then everything will work out well for us all, I know. We shall all be looking at things differently . . . more normally, more naturally.'

I hoped she was right.

I thought a great deal about what she had said. Robert would go away soon. Perhaps I should never see him again. Perhaps my mother and Sybil were right. Perhaps I should marry him. It was what he wanted. Sometimes I thought I wanted it too.

Why did I hesitate? Because I was not like Marcus and could not turn to another so easily. He was so different from Robert – what they called a 'man of the world'. He had a secret family and had been almost nonchalant about it, as though it were natural for a man in his position. Perhaps it was.

I did still think of him with pangs of longing, and I often wondered how he and Annabelinda were getting on together.

I found during that period that I wanted to be alone, to think about what was happening. Perhaps in wartime, with death and separation constantly at hand, one saw things less clearly than one did in the calmness of peace. Then life went on predictably – or more or less so. During war, one never knew when one was going to hear bad news; one never knew what catastrophe was going to strike.

I liked to sit on an overturned tree-trunk in one part of the forest which had been lying there for as long as I could remember. It was quiet and peaceful there; the trees growing thickly round it made it a secluded spot.

I was constantly asking myself why I hesitated about accepting Robert's proposal.

Accept him, said common sense. You should marry one day. You want children. Look how you feel about Edward. As my mother said, I had seen Marcus in a romantic light . . . escaping from danger with him when he was like some hero from an old legend. But he had not turned out to be what I had believed. He had made me care for him and then had quickly turned from me to Annabelinda. And then I had made that discovery about his secret life. I wondered how many secrets there were in his life. With Robert one would always know. Everything he did would be open and honest.

And as I sat there brooding I was aware of the sound of horses' hoofs. Someone was riding nearby. I heard voices. Andrée and Edward. I would surprise them. I made my way through the trees. There was a small clearing just beyond and it was from this direction that the voices came.

I emerged from the trees and there they were. Edward was on his pony; Andrée was holding the leading rein and with them was a man.

Immediately I remembered my conversation with Edward when he had told me that they met a man in the forest.

'Hello,' I called out.

There was silence, broken by Edward who shouted: 'Lucinda.'

I advanced: and then I clearly saw the man to whom Andrée was talking. For a few moments we stared at each other.

Andrée said: 'Oh, hello.'

The man took off his hat and bowed.

'Goodbye,' he said. And to Andrée: 'Thanks.' Then he disappeared through the trees.

I thought I was dreaming. When he had taken off his hat, I was sure. I recognized that thick yellow hair. It was Carl Zimmerman.

I felt stunned. Then I wondered if I had been mistaken. True, it was only the third time I had seen him and always in strange circumstances: long ago outside the cubbyhole; in the gardens of La Pinière; and now, here in the forest, talking to Andrée. What could it mean?

I said: 'Who was that?'

'He was asking the way,' she said.

'I . . . I thought it was someone I knew.'

'Really?'

Edward said: 'You found us, Lucinda.'

'Yes, I found you.'

'Like hide-and-seek. Can we play hide-and-seek when we get home?'

237

'I dare say we might,' promised Andrée.

I wanted to ask questions about the man whom I believed to be Carl Zimmerman, but I did not feel I could do so in front of Edward. One can never be sure how much children understand. They often appear to be not listening when they are taking in everything. I kept thinking that, if it had been Carl Zimmerman, he would be seeing his son for the first time. He would not know, of course, but what might have been an ordinary encounter in the forest had taken on a dramatic turn.

Secrets, I thought. Everywhere there were secrets.

I took the first opportunity of talking to Andrée.

I said: 'That man you were with . . .'

She wrinkled her brows and looked puzzled.

'The man you were talking to when I came upon you in the forest.'

'Oh, you mean the one who was asking the way?'

'Yes. I just wondered if you'd seen him before?'

'No. Why should you think that?'

'Oh, it was something Edward said about your meeting a man in the forest.'

'Edward?'

'Yes, he said he'd seen a man.'

She flushed slightly. 'Oh, he must have meant Tom Gilroy.'

'Isn't he one of the male nurses?'

'Yes. The big strong one.'

'Oh, I know.'

'Well, we have been rather friendly, and we have met once or twice in the forest.'

'Oh, I see.' I smiled. It was natural that a girl like Andrée should have an admirer. But I was still shocked by the encounter with Carl Zimmerman. Then I began to think I might have been mistaken.

The stranger who had asked Andrée the way must just have looked like him. After all, the meeting had been over in a few minutes.

*

1917 was coming to an end. It had been a momentous year. There had been a revolution in Russia and the armistice between that country and Germany had released more German forces to be used on the Western Front.

Nearer home, just before Christmas, Robert had been called to the medical board in London and pronounced fit for military service. The news depressed us considerably, though Robert took it philosophically.

'Couldn't hang on much longer,' he said with a grimace.

'Oh Robert,' I cried and clung to him.

I almost said that we should become engaged. If he had pressed me then, I should have said I would marry him. I kept telling myself that I loved him. He was far more perceptive than he pretended to be, and I believe he did not want to force me to a decision until I was absolutely sure.

Just after Christmas he came down to Marchlands and told us that he was going to do a course on Salisbury Plain and would be there for six weeks.

We were jubilant.

'Six weeks!' said my mother. 'And the course does not start until mid-January. It's a reprieve.'

'You're very fond of Robert, aren't you?' I said.

'My dear Lucinda, who could help being fond of Robert? He's one of the nicest people I know.'

I felt that I was being gently nudged towards Robert, which made me feel I wanted to hold off. I could see what the future would be. The Denver estate would be my home, Aunt Belinda my mother-in-law, Annabelinda my sister-in-law.

I should be close to my own family, of course. I should see Marcus often. But perhaps he and Annabelinda would go off to foreign places – Bombay, Madras, Colombo. My life would be very little different from what it always had been.

My father came down to Marchlands for most weekends.

'He looks a little strained,' said my mother. 'I do hate his being alone up there for most of the week.'

He and my mother went for walks in the forest. I think he

had very few secrets from her and I sensed that they were both uneasy.

It was January. Robert was no longer at Marchlands, for he had left for the course.

My mother said: 'It doesn't seem the same without him. He is always so cheerful, so understanding. I think you miss him very much, Lucinda.'

'Yes, I do.'

'I have an idea. Why don't you get away from Marchlands for a while? Why not go to London and be with your father? I worry about him up there on his own. You'd be company for him.'

It did seem a good idea, for I was missing Robert very much.

I was getting worried. There was no sign of an end to the war, and when the course was finished, Robert would have to go out there into danger. There would be less to remind me of him in London and I should see him when he came back from the course.

I said: 'I should miss Edward. And I think he rather depends on me.'

'Perhaps he and Andrée could go up with you. Then you'd have plenty to do.'

'Andrée might not be so eager.'

'She seems to enjoy trips to London.'

'Yes. But now she is getting friendly with Tom Gilroy, I think.'

'Really? Nice man, Tom.'

'So I think and, apparently, so does she.'

'How did you know?'

'Edward rather betrayed it.'

'Edward?'

'He told me that they met a man in the forest. And Andrée told me it was Tom Gilroy.'

'Oh, I'm glad.'

'Why do people who are happily married want to arrange marriages for everyone else?'

'Because they want them to enjoy similar marital bliss, of course.'

We laughed.

'Sound out Andrée,' said my mother. 'See what she says. She need not be there all the time if she's so anxious to be with Tom.'

I did sound out Andrée. I was amazed at her response. Her eyes lit up.

'Oh yes, I should like to go to London for a spell,' she said.

'I thought perhaps you might not . . . now . . .'

'It would be exciting for a while.'

'Do you think Edward would like it?'

'He'll like it if we're there, though he might have a few qualms at being parted from his new pony.'

'We shall come back most weekends.'

'Then there will be a reunion with his pony. He will love it.'

At dinner that night, my mother said to my father: 'Lucinda is coming up to London for a while to look after you. She thinks you're looking peaky.'

He smiled at me. 'Thank you, Lucinda. Let's go for a nice long walk tomorrow morning, and we'll have a chat.'

I felt there was something significant about that remark and that there was some special reason why my parents wanted me to go to London, apart from the fact that they both thought that a change of scene might stop my brooding over Robert's departure for the Front.

I was right, as I learned in the forest next morning.

It was an ideal day for walking. There was a brisk chill in the air, but a wintry sun could be seen between the clouds and the wind was less penetrating among the protective trees.

The forest was the natural place to walk. We had done so all our lives. There was a certain feeling of security there. One could talk without being overheard.

My father took my arm and said: 'Lucinda, I want to talk to you very seriously. I have discussed this with your mother and we both think you might be able to help.'

241

'I?'

'Yes, listen. We are very distressed.'

'Distressed? Who?'

'I . . . and my friends. You know, don't you, that I am involved in certain work?'

'I know there has always been something of a mystery . . . and that it was not concerned with your parliamentary life.'

He nodded. 'There is no need for me to tell you that I am talking to you very confidentially.'

'I do understand that.'

'Lives could be at risk. There is no doubt of that. A careless word . . . you know how it is. You remember what happened at Milton Priory?'

I nodded.

'That was sabotage. It was due to a leak of special information which was in my possession.'

'I knew there was something mysterious about it and how upset you were.'

'It is not the only instance. I keep certain papers at the house in London. You see, my part in all this is in a way unofficial.'

'I realized it was something like that, ever since Mama told me about the time when you were in Africa and were reported missing . . .'

'Well, even she doesn't know all the details, but I want you to come up to London because I think you can be of help to me.'

'How can I do that?'

'There is nothing much, except to watch.'

'In the house, you mean?'

He nodded. 'There are certain papers of mine which are being seen and copied . . . and passed on to the enemy.'

'Do you mean there is a spy in the house?'

'Well . . . there has been no break-in. It seems as though someone in the house . . .'

'One of the servants?'

'Perhaps. Or someone they are acquainted with. A friend . . . a visitor . . . a workman.'

'Looking at secret papers and passing them on to an enemy! I can't believe it.'

'I am away for most of the day. It would not be impossible for someone to be let into the house . . . to get to my room.'

'What a terrible thing! Someone in the house . . . a traitor! I suppose someone has to go into your room to clean?'

'I have told Mrs Cherry that I do not want anything disturbed there and for that reason I have asked her to clean the room herself. She has a special day for doing it, and for the last few weeks I have made sure that on that day there is nothing of importance in the room.'

'I see. So important papers are normally locked away in your bureau.'

'I make sure that they are.'

'And you have the key to the bureau?'

'Yes, and it never leaves me. Until a few months ago, I used to have a spare key in a drawer. Now the two keys are in my possession all the time. What I want is for you to be watchful. My study will be locked from the outside. Only I and Mrs Cherry have keys. You will be in the house while I am away. You can be alert for anything you consider to be suspicious.'

'It's very melodramatic.'

'We live in melodramatic times.'

'I do hope I am going to be of use to you.'

'Your mother is sure that you will be. But more of all this later . . . when we are there.'

It was with considerable excitement that I made my preparations to leave for London.

The House in the Square

I left Marchlands with my father. Andrée, with Edward, was
to come the following day. When I arrived at the house which
I had known all my life, it seemed to have a somewhat sinister
aspect. It harboured a spy!

My mother had been right about my coming to London. I
was stimulated. I had not thought about Robert's going to the
Front for several hours.

I went straight to my old room. So familiar and yet . . . But
of course it had not changed. There were the banisters through
which I had watched guests arriving at my parents' parties;
there was the staircase at the top of which they had stood to
receive guests; there was the dear old cubbyhole where I had
shared secrets with Annabelinda, and where Charles had tried
to listen to what we were talking about. But the old familiar
places seemed to have become a little different. It was a house
in which a spy was lurking.

A German spy, I thought! I wondered what he would look
like.

But my father did not really think he was a member of the
household. That seemed impossible. The staff was depleted
now. Fewer servants were needed. Just enough, as my mother
said, to keep the place ticking over. Some had gone to Marchlands, some had been called up to the Army, others were doing
war work of some nature.

'It's different in wartime,' said my mother. 'We only need
a skeleton staff.'

That was what we had in London now.

I considered them all. There were the Cherrys, butler and

244

housekeeper, who really had become custodians, there to make sure that everything was kept in order and that my father was looked after while he was in residence. They had been with us for years. I could not imagine them, in any circumstances, turning into spies. Mrs Cherry was extremely patriotic and ready to tackle anyone who had a word to say about the old country. Mr Cherry was a firm supporter of Mr Lloyd George and talked knowledgeably about the Welsh Wizard. Mrs Cherry looked up to Mr Cherry. She was the loyal, adoring wife, accepting his superiority on all matters concerning the war while she herself remained controller of the household.

For the rest, there was only the housemaid, parlourmaid and tweeny, Alice, Meg and Carrie. Alice was fortyish and had been with us since she was twenty; Meg was eighteen or so and deeply involved with a young man who was somewhere in France; and Carrie was fifteen and simple.

'You take what you can get in wartime,' my mother had said of her.

I could not imagine any of them copying documents and conveying them to the enemy. I believed Carrie could not write; and when Alice corresponded with her sister in Devon it was a laborious business; she would sit at the table, holding a pen, which she regarded as though it were a dangerous implement, her tongue peeping out at the corner of her mouth while she showed the utmost concentration. As for Meg, she might have been more able, but she seemed to think of nothing but when her Jim was coming home and they would 'get engaged'.

There were, of course, people in the mews. Mr and Mrs Menton had been there for years. And there was young Eddie – I don't remember hearing his surname – who had come in when James Mansell had been called up for the Army.

Much to the delight of Mrs Cherry and the other females of the household, Andrée arrived with Edward the next day.

There were gasps of wonder at the sight of Edward.

'My goodness gracious me, hasn't he grown?' cried Mrs Cherry.

'How old are you, love?' asked Alice.

'I'm four and a bit,' Edward told her. 'Next year I'll be five.'

'Would you believe it?' said Mrs Cherry. 'Some people are clever. Five and all.'

'It is not clever,' Edward told her rather scornfully. 'Everybody is five after they're four.'

'My word, here's a sharp one.'

Edward looked a little dignified. I could see he was determined to make them understand that he was no longer a baby and must not be treated as one. Mrs Cherry made the mistake of calling him 'Eddy-Peddy' which aroused his indignation.

'It is an Edward,' he told her. 'Not an Eddy-Peddy.'

How they laughed at his 'old-fashioned ways'!

'He's a real caution,' said Meg. And they enjoyed having him in the house, as I knew they would.

In the evening I dined with my father. I said the mystery had deepened for me since I came to the house, for I was certain that none of the people here could possibly be concerned with the leakage of information.

'I am coming more and more to the conclusion that it must be some workman. But it has happened fairly consistently, so be on your guard.'

I assured him I would be.

Three days after my arrival, Annabelinda came to the house. She was quite exuberant and seemed very happy.

'Oh Lucinda!' she cried. 'It is wonderful to see you. I'm glad you're going to be in London for a while. We'll be able to see something of each other. How are you?'

'Very well. No need to ask how you are.'

'Everything is perfect. I am so happy, Lucinda. Marcus is just marvellous. I'm meeting lots of people, too . . . interesting people. Army and all that. The trouble is we can't entertain as we would like to. This place we're in . . . well, it is only temporary, and when Marcus was there just alone it was all right. But it's different now.'

'Now that he has a dazzling wife to show off to his friends.'

She smiled. 'I've made him see that we have to get a house.'

'What, now? With everything so uncertain?'

'We have to have a place in London!'

'What about this ancestral home we have heard so much about?'

'Very grand . . . oh yes, very grand indeed. But to tell the truth, it's too close for my liking.'

'Too close to what?'

'My feudal in-laws.'

'Are they so bad?'

'Worse.' She grimaced. 'So stiff and formal. My mama-in-law is determined to make me into a model Merrivale . . . one of the family. An insurmountable task, I am sure, and it is more than I can endure.'

'So you are all for the London life.'

'Yes, I shall see that visits to the ancestral home are few and far between.'

'Sounds a good basis for a happy married life.'

'Why do you always spar with me, Lucinda?'

'If I do, it is because it seems the natural thing to do.'

'Are you just a little bit jealous?'

'Not the tiniest little bit.'

'Then you ought to be. I suppose you are going to marry Rob.'

'Nothing has been arranged.'

'It will be. Poor darling. They don't like it much – our parents, I mean – Robert's having to go out there again. There is this course, though. It could be extended for a week or two, and then I suppose he'll be properly equipped to go out and do what he has been trained for.'

'I do wish they would stop this fighting.'

'Don't we all? I'm lucky that Marcus is at the War Office.'

'How does he feel about that?'

'You know how he is about everything! He laughs it off. It's no life for a soldier, he says, but I think he had enough of fighting at Gallipoli.'

'You must be delighted to have him home.'

'But of course. I'm going to have lots of fun when we get this house. I'm searching for it now. I want something rather like this one. I love the staircase. Can't you just see Marcus standing up there, with me beside him, receiving the guests?'

'Quite clearly.'

'Oh, this wretched war, surely it can't last much longer? Just imagine when it is all over.'

'It will be wonderful,' I said, thinking of Robert's homecoming.

I said: 'Andrée is here . . . with Edward.'

'Oh really?' She looked faintly hurt, and gave me a suspicious look, which she often did when I mentioned Edward.

'Why have you brought them?' she asked.

I replied sharply: 'I expect you will be surprised to hear that I hate parting from Edward, and, do you know, I think he misses me, too, when I am away; and as I shall be up here for some little time – though we shall be going to Marchlands for the weekends – I thought he should come with me. Why don't you come and see him?'

She hesitated, and I went on: 'Andrée is always so interested in you. She thinks you are very attractive and she admires you so much.'

She brightened a little and allowed me to take her to the nursery where Andrée was sitting at a table writing and Edward was on the floor with a jigsaw puzzle.

'Mrs Merrivale has called,' I announced.

Andrée sprang up. 'How nice to see you, Mrs Merrivale.'

'Brings back old times, doesn't it?' said Annabelinda. 'We shall never forget, any of us, that trip across France.'

'That's true,' replied Andrée, taking in every detail of Annabelinda's appearance and clearly expressing her admiration.

'It seems ages ago.'

'It does indeed,' agreed Andrée. 'A great deal has happened since then . . . you and the Major marrying . . .'

'It all turned out wonderfully for me,' said Annabelinda.

'I think I was lucky, too,' added Andrée.

'Edward wants to say "how do you do",' I said to Annabelinda.

'Hello, Edward,' she said.

He looked at her with curiosity and replied: 'Hello,' and added, 'Why do you wear that funny hat?'

I said: 'Edward's appreciation of *haute couture* is not fully developed.'

'It's not funny, Edward,' chided Andrée. 'It's beautiful.'

'Thank you,' said Annabelinda. And to Edward: 'I'm sorry you don't like my hat.'

'I do like it,' he insisted. 'I like it because it's funny.'

'What are you making with your puzzle, Edward?' I asked.

'It's a cat. His whiskers are on this one . . . and this is the start of his tail.' He turned to Annabelinda. 'At the bottom,' he went on, 'it spells CAT.'

'So clever,' she murmured.

Edward turned away and said: 'Shall I do the elephant?'

'Well, he is your favourite.'

He was not really interested in Annabelinda beyond her hat. I thought how strange it was that he should not know her for his mother. It occurred to me that there might have been some instinct which would show itself; but there was not.

I squatted on the floor and we completed the cat and started on the elephant while Annabelinda chatted with Andrée.

Annabelinda talked mainly about herself, and Andrée seemed quite content to listen. She was explaining that she was going house-hunting. 'Always such fun.' The Major would be giving her a free hand; as long as it was somewhere suitable, that was all he would care about; and she knew exactly what he wanted.

They were deep in conversation about houses while Edward and I finished the elephant and started on the giraffe.

The first week at the house passed very quickly, though fruitlessly as far as any discovery was concerned. I was beginning to be certain that the spy could only have been some visitor to the house.

Mrs Cherry was friendly with the housekeeper of one of my father's friends and she occasionally came in to take a cup of tea. I could not believe that the portly Mrs Jordan, who complained a great deal about her rheumatics, could possibly creep about the house searching for vital information without Mrs Cherry's being aware of it.

The mystery deepened. It could only have been some casual workman who had called at intervals perhaps, as had happened more than once. It was a pity my father could not question Mrs Cherry, but the one thing he did not want was to call attention to his suspicions.

I was watchful. Sometimes I would wake in the night and sit up listening. One night I even went down to the study. The door was firmly locked and everything was in darkness.

We went to Marchlands on the Friday afternoon. Edward was joyfully reunited with his pony, Billy Boy, and enjoyed the animal even more because of the short separation; and on Monday we were on the move again.

During the second week Robert called.

I was delighted to see him, yet fearful because I knew what this meant. The course was now completed and he would be going away.

I was right. He was to leave at the end of the week.

'Oh, Robert,' I said. 'How I wish . . .'

He gripped my hand and said: 'I'll be back soon, you'll see. I'll tell you what I'd like to do. I'd like to take a walk in the Park . . . just like we used to. Just go over the old ground to remind myself while I'm away. Not that I shall need reminding.'

'Let's do it.'

We walked through the trees and down to watch the ducks which, years ago, we used to feed.

'Everything looks the same as it always did,' said Robert. 'We're lucky not to have the enemy invading this country.'

'Oh, how I wish it could all be over . . . and that you had not to go away.'

'It can't go on much longer. Things are moving in the right direction. It just means hanging on a little.'

'It will be four years in August,' I reminded him. 'People keep saying it will be over soon, but it goes on.'

He put his hand over mine. 'The end is coming. I am sure of it,' he said.

'But you are going out there again. You're so calm about it . . . almost as though you don't mind.'

He was silent for a moment, then he said: 'I suppose I am one of those people who don't always show what they are feeling. At the moment, I am wishing I could sit on this seat for ever . . . with you.'

'I do love you, Robert.'

'I know. Do they say "like a sister or brother". . . as the case may be?'

'No, more than that. It's true I have always thought of you as part of the family, because your mother and mine were brought up together for much of their childhood. No, it is more than that. Especially with you. I could not bear it if you did not come back.'

'I'll come back,' he said. 'I'll come back to you.'

'You asked me to marry you. Is the offer still open?'

'It will be open until you accept it . . . or marry someone else.'

'It is time,' I said, 'that we were thinking about the future.'

'Do you mean . . . ?'

'I mean that I am getting older and wiser. I'm beginning to understand myself. The thought of your going away has made me realize how much you mean to me. Robert, you must come back to me.'

'I'll have everything I want to come back to now.'

'I should have told you before . . .'

'We could have had a hasty wedding before I went. Perhaps this is best. I never wanted to hurry you. I could see how you felt. You've known me all your life. There was no sudden realization. Love did not have to be implanted by Cupid's arrow in one exciting second. It was always there for me. It

251

started when I first saw you nibbling the edge of your blanket in your pram in this very park. All the tricks of romance were missing. We didn't have to go through the preliminary stages. It made it difficult to realize.'

'For you too, Robert?'

'Oh no . . . no. I could see it more clearly. When you were seven years old I decided I wanted to marry you. I was a little put out by the difference in our ages at that stage, but thank Heaven, when you get older the gaps don't seem so wide.'

'Wise old Robert!'

'Not very bright in some things, I fear, but in this I knew exactly what I wanted, and what is right for me and, I hope, for you.'

'I know it is right.'

'Then we are engaged to be married. Is that so?'

'It is.'

'How wonderful it is sitting here with you. Look at that small boy feeding the ducks. You see that greedy one . . . oh good, he's been pushed aside and the little one's got the piece of cake, or whatever it is. Oh, it is wonderful to sit on this seat and become engaged!'

I slipped my arm through his. I sensed his contentment and shared it until I reminded myself that in a few days' time he would be in the midst of danger.

'I wish we were still at Marchlands,' I said. 'I wish your leg was so bad you couldn't go. I'd wish anything to keep you here.'

'This is the happiest moment of my life. I just want to enjoy it.'

'How can I enjoy it when you are going away, when I don't know when I shall see you again?'

'I *will* come back.'

'How can you be sure? How can anyone be sure of anything in this fearful world?'

'I shall come back. We shall sit on this seat and there will be nothing to fear.'

'If only that can be! I am sorry to be so uncertain, Robert. We have wasted so much time because I was foolish. But at last I have had time to see things as they really are. What I want more than anything in the world is for you to come back safely to me.'

'I shall. I promise you. Dearest Lucinda, I shall come back.'

I had to believe him, for I could not bear to contemplate a future without him.

I spent the next day with Robert. I was catching his mood of optimism. We made plans for the future as though it were certain to come.

Then I said goodbye to him and he went off. I guessed it would not be long before he was on the battlefield. I tried not to think of it. I forced myself to plan for the future, to believe in it as he had.

Over dinner I told my father about my engagement.

He was delighted. 'We – your mother and I – could not be more pleased,' he said. 'It is what we have always hoped for. Robert is a wonderful young man. Not appreciated by some because he is so modest. Such people are often taken at their own estimation, which can be a great mistake. Robert's family will be pleased also. Perhaps Belinda would have liked a duke's daughter for her son, but at least she is gratified by her daughter's elevation to the aristocracy. At one time, your mother and I thought that you and Marcus . . .'

'Oh no, it was Annabelinda for him.'

'I'm glad. There is no one we would rather see you marry than Robert Denver.'

'I know . . . but I'm afraid because he'll be out there . . . in the thick of it.'

My father nodded his head gravely. 'Robert has always struck me as a survivor in his calm, quiet way,' he said.

I could not bear to think of Robert's being in danger and my father changed the subject quickly. He said: 'By the way . . . you haven't seen anything?'

I knew what he meant and replied: 'No, and I can't imagine who could possibly get in there.'

'I think it is certain that someone has been in there.'

'When?'

'Within the last few days.'

'I have been watchful.'

'You can't be everywhere at once. The essence of this is secrecy. You must not let anyone see you are on the alert. I don't like that key being in Mrs Cherry's possession. Not that I suspect her. But of course she doesn't realize the importance of that key, and I can't tell her. It's a pity the room has to be cleaned.'

'I wonder if I could get the key?'

'How?'

'I mean, ask Mrs Cherry to give it to me. Suppose I offered to clean the room?'

'Wouldn't that be rather unusual?'

'Well, everything about it is unusual. Your study having to be kept locked, for one thing . . . no one but Mrs Cherry having the key. I don't see why I shouldn't clean the room. If I had the key we could be sure no one could get in.'

'I think it would arouse too much suspicion if you asked Mrs Cherry for it.'

'I'll think of something.'

'Lucinda, be careful. You do realize how important this is, and if there is someone in this household, someone who is working for the enemy . . . well, such people could be dangerous.'

'I do know, but I am sure I can make it all seem natural.'

'I certainly don't like the idea of there being a key which is not in my possession. I don't like the thought of Mrs Cherry's going in. While she is working the door will be open. She could be called away suddenly. I am certain that someone is getting into that room.'

'Well, I am going to find out, and the first step is to get the key, without which no one can get into the room, unless they come through the window, which is always locked; and as the room is on the second floor, an intruder would need the agility of a cat to get in. There's not so much for me to do here as there was at Marchlands. Walk in the park . . . and play with Edward. I really don't see why I should not clean that room. After all, there are not many servants in the house now. I could make that an excuse. Leave it to me. I'll get that key and that will set our minds at rest on that score.'

It was not so difficult to manage. I had always been on good terms with Mrs Cherry, and Edward had made a special bond between us. She had thought the story of my bringing him from France was very 'beautiful' (her word). It was heart-warming, she said, like something out of a novelette.

'Some would have left him behind. I mean to say, a young girl bringing home a baby like that. Well, of course, there was Mrs Greenham. She'd never turn anyone away from her door, let alone a little baby. So I reckon it's a beautiful story. And there he is, the little mite, as cocky as they come. What would have happened to him if he'd been left to those terrible Germans?'

She had always been fond of my mother, and now I had become almost a war heroine in her eyes, so I was on especially good terms with her.

I began by asking her for the key of my father's study as there were some papers he wanted me to look out for him.

'Oh, that key,' she said. 'It worries me a bit. Your father says I am never to let it out of my sight.'

'And you don't, do you? It is just because he doesn't want his papers moved about, you know.'

'I never touch papers. Besides, I thought they were all locked away.'

'Oh yes, they are, I believe. But let me have the key.'

'I'll get it for you.'

'Where do you keep it?'

'In the dresser drawer, right at the back of the cloths and things. It's well hidden away there.'

She went to the drawer and produced the key which I took from her.

'Mrs Cherry, shall I keep the key?'

'Well, there's times when I have to go in to clean.'

'You could ask me for it then, then I'd come and help you with the room.'

'*You*, Miss Lucinda!'

'I used to do all sorts of things at Marchlands. The hospital, you know. There's not much for me to do here. I'd enjoy it. We could have a little chat while we worked.'

'Well, Miss, I don't rightly know what to say. Your father did tell me . . .'

'I'll explain everything to him. I'll keep the key and when you want it, just let me know.'

'Well, if that's all right with you . . .'

'I think it will be. Let's try it, shall we? I don't like having too little to do.'

I put the key in my pocket. I thought: I shall always keep it with me. I went to my room telling myself I had managed that rather cleverly.

Alone in my room, I took out the key and looked at it. Things could fall out of pockets. I found a strong gold chain and hung it round my neck, tucking it down the bodice of my dress. There it would be safe.

When I told my father what I had done, he was clearly pleased.

'I shall feel much happier now,' he said. 'And if anything else happens, we shall have to consider whether someone had a key to the room besides ourselves.'

'How could anyone come by that?'

'If they had stolen it from Mrs Cherry, they might have had another made.'

'Wouldn't they have to keep it some time to do that?'

'Not very long, I suppose.'

'She would have missed it. She was certainly worried about having it and was glad to pass it over to me. I shall see that no one goes into that room without my knowing.'

'It's a comfort to have you here, Lucinda.'

I was susceptible to every sound in the house. I was sleeping lightly. Often a creaking floorboard would awaken me. I would imagine I heard someone creeping down the stairs . . . the sound of a key in a lock. Then I would feel for the key which I kept round my neck, even in bed. I realized that I was over-sensitive. I knew this, but there was a night when I thought I heard noises. I put on my dressing-gown and went down to the study. I turned the door-handle. The door was locked. I stood there listening.

Then someone called. 'Oh . . . it's you, Lucinda.'

I looked up. Andrée was leaning over the banisters.

'Is everything all right?' she asked.

'Yes. I thought I heard someone down here.'

'False alarm?' said Andrée.

'I'm sorry I disturbed you.'

'I'm a light sleeper, particularly since I've been looking after Edward. The least sound and I'm awake.'

'I must be the same. It's chilly here. We mustn't get chilled. Good night.'

I went into my room and shut the door. How foolish I was! Yet, on the other hand, if someone had been there, I should have caught him . . . or her. I had to be on the alert.

Spring would soon be with us. There was a certain hope in the air. We were forcing the enemy back with some success. The battle for the Somme had started and the fighting was fierce. Robert was constantly in my thoughts and I was tortured by speculations of what was happening out there. There was not much news, but the German successes which had occurred in the beginning were definitely halted. People were saying that we were winning the war of the U-boats and it would not be long before we were triumphant on land.

Frequently I saw Annabelinda. I had been to look at two houses with her. I told her I did not know why she wanted my opinion because she never took any notice of it. She retorted that she knew exactly what she was looking for. It had to be something more splendid and grander than anyone else could have. I told her she would never find perfection, but she believed she would. However, I did find looking at houses a fascinating experience. I liked to explore the rooms, imagining all the people who had lived in them, while she was calculating how impressive those rooms could be made to look.

One day at the beginning of April she came to the house and I could see that she was not her usual exuberant self.

At last we were alone in my room and she burst out: 'Lucinda, I'm worried.'

'I thought something was wrong.'

'Is it so obvious?'

'To me, yes. But then I know you so well.'

'I've had a note,' she said.

'A note? From whom?'

'From Carl.'

'You mean *Carl* . . . Carl Zimmerman?'

She nodded.

'And it has upset you, of course.'

'He wants to see me.'

'You won't see him, will you?'

'It's difficult.'

'Why? And what is he doing in England?'

'He was attached to the Swiss Embassy.'

'But I thought he'd gone from there and that was why he was able to work as a gardener at La Pinière.'

'He must have sorted that out. Anyway, he's in England.'

'How did he get here?'

'I expect he is back in the Embassy.'

'What does he want?'

'To see me.'

'Does he know . . . about Edward?'

'How could he?'

'He is his father. Perhaps it is about Edward that he wants to see you.'

I felt alarmed. What if he wanted to take Edward away?

'He wants to see *me*,' she said. 'I don't know what to do.'

'Why don't you tell Marcus?'

'Tell Marcus!'

'Why don't you tell him everything?'

'How could I?'

'Just tell him . . . that's all.'

'How ridiculous! Of course I couldn't tell him.'

'Then what are you going to do?'

'I don't want to see Carl. I don't want ever to see him again.'

'Well, don't answer the note.'

'But he knows the address. Though how he got it, I can't imagine. He'll write again.'

'Then write and tell him you can't see him.'

'Well . . .'

'Well what?'

'That note he wrote . . . it doesn't sound as though he will take no for an answer.'

'As long as he doesn't know he has a son.'

'You would bring that up!'

'It's rather a salient point, isn't it? It's the only thing you need worry about. If he doesn't know about Edward, all you have to say is, "I don't want to see you again. I'm a happily married woman, no longer a romantic schoolgirl. Goodbye."'

'You make it sound so simple.'

'Other people's problems always seem simpler than one's own. But it does seem a clear case to me. All you have to do is tell him you don't want to see him.'

'It's the way he writes. It's almost like a threat. I've got to go and see him. I think he is still in love with me.'

'It might be blackmail.'

'What do you mean?'

'He may be desperate. What was he doing working as a gardener? Really, Annabelinda, the best thing you can do is to tell Marcus everything. Then you will have nothing to fear.'

'How could I tell him!'

'I'm sure he would understand.' I thought of Emma Johns and Janet. How could he judge Annabelinda harshly because she had taken a lover before marriage? He was, of course, what is called a 'man of the world'. I guessed his emotions had not been deeply involved with Janet. So . . . surely he would understand.

'And then,' she went on, 'what about Edward? Isn't this awful bad luck? All this to come up now I am so happy, and everything is going perfectly.'

'One's actions do have an effect on one's life and one cannot be sure that the consequences will make themselves felt only at convenient moments.'

'Stop moralizing! What am I going to do?'

'If you are asking my advice, I would say go to him and explain. If he makes a nuisance of himself, then there is only one thing to be done, and that is to tell Marcus.'

'It's not only Marcus . . . it's his family. Just suppose Carl went to them.'

'How would he know about them?'

'How did he know my address? Oh, it was all so wonderful . . . and now this.'

'Go and see him, Annabelinda. Explain that you are now happily married. He can't possibly know that there was a child.'

'You've never betrayed me, Lucinda.'

'Of course I haven't.'

'You might have done . . .' She looked at me tearfully and flung herself at me. 'Oh, you are a good friend, Lucinda, and I'm not always good to you. Why do you put up with me?'

I heard myself laugh. 'I don't rightly know,' I said. 'But you are Annabelinda, the intimate and tormentor of my youth. I'd always do what I could to help.'

'I don't deserve it, Lucinda. I really don't.'

Such an admission really disturbed me. Poor Annabelinda! I had rarely seen her so frightened. The only other time was when I had told her I knew about the indiscretion and Edward's birth.

I truly wished that I could help her, but there was nothing I could do but advise her, and who could say that my advice was any use?

'Do go and see Carl Zimmerman,' I said. 'Explain how you

are placed now. Tell him it is finished between you, and say goodbye. If he's a decent, honourable man, he'll disappear and won't bother you again.'

'All right, Lucinda. I'll do that. I'll go and tell him.'

I heard nothing from her for several days, and I was growing anxious.

I called at the house.

The parlourmaid said that Mrs Merrivale was resting and should she tell her that I had called?

I was amazed when the maid returned and told me that Mrs Merrivale had a headache and was sorry she could not see even me. She would be in touch with me and she was sure that she would have recovered by the next day.

I guessed something was very wrong. It was unlike Annabelinda not to want to talk about her troubles, so I guessed she was very worried indeed.

I returned to the house. Andrée was sitting in the garden with Edward. The London garden was a square patio at the back of the house in which a few flowering shrubs were now beginning to show signs of spring blossoms.

Edward was reading aloud to Andrée in a halting fashion.

'Hello,' said Andrée. 'How is Mrs Merrivale?'

'How did you know I was going to see her?'

'You said you were.'

'Oh, did I? I didn't see her actually. She isn't well.'

Andrée smiled. 'Do you think . . . ?' She nodded towards Edward.

Pregnant, I thought? It was a possibility, but I thought it was more likely something to do with Carl Zimmerman.

I shrugged my shoulders. 'I couldn't say. She had a bad headache.'

'I suppose she leads rather a busy life, with all the people in military circles she has to see.'

'Perhaps.'

I sat there while Edward went on reading. I was thinking

261

of Annabelinda and Carl Zimmerman. What a big part he had played in our lives, and yet I had seen him so rarely.

I remembered the first time outside the cubbyhole when he had lost his way – and there was the amazement at seeing him working in the gardens at La Pinière – and lastly in Epping Forest with Andrée.

I said on impulse: 'Andrée, do you remember that man in Epping Forest – the fair-haired one who asked the way?'

She looked puzzled.

'You remember – you were with Edward and I met you there.'

'I can recall several people who asked me the way while I was there.'

'This was not long ago.'

'Oh, I vaguely remember. Why? What was so special about him?'

'I just wondered what he said? Did he just ask the way or any questions . . . about us . . . or Mrs Merrivale? I think Major Merrivale might have been in the hospital at the time, though I'm not sure.'

Andrée continued to look puzzled.

'Questions?' she said. 'I don't remember anyone asking anything but the way. Why?'

I thought to myself: I'm being rather foolish, and I said quickly: 'Oh . . . it's of no importance . . . no importance at all.'

Annabelinda came to see me the following day. I noticed at once that there was a feverish excitement about her. I thought: Andrée is right. She must be pregnant.

I was in the garden once more with Andrée and Edward. We were playing Edward's favourite game of the moment, 'I spy with my little eye, something beginning with a . . .' and then the first letter of the object, only Edward was not quite sure of the alphabet just yet, so we used phonetics. Something beginning with a 'Der' or a 'Sha' or 'Ber'.

Edward was saying: 'I spy with my little eye, something beginning with a Ter.'

We pretended to ponder before one of us suggested it might be the tree . . . when Annabelinda appeared.

'Oh hello, Lucinda,' she said rather too heartily. 'I'm sorry about yesterday. I really did have the most awful head.'

'Oh, I quite understand.'

'But I did turn you away.'

'That's all right. You're better today, I hope.'

'I'm fine.'

Edward said rather reprovingly: 'We're playing "I Spy".'

'What fun,' said Annabelinda absent-mindedly.

'It was something beginning with a Fler,' went on Edward.

I looked at Andrée and smiled. We should have to devote ourselves to Annabelinda now that she had arrived. So we brought the game to a timely end by saying the answer must be a flower.

'Yes,' cried Edward, delighted.

'Well, we'll play again later,' I said. And to Annabelinda: 'Why don't you sit down?' I made way for her on the wicker seat.

'I've found the most marvellous house,' said Annabelinda. 'You must come with me to see it.'

'Where is it?'

'In Beconsdale Square.'

'Where's that?'

'Not far from here. I've got the cutting. Listen: "Country mansion in the heart of London". Doesn't that sound nice?'

'I can't imagine a country mansion here.'

'That's because you don't use your imagination.'

'"Beconsdale Square, Westminster,"' Annabelinda went on reading. '"In a quiet London square, large family house built circa 1830. Drive-in, garden of about half an acre. Large drawing-room suitable for entertaining, eight bedrooms, four large reception rooms, spacious servants' quarters . . ." Then it goes on for a bit. It sounds just right. I like the sound of the drive-in. It sets it apart. I have a feeling that this is the one. . I shall go to see the agents and make an appointment to see it. Promise me you'll come with me, Lucinda.'

'Of course. I'm all agog.'

'I'll let you know when.'

She was silent for a while. She was sitting still and rather tense.

'Do you feel all right, Annabelinda?' I asked.

'I'm just feeling . . . not very well. I wonder if I could go and lie down for a while?'

'Of course. Come on.'

I went into the house with her.

'I'll take you to the room you use when you stay here,' I said.

'Oh, thank you, Lucinda.'

When we were there, she took off her coat, kicked off her shoes and lay on the bed.

'Annabelinda,' I said. 'Something's wrong, isn't it?'

She shook her head. 'Just . . . not very well.'

'Is it . . . Carl?'

'Oh no, no. I'm settling that.'

'You've seen him, then? You've told him that you can't see him any more?'

'Yes, I've seen him. It's just that . . .'

'Do you feel sick?'

She nodded.

'Are you pregnant?'

'It . . . it could be.'

'Well then, rest a little. It'll soon pass. I'll stay with you.'

'No . . . no, Lucinda. You go back to the garden. I'll be all right. I feel I just want to be quiet . . . alone. It'll pass, I know.'

'All right. If there's anything you want, just ring. Meg will come up.'

'Oh, thank you, Lucinda. I'd feel better if you went back to the garden and there was no fuss. I'll feel better, I know I shall. It doesn't take long for this to pass.'

'So you've had it before?'

'Once or twice. I hope it's not going to be a regular thing.'

264

'It's only in the first weeks, I've heard.'

'Thank you, Lucinda.'

I went out and joined them in the garden. We must have been there for about half an hour when Annabelinda came out.

She looked better, relieved, I thought.

'How are you?' I asked.

'Oh, I'm all right now.'

'You look flushed.'

'Do I?'

'Well, you're all right. That's the main thing.'

'Yes. I'm all right now. I'm sorry it happened.'

'Never mind. Tell us about the house.'

'It really seems that this will be it,' she said.

'Annabelinda! All you've seen is this advertisement.'

'I have a feeling in my bones.'

'What does the Major say about it?' asked Andrée.

'Oh, he doesn't know. I want to find the house and then take him along and show him how wonderful it is. It seems just right. Secluded. It's not easy to be secluded in London. It will be wonderful for entertaining. The war must be over one day. It can't go on for ever. Then this will be just what we need.'

When she left I walked back with her. 'Just in case you don't feel well on the way back,' I told her.

'Oh, Lucinda, you do take good care of me.'

'I always have in a way, you know. You think you are the worldly-wise, clever one, but when you come to think of it, I have looked after you far more than you have me. Yet you always behave as though I'm the simple one.'

'Forgive me, Lucinda. I wish I had been better to you.'

'I can't understand you, Annabelinda . . . and I think it is for the first time in your life: you're becoming human.'

She laughed and when we reached the house she said: 'Come in for a while.'

'Thanks, I don't think I will. I ought to get back.'

'All right. And thank you . . . for being such a good friend.'

Change indeed, I thought, as I walked home.

Perhaps it was because she was contented in her marriage and she was going to have a child. Motherhood changed people, softened them; and this pregnancy, unlike that with Edward, would be a happy one.

She must be thankful that she had come to this happy state.

There was an account in the paper of a derelict farmhouse along the coast three miles from Folkestone which had been the scene of an explosion. There was no explanation as to what had caused this.

There were comments from the local people. 'I heard the noise. Deafening it was, and then I saw the flames. The place went up like a matchbox on fire.'

The verdict was that it was an example of wanton arson. There were no casualties.

My father asked me to meet him in his study, and when I arrived he shut the door and said: 'I want to talk to you, Lucinda. You are absolutely sure no one has been in here? You have had the key in your possession all the time?'

'Yes.' I pulled out the chain and showed him the key. 'It has been with me all day and night.'

'I don't think any strangers have been in the house this last week?'

'I am sure not.'

'I must explain to you. You know everything is speeding up over there. The Germans are getting desperate. They firmly believed that they would have brought the war to a satisfactory conclusion long before this. The fighting on the Somme has been fierce. As you know, our factories are working at top speed. We have the arms now, and the only difficulty is getting them over there. The enemy is determined to stop them reaching their destinations. It is vital for them to do so. They have to be stored in arms deposits before we can ship them across the Channel. The site of these storehouses is known only to a few, and certain information is leaking. It seems to come from me. I set a trap.'

Understanding dawned on me. I said: 'That place in Folke-stone?'

'Yes. There was nothing there. I had a document in my bureau. On it there were lists of ammunition that were sup-posed to be stored in this farmhouse which was derelict. It was near the coast and, according to this document, was due for almost immediate shipment. Lucinda, there was only one reason for blowing up that farmhouse, and that was because it was believed that we had stocks of ammunition there. And this happened because in my desk was this document. It was placed there as a test.'

'So then – it is someone in this house!' I cried. 'Oh, I can't believe it. What can we do?'

'Short of having a watcher always in the room, I can't say. I shall not keep anything of importance there now. But what is vital is to discover the spy. We know now that there is one – in this house.'

'What can we do now?'

'We just go on as before. Always be on the alert. If anything extraordinary happens, however trivial, let's talk about it.'

'Yes, Father. I understand,' I said soberly.

I felt very uneasy. It was an eerie feeling, to know that someone near to us was working for the enemy. It had been proved.

I felt the need to be alone to think. I could not believe Mr and Mrs Cherry could possibly be concerned. Yet Mrs Cherry had had the key. If any workmen came to the house, she would be the one to deal with them. Alice, Meg, Carrie – impossible! The Mentons? Eddie? Eddie was the most likely. He had not been with us so long. He was young. Perhaps he would be tempted. Whoever wanted such information would pay well for it.

I went for a walk and was wandering rather aimlessly when suddenly I saw the words 'Beconsdale Road'. There was a familiar ring about it. Of course, Beconsdale Square was where the house Annabelinda was going to see was situated.

The Square must be near the Road, I presumed, and it did not take me long to find it.

The houses were certainly grand. They were all different, which added to their attraction. Most of them were well set back from the pavements and had their drives.

They all appeared to be occupied by the affluent, which was what I had expected. I wondered which one was for sale. I walked round the Square, in the centre of which was a well-kept garden which I supposed was for the use of residents, in accordance with the custom.

I found the empty house. It was certainly impressive, and I felt sure Annabelinda would be pleased.

I could not resist opening the iron gates and looking along the drive. The grass on the lawn needed cutting and the shrubs surrounding the house were overgrown. That gave the place an air of mystery. That would all be different when Annabelinda took charge. I could well imagine that the house offered just what she wanted.

I walked up the drive. If I met anyone I would say that a friend of mine was interested in the place and I should shortly be coming along with her to see it. There was a big brass knocker and I could not resist knocking. It sounded quite deafening in the silence all round.

The place was quite isolated because of the grounds surrounding it. I guessed it had been empty some little time.

There was no answer to my knock, which was perhaps just as well as I felt I was probably being a little officious. I went round to the back of the house and looked through windows. I could see the hall and wide staircase. It would be grand enough for Annabelinda, I was sure.

Yet I could not cast off the eerie feeling the house aroused in me. But empty houses did have that effect – particularly one which, in spite of being situated in a London square, was somewhat isolated.

*

It must have been two days later when Annabelinda called. She was in a state of tension still, and I wondered what was happening, for I certainly felt that something was.

On this occasion she was anxious to be alone with me.

She said rather breathlessly: 'I have decided that I am going to tell Marcus.'

'Tell Marcus!'

'Yes. I am going to tell him everything.'

'Everything?'

'I – I'll see. I am going to tell him about Carl. I have to, Lucinda. I can't go on. I can see I have got to.'

'You've seen Carl again?'

She nodded.

'And he is being difficult?'

She nodded again. 'I can't go on, Lucinda. I just can't.'

'Don't work yourself up into a frenzy. I think you are doing the right thing. I am sure Marcus will understand. After all, he is a man of the world.'

'People expect women not to have lovers.'

'Well, things don't always work out as people expect.'

'You seem to think it is so easy.'

'Of course I don't. But I feel sure it will be all right. If you didn't tell him, you'd be worrying about Carl for ever. If you tell him the truth, you'll know that is the worst that can happen. At least you've faced it.'

'I shall choose my moment.'

'That's sensible enough.'

'I'm thinking of it all the time. I am going to tell Carl I can't do what he wants.'

'What does he want?'

'He – he's still in love with me. He won't give me up. He'll make trouble, Lucinda.'

'I am sure you should tell Marcus. Then you'll be well rid of Carl. Let him know you don't care for his blackmail, for that's what it is, isn't it? Marcus will send Carl about his business.'

'It's not easy, but I have to do it. Who would have thought all this could have come out of . . . that?'

269

'Poor Annabelinda! But you are doing the right thing at last. Marcus must understand.'

'Do you think so?'

'He must,' I said firmly. 'Come and see Edward.'

'I don't feel up to it.'

'It will do you good. Andrée always likes to see you. She thinks you are so attractive and lead such an interesting life.'

'Well, I suppose I could.'

'Of course you could.'

I took her up to the nursery. Edward was sitting on the floor colouring pictures. Andrée was sewing.

Edward looked up and said: 'Hello,' while Andrée laid aside her sewing and said: 'Good morning, Mrs Merrivale.'

'Good morning,' replied Annabelinda and sat down.

'You are better today, Mrs Merrivale?' asked Andrée.

'Yes, thanks. Much.'

'I'm so glad.'

'You haven't brought your funny hat,' commented Edward without looking up from his painting.

'You don't appreciate this one?' asked Annabelinda.

I could see that Edward was mouthing the word 'appreciate'. A new one for him. He would use it soon afterwards in the way he always did. If he decided he liked it, it would figure in his conversations for the next days to come.

The newspaper was lying on the table. Annabelinda glanced at it. 'They are still going on about that explosion,' she said.

'What a mercy there was no one there,' commented Andrée.

'I wonder who did it?' I said. 'It seemed pointless. Like that place – remember – Milton Priory.'

'Wasn't that something do with the gas?' asked Andrée.

'They did say something about that at the time.'

'Perhaps it was the same with this one,' suggested Andrée.

'I'm glad no one was hurt,' put in Annabelinda. 'I'm very glad about that.'

She's changed, I thought. She sounds as though she really cares. A little while ago she wouldn't have given the matter a thought.

'By the way,' said Andrée, 'did you ever see that house you were interested in?'

'Oh, I was forgetting. That was really what I came about.'

'Is this the one in Beconsdale Square?' I asked.

'Yes, of course. It sounds exciting.'

'I forgot to tell you. I took a look at it.'

'Really?'

'Only from the outside. At least, I suppose it was the one. It was the only one, as a matter of fact, that seemed to be empty in the Square.'

'So you actually went there?'

'I came upon Beconsdale Road by chance and thought the Square must be close by, so I did a little investigation. I went along the drive and looked in at the windows. If it is the one I saw, it is going to suit you.'

'Well, I am going to see it tomorrow. I want you to come with me, Lucinda.'

'I'd love to see more of it.'

'You know exactly where it is. Could you meet me there at two-thirty? The agent will be there to let us in.'

'I'll be there,' I said. 'I must say I found it most intriguing.'

The next day I set out for Beconsdale Square. It was about two-fifteen which I thought would give me just enough time to reach the house by two-thirty. I guessed Annabelinda would be on time, although normally she was inclined to be late. But this was something she would be enthusiastic about, even though she had Carl Zimmerman on her mind.

I arrived about a minute or so before two-thirty. There was no sign of the agent who was to meet us there.

I went up the drive and stood at the door. It was very silent. I was surprised that Annabelinda had not arrived. I strolled back to the gate and as I did so a man appeared. He was in striped trousers and black coat and, as he carried a briefcase, I guessed that he was the house agent.

'Good afternoon,' he said. 'I am a few moments late . . . the traffic. Shall we go in, Mrs Merrivale?'

I replied: 'I am not Mrs Merrivale. I'm a friend of hers. She wanted me to see the house with her.'

'Oh, of course. May I have the pleasure . . . ?'

'Miss Greenham,' I said, and we shook hands.

'My name is Partington; John Partington of Partington & Pike. Well, I am rather relieved that Mrs Merrivale is a little late. I hate to keep ladies waiting.'

'Yes, I'm surprised she's late. She is so eager to see the house. As you say, the traffic can be a problem.'

'I am sure she will be attracted by this house,' he went on. 'There is really something very special about it.'

'Yes, it looks interesting. There is quite a sizeable garden, by London standards.'

'It really is the country house in Town, and that's the truth.'

'I'm very much looking forward to seeing it.'

He glanced anxiously along the drive. There was no sign of Annabelinda.

'She must be along soon now,' I said.

'Oh, I'm sure she will.'

A few more moments passed and still there was no sign of Annabelinda. He was beginning to be uneasy, and so was I. It was twenty minutes to three.

I said: 'Why don't we go in?'

He was thoughtful for a moment, then he said: 'Yes, why not? If something has prevented her coming, you can tell her what you think. But I have no doubt that she will be here soon.'

He took a last look round and opened the door, and stood aside for me to enter.

I stepped into the hall. It was spacious and there was the grand staircase which I was sure would please Annabelinda.

I walked across the hall, the sound of my footsteps echoing on the wood floor.

'It is lovely!' I said.

'A very desirable property.'

'Where do these doors lead?'

'Well, one would be to the kitchen and the other to one of the reception rooms.'

I opened that door. I was unprepared for what met my eye. Annabelinda was lying on the floor, very still, and there was something about her which filled me with an increasing horror.

I stood for a few stunned seconds staring at her. I heard myself gasp: 'Mr Partington . . .'

'What is it, Miss Greenham?'

He came and stood by my side.

'My God,' he said. 'She's been strangled.'

I had knelt beside her. 'Annabelinda,' I said. I kept saying her name over and over again.

She lay there inert. There was a look of surprised terror on her face which was white and lifeless.

'Annabelinda,' I sobbed. 'What was it? What happened?'

I heard Mr Partington say: 'We've got to get help . . .'

I could not rise. I just knelt there, looking at her.

Disclosures

It was like a bewildering dream. There were people . . . doctor . . . police . . . and others.

What had happened, they wanted to know. Why were we there?

'I was to meet her here,' I told them. 'It was half past two. We thought she was late. We went into the house. We thought she would come . . .'

Someone took me home. My father came soon after. They must have sent for him.

I was lying on my bed and he was sitting beside me. The doctor had given me a sedative. He said I needed it.

So I lay there with my hazy thoughts and I could think of nothing but Annabelinda . . . lying dead in that empty house.

Later there were questions. Two men had come to see me. My father explained. 'They are from the police. You see, you were the one who found her, you and the house agent. The general opinion seems to be that it was some madman. Someone sheltering in the house perhaps, who did not want to be disturbed.'

'But other people must have looked at it. And how did she get in? The house agent had the key.'

'We don't know yet,' said my father. 'However, you'll have to talk to the police. I don't suppose they will be here long.'

'We are sorry to disturb you, Miss Greenham,' said one of them. 'Just a few questions. Mrs Merrivale was a great friend of yours, wasn't she?'

'Oh yes. Our families have been close all our lives.'

'And you were going to look over the house with her?'

'Yes.'

'She did not arrive at the appointed time of two-thirty.'

'That is so. I cannot understand how she got into the house. The agent was to have let us in with the key.'

'He it was who took you in.'

'Yes. We thought we might as well go in. We left the door open so that when she came she would see we were there.'

'Do you know any reason why she should have arrived before the appointed time?'

'No. And I still can't imagine how she got into the house.'

'She was let in by someone. Possibly the murderer.'

'You mean . . . the murderer was in the house?'

'It may have been a trap. As a matter of fact, there was a broken window which had not been noticed before. It could have been that someone was in the house waiting for her. Someone who let her in and posed as the house agent. Did Mrs Merrivale not say anything to you about the appointment's having been changed to an earlier time?'

'No. If she had, I should have been there earlier.'

'Naturally. Well, I don't think there is anything further at the moment, Miss Greenham.'

I was glad when they went.

My father came into the room. He was very disturbed.

'It is so mysterious,' he said. 'Poor girl! What a dreadful end . . . and she was so young.'

'She was happy. She thought she was going to have a baby.'

'How tragic!'

'And Marcus?'

'He's having a bad time. He's had a gruelling by the police. Heaven knows what this will do to his career.'

'Do you mean they suspect him?'

'In cases like this, the husband is always the first suspect.'

'But they were so happy together.'

'That won't stop suspicion. Oh, Lucinda, I wish you were not involved in this!'

I felt sick and bemused.

My father said that the doctor's opinion was that, as I had had a terrible shock, I should rest for a while in my room.

How could I rest? I could think only of Annabelinda entering that house . . . that strange, eerie, empty house, as it had become in my imagination, and meeting her assassin.

I wished I had been with her. How was I to know that she was going to be early? Why had she? Why had she told me to meet her there at two-thirty? What had made her go early? She must have had some message. And why? Because someone was lying in wait for her . . . to kill her.

The answer to that question was not long delayed. Mrs Kelloway, Annabelinda's housekeeper, was able to supply vital information.

Someone had called at the house during the day Annabelinda had met her death. He had seemed in a great hurry and said he came from Messrs Partington & Pike about the house in Beconsdale Square. He had waited at the door and asked if Mrs Kelloway would take a message to Mrs Merrivale.

Mrs Kelloway had invited him in, an offer which he declined.

'Excuse me,' he had said very politely. 'But I am pressed for time.' He spoke in a funny way, she said. 'Not quite natural. It might have been from another part of the country, but it was not familiar to her. He had insisted on waiting at the door until she took the message, which was, could Mrs Merrivale be at the house half an hour earlier, at two o'clock? He had a quick call to make and he was going straight there. He had got a little hung up with his appointments and he was afraid he would not be able to spend as much time with Mrs Merrivale as he would have liked if she could not meet him at the earlier time. He just wanted to know if she could oblige.

'Mrs Merrivale was at the top of the stairs when I called to her, and I told her what he had said. She said she'd be there. He said he was grateful, then he hurried off before she could get down the stairs. Mrs Merrivale said there wasn't time to let Miss Greenham know, but it would be all right.

She would already be there when Miss Greenham arrived.'

Mrs Kelloway had assumed great importance. She was proving of inestimable value to the police. She was the only one who had seen the man who had most likely murdered Annabelinda.

The house agents quickly confirmed that Mr Partington was the man in charge of that particular house, and he was the only one from the firm who had arranged to meet Mrs Merrivale, and the appointment was for two-thirty.

When pressed for a description of the man, Mrs Kelloway again proved her worth. She could not say what age he was. He had a beard which covered half his face. He seemed young in a way, but the beard gave him a middle-aged look. But there was one important clue. He was holding some papers in his hand and as he was talking to her he dropped them.

She stooped to pick them up and so did he, and as he did so, she saw the fingers on his hand very clearly. There was something odd about them . . . something different. One of his fingers looked what she called 'a bit funny'. It seemed as though part of one of them was missing.

How grateful they were to Mrs Kelloway! She had become a celebrity overnight.

Soon the press was interviewing her. We had headlines. 'Who is the mystery man in the case of the Empty House Murder?' 'Police seeking man with maimed hand.'

'If Mrs Kelloway was right about the deformed hand, it should make the search for the murderer easier,' said my father. 'But why? Why lure her there . . . to be killed? For what reason? Can you think of any, Lucinda? You knew her well.'

I wondered. I felt I could not uncover her devious past. I seemed to sense her beside me, begging me not to.

Suppose the story of her misdemeanour was brought to light now? What good could it do? Poor Marcus, and his proud family! They were suffering enough already.

What good would it do to tell?

*

277

Those were strange days. It was as though a pall hung over us. Aunt Belinda and Uncle Robert came to London. They were very subdued and sad; I had never seen Aunt Belinda like that before. Sir Robert looked bewildered. He loved his children dearly. I wished Robert would come home.

Sir Robert had aged in a few weeks, but it was Aunt Belinda who surprised me. My mother was very gentle with her and they spent a great deal of time together.

Annabelinda was never out of my thoughts. She had lived dangerously, of course, and these were dangerous times. But who could have wanted to lure her to an empty house to kill her?

I was in a dilemma. I could not get out of my mind that Annabelinda had been deeply worried just before her death. I had never seen her like that before. Of course, she had been terrified that Carl would insist on seeing her and possibly try to break up her marriage, but that was no reason for killing her.

I wondered whether I should tell my father or mother and ask advice. I had promised Annabelinda that I would tell no one. How could I break my word now?

I would lie awake at night . . . wondering.

I had thought that my mother should know who Edward's parents were. After all, she was his guardian. I tried to convince myself that Annabelinda's involvement with Carl had nothing whatever to do with her death. But why?

The days passed. We heard that the police were continuing with their inquiries. Mrs Kelloway was questioned once more, but she had told all she knew. And the mysterious man with the beard and the maimed hand had not materialized.

I think they had begun to wonder whether he existed outside Mrs Kelloway's imagination. There was no doubt that she had enjoyed her temporary importance.

I saw Marcus alone when he came to the house to see my father, who was not just then at home.

There was a certain embarrassment between us.

'Oh, Marcus,' I said. 'I am so deeply sorry. This is all quite terrible.'

He nodded. He had changed. He must have loved her dearly, I thought. This was more dreadful for him than for any of us. And if there really had been going to be a child, it would be a double tragedy.

'How could it have happened, Lucinda?' he said. 'You were in her confidence more than anyone else.'

I shook my head. 'It is what they are trying to find out.'

'To what purpose? It won't bring her back.' He looked at me ruefully. 'They suspected me.'

'Not now . . . only just at first.'

'That's so. I was with people all that day, so they had to eliminate me. Rather reluctantly, though.'

'I'm relieved about that. It must have been dreadful for you.'

'Yes, it was.'

I thought of his family. How distressed they would be! They must never know that Edward was Annabelinda's child. Nor must Marcus. He himself had had a secret family life, but he was arranging that in a manner which was presumably satisfactory to all concerned.

'Lucinda,' he said. 'Let us meet some time. This will all be cleared up one day.'

'Perhaps,' I said.

I was glad when my father came home.

So thus we continued, and the mystery of Annabelinda's death seemed as far from a solution as it ever had.

Sometimes I walked through Beconsdale Road to the Square. I walked past the gate where I had stood with Mr Partington and waited for Annabelinda.

I glanced at the house. It certainly looked eerie. The shrubs were more overgrown than they had been. The place looked desolate – a house where a murder had taken place, a brutal, unexplained murder of a beautiful young woman by a man with a maimed hand.

Then one day we had a visitor.

When I came into the drawing-room I saw him sitting there. I could not believe it. I had not seen him since before the war.

Jean Pascal Bourdon rose as I entered and, advancing towards me, took both my hands in his.

'Lucinda! Why, you are a young lady now . . . and a beautiful one at that!' He drew me to him and kissed me on both cheeks.

'I have wondered about you,' I stammered. 'How . . . how did you get here?'

'With some difficulty . . . as was to be expected in wartime. But here I am and it is good to see you. These are terrible times.'

I nodded in agreement.

'This is a great blow. My granddaughter. Such a beautiful, vital girl . . .'

I thought immediately of the adroit way in which he had extricated Annabelinda from her trouble.

'Is the Princesse with you?' I asked.

'Oh no, no. It was not easy to get here. I have come alone.'

'And she is well?'

'As well as anyone can be in these circumstances. It is not a thing we like . . . to have an enemy on our land.'

'I understand the situation is getting better.'

'Perhaps. But until we have driven the lot of them out of our country we shall not be content.'

'You came because you have heard of Annabelinda?'

'I heard, yes. It is one reason why I have come. I wish to see your father. It may be that what I have to tell him may be of some importance.'

'He will be here soon.'

'Then we shall talk.'

'What happened to Madame Rochère?'

'Madame Rochère! That great spirit! She stayed as long as she dared. She would have dared further, but she is no fool. Indeed, she is one of the shrewdest ladies I know. There came a time for leaving. She is with us near Bordeaux.'

'And how do you manage there?'

He shrugged his shoulders and lifted his hands in a despairing gesture. 'It is not good. But our day will come.'

'And the school?'

'The school became the enemy's headquarters, I believe.'

'Will it ever be a school again?'

'Indeed it will. But not in your time, *chérie*. By that time you will have left your schooldays long behind.'

When my father arrived, he was delighted to see Jean Pascal.

'I heard you were coming,' he said.

'Ah. The news travels.'

'You did not tell me,' I said. 'I should have been so glad to hear it.'

'Thank you,' said Jean Pascal, with a little bow. He has not changed at all, I thought.

'You must dine with us,' said my father. 'And we will talk later. Is that in order? Or would you prefer to talk first?'

'I think it would be delightful to sit at the dinner table in a civilized manner. We have had the enemy at our gates for so long. The peace of this place is too enticing for me to resist. Let us eat and chat of happier times than those which have recently befallen us.'

So we dined together – just the three of us. Jean Pascal talked of the life in France, the dangers, the uncertainties, and the difficulties of getting to England. It was all of immense interest, but I had the impression that both he and my father were biding time before they discussed the really important matters which were the reason for his visit.

As soon as the meal was over, my father said: 'I think we should go to my study.'

Jean Pascal nodded, and my father looked at me and then questioningly at Jean Pascal.

Jean Pascal said: 'I think it is necessary that Mademoiselle Lucinda shares our talk. I think she already knows more than you realize.'

My father looked surprised and I was overcome with a feverish desire to know the real reason for Jean Pascal's visit.

When we arrived at the study and entered it, my father locked the door.

'Yes,' said Jean Pascal. 'This must be very secret.'

'I guess,' said my father, 'that you are very deep in things over there?'

'Ah, *mon cher*, there is a great deal going on. Do not think we calmly accept them on our soil. We are working against them all the time. And with some success, I may tell you. It is because of our discoveries that I am now in England. There are certain people here who we are very anxious to bring to their deserts.'

He took a large envelope from his pocket and from it took a picture which he put on the table.

'Do you know this man?' he asked my father.

I gasped, for I was looking at a picture of Carl Zimmerman.

I said his name aloud.

'No, no,' said Jean Pascal. 'This man is Heinrich von Dürrenstein. He is one of the best and most experienced spies the Germans have.'

'Carl Zimmerman!' said my father. 'He was with the Swiss Embassy before the war broke out.'

'Certainly he was here in the Swiss Embassy. He did some very good work there. Not so good for the Allies, of course. You know him then, Lucinda?'

'Yes. I first met him here in this house. He said he had lost his way.'

I told them how I had seen him outside the cubbyhole.

'I remember,' said my father. 'We thought there had been a robbery. Papers were disturbed. That was before I had any suspicions of the real motive. He made it appear like a robbery. The jewellery we thought had been stolen was later found. It is all coming back to me.'

Jean Pascal nodded slowly; he turned to me. 'And you saw him next . . . ?'

'In the gardens of La Pinière.'

'He did a good job there. He reconnoitred, found all the weak spots in the surrounding country and arranged for the German army's headquarters at the school.' He looked at me. 'I think, Lucinda, your father has to know. He has to see the whole picture clearly. This is too important a matter for us to hide anything.'

He looked at my father and went on: 'He managed to seduce my granddaughter at the same time as he was working so assiduously for his country.'

My father was aghast.

'There was a child,' said Jean Pascal calmly. 'I arranged for the birth and for the child to be cared for afterwards. His foster-parents were killed during the bombardment of Mons and Lucinda stepped in. She rescued the child and brought him here.'

'Edward!' said my father. 'And you . . . Lucinda . . . ?'

'Lucinda was noble. Lucinda was wonderful,' said Jean Pascal. 'She brought my great-grandson out of danger. She knew who he was, you see. She was in my confidence. She had to be, because of the way everything had worked out. With the help of Marcus Merrivale, she brought him out of France.'

'This is fantastic,' said my father. 'I can't believe it.'

'Strange things happen, particularly in wartime, and all this brings us to where we stand today. Now, Lucinda, I want you to tell me exactly what happened when you made your journey across France. You acquired a nursemaid for the child, did you not?'

I told him how we had met Andrée and her brother and how Andrée had accompanied us to England and had become Edward's nurse.

He sat there nodding, and then he took more pictures from the envelope which he was still holding. There were six in all and he showed us one of them, which was of Andrée.

I looked at it in amazement. Jean Pascal smiled at me. 'This is Elsa Heine. At least, I think that is the name to which she has most claim. She works in close contact with von Dürrenstein.'

'It's . . . Andrée!'

'They are clever, these people. So adaptable. They have to carry out their duties with efficiency. They can become nursemaids or gardeners – whatever the occasion warrants.'

'But Edward is so fond of her.'

'Of course. She is an excellent nursemaid, and a very clever young woman into the bargain. Let us think about her. She has frequently been in this house since you came back from France. What luck for her that you brought her in! It was what was intended, of course.'

'Her brother . . .'

'More of him later. Let us consider your Andrée first.'

'I knew someone was getting into my room,' said my father. 'We could not understand it. Mrs Cherry was the only one with the key, until Lucinda had it.'

'The problem of a key to these people is quite a simple one. Clever Andrée would have managed to get a copy of that key very quickly. She would find some means of stealing it long enough for her to do what she wanted. It explains how information leaked out. She had been systematically passing on what she was getting from this house.'

'How could we have been so stupid!' cried my father. 'It is all so obvious.'

'Everything is obvious when one is aware of it,' said Jean Pascal. 'So . . . we have the spy in the house. That was all arranged by the clever group. They worked well together. Now, my granddaughter's death. It is involved in this, I am sure. Lucinda, my dear, you knew Annabelinda as well as anyone. Did she confide in you?'

'Yes, she did to a certain extent.'

'Then perhaps you can throw some light on this. The man she had known as Carl Zimmerman has returned to London. Did he try to see her, do you know?'

'Yes, and he wanted to see her again. She told me that he had threatened to tell her husband if she did not continue their affair.'

'The persistent lover! It is hard to believe von Dürrenstein was that. The only thing he is ardent about is his work. He could not be so proficient at it if he allowed himself other interests. We have to look at it this way. Why did he come to see Annabelinda again? He was ardently in love with her? He had heard about the child and wanted to see him? That makes me smile. No. He came for a purpose. This could be useful. A husband in the War Office. Close friendship with this house. They already had Andrée installed here. But they could do with another to work for them. I'll guess that he blackmailed Annabelinda, threatening her that if she did not help him in his work, which she was qualified to do because of her connections, he would expose her to her husband. Go on from there, please, Lucinda.'

I told them how uneasy she had been. 'She was really distrait,' I said. 'I have never seen her like that before . . . except on one occasion. I remember we were in the garden and she was not well. She wanted to go and lie down. I said I would stay with her, but she did not want that. So she went into the house. She was most insistent that she should be left alone.'

'For how long?' asked Jean Pascal.

'It must have been about three-quarters of an hour.'

'Long enough to go to the study and get something from the bureau.'

'She could have taken that information about Folkestone,' said my father.

'Von Dürrenstein would have given her the key and the nursemaid kept the coast clear while she did the job,' said Jean Pascal.

'But why make her do it when Andrée could have done it so easily?' I asked.

'Probably to test her. To give her an easy task and, once she had committed this, she could not turn back.'

'But that was what she planned to do when she realized the enormity of what she had done. She was very upset about the explosion at Folkestone, and she said she was going to confess everything to Marcus.'

'And do you think she told von Dürrenstein that she was going to do this?'

'Yes. She was plucking up her courage to. She said she was going to choose the right moment.'

'If she told von Dürrenstein that, she was signing her own death warrant.'

'And she was killed by these people, because of this?'

'It may well be. She was going to confess "at the right moment". She would tell him about the stolen document she had passed to von Dürrenstein. Her husband was at the War Office. The entire network of spies could be betrayed. Our service would have been alerted. For a long time they have been trying to rout out von Dürrenstein and his gang.' He was thoughtful for a moment. Then he went on: 'These little facts we have pieced together are why I am here in England. When I heard that my granddaughter had been murdered, I wondered why. I was all impatience to come here and find out. You see, there was this unfortunate connection with von Dürrenstein. When all is said and done, this man is the father of my great-grandson.'

'You think it was this gang who lured Annabelinda to her death?'

'I think it is a possibility. The bogus nursemaid would know of the house she proposed to visit. She would know that she was going to meet the house agent there. One might ask, why did they need such a complicated set-up? Why not just climb into her room one night and strangle her? Why go to all the trouble of going to an empty house? There was a great deal at stake. The murder of the poor unfortunate girl was of no great significance to them. She was someone who got in the way, who could have been a danger, and they could not afford dangers. They just brushed her aside in the manner which seemed least hazardous to their organization. The nursemaid knew of all the arrangements. The empty house must have seemed the best spot. The murderer could have been a tramp . . . a robber . . . anyone, and he could make his escape with ease. That is how I see it. Von Dürrenstein was not going to

286

be seen near the scene of the crime, for he had already had some communication with the victim. Although the meeting had been secret, someone might have seen them together. One never knows what investigations are going to reveal. So it was better for him to be as far removed as possible. I have read all about the case, of course. I know of the bogus house agent who called and was seen by the housekeeper – Mrs Kelloway, I believe.'

'Yes, that is right.'

Jean Pascal turned back to the envelope and drew out a picture. There was something familiar about the face.

'This is Hans Reichter, one of their cleverest. He is a very worthy member of this nest of spies.'

'Surely I have seen him somewhere?' I said.

'Oh yes, you have. It was when you were travelling across France and he joined you with Elsa, who was his sister for that occasion.'

'I can't believe it. How we were duped! The car broke down. He fixed it . . . and then Andrée came with us and he went to Paris.'

'All neatly arranged, no doubt. Elsa wanted to get to England. It would not have been very easy for her. But there you were, in the company of a high-ranking officer of the British Army. They knew who you were, Lucinda.' Jean Pascal turned to my father. 'Your work, *mon cher*, has not gone unnoticed. To get into your house was Elsa's project. And how well she managed it.'

'With our foolish help.'

'Oh, come! You must not say that. You were in ignorance. How could you have been otherwise? You have contributed to my knowledge, as I now have to yours, and we can help each other in tracking down these people and putting them where they belong.'

I was looking at the picture, remembering it all, seeing him walking across the dining parlour, joining us at our table with his 'sister'. All lies! How could we have been so easily deluded?

I said: 'The man Mrs Kelloway saw had a beard.'

'It is not difficult to grow a beard,' commented Jean Pascal.

I was thinking of the scene in the parlour. I saw the man sitting there. There was something wrong with his hands. He had lost part of his little finger. I could hear his words: 'I was playing with fireworks.'

It was all beginning to fit. Jean Pascal might not have discovered the entire truth, but he was somewhere near it.

'That young man,' I said. 'There was something about his hands.'

'It is a distinguishing feature which has helped us considerably.'

'It was quick of Mrs Kelloway to notice,' said my father. 'It was a vital clue . . . and seized upon.'

'It is strange how a little carelessness can bring disaster, after all the careful planning that went into it.'

'Yes,' said my father. 'He dropped the house agent's brochure which he had carefully obtained to increase his credibility, and in picking it up, showed his hand to the housekeeper . . . and so he was identified.'

'Do you think he was the murderer?' I asked.

'Undoubtedly. He is known as a killer. He would have broken a window, got into the house and been waiting there when my poor Annabelinda arrived. He would have let her in and chatted about the house for a moment. She had seen him before, it is true, on that journey through France, but his beard would have been sufficient to disguise him for that brief period.'

'I can't bear to think of her walking into that house,' I said.

'Poor child. She was little more. I shall not rest until she is avenged. Now, no sign must be given of anything we have talked of. I shall have the woman watched, and in time she will lead us to the others. She is only a small fish. It is von Dürrenstein whom we want. We are well on the track. She will be watched night and day, and before long there will be results. It is of the greatest importance that they shall not be aware that we know who they are. You must not betray, by a look or an inflection of your voice, that anything is different.'

'I hate to think of her looking after Edward,' I said.

'Have no fear. She will look after the child. There is nothing to be gained by not doing so. It might be that she is genuinely fond of him.'

'He certainly is of her.'

'There you are. Looking after the child is all in her line of duty. How much her feelings are involved we do not know, but the boy is no threat to what she would consider her real work, therefore she will care for him. Every movement she makes will be watched, and I doubt not that before long we shall have this group where we want them.'

'The police will be eager to arrest the man who killed Annabelinda.'

'It may well be that he is wanted in other connections. We shall see. But rest assured, they will pay for their sins.'

We went on talking, going over everything we had discussed. It was late when we retired to bed – but not to sleep. I could only go over everything that had been said that night with a feeling of incredulity. But the more I pondered about it, the more it seemed to me that there was much truth there among the conjectures.

The days that followed were tense. I did not see Jean Pascal during that time. I fancied he thought it wiser to keep away. I tried not to make any difference in my attitude towards Andrée, as Jean Pascal had warned me emphatically about this. It was not easy. Andrée had become a different person in my eyes. I could not help marvelling at Edward's love for her, but he had known her almost all his life. It was hard for me to accept the fact that indirectly she could have had a hand in his mother's murder.

What a web of intrigue we had stumbled into, and largely because of Annabelinda's light-hearted dalliance with a man who was spying for his country.

I knew that we could not go on as though everything was as normal. Something had to happen soon.

It did. One day Andrée went out alone and did not come back.

There was great consternation in the house. At first Mrs Cherry was quite indignant. The nurse had no right to stay away so long. She was lucky to have so much free time. She would soon discover that if she took a place somewhere else. But when evening came and she had not returned, Mrs Cherry changed her attitude. She began to wonder whether Andrée had been murdered. When there was one murder connected with the house, you began to think there might be another. 'We're living in shocking times, Miss Lucinda. And where could she have got to?'

I spoke to my father.

'We must do something about Andrée,' I said. 'They will start a rumour and it will spread in no time. We'll have to think of something.'

My father agreed. 'I'll take up the matter,' he said. 'By the way, we've got them all. Von Dürrenstein himself. It's our best bit of luck for a long time. They were in a house in Battersea, having some sort of conference. She led us right to them.'

'That was what was hoped would happen.'

'I've seen Bourdon. He's been working hard underground ever since the start of this war. It's a great triumph for him.'

'What will become of Andrée?'

'The fate of all trapped spies, I suppose. There may be a murder charge too against Reichter. They're all accomplices, of course . . . all guilty. That will be sorted out. I doubt the public will ever hear the truth. Annabelinda's murder will be one of those unsolved crimes.'

'Lots of people will be careful about viewing empty houses, I suppose.'

'Inevitably.'

'What are we going to tell the servants about Andrée?'

'I'll consult with the powers. I agree, we should think of something to stop talk. We can't have people just walking out of the house and never being heard of again.'

He very soon came up with the solution. Andrée had had a communication from the French Embassy to get in touch with them without delay. Her brother was dying and they had arranged for her to leave immediately. A message had been sent to my father explaining all this. There had been a little delay in his receiving it, but Andrée was now with her brother. We did not know when she would come back.

It was not very convincing, but after the first reaction of incredulity, the story was accepted. The fact that it was wartime, when the most extraordinary things could happen, was a help and in a week or so Andrée's disappearance ceased to be the main topic of conversation.

It was different with Edward.

'Where is Andrée?' he asked.

I told him she had gone to her home to see her brother.

'This is her home,' he insisted.

'Oh no. She had a home before she came here.'

'Are we going there?'

'No. We shall stay here.'

'When is she coming back?'

I fell back on the old vague answer which had become a byword since Mr Asquith's famous statement: 'We shall have to wait and see.'

But he continued to ask about her. He cried a little when he went to bed. 'Want Andrée,' he said.

I would kiss and cuddle him, telling him stories until he slept. It amazed me that a woman who had been involved in the murder of his mother could have become so dear to him. He had seen Annabelinda only a few times and she had made no impression on him, apart from her hat; and yet he mourned Andrée.

I used to say to him: 'Never mind. You have me . . . and all of them at Marchlands. You have Billy Boy there, and Mrs Cherry and everyone here.'

'I know,' he said. 'But I really want Andrée, too.'

I spent more time with him, but he continued to ask for her.

Victory

As we advanced through the year, the aspect of the war began to change.

It was September and the great Allied attack had begun. There was a feeling of light-heartedness in the air and with the passing of each day the news grew better.

We knew now that that for which we had been longing over the last four years was about to happen.

Then came that November – darkish misty days, yet brighter than the days had been for years – made hopeful by the news.

If only Robert were home, how happy I could have been, but my fears were still with me. I longed to see him. I wanted to tell him how foolish I had been to hesitate, to have been swayed this way and that when I should have known full well that he was the one for me. How could I ever have doubted it? I was now obsessed by a terrible fear that he might not come back. They were still fighting out there. Oh, why would they not stop! Was it not now almost all over? How tragic it would be if anything happened to him now.

I prayed for him. I wanted the chance to tell him how much I loved him. These last years had made me realize that.

My father came home in a state of great excitement. Germany was in revolt. They had given in. The Kaiser had fled to Holland.

The Armistice was signed at eleven o'clock on the eleventh day of November. 'The eleventh day of the eleventh month' as everyone was saying. A day to remember for the rest of our lives.

The war was over.

*

There was rejoicing in the streets. Flags hung from windows; bunting was strung across the streets; and the bells rang out. People crowded on to the streets. There was the sound of music everywhere; bands were playing patriotic marches and barrel organs rolled out their tinkling tunes.

There was euphoria everywhere except among those to whom victory had come too late.

Mrs Cherry said the servants all wanted to go out to join the throng and I said they must. She and Mr Cherry wouldn't mind taking a turn out there themselves. At a time like this, it didn't seem right to be left out of it.

Marcus called. He was exuberant.

'What a great day this is!' he cried. 'You'll have to join in the general rejoicing.'

My father said that Marcus was right. He suggested that we go out and celebrate. It would be amusing to go to the Ritz or the Savoy for a meal.

We went into the drawing-room for a while and talked about the cessation of hostilities, and fell to wondering how long it would be before the men came home.

'It is good to know the firing has actually stopped at eleven o'clock this morning,' said my father. 'That will put a stop to the senseless slaughter.'

He added that we should drink to victory, and while we were doing this a messenger arrived for him. His presence was required elsewhere.

It was an accepted rule in the household that we never asked questions about anything connected with his work.

Marcus said: 'I shall do my best to entertain Lucinda, and perhaps you will be able to join us later.'

My father thought that he might be detained for some time, so he would not arrange to meet us.

'It would be no use to make a rendezvous,' he said. 'I dare say the restaurants will be crowded tonight with the whole of London wanting to celebrate.'

'Then you will leave your daughter in my care?'

'I shall be happy to do that,' replied my father.

Thus I found myself seated opposite Marcus in a smart restaurant overlooking the river.

The place was full of people clearly bent on rejoicing. There was laughter and chatter and people calling to each other from the tables. The orchestra was playing patriotic tunes.

When we appeared a waiter rushed forward and shook Marcus's hand. Several people clapped. All men in uniform were greeted rapturously, and Marcus, of high rank and looking extremely handsome in his uniform, stood out amongst them.

I noticed envious glances directed towards me. Marcus smiled and lifted his hand in greeting and acknowledgement of the acclaim with that nonchalance which was essentially his own.

When he had ordered dinner, Marcus smiled at me and said: 'This is a happy occasion. Thank God the war is over. How long it seems since I came to La Pinière and we first met. From the first moment I saw you – a schoolgirl, so fresh and innocent – I loved you.'

'It is four years ago. It seems much longer.'

'So much has happened. For some time I have been wanting to talk to you and have wondered whether I could . . . whether it was too soon. This dreadful thing has happened. Poor Annabelinda! What a terrible fate to be caught up as she was.'

'You know? They have told you?' I paused, embarrassed. I was afraid that I might have said too much. I knew that Annabelinda's murder was to be a well-guarded secret. Would that mean excluding her husband?

'For two reasons they would tell me,' he explained. 'I was involved in the case. I was on the hunt with your father for those saboteurs. The other reason is that I was her husband.'

'Then you must know . . . everything?'

He looked at me very solemnly and said: 'I had to know, Lucinda.'

'It must have been a great shock.'

'Remember the police first suspected me, until I could prove conclusively that I had been nowhere near the house. It was one shock after another. First her death and the suspicion against me . . . and then to learn the truth. I was a fool, Lucinda. I might have known, I might have guessed. But it all fitted so neatly. After all, you were the one who would not give up the child. You were the one who was most concerned for his welfare.'

He was looking at me with an expression I had never seen on his face before. It was contrition, humility and – most unusual – he gave the impression that he did not know how to express what was in his mind.

'I was deeply upset,' he went on. 'I could not believe it. And yet it seemed so plausible.'

'What do you mean, Marcus?'

'I am talking about the child. What Annabelinda told me.'

I was puzzled.

'You haven't realized, Lucinda, you were the one. It was you whom I loved. And when she told me, I could not believe it . . . and then it seemed obvious. If it had just been myself, well, I was shocked, but I would have got over that. I loved you. You were different from any girl I had met. I knew that we would have been good together, but for that. They could have found out, my parents, I mean. They would have cut me off. I know how their minds work. They would have considered you a loose woman. You have no idea how rigorous their ideals are! They had been harassing me for a long time. I should have married. The all-important duty was to produce more Merrivales for the family. I know it is hard to understand, but they are quite feudal – medieval in their ideas. We have been brought up to believe that the family comes first.'

'Marcus, why are you telling me all this now?'

'Because I want us to wipe out the past. I want us to start afresh from now on – from this first night of peace. I want us to start and build up from there.'

'Oh no, Marcus.'

'Listen to me. I have been foolish. I should have known. It was the scandal I was afraid of, if it became known. We should live in fear of it. Scandals have a habit of coming to light at awkward moments. I just could not face it. And all the time, the child was hers. She is dead now. Poor Annabelinda! She knew that it was you I cared for – and she cared so much for me that she lied to me, she could slander her best friend. But it is over now. We have to forget. We have to go on from here.'

'What are you saying, Marcus?'

'Annabelinda knew I was about to ask you to marry me and she told me that when you were at school you had a love-affair, that the result was Edward. She said you had had the child put out with foster-parents and when they had been killed your conscience smote you so deeply that you had the idea of bringing the child home to your parents. It was a way of keeping him with you.'

'Annabelinda told you that!'

'I know now that the child was hers. It all came out when she was killed, when the German spies tried to snare her into working for them. I see it all clearly now, Lucinda. But we've got to forget poor Annabelinda. What a terrible price she paid! We have to build up from there. We'll let a reasonable time elapse and then –'

'I think I ought to tell you this, Marcus. I am engaged to marry Robert Denver.'

'Oh, but you decided to marry him because I was married to Annabelinda. He'll understand.'

'It is you who have to understand, Marcus.'

'I do understand how you feel. I should never have done what I did. I should have realized –'

'You realized that it would never have done for you to marry a girl who had committed a social misdemeanour – if that is what your family call it. And having committed the further error in acquiring a child in the process, she had put herself quite beyond acceptance. You acted in accordance with the rules. You did the only thing possible for you. It was unfortunate that in trying to avoid the inconvenience you stepped right into it.'

'You are understandably bitter.'

'No, I do not think I am. I think it has all worked out for the best.'

'I love you, Lucinda. I want to start afresh.'

'Life rarely gives us that opportunity. Who would not like to start again when things have gone wrong? And you did not love me deeply, Marcus. It was probably as well. It suits you to be as you are. You will marry. Your family will wish you to remember your duty. You will find a charming wife who will be all that you desire; you will have model children who will be a credit to you and your family. But love? You have never loved deeply, Marcus, and it is better that you should not. You were fond of me. I was quite suitable and you would have asked me to marry you. But that misdemeanour – as you thought – stood in the way. If you had truly loved me, you would not have allowed it to. You were fond of Janet, but there was no question of marriage there. You are fond of the children you had together, but you cannot acknowledge them openly. You see what I mean? You will have a happy life, I am sure of that. People like you. See how they cheered you tonight.'

'That was the uniform. All over London, soldiers are the heroes tonight. Tomorrow they will be forgotten.'

'And you looked so gallant. There were special cheers for you. You deserve them. You have fought for your country. But for men like you there would not be the rejoicing there is tonight. You deserve it, as I say. You deserve a good life. But you don't deserve the kind of love I want in my life – simply because you could never give it.'

'Try me, Lucinda.'

'I have told you, I am already engaged to be married.'

'It is not too late.'

'It is not a matter of lateness. It is a matter of what is real to me, of understanding – rather belatedly – what I want in my life and with whom I want to share it.'

He was finding it hard to accept what I was saying. He had been sure that when he had explained to me the reason why

298

he had not asked me to marry him in the first place, I would be ready to give up everything for him.

Self-confident, indeed. But then he had some reason to be.

I looked across the table at him with great affection. I lifted my glass and said: 'All happiness to you, Marcus.'

'How will that be possible without you?'

'With a man like you, it is possible.'

I had made him see what I meant. I was going to marry Robert and, more than anything on Earth, I wanted him to be safely back with me.

Marcus was silent for a moment, staring into his glass. I saw that he accepted what I was telling him, though up to that time it had seemed inconceivable that I could have chosen Robert in preference to him.

I saw the look of resignation steal across his face and I felt relieved.

People were dancing all around us. They were singing 'It's a long way to Tipperary' and 'There's a long, long trail a-winding'.

It was late when we left and walked home through the crowded streets where people went on celebrating far into the night.

I saw Marcus a few days later. He called at the house and Mrs Cherry told me he was in the drawing-room waiting to see me.

When I went down, he came towards me and took both my hands.

'I have news for you,' he announced. 'I thought you should hear it at the earliest possible moment. Captain Robert Denver will be arriving in London tomorrow.'

Great floods of joy swept over me. I could not help betraying my emotion. All the pent-up fears, the anxieties, the horrible possibilities, the tortured doubts which had filled my mind, were dispersed. He was coming home.

Marcus had put his arms round me; he held me against him

for a few seconds, then he drew back and kissed me, first on one cheek and then on the other.

He smiled and said: 'I thought you would be pleased to hear that.'

I heard myself say: 'Captain Denver,' as though his new rank were important.

'Well, naturally, promoted in the field. He has been a good soldier.'

'Oh, Marcus, it was good of you to come and tell me.'

'I am not sure at what time he will be arriving, but as soon as I am, I will either come myself or send a messenger to tell you.'

'Oh, thank you.'

'All that remains now,' he said rather whimsically, 'is for you to live happily ever after.'

'Oh, Marcus,' I said. 'I do wish the same for you.'

The next day a messenger came from him. He brought a note which just said: '4.30 Victoria.'

I was in a state of great happiness. I wanted to shout to everyone, 'Robert is coming home! After all this time he will be here. Safe! All the time I have been worrying, he has been safe.'

I thought the day would never pass. I would go immediately after lunch.

In the late morning Jean Pascal Bourdon called.

He said: 'I've come to say goodbye. I shall be going back to France very soon now. There are just one or two things to clear up.'

I told him that Robert was coming home.

'I thought there was something different about you. I can see it shining through. My dear, I wish you all the happiness in the world. It will be the same in my country. The war is over. Let us hope that it never happens again. Now all that is left for us is to enjoy the good things which life provides. Lucinda, my dear, you look radiant.'

'He is coming this afternoon. Four-thirty at Victoria.'

'And you will be waiting for him. Good luck. He is a fortunate man.'

'It is I who am the fortunate one.'

'Then there are two fortunate ones. There is one thing I should like before I go, Lucinda.'

'Yes?'

'To see my great-grandson.'

'But of course. We have a new nursemaid for him now. He is just getting used to her. He still misses Andrée. It never ceases to amaze me that someone involved in such work could at the same time be such a loving nurse to a little boy.'

'It is just another instance of the complexities of human nature. We can be all things at times. We are not simple – good and bad, black and white. Perhaps there is no such thing as a wholly bad person. That is a theory which appeals to me when I look back over a life which has not been entirely free from sin.'

'I know that there is a good deal of good in you.'

'I am not sure of that. But a modicum perhaps. Well, may I see my great-grandson?'

I took him to the schoolroom where Edward was occupied at his favourite pastime of the moment: colouring pictures.

'It's a dinosaur,' he explained to Jean Pascal, who sat down beside him.

'A red dinosaur?' said Jean Pascal. 'Are there red dinosaurs?'

'I like red ones,' said Edward, as though that settled the matter.

'Shall we give him some whiskers?'

'Dinosaurs don't have whiskers.'

'Well, if you can have red ones, why not whiskered ones?'

Edward considered. 'I suppose you could,' he said.

I watched Jean Pascal studying the child with interest. There was a gleam in his eyes. Jean Pascal had always had a strong family feeling.

When Jean Pascal rose to go, I could see that Edward was

loath to lose his company. Jean Pascal was aware of this and there was no doubt that it pleased him.

Back in the drawing-room, he said: 'What a delightful child!'

'I think so too.'

'I can't help marvelling that he is my great-grandchild.'

'Life is very odd, isn't it?'

'You must bring him to visit me. He would be interested in the vineyards.'

I could see there were plans in his eyes.

When I considered this, I said: 'It all seems so incongruous. Edward is your great-grandchild. His father is a spy involved in the murder of his mother. Will he ever know it?'

Jean Pascal was silent and I went on: 'Should he know the truth? Is it right to keep it back? Hasn't everyone the right to know who he or she is?'

Jean Pascal said slowly: 'That is a point which can be argued from several angles. Is the truth sacrosanct? Someone once said, "Speech is silver, Silence is golden", and someone else said, "Where ignorance is bliss, 'Tis folly to be wise."'

'I know. But what will happen when he is a man and he might want to know? It is certain that he will.'

Jean Pascal was thoughtful. Then he said: 'Edward believes he belongs to you now. Soon he will be asking questions which will have to be answered. What does the world think? Here is a boy whose parents were killed during the bombardment of Mons. You, a young English schoolgirl, who had struck up a friendship with his parents, found him in the garden of the wrecked cottage. You were getting out of France before the German advance and you brought him with you. That is best. His father responsible for the murder of his mother? His mother putting him out with foster-parents, ashamed of his birth? No, no. Let us keep to the more pleasant account. There is often a time for talking, Lucinda, and there is a time for silence. As regards this matter of Edward, it should always be a time for silence.'

I smiled at him. This man who had experienced most things

302

life had to offer was knowledgeable in the ways of the world, and I believed he was right.

This was a time for silence.

It seemed a long time before the train came in. The platform was crowded with people, for it was the troop train bringing back the heroes from the Front.

A great cheer went up when the train steamed into the station. We surged forth, everyone there, men, women and children, seeking the one person whose return meant so much to them: the end of fear, the new hope in a future no longer tormented by thoughts of war and the fearful desolation of bereavement.

It was some time before we found each other.

And there he was. I saw him a second or so before he saw me. He looked older, a little worn, but there was a wonderful light in his eyes.

Like others on that crowded platform, we flung ourselves into each other's arms, unashamed of our emotion.

'Robert!' I cried. I could think of nothing to say but his name.

'Lucinda, Lucinda,' he said. 'I've come home.'